PRAISE FOR STEVEN-ELLIOT ALTMAN AND HIS WORK ON *THE TOUCH* AND ITS SEQUEL, *DEPRIVERS*

"*The Touch* will take you to a terrifying and disturbing tomorrow and make you feel like you live there."
—**David Brin**

"*The Touch* is one of those rare anthologies whose contributors have managed to tell an impressive breadth of tales.... If this doesn't challenge you, move you, and, most importantly, make you think, then you're deprived already."
—**Brian Hodge**

"In the tradition of King and Koontz... a timely, thought-provoking and unfortunately, relevant story."
—**Alan Cabal**, *New York Press*

"Fans of everything from *The Hot Zone* to *The X-Files* take note, THIS BOOK IS GOING TO BLOW YOU AWAY!"
—**Rockne S. O'Bannon**
creator of *Alien Nation* and *Farscape*

"A book that gets under your skin and on your nerves. The science is impressive; the fiction is haunting. It has a lot on its mind and it will touch you."
—**Mark Frost**
bestseller and co-creator of *Twin Peaks*

SCIENCE FICTION COLLECTIONS
published by ibooks, inc.:

The Ultimate Cyberpunk
Pat Cadigan, Editor

The Best Time Travel Stories of All Time
Barry N. Malzberg, Editor

Morning Child and Other Stories
by Gardner Dozois

Sailing to Byzantium
by Robert Silverberg

Troublemakers
by Harlan Ellison

The Last Defender of Camelot
by Roger Zelazny

Straczynski Unplugged
by J. Michael Straczynski

THE TOUCH

epidemic of the Millennium

created by

STEVEN-ELLIOT ALTMAN

edited by

PATRICK MERLA

**a WRITE AID project to benefit the charities
HEAL and F.A.C.T.**

ibooks

new york

www.ibooksinc.com

DISTRIBUTED BY SIMON & SCHUSTER, INC

A Publication of ibooks, inc.

Distributed by Simon & Schuster, Inc.
1230 Avenue of the Americas, New York, NY 10020

ibooks, inc.
24 West 25th Street
New York, NY 10010

The ibooks World Wide Web Site Address is:
http://www.ibooks.net

ISBN 0-7434-9298-6

PRINTING HISTORY
First ibooks, inc. trade paperback edition October 2000
First ibooks, inc. mass-market edition September 2004
10 9 8 7 6 5 4 3 2 1

Printed in the U.S.A.

For every individual who has ever suffered
societal alienation, of any sort,
due to afflictions beyond their own control.

Welcome to *The Touch*, a literary work created to benefit the charities HEAL (Health Education AIDS Liaison) and F.A.C.T (Foundation for Advancement in Cancer Therapy). The contributing authors have graciously donated their work to this project without compensation in the hope of spreading enlightenment and promoting future charitable works.

The common thread winding through each of these collected stories is the onset of a fictitious epidemic created by Steven-Elliot Altman, referred to as "The Depriver Syndrome." The guidelines for the epidemic, distributed to the various authors, were in the form of a government Public Safety Notice.

SPECIAL THANKS TO:

Carl Jaynes and Patrick Merla, John Morrone at PEN, Michael Ellner at HEAL, Ruth Sackman and Consuelo Reyes at F.A.C.T, Franka O'Keefe, Paul Maragay, the law offices of Edelstein and Faegenburg, Maria Vargas, Leslie Kaminoff of The Breathe Trust for allowing the writers to use the sensory deprivation tanks, Lubna Abu Osba, Christopher Wodtke, Stephen Mark Rainey, Alexia Meyers & Tim Travaglini, Dawn Emory Thorne, Sari Scallin, Edward Gorey, Doug Stewart, Steve Roman, Byron Preiss and Katherine Dunn.

table of outbreaks

CONTENTS

INTRODUCTION

TOUCH

The stories in this powerful collection explore, and occasionally explode, elements of human culture so basic that they are rarely discussed; as essential and unconsidered as gravity. The core of the Depriver Syndrome is touch, the sense that forms our surest anchor in physical reality.

The simple act of humans touching, skin to skin, has always been loaded with power and significance. Touch heals or hurts, soothes or arouses, and conveys the entire emotional spectrum from love to hatred. Whole judicial systems emerge from the question of who gets to touch who, when and how. If my right to swing my fist terminates some fractional distance from your nose, that violable "personal space" shifts between cultures, eras, ages and genders.

Touch is so potent that it requires ritualization. The ritual combat challenges of touch stretch from counting coup to the touché of fencing, through the duelist's slapped face and the crude jostling from rock-paper-scissors to professional football.

That pervasive Western tradition, the handshake, is a more civil example. It's often viewed now as a cheap character diagnostic to separate the limp, moist or the bullying show-off from more respectable grips. But folklore says the custom grew out of dark eras when most men went armed with knives or swords and showed each other empty hands when they met, to prove peaceful intentions. The clasping of hands was an exchange of faith—an expression of trust.

For a long time women did not shake hands, maybe because they were supposed to be noncombatants. Kissing a woman's hand identified her as a superior creature, revered with the same gesture as popes, potentates and godfathers.

But the meaning of that odd grasping ritual, the handshake, fluctuates endlessly. In the early '80s when public information about how HIV was communicated was still confused and contradictory, I watched a serious young reporter stand in his office deciding whether to shake hands with a man who was dying of the disease. The polite visitor was new to his own mortality and, as he was introduced, he automatically extended his hand. Then, seeming suddenly to recollect his situation, he jerked it back and a terrible blush spread up his neck. The reporter was the father of toddlers, the husband of a brilliant beauty. The reporter did not know whether touching this man's hand would destroy his life and endanger his beloved family. The pause was brief—an ice instant. Then he reached across his desk and waited as the patient gingerly extended his hand for a quick, grateful clasp.

The idea of contagious touch is ancient, reaching back through ignorant eons of plague and lepers exiled or murdered. It is evident in the universal predator-prey games of tag or touch-and-run in which the slightest tap from the monster, "It," transforms us into "It."

The other original meaning for the handshake was gift-giving. It was a symbol of the transfer of power, usually from a god to a mortal. Once a year the Babylonian kings clasped the hand of a statue of the god Marduk to preserve their throne. Michaelangelo's Sistine Chapel God is reaching for Adam's outstretched hand to bestow a gift.

Neither theory of handshake origin covers the common practice of holding hands. The power of shared touch is a mystery that science has only begun to explore. So far there is evidence suggesting that skin to skin contact between living creatures is a powerful antidote for depression. It reduces stress symptoms, lowers blood pressure. Two bodies entwined over time gradually synchronize heartbeats. Some preachers claim to cure with a laying on of hands, but the gentle application of loving lips is a proven anesthetic for bumps, bruises, stubbed toes or offended funny bones.

As mammals, nurtured first inside another body, it seems somehow reasonable that our need for the touch of other humans is profound. The infant monkey alone in a cage, fed by a bottle in a wire frame, grows hysterically deranged. The monkey is comforted, made saner, by the addition of a terry cloth cover for the wire frame. The orphaned child in an institutional crib starves for touch, fails to thrive, and retreats into mechanical autism. Some part of the lunacy of adolescence must be that touchless limbo where we are too big to sit on laps but too young to mate.

These clear, fierce stories usher us into a fear-spawned isolation that leaves Deprivers utterly deprived. It is a dark place, and the authors lead us there by the hand.

—Katherine Dunn

THIS IS A PUBLIC SAFETY NOTICE
FROM THE CENTER FOR DEPRIVERS CONTROL

What Does It Mean To Be A Depriver?

A Depriver is someone who, for reasons still under scientific investigation, possesses and employs a defense mechanism that can drastically incapacitate other human beings.

Deprivers are prohibited by law from touching other human beings due to the inherent adverse effects of their touch.

Deprivers need special attention and care during most activities that most of us take for granted. A brush with someone on the bus could have life-threatening results.

Hopefully, this safety notice will answer several of your questions and help you protect yourself and your loved ones from any negative contact.

Things you need to know if you or someone you love is a Depriver:

Some people don't even know they're Deprivers.

Depriver tendencies often develop soon after puberty.

Deprivation affects both the spinal column and brain centers directly.

Deprivation can occur either immediately after contact with a Depriver individual, or for up to two hours after contact has been made.

You can be deprived of sight, sound, touch, taste, smell, memory, pain, balance or sense of direction . . . indefinitely.

There is currently no cure for the Depriver condition.

If you are a Depriver or suspect you may have a Depriver tendency:

Call the Depriver hotline immediately and register, a qualified technician will tell you how to proceed.

If you must make physical contact with a child or pet in a life-threatening situation — wear gloves and avoid skin contact.

Do not donate blood, receive blood or become an organ donor.

Frequent misconceptions about Deprivers:

Deprivers gain something from you when they touch you.

Not true. Although the senses of a deprived person are diminished, the Depriver's senses are in no way enhanced.

After you've been deprived you'll become a Depriver.

Not true. Deprivation has never been observed to cause genetic mutation or the development or display of any Depriver tendencies.

Once you're deprived, that's it . . . you're deprived forever.

Not true. Most deprivations are temporary, only one out of ten afflictions have been labeled permanent. However, there have been cases whereby the deprived was rendered senseless permanently. Blindness, unfortunately, appears to be the easiest permanent affliction due to the delicateness of the optic nerves involved; the deprivation may actually expire yet the damage is often extensive.

Scientists have already developed a suppressant.

Not true. There is no known Depriver inhibitor.

Using public facilities after a Depriver has used them is dangerous.

Not true. Deprivation occurs only after skin on skin contact has been made.

Only certain types of people can be Deprivers.

Not true. Anyone could be a Depriver. Anyone.

Steps to take if you or a loved one has been Deprived:

Safely remove yourself from the situation, as not to cause repeated exposure. Repeated exposure may compound the sensory deprivation or extend its duration.

A typical deprivation lasts from forty-five minutes to two days, may clear suddenly and often leaves no permanent side effects.

Call your local Depriver hotline and allow a qualified technician to direct you.

Do not attempt to travel. In a deprived state, you may make poor or incorrect sensory choices that could be life threatening. The major percentage of fatalities occur when a deprived person makes a panicked attempt at transit. A minor optical deprivation could cause a slip or a fall. An audio deprivation could be dangerous in any and all traffic situations.

Frequently asked questions:

1) *Can a Depriver affect more than one of my senses?*

At this point, there are no documented case studies of multi-depriver capabilities, however there is much speculation in this field.

2) *Can Deprivers deprive each other of their senses?*

Yes.

3) *What about people who get purposely deprived by Deprivers just for the experience?*

There are thrill seekers out there who will seek out Deprivers to see "what it's like." They usually seek a Depriver whose deprivation duration is relatively short for obvious reasons.

4) *Are there any side effects of deprivation?*

Some report that it is consciousness expanding, but there is no empirical evidence to suggest any benefits beyond those attainable in a man-made sensory deprivation tank.*

*However, it has been frequently reported by patients who have been deprived that afterwards, also for an indeterminate duration, they will notice a blue-colored, prismatic afterimage, or aura around other Deprivers. In simpler terms, once you've been deprived you may now recognize a Depriver in a crowd.

Stay safe, don't touch strangers!
A message from your National Health Affiliates.

THE TOUCH

THE PENITENT

LINDA K. WRIGHT

When Gerald Williams called and asked me to meet him at the El Station at 48th and Market at three in the morning, I didn't give it much thought. I'm a city newspaper reporter and I'm used to getting calls in the middle of the night. I don't sleep well, anyway. The meeting was in the heart of what they call a rough area, but I'd grown up in one equally rough. You had your share of people who helped you and you had your share of assholes. What neighborhood doesn't?

They also said it was where people went to score drugs big-time. I'd had what people call a "substance abuse" problem and, truth be told, the neighborhood in which I was meeting Gerald wasn't either the best or the cheapest place to score. "They" really should check their facts.

But, if I met Gerald, I'd find out what had happened to Donna Kate.

Donna Kate Williams had reigned as the lead dancer for years with New York's Alvin Ailey Dance Company. She'd taken over from the legendary Judith Jamison and given

Black teens—male and female—another role model. When she wasn't touring the world with the company, she was speaking before civic associations, classes in high schools, everywhere, providing the message that people should pursue their dreams, regardless of the obstacles. After Donna Kate retired, she'd come back to Philly, her hometown, and founded her own modern dance studio. She wanted to teach the next generation of dance stars and preach the gospel of getting what you wanted.

This woman who had achieved her own dream and earned everyone's acclaim for doing so, had recently disappeared from public view, amid a huge scandal involving the death of her protégé. She'd been lambasted by the press, the girl's parents, and the community that had so worshiped her. For several months, she had refused to talk to anybody.

Now her husband, who had gone into seclusion with her, had resurfaced. He said Donna Kate wanted to talk to me, and warned me not to tell anyone about the meeting.

I didn't tell anyone where I was going. That didn't mean I didn't leave some word in my tiny apartment, in case I didn't return. I had to make sure people could trust me—up to the point where I could trust them.

I met Gerald at the El stop. The last time I'd seen him had been at some ritzy charity ball, this Black man poured into a tuxedo, looking really fine. But now he looked haggard; some of the polish was off. He didn't take the hand I offered.

"Thanks for coming," he said, his voice still wonderfully deep. He looked around, watchfully. "If you'll get inside, we'll be on our way." He waved toward the dark car almost hidden in the shadows of the El Station. I got inside. He didn't even open the car door for me. He waited till I'd fastened my seat belt and drove off. I gave him a minute, then started asking questions, but he told me I should wait and talk to Donna Kate.

Had Donna Kate pushed her protégé—Lisa was her name—too hard? That was the question everyone was asking. It had been rumored that Lisa had started to slip in her performances before she'd died. Had she started taking drugs? Did Donna Kate know something about it? Donna Kate had never gone in for drugs herself (not that anyone knew), but she was part of that artistic world. They did whatever it took to sustain their artistic reigns. It wouldn't be the first time a star had tried to manipulate a protégé.

I had my information from the press reports and the investigating I'd done on my own. But I also had Beverly, the twelve-year-old I'd adopted as a Little Sister. Having helped to raise my own four younger brothers and sisters, I couldn't seem to get away from raising somebody. Beverly's foster parents had enrolled her in Donna Kate's Dance Studio to help curb some of her anger. Beverly had loved it. Every time she and I had gotten together, she couldn't wait to tell me about all the new steps she'd learned and how excited everyone was for Lisa. If Lisa made it, they could, too. After Lisa's death, with the resulting publicity over unanswered questions, the Studio had shut down. Beverly became very quiet.

Lisa had jumped off the top of the Donna Kate Dance Studio. Why such a violent statement? The rumors were everywhere; but the police couldn't prove anything and they had to let it go. They had more pressing cases, with more promising leads.

Lisa's parents were inconsolable. Their grief had turned to anger. They told any reporter who would listen (and I'd been one of them) that famous people were always using children. You thought they cared, that they wanted to give back, but they didn't. They just wanted to use the children, stand on their backs. What recourse did hurting parents have?

Gerald Williams led the way inside the clean but run-down building. It had a fire escape, providing a quick exit if the press or the police got too close. You could just jump from the fire escape to the next building. I'd done it in the building where we had lived when I was growing up. But if I had noticed it, so would others. Donna Kate wouldn't jeté very far.

We climbed the steps to the third and top floor in silence. Gerald opened one of the doors on the left and motioned. He didn't follow as I stepped inside. I heard the door click behind me.

The woman I saw stretching her leg at the makeshift barre along one wall could have been the model for any dance magazine photo—she had been. From her bent-over position, she murmured, "Just a minute." Donna Kate took a deep breath as she lifted up, moving her leg off the barre. It was the middle of the night and this woman was warming up.

She grabbed the towel hanging over the end of the barre and draped it around her neck, then waved her hand toward the solitary chair in a corner of the room and started flexing her foot back and forth.

"I know this is an inconvenience. Thank you for coming," she said, all business. I looked at this tall, thin woman who'd become a pariah—her braided hair pulled back and her hands behind her.

"I'm glad your husband called me," I said. "How are you doing?"

"I asked Gerald to contact you because you have a reputation around the city. You aren't the first to jump on anyone's bandwagon—either for or against."

I watched as she kept flexing her foot.

"So, what happened?" I asked, getting to the point.

"Lisa Jenkins was my star pupil," Donna Kate answered, just as directly. "She had a *phenomenal* talent." She gave me a look. "I know you and others outside the arts see us as full of hyperbole, but Lisa really had it. She could execute a flawless–." Donna Kate stopped herself. "I wouldn't *knowingly* be a part of hurting that child. Why would I?" I saw tears in her eyes. "She was following in my footsteps. We took every spare minute to practice together." She looked down at the floor.

I tugged her back.

"You created a piece specifically for her?" Beverly had told me how Lisa had been practicing a special dance. The other students had talked of nothing else.

"Yes." Donna Kate shivered then composed herself. "Yes, I did," she said in a stronger voice. "I created my best work for her–in the tradition of the spiritual. It is called *The Penitent*. The Company in New York was sponsoring a competition and this piece, properly done, had everything that the true admirer of the dance would appreciate." Donna Kate whispered fiercely. "And Lisa could *do* it."

I sat and watched as she lost herself again in the telling, half-walking, half-dancing across the floor.

"The Penitent comes before God and her dance is a plea for forgiveness. She has willfully committed many sins and knows that only God can grant her the forgiveness that she seeks.

"There was one day we practiced that was particularly intense. We were working on the part just before the Penitent is blessed by God. It is especially dramatic, entailing a series of jumps, and must be done just so. I had taken Lisa through every step, every sequence, over and over. I straightened her feet–" Donna Kate pinched her fingers together "—if they were even a millimeter off. I molded her arms, her body." Donna Kate shrugged her shoulders. "The practice was more intense, perhaps, than other days, but nothing unusual when preparing for a competition.

"Lisa came in the next day feeling off-center. She kept checking everything she did. I was puzzled. She'd never done that before; she'd never had to. She kept touching things, as though to reassure herself. I thought maybe it was the tension. I told her to do her usual practice and then go home, take it easy.

"Every day after that, she was worse. I'm used to dealing with teenagers. They're all drama queens. I thought, Maybe it's not the tension over the competition. Maybe it's some school problem, a boy, something. Lisa kept saying she couldn't feel the movements. We repeated everything again and again, and she kept saying the same thing. She couldn't feel. Couldn't feel the floor underneath her feet, couldn't even feel if she were truly pointing her toe. At one point, she took my hand and hit her arm with it—several times. 'I can't *feel* it!' She looked at me, daring me to tell her she was wrong.

"What did you do?" I'd brought my notepad but I wasn't taking notes.

"I pulled away, of course." Donna Kate looked at me as if talking to an idiot. "Her hand was warm; I thought she must have a flu. I couldn't afford to catch it. Lisa stared at me, looking at me for so long that I felt a little unnerved. That would have been anyone's reaction. I asked her what she was staring at. She said she saw a blue light around my head. I thought she was delirious. I telephoned her parents.

"They took her to see one doctor and then another. They didn't help.

"I wondered if it might be a neurological problem. I got

8

in touch with one of the best doctors I knew. I told her parents I'd even pay for the visit. I *personally* walked her through all the tests, encouraged her—everything. The hospital took her through the mill; they didn't find anything. Finally the neurologist said that it had to be in Lisa's head. Her parents had no choice but to believe this. They took her home.

"After that, Lisa became more determined to act as if everything was normal. But that didn't stop her from checking everything. I'd find her staring intently at the mirror while she did a step or as she touched a partner's hand during practice. It's like she was seeing how it *looked* to apply the right pressure.

"I would have her dance *The Penitent*, and she kept pushing too hard. She'd lost her light touch with the movements. I tried not to get impatient. If this child could just get through the competition, she'd have access to any company in New York. She could rise to the top and take her family with her, just like I did.

"It didn't work. She kept flubbing it. Finally, I told her she was going to have to get the series of jumps right that day or I'd have to choose someone else to do the competition. I guess I thought even then she was exaggerating her symptoms and when she got her nerves under control, she'd get it right.

"She did the jumps. I could see her straining, giving it everything she had. I hadn't gotten it before—she was visibly trying. She had made it look so effortless before. She came down too hard. That's what made me realize, she really *couldn't* feel. She couldn't feel how hard she came down. She broke her leg.

"The weird thing is that when she came down and everyone around us was screaming—I mean, the blood was everywhere and you could see the bone sticking out—she didn't react! While we waited for the ambulance, she just sat there, looking at me.

"I had to assign her role to another student. His dance wasn't up to Lisa's level, but he would give the Studio a chance in the competition. I had to think about the Studio.

Donna Kate looked at me defiantly. "This is art. You can't skimp on it."

"How did *Lisa* feel?" I asked.

Donna Kate held out her hands. "How do you expect? How can a dancer dance unless she can *feel* what she is doing? How can she do an arabesque?" She did one. "You have to *feel* your foot pointing upward! How can she do a *pas de chat*?" Donna Kate bent her leg and darted like a cat. "She has to be able to *feel* it." Her voice became louder. "A pirouette?" Her execution was as controlled as her voice was not. "She has to be able to *feel* the turn. She has to be able to feel the floor under her feet!" Her eyes filled with tears. "I took this child's dreams away."

"Wasn't it the illness, whatever it was, that took her dreams away? Why do you think it was you?" I didn't like Donna Kate's cavalier attitude. But, unfeeling as it was, I didn't understand how this woman, who hadn't blamed herself for her behavior up to now, was feeling the bite.

"It was funny, I didn't take it seriously when Lisa kept saying she could see a blue light around me. I thought she was getting dramatic again; it sounded so religious. You know. But a few days after I'd been working with Derek, the student I'd assigned to do the competition, he started acting like Lisa. He didn't say anything to me at first, but I saw him doing the same coping things Lisa had done. Checking every move in the mirror because he couldn't *feel* what he was doing. I asked him about it. He told me the same things

Lisa had. I thought he was playing games, maybe had overheard Lisa saying something. I sent him home.

"This had just been so hard on me. I took a few days off. Gerald knew I was uptight, even though I hadn't told him any details of what was happening. He rearranged his schedule and we went to Cape May for a long weekend. We are so attuned to each other. I thought I'd get reconnected and come back to the Studio refreshed and figure out what I was going to do about the Competition. We made love quite passionately the first two nights. The third night, just before we were to come home, I felt my husband was just going through the motions. You've seen him," Donna Kate cocked an eyebrow. "It doesn't take much for either of us to get stirred up. I'd never tired him out before. He just wasn't responding the way I wanted, the way I expected.

"The bottom line," she said flatly. "He couldn't feel me. Have you ever made love, with total abandon, and known that your partner wasn't feeling what you felt? He felt *nothing* I was doing to him—nothing!" Her tone was no longer flat. "I took him inside me and he felt nothing!"

Donna Kate looked down at the floor, started to speak, then tried again. She looked up. She spoke slowly, succinctly. "He said . . . he saw . . . a blue . . . aura around me. I knew then, whatever it was, I had something and I was hurting people with it. Lisa, Derek, and now Gerald? I don't touch many people; I don't need to. The other teachers train the general dance student population." Donna Kate shrugged helplessly. "Only the people I touched were getting hurt!

"I took the risk of going to a doctor outside the state. I didn't tell him anything, just had him give me his most thorough examination. He found nothing! I called his office a few days later to check on the test results. The nurse reported that I was perfectly healthy. I asked if I could schedule a follow-up with the doctor. She said she'd give me the name of one of the doctor's associates. The doctor who'd seen me had taken a medical leave."

She looked at me, no defiance left. "You're a reporter. I'll give you his name and you confirm what's wrong with him. I already know.

"Out of all of this, you want to know what gets to me?

"Lisa couldn't feel her *bed*! When she was in the hospital with her broken leg, I went to see her. She waited till her parents had left the room. She had told them that her sense of feeling was coming back. She said she told them that so they wouldn't worry. But she still couldn't feel, she said. Even though she knew her body was horizontal on the bed, she couldn't feel it. She couldn't rest because she couldn't feel what it was like to release her body into the bed. I'd never thought about it before; you have to *feel* the bed underneath you in order to rest. And she couldn't feel it. I had not only taken this child's dreams away, but I'd taken away her ability to dream more dreams. She couldn't rest. How could she live?

"The day they let Lisa out of the hospital, she waited till it was dark and snuck out of her house. She got a hack and came here to the Studio after hours. She hobbled up to the top of the fire escape—and jumped off. Her parents asked me, at the funeral, why their daughter had died and what the note she'd left meant. They'd found a note in her room. In it she asked them not to worry. She'd chosen to go this way. She told them she wouldn't feel the pain of hitting the ground—just release. Only I knew what she really meant.

"What could I tell her parents? What can I tell them now? They think it was because I pushed her too hard. They blame me. They should, but not for the reasons they do.

"Besides," Donna Kate sighed, "the 'why' doesn't make a difference to them. Their daughter's dead. And what they *think* caused Lisa's death is probably a lot less scary.

"Something's wrong with me and they can't find what it is. I'm not an hysteric. And if you think I am, you're more than welcome to come over here and let me touch you."

I remained sitting where I was.

Donna's bravado cracked. She asked, in a whisper, "You don't see anything around my head, do you?"

I looked. Her braids were beautifully done, but I saw nothing around her hair or her head.

Gerald took me back to the El Station. I noticed there were suitcases in the back of the car. I asked him about them. All he said was that I needn't come back for a second interview.

When he pulled up at the El Station, I said. "I appreciate the care you took not to touch me."

Gerald turned his head and looked at me. "I don't know if I have whatever it is. I don't even know if I got it from my wife. It just seems wise not to touch anyone."

He turned to stare straight ahead and waited till I got out of the car. I looked at this man and remembered how he had used to look—handsome, tall, and built. I watched him drive away.

If Donna Kate's story was true, and I would check it out, what did it mean? I knew neither Gerald nor Donna Kate had touched me, but what effect did close proximity have? Had I been exposed to whatever it was, anyway? Even though Beverly had trained with the other dance teachers, had Donna Kate touched her, even once? A pat on the arm, maybe? Was I sure I hadn't brushed up against Gerald in the car?

I heard the El coming. I could catch it if I hurried.

I didn't hurry. I didn't take the El that night.

I walked the 15 blocks back to my apartment in West Philly.

I wanted to feel the ground underneath my feet.

AFTER THE WAR

KARL SCHROEDER

I rina stood in line, trying to imitate the look of dejected patience worn by other women. The sky had decided to be gray, darkening the shot-out windows in the houses around the square.

"Who is working the table today?" Irina asked the woman in front of her.

"Gersamovic." The woman drew her shawl more tightly around her shoulders. "He is a butcher."

"I know."

"Six times he's made me line up. Something's not right each time."

"They say he lets younger women through."

The other gave Irina a once-over. "Oh, yes," she said. "You're his type. He'll certify your papers. But at a price."

Irina shivered. "Anything to escape this godforsaken country." She let her eyes rest on the vista of broken rooftops that, when she was a girl, had glowed gold like magic in the evening light. She saw only gray slate and upthrust splinters now.

A commotion had broken out on the other side of the square. Probably another squabble over food.

"I hope somebody kills him soon," said somebody behind Irina.

"Hush," said the first woman. Irina didn't know either of them; the town was overrun with strangers these days. "Don't even think anything like that. Ostovac's men have immunity. Even the UN won't touch them."

"Yeah, I hear he had his own lieutenant shot. An old boyhood chum. Dumped the body in the river, then went swimming."

"Ostovac," said Irina under her breath.

They were nearly at the head of the line. Just a few more minutes, and she would have what she wanted . . . or not.

"Witch!"

All heads turned. A man had burst into the empty center of the square. He stood, a grey pillar in the red mud. He held a rifle in his hands.

"I know you're here!" he shouted. "Show yourself, or by God I'll kill all of you."

"That's Terajic," said the woman behind Irina.

Other men, members of Ostovac's private police force, ran over. Two of them began struggling with the man.

"You don't understand! She's here! She'll come for you too if we don't find her now." Terajic broke free, staggered, and raised his rifle. It was pointed at the line of visa applicants.

Irina and the other women hit the dirt. Nobody screamed, the way they might have in the early days of the war. There was a shot, then another. Then only the sound of men cursing.

Irina ventured a peek. Terajic was down, slumped with the unnatural looseness she recognized as death. The other soldiers were clumped around him, babbling to one another, shouting and accusing, ignoring the still crouching women.

Gersamovic stood up from the metal table they'd hauled into the street that morning. "Get him out of here!" he shouted. "You! Tell Ostovac that Terajic's dead. Nobody's to blame, I saw the whole thing. Go on! Get on with your business."

He sat down again, puffing out his swarthy cheeks. "Come on! Next!"

The women stood. Irina heard someone behind her weeping. The two she had been talking to wore pragmatic frowns, like herself, as they examined their muddied clothes.

"What was that all about?"

"What do you mean? Isn't it obvious?" He snapped.

"But why?"

Irina looked down her nose at them. "Guilt," she said, with satisfaction.

"Next!"

It was her turn. Irina walked slowly up to Gersamovic, smiling as winsomely as she could. The effort to hold the expression hurt her face.

"I haven't seen you around here before," said Gersamovic. He took a posture characteristic of him, fingers wrapped around the far ends of the desk to emphasize his size as he leaned forward. "Just arrive?"

"Actually, I grew up here." *So I've known the alleys to take to avoid you.* "I've seen *you.*"

"I'll bet you have. So, you want to leave, do you?"

. Irina looked around pointedly, and shrugged.

Gersamovic laughed. They said he laughed when he shot people. She didn't place much stock in stories, but he was Ostovac's man, and part of the occupying force. Irina didn't need extra incentive to hate him.

"Tell you what," he said. "I'll stamp your little paper there, and you can go see Ostovac tomorrow. But first you see me. Tonight."

She held out her papers, unable to continue smiling. Gersamovic's stamp was necessary for her to get in to see Ostovac for the actual emigration interview. It was joke bureaucracy, of course, there to satisfy the letter and flout the spirit of the UN peace terms.

Irina turned her hand as Gersamovic reached for the papers, so that his fingers collided with the inside of her wrist. She let her skin slide over his fingertips and dropped the papers in the center of the desk.

He blinked at her, squeezed his eyes shut for a second, then looked down at the papers.

Mechanically, he reached out and slammed the stamp down on the top sheet.

"Thank you." She snatched up the papers and walked quickly in the direction of the crowd that was gathering because of the shooting. She spared a quick glance at Terajic, who was being dragged away by three cursing men. She smiled. When she reached the crowd she looked back at Gersamovic. He was staring at the face of the woman who had come after Irina. His face held an expression of almost comic bewilderment.

Suddenly he stood up. "Shit!" His chair toppled back, and the woman recoiled with a shriek.

"Stop her! Where is she?"

Two of his men ran up. "Who?"

"The woman! The one who was just here. Where did she go?"

The men exchanged a shrug. They had been watching Terajic's corpse leave the square.

"What's she look like?"

"Like . . . like . . ." Gersamovic's face was turning red.

Irina smiled. She was dressed with absolute conservatism today. She could be any of these women, or they her. Only her face might betray her, to a man who could remember it.

In the moment when she touched him, Gersamovic had lost that ability.

It was terrifying, but exhilarating, to stand there while Gersamovic stalked up and down the square, grabbing people and staring at them as if he didn't know what he was seeing. Well, he didn't, in fact, and when his eyes lit upon her there was no recognition in them at all.

"What's she look like?"

"I don't know." Finally he stood there, shaking, tears starting in the corners of his eyes. "I don't know, I don't know, I don't know."

Satisfied that he wasn't going to seize upon an innocent bystander at random, Irina turned and walked away. She let one hand caress the papers in her pocket. She was one step closer.

When the emptiness came over her, late that night, she was ready for it. This was the fourth time she'd deliberately used her curse, and she was beginning to understand the way of it. She lay in bed, biting her lower lip, blinking away the tears, but curiously calm under them.

Yes, there was a pattern. First the anger came, and the gloating ambition to take revenge on the invaders who had destroyed her family and her life. She would walk the streets, tingling with anticipation, feeling that for once her affliction was her ally. She would hunt her prey single-mindedly and, in the moment of touching them, feel a terrible satisfaction.

Then, in the night, would come the despair. She had destroyed another man's life, and still her son remained dead. No amount of revenge upon those who had killed Mikhail would bring him back.

Irina let herself cry. Her breath steamed in the dark air. It was utterly silent after curfew; she was sure everyone within a block would hear her, but who would notice one more woman crying these days?

The first time, she had wanted to die. She hadn't believed she could deliberately do to these men what she had accidentally done to her own husband and son years ago. Do it—and like it. She was evil, an abomination.

Irina had never told her old friends here the truth about her return to her hometown. Her husband had cheated on her, she'd told them, and lied well enough to get custody of Mikhail at the end of it all. They'd believed her; she was shattered enough for the story to be convincing. No one asked why she wore long gloves even in the summer, and took no new lovers. People here were used to the strange grief of widows and cast-outs. She moved among them like a ghost, tracing long circles through town that began alone at her front door and ended there the same way, carrying the few spoils she could afford from occasional accounting jobs. She read, she watched the streams of people, and she hid her face from the sight of lovers kissing.

She hardly noticed the war until the day refugees from her husband's town began streaming down the road. They were all women or girls. The men were dead. The boys were dead. Ostovac had come and purged the countryside in the name of his own people.

Taking station in a field on the edge of Brcko, Ostovac had made the townspeople parade past him. He'd separated them by ethnic type. His own people he sent back into the town. Of the others, the women were sent down the road, while the men—including her husband, who could not tell invader from neighbor—were marched to the woods behind the field. Irina had heard that the gunshots went on for hours. Ostovac was indiscriminate. He allowed himself to make mistakes, erring on the side of thoroughness. Mikhail was dead, along with a dozen boys who were probably Serbian and could have been saved.

Irina had let that knowledge prey on her. In the silent times before dawn, when she couldn't sleep, she would sometimes admit to herself that she felt better blaming Ostovac's men for shooting Mikhail. It lessened her own guilt. The more she focused on that blame, the less she hated herself.

So she had begun to stalk him. And tonight she finally had the pretext she needed to get within touching distance. These hands that had maimed her husband and son, forever separating her from them, could at least be revenged on the one who had killed Stefan and Mikhail.

Or so she told herself, as she lay staring at the ceiling and crying. It had taken weeks for her to recover the anger, and strike again after the first time. Days, after each of the next two. Meanwhile she would wallow in self-loathing and horror. She felt it now, overwhelmingly.

She closed her eyes and gritted her teeth. Gersamovic would talk. They would figure it out. If she was going to go after Ostovac, it would have to be tomorrow. She couldn't wait to feel better about herself, or remind herself of all the reasons why he deserved it. She was going to have to decide if she was going to do it despite her guilt.

Irina didn't sleep that night.

Most of the houses in the town were of new, cheap construction. Irina had grown up in one of these—cinder block walls, metal roof, some attempt at ornamentation around the windows. The house Ostovac had taken over was old, at least two hundred years. Its roof had been replaced with corrugated iron recently, but the windows were of leaded glass that looked pebbly and uneven, as if those bullets had miraculously missed the original glass all these years. As she approached, she could make out a patina of bullet holes in the whitewash. If she looked closely, she recognized hundreds of older dents in the stonework, made by bullets in previous wars. The house had remained standing through all of it; who knew how many times it had changed sides?

Two of Ostovac's thugs stood guard behind the concrete pylons that ringed the front door. Although hostilities were officially over, the guards were armed to the teeth; Irina even spotted a rocket launcher leaning in the shadows near the door.

She held out her papers, looking closely at the face of the man as she said her name. "Irina Ulaj." Had they made the connection between herself and Gersamovic? It wouldn't matter if they figured it out within the next ten minutes; it was just a case of whether she could get in this door.

The guard made a good show of looking over the papers, then shrugged indifferently. "Go in." But he didn't hand the papers back. She eased around him, thankful again for the cold weather that allowed her to cover so much of her skin.

Inside she smelled cigar smoke, cooked sausage and the particular, unidentifiable smell that distinguishes individual houses. It was cold in here, almost as cold as outside. Five men bundled in greatcoats were playing cards in the living room; sunset light through the windows made crosses on the far wall. One looked up, said, "Upstairs, second room," and went back to the game.

Ostovac had made his office in the smallest room, presumably because it was easy to heat. He sat in a metal-frame chair with his hands behind his head, back to the small fireplace, in an attempt to soak up as much heat as possible, more than an arm's length from the battered desk strewn with papers. She wondered why he didn't just drag the desk closer to the fire?

There were two other chairs in front of the desk; aside from that, the room was empty, except for pyramids of paper stacked everywhere. The floor was wood. The wallpaper was a dull green.

His eyes followed her as she entered and sat at the desk. He had a wide face and black hair, with the wide mustache that seemed like a military standard these days. He reminded her of Stalin, and she remembered reading how Stalin's mask of calm had become so second nature that even during the war he neither wept nor smiled at misfortune or victory. God forbid any son of hers should grow up this way.

"My name is Irina Ulaj."

"I know." He continued watching her. His voice was a baritone, pleasant even. His continued gaze unnerved her, and deliberately, she stripped off her gloves, allowing herself a glance at the white skin of her fingers as she laid them on her knee. Her weapons were ready.

"They . . . took my papers at the door."

"You want to leave the country?"

"Yes. I want a passport."

"All right." He finally moved, hopping the chair up to the desk, where he picked up an envelope. He tossed it across the table; she caught it as it was about to fall off the edge.

He's tense, Irina realized. She cleared her throat. "That's it? That's all there is to it?"

"No." He looked somewhere distant over her shoulder as he said, "You'll have to earn it."

Just like Gersamovic, she thought. But her mouth was dry as she said, "How?"

Ostovac finally looked at her. He allowed himself a small, ironic smile. "By doing what you presumably came here to do anyway."

Her heart began to race. "And that was?"

"Whatever it is you did to Gersamovic yesterday."

Irina's mind went utterly blank. All she was aware of was his eyes, dark and calm, gazing into hers.

"You killed my son," she heard herself say.

Ostovac lost the smile. He sat back. "I've killed many women's sons," he said, not proudly, matter-of-fact.

"Other women's sons are not my concern," she said. She had crossed the Rubicon; she was dead now, or worse, so it no longer mattered what she said. She would say what she felt. "I don't want impersonal justice for you, not some anonymous war-crimes trial. No, I want you to know that it is for Mikhail my son that . . ." *I'm going to do this*, she finished in her mind as she silently watched him unbutton his shirt cuff and stretch out his arm.

"How is it done?" he asked mildly. "Is it enough for you to touch my hand?"

A momentary silence hung in the air.

"So, now you mock me," she scowled. He was going to snatch his hand away at the last minute. Ostovac was an adrenaline addict, she guessed. Of course, what other man would rise to his sort of position?

"I'm not mocking you. I saw what you did to Gersamovic. We had a doctor look at him. He said it's something called—aphasia. He'd seen it before, in a soldier who had the side of his head shot off. Gersamovic can't recognize faces anymore, and he has trouble with names—though he did remember yours from the papers. Good thing. He's sedated right now, by the way. It's hit him hard."

"Good." She was surprised at the viciousness in her voice.

"You know why I became a soldier?"

"I don't care. Did Mikhail know?"

Ostovac sat back. "Ah. Well, that's hit the nail on the head, hasn't it? But let me explain. My parents were killed

when I was twelve. It was one of you who shot them. Who?
I don't know. Might have been someone you know, a relative, your father, even. I didn't know; that's the problem.
Every day while I was growing up, I saw you people, I wondered, Is that one there remembering how he shot my parents? Is he laughing at me inside? Somewhere out there was
the man, or woman. I couldn't hit them directly. But I *had* to
hit them."

"By killing my son."

Ostovac shrugged. "It can take a lifetime for a man to
grow up. It took me my whole life to reach this point—this
day, this room and you."

"What do you mean?" She had no idea what he was
talking about, and that was more frightening than any cer-
tainty about her fate. She had a death-grip on the arms of
her chair. Well, it will never identify me, she thought, and
almost laughed at the absurdity of the thought.

"You see," Ostovac went on, "you and I are both driven
by the same thing: revenge. Even a month ago, I would
have said there was no difference between us. I'd have shot
you there in that chair without a second thought."

"So? Why don't you?" she managed to say.

His eyes were darting around the room again. "I'm sure
you heard about it. Two weeks ago, I gave the order to have
an old friend shot. It's raised my standing in the eyes of our
fighters, because Vlacic was a peacemonger. Well, maybe.
At the time, that was how I was thinking. Afterward . . . I
remembered our times together. We drank together—here,
actually, down the street. Used to be an inn, but of course it
was burned down in the first days of the war. I remember
that night . . ." His eyes focused on her again. "Was that
revenge? I don't think so."

He laughed, nervously shuffling the papers on the desk.
"After that, I thought about killing myself. I never had any

trouble shooting you people. Christ would have us make no distinction between others, but I do. I do, and I can't stop myself. I look at you and I see a damned Croat. I'm not going to lie to myself, I'll never forgive and forget. So what, then? Shoot myself and go to Hell? I've seen men do that.

"I would have, though, except that something happened. One day Malacek went crazy. He didn't recognize anybody, started shooting wildly. We had to take him down. Two days later, same thing happens to Terajic. But all he did was babble about witches: he meets a mystery woman, and she steals people's faces. A mystery until yesterday, when Gersamovik lost it in the market square."

Ostovac fumbled in his khaki shirt, drew out a cigarette. Absently, he offered it to her. She shook her head. He lit it and blew smoke down at his lap.

"At first, I was horrified. To be unable to tell the enemy from your own! But as I thought about it, the words *all are one* kept coming back to me. The more I thought about it, the more it seemed like the answer I had been looking for."

Irina stood up, knocking her chair over. "No! I'll not save you from yourself!"

He had rolled himself back to the fire. Now he absently put one hand down to the warmth while staring at her fixedly over the glowing end of his cigarette.

"I could force you," he said. "All I have to do is grab your hand. That's true, isn't it?"

She stood poised, ready to run for the hall. He could shout, and his men would block her way in an instant.

"Well, I asked myself this morning, when does a man begin to atone for himself? You have to draw the line somewhere. Go if you want, and maybe I will shoot myself. Just answer me one thing first."

"What?"

"If you were my mother, what would you want Irina Ulaj to do?"

"Bastard!" She launched herself around the desk. Ostovac didn't flinch as she raised her hand, then she slapped him so hard that her hand stung with the force of the blow.

He fell off the chair and lay on his side, hand to cheek. Then, he levered himself up onto his elbow. He looked at her, utterly serious.

Trembling, Irina reached out and took his face in her hands.

It was hours before the feeling that she was having a heart attack subsided. The pain in her chest was intense, but she knew it for what it was: grief. So, she walked with it, not seeing the faces of those she passed or the bullet-scarred facades of their houses. Eventually, she found herself sitting in her own parlor, the envelope from Ostovac on the desk before her.

They had just let her go. That seemed the cruelest thing: she had been allowed to live with it. Ostovac's men didn't know what she had done, and she didn't know how long he was going to try to keep it from them. It couldn't work for long. Unless she used the contents of this envelope now, and left the country, they would come for her soon. Maybe that would be best.

As evening fell, she rose automatically and lit a lamp. In the flickering light she had a sudden moment of perception; seeing the small room as it had been before the war, during one of the periodic blackouts that plagued the towns during the communist period.

Irina and her mother had sat together in this kitchen with just a candle between them, joking to pass the time. Her mother had told Irina how she had baked with *her* mother before they had electricity; in the evenings, they would wrap the cooling bread for tomorrow's market. Her mother associated candlelight with such times.

Irina would forever associate it with the war.

What would mother want for me?

Tears starting in her eyes, Irina plunked herself down at the table and tore open the envelope.

A travel visa fell out. Then a second visa.

Irina blinked. Was this a mistake? Ostovac must have given her the wrong papers. She picked up the visas.

One was made out to Irina Ulaj. The other was made out to Mikhail Ulaj. It had a sheet of paper clipped to it.

Hands shaking, she spread out the paper by the candle. The first thing she saw was Ostovac's signature on the bottom of the white sheet.

"Irina Ulaj," he had written. "When I learned it was you, I checked your background. They told me about your husband and son, so I checked our records. Atonement has to start somewhere."

The only other writing on the page was an address:

APARTMENT 12

782 BYELOSJ STREET

BRCKO

Irina began to sob. "Mikhail, Mikhail," she murmured through her tears, and, for the first time in five years, she knew she was not speaking to the dead. "You won't know me."

Mikhail wouldn't recognize her, no matter how much time she spent with him. No matter how she loved him, his eyes would never light up when she entered the room. The last time she had seen him, he had barely known the sound of her voice. By now, even her name might be a fading memory.

Ostovac had stepped willingly into that same shadow world. He no longer wanted to be able to tell people apart. Such blindness was his only hope of salvation.

Funny, that. As her tears dried, she found herself stroking the visas, thinking about Ostovac walking into the night, hands outstretched for the touch of another human—innocently indiscriminate, unjudging, pure.

Had she ever held the hand of another and not judged them, by age, race, sex or color? Of course not. At last she knew that she had walked away from her husband and her son not because of guilt, but because she could not bear the thought that *they* could not judge her. Because they could not punish her, she had punished herself.

By morning, she was packed and on the road to Brcko.

A BLIND VIRGIN
LIKE A LOADED GUN

STEVEN-ELLIOT ALTMAN

She had no idea that I'd killed a man earlier that morning. His name was Osbourne and I'd waited for him for just under an hour. I bore his tardiness no ill will. After all, I was there to kill him. Maybe he'd sensed it? Maybe he'd stopped off to enjoy a final cup of coffee or taken the longer path through Central Park, the grassier one? Who knows? Wouldn't affect my paycheck. He came in and was startled pale to see me sitting there enjoying a glass of wine on his veranda. One of the dustier bottles from his collection, quite a charming wine, effervescent, a cherry pick.

I motioned to him with a finger. He hesitated at first, then came striding over and slapped his hat down on the table before me.

"Who are you and what do you mean breaking in here like this?"

I swished the wine in the crystal and took a sip, gave him a wink. "I'm Robert," I told him, "and you have a fine taste in wines. May I pour you a glass?"

"No," he said, shaking his jowled face in confusion. "Why are you here, what do you want?"

I slowly rose, offering my right hand. "I wish to make your acquaintance, Mr. Osbourne . . . and then to discuss a business proposition from a mutual friend."

He reluctantly shook my hand—rightly so, but his options were, after all, limited. It was a firm contact. He sat down then and allowed me to pour him a drink.

"Now then," he began, finding again the sense of authority that had brought him to such a high position in the world. "Which friend and what business proposition?"

"Prescott. I believe you were supposed to make a certain phone call to a specified politician, you know the one?"

He nodded, the remaining color draining from his face.

"You never made that call and my client is very disappointed."

"I'll make restitution!" he broke in feverishly.

I shook my head and sipped his wine. "Sorry," I said. "The contract has already been posted and I'm the collection agency." I removed a small case from my coat pocket and placed it on the table.

Osbourne panicked. He tried to rise, but was already paralyzed. Only his eyes were capable of movement.

I checked my watch: three minutes. Not bad. I unzipped the case and brought out the syringe, checked for the air bubble. Funny how air is one of the key ingredients of life and yet a tiny bubble injected into the bloodstream ends it all so abruptly.

"Don't struggle," I said, tapping the needle. "I don't want to hurt you."

I don't have an alarm system in my own apartment because I've always considered my special trick to be enough to get me through any situation. Nobody knows where I live anyway. Cops poking blind? A rare instance. Clients? All satisfied customers. Friends? None to speak of.

I opened my door and there she was sitting on the couch smoking a cigarette; blonde, teen-ager, body posture relaxed and non-threatening. I laughed out loud. I thought about running, but all I had to do was get close enough to touch her, right? I took my coat off, hung it up, took off my gloves, stowed them away in the coat, all beneath her watchful eyes.

I came up around the couch within arms-length and saw her stiffen as she rose. I offered my hand: "Robert Luxley. To whom do I have the pleasure?"

"As *if* I would reach out and touch you," she said, and took a drag off her cigarette, flicking ashes indiscriminately on my priceless Persian rug.

Fascinating. A thousand responses flickered through my brain. *She knows. She knows about my special trick. How in the hell can she possibly know?* And yes, she was in range. I could easily have reached out quickly to touch her and that would be that. But I was intrigued, like never before. *Son of a bitch, she actually knows.*

"Darling . . ." I said. This was a bad choice of words. She suddenly displayed a .38 caliber pistol, plunging the barrel into my mouth.

"Not darling," she whispered. "Cut the bullshit and tell me who you work for."

Screw her. I reached out for her bare stomach. She moved like she was expecting it and cocked the hammer, her lips contorted. "Don't you ever try to touch me, Mister. I will blow your brains right outta the back of your skull!"

I dropped my hand slow and steady. I wanted to apologize but it was futile, what with the gun in my mouth and all. She said, "I know what you are," then let the hammer slide back, inching the gun from my face, and stepped out of range. Still aimed, of course.

What I am? I smiled and inquired, "Would you like something to drink? I could really use one right about now myself."

"Yes. Water, please," she replied.

I thought the *please* was rather odd after a break-and-entry and the forced intimacy of the pistol, but I poured two glasses as she stood over me. Handing her the glass of her choice, I sighed. "Well, then, would you mind explaining exactly what it is you seem to think I am?"

She seemed puzzled, judging from the slight curl of her lip. That movement was so attractive in her that I was thankful I hadn't touched her. "Don't jerk me, Mister!" she said with a sneer as she regained her composure—and aimed at a most sensitive part of my anatomy.

"Hang on!" I yelled. "I'm not *jerking* you. I don't know you and I don't know what you want from me. How do you know about my trick?"

She looked me dead in the eyes and laughed—a beautiful, frightening thing. "You really don't know, do you? You don't know what you are? You can't sense what I am?"

Questions, more questions. Keep her talking.

"I honestly don't . . . I've been doing it since I was fourteen years old. Are you a relative of someone that . . . ?"

"Oh, I'm a relative of yours all right," she expelled between hysterics. "I'm the same genetic stuff, but you . . ." Laughter again; I thought she'd double over. "You think I'm here because you killed some mark, don't you, you sick fuck? You think I'm here seeking vengeance? Oh, God, you're too pathetic. You really don't know. I can see it on your face."

She was pissing me off but there was little I could do. The fact that I was an assassin was laughable to her. Okay, if she's not here because of business then what does that leave? It was all too obvious that she knew things, things I needed to know and would pay good money for. She evidently sensed this as well because she slipped the gun back into the front of her jeans, flopped down on my couch, and put her boots up on my ten-thousand-dollar crystal coffee table.

I sipped my water. "How do you know about my trick?"

She licked her lips. "It's *your* trick, huh?"

"How did you know where I lived?"

"I saw you on the street. You're unmistakable, but you wouldn't know that either, Mister *un*touchable, *un*touched."

She held all the cards and I couldn't stand it. "What if I touch you?"

At that she smiled, somehow eager to fill me in. C'mon baby, keep talkin'.

"What if *I* touch you?" she said with a smirk.

That thought blew me away. I sat down on the divan across from her. She was telling me that she didn't just *know* what I was, she was implying that she *was* what I am. I'll be a sonofabitch.

"You do it, too?"

She nodded, lit up again. "Hate to break it to you, but a lot of people can do what we can do."

"So, if we touch each other, we're both paralyzed?"

She smiled again and stretched out. "A paralyzer, huh? Rule Number One: Never tell what you can do."

"Oh," I replied. "There's something else that you do to people when you touch them?" I just sat there calmly, wanting to scream. This girl held the answers I'd looked for without a clue for sixteen long, puzzling years.

She pursed her lips and shook her head. "My questions first, Robbie."

I could do nothing but nod in agreement. She had me cold.

"How long do normals stay zapped when you touch them?"

Normals? That took painful calculation. "Twenty minutes or so," I replied. "And you?"

She rolled her eyes and then, "If they come out of it—if you don't do something nasty, I mean—are they like, still healthy after?"

Another heavy question, one I didn't like to dwell on for too long. I'd touched this girl I knew in college ungloved once by accident and had spent half an hour praying to God that she'd be okay. She'd seemed all right, I think she was all right. Didn't seem psychologically screwed-up or anything. Damn, this was getting personal. "Yes," I replied. "If they live, they're always healthy afterwards, as far as I know."

She was ready to fire the next question: "Does it always happen with you, or only when your heart starts beating really fast?"

That did it, no more doubts, this is the real deal on my couch. "It only happens when I am either excited or stressed. But I never trust it. Always gloves. Believe it or not, I go far out of my way to avoid touching normals who aren't contracts."

She sagged a bit at that, and her eyes were far away for a moment. She bit her lip ever so lightly.

"It always happens with you, doesn't it?" I asked softly.

She looked back to me, tears starting in her eyes, and she nodded. She almost touched me there—emotionally, I mean—but I'm not one to pass on an advantage.

"You could at least tell me your name, couldn't you?"

A drop released itself and came slithering down the

curve of her young cheek, entering her mouth. "Cassandra," she told me. "My name is Cassandra."

I got down on one knee before her. "Tell me, please, Cassandra. I want—I *need* to know. What are we that we can't touch them?"

She wiped at her face with the back of her thin fingered hand and said, "We're Deprivers, Robert. They call us Deprivers."

Yes! That is the perfect name. Deprivers! That is exactly what we are!

I asked her if she might not care for a glass of cognac.

The next morning I awoke with a hangover and went to check if Cassandra was still passed out on the couch. She was. What to do?

I made us coffee, orange juice, eggs benedict and toast before moving to wake her, all the time thinking, My life is changing now, nothing will be the same again. I was about to tap her, then thought better of it.

"Cassandra, Cassandra, wake up. I've made us some breakfast. Cassandra."

She startled awake and was over the side of the couch in a blink, eyes wild. "Don't touch me!"

"It's Robert, remember? You slept on my couch last night."

"Yeah," she said, catching herself. "I dreamt that you touched me and I was never gonna wake up again."

"I had the same dream. Well, both still intact, eh?" Actually, I'd stood over her, considering just that act, for a good half-hour before retiring. Her touch would have affected me also, but how? Certainly I'd have been able to kill her—strangled her, or utilized any number of weapons I owned—but at what cost? I feared the loss of opportunity. Stalemate.

I directed her attention to the table I'd set. "Hungry?"

"Yeah."

"Shall we?"

We sat down and ate together.

"How many people . . . like us?" I asked.

"Deprivers," she replied harshly. "It's not the word that'll kill you, Robert. For a killer you are way too uptight. I've known about two dozen or so. Most on bad terms. Good eggs, just the way I like 'em."

"Thanks. What terms are we on, provided I can forget the gun in my mouth?"

"You're not dead or deprived, are you?"

"No. And neither are you."

"I've noticed. Thanks."

"Most welcome. Mind telling me why you're here? Are you the Depriver welcome wagon?"

She lowered her eyes to her plate and spoke into it. "I tagged you in the park and I thought you might be working for someone. I thought you were hunting me. I get followed a lot. I wasn't taking chances. I'm still not."

A Depriver working for who? A Depriver employment agency? A government agency? Hunted? Why?

"I emptied the cartridges from your gun," I said, raising a forkful of egg.

She grinned at that. "Did you, now?"

"Yes, I did. Pass the juice, please."

"Do I get them back?"

"If you're a good girl and eat all of your breakfast I'll consider it. Ever think of entering the cleaning business? I think you'd excel."

"*No,*" she snapped. "I don't kill people. I'll deprive in self-defense, but I've never killed anybody!" She was either being totally honest or she was an olympic class liar. "I might need to, though, soon," she said, lowering her eyes again. "How much do you charge?"

I munched my toast. "You can't afford me."

"Not with cash, but with information you need badly. You're a sitting duck to any of us with sight."

"Deprivers who can't touch me any more than I can touch them."

"*Wrong,*" she broke in. "By those with much nastier touches than you who don't mind a twenty-minute out while the others turn you off. Or by sighted normals who want you either with them or dead."

Sighted? "Well, nobody's hassled me before. I'm not bothering them."

She pulled her hair off of her face in desperation. "You just don't get it, Robbie. You're either allies with other Deprivers or you're a threat, period. There's no room for neutrality in this shit. You're alive because you're a hermit. If you'd worked in a grocery store, blind like this, you'd be dead and forgotten by now."

I got up and pushed two more slices into the toaster. "Make me an offer, I'm listening." What was I doing, forming a contract with a seventeen-year-old psychopath?

She left the table, grabbed her cigarettes from the living room, and came back lit. I hate smoke while I'm eating, but decided to suffer it. She dragged incessantly as she spoke.

"I'll get you sighted and offer you safe haven through friends I have, and in return you help me rescue someone. The rescue could include some killing, but it's not mandatory or anything."

The toast popped up, startling her as I'd expected.

"Who would we be rescuing and who *might* we be killing?"

Long, hard drag. "My brother, Nicholas. Ya see, there's a whole group of Deprivers banded together under this man Deveraux. He's plugged in just about everywhere. He contacted me and my brother and we said no. He didn't like no, and we had to jam. I've lost contact with Nicky and I know they have him. I want you to help me get him back."

I let it sink in for a bit. Maybe she lies, maybe not? Either way, a band of unfriendlies could easily be coming my way. And could she really offer me some sort of extra sight? She did, after all, find me. Depriver sight is starting to sound more and more like an imperative.

"What kinds of things could these other Deprivers do . . . to me?"

"Depends on the Depriver. Hearing, taste, touch, smell, sight, balance, paralysis—or anything else that can get screwed-up in your nervous system."

Breathtaking. "What is it that your brother, Nicholas does?"

She tensed at that, but she knew it was time to either put up or shut up. "I'll tell you as a token of faith. He's a blinder. Full visual impairment. He's a shy kid. Has to be. You don't get your sight back in twenty minutes, or twenty years. He's permanent."

"No wonder they'd want him."

"But he freaks at the idea of touching anyone." She gave me a cold stare. "Like I do. But I will if you cross me or join them, I swear it, Robbie. I swear."

"Relax," I said. "I'm a loner. We just do this and I get this sight of yours and then I'm going back to business all the wiser and you go your own way, right? I won't be signing up with anyone. Just relax. Now, how come you're not blind? He must have touched you a million times, growing up."

She crushed out her cigarette in the remains of her eggs, thoroughly turning my stomach. "Nicky can't affect me and I can't affect him. We give each other headaches sometimes. It's like that with brothers and sisters for some reason."

"And your parents?"

Long pause, then: "My mother . . . was blind."

"Because of Nicholas?"

"Yes. Because of Nicholas."

Just then my telephone began to ring. Damn, not a client now!

We let it ring three times, neither of us moving. To not answer would be bad. To lose this intimacy would be bad. I had to make the choice as a matter of self-preservation.

"How do we proceed?" I asked her. *Ring-ring, ring-ring!* She warmed.

"I have to set some things up to get you sighted. Meet me at the head of the Astor Place subway station in three hours. No weapons. And I'll take back my cartridges."

The phone stopped ringing. I sat buttering my toast as she waved, then closed the door behind her, feeling more vulnerable than I had ever felt before.

I shaved, showered, and checked my various answering machines in all of my various apartments around the country. No new clients. Good. Missing an assignment would be bad, could have a serious effect on my life. My hangover persisted. I took some aspirin.

I dressed and put together a few bare essentials. Glass knife, handy for unforeseen metal detectors and close-range unfriendlies, into my coat sleeve sheath. Pocket telephone scrambler, rearview glasses, and micro-binoculars.

One hour early, I was downtown scoping out Astor Place. Cross streets merging, continuous car and foot traffic, bookstore, drugstore, shishkebab stand, ice cream cart, subway entrance—and large wrought-iron sculpture of a precariously poised cube in the center of it all. People milled about on their lunch breaks, buying and selling drugs, feeding the pigeons. I sat on a bench with my back to the subway, rearview scanning and eating an ice cream sandwich, *a Depriver waiting for another Depriver, who is being pur-*

sued by still more Deprivers as she enlists my Depriver abil-
ity in the hopes of rescuing her Depriver brother.

I caught a glimpse of yellow hair bobbing up in the distance and brought the binoculars up in my palm. Cassandra,
running this way, dodging in and out of the crowd. Running
makes me nervous. She would be in range within moments.
I made a fast decision and went with it.

Reaching from behind the wall of the subway entrance,
I grabbed her by the arm and pulled her out of view. "You're
being chased?"

She nodded frantically, an ungloved hand on my coat,
catching her breath. "Dark suit. Sunglasses. Works for Deveraux. Not a Depriver."

Suddenly there he was, between the vendors—about six
feet, medium build, dark gloves. No gun yet, but I anticipated one soon. He was no more than five feet away and I
was about to pop my knife.

Then Cassandra shoved me backwards and dove for
him. He wasn't any more ready for it than I was. She slapped
him barehanded across the neck and rolled behind the ice
cream cart, tripping one of the pigeon feeders as she went.

Dark Suit never flinched. He proceeded to draw a Smith
and Wesson from his underarm holster, aimed the gun, and
indicated I should rise. I did so with hands in clear sight.
Pandemonium broke out all around us. I heard shouts,
screams, and running feet, but saw only one thing: the barrel of the gun. I'm dead. Game over. Goodbye.

And then Dark Suit took a step backwards, shook his
head, and fired off three rounds—the first about ten feet
over my head, the second at the concrete in front of me, and
the third into the chest of the ice cream man. I was baffled,
but happily so.

Dark Suit tripped over his own feet, fell flat on his back,
fired his remaining rounds straight up into the air, as if he

were aiming at the sun or something. I wanted to run over and kill him for pointing a gun at me. Then I felt Cassandra pulling at my elbow as she yelled, "Let's go, there'll be more of them any second!" We ran three blocks or so, then flagged down a cab. "Drive!" she yelled at the driver, and off we sped.

A few lights later I was breathing better. I tried to get a handle on what had happened. Death and I had never had so close an encounter, save that time in Vegas when I was almost shot in an alleyway, not even job-related. His cheap pistol jammed and I ended up first paralyzing him, then kicking him to death. He was just a common street thug. Dark Suit was a professional, at point-blank range with Harbinger of Death written across his face. He'd just . . . missed.

I looked to her; she was scanning as we drove.

"You touched him, right?"

"Shut up," she snapped; then, to the cabbie: "Let us out here."

She threw the guy a fiver and we went down into another subway entrance.

"Where are we going?" I whispered as she bought us two tokens. A wino was eying her.

"Port Authority," she replied.

I sat next to her on the train, reading a banner advert for Colgate in Spanish and trying to piece together what had happened. She touched him and there was maybe a thirty-second reaction time. It wasn't his sight that went. Maybe a physical spasm on the trigger. No, it was his aim that was off, and his balance.

"Causing a loss of one's sense of direction?" I asked like an unsure game-show contestant. "Is that it?"

She averted her eyes and nodded.

"Not very aggressive."

"No, but it saved your ass," she snapped back.

"True," I had to admit. Losing your sense of direction, *hmm?* No driving, no sports, no shooting, no a lot of things. No fun. "How long does it last?"

She wouldn't answer.

"What, Rule Number Two? Don't tell your duration?"

She raised an eyebrow and looked right through me. "Eternity, Robbie-boy. It lasts for all eternity."

We pulled into Port Authority and headed upstairs to the buses. Cassandra took money from me to buy our tickets and a pack of cigarettes, and I bought myself a soda and a candy bar. We located our bus and took seats in the back. She fell asleep on my shoulder. I was very careful not to touch her. She wasn't a bad kid, I decided. I wondered if touching her hair would be dangerous.

She awoke when we stopped in Freehold, New Jersey, around dusk. We got off and I looked around at a whole lot of nothing. She stretched and yawned and said, "Still a bit of a hike yet."

"No cabs?"

"Nope." She lit a cigarette as we began walking.

"Mind if I ask you again where we're going?"

"Safe House," she said, absentmindedly pulling the tabs on her sweatshirt. "Where Deprivers can gather in peace."

"Like an underground railroad?"

"Yeah. Let's stop a sec." She moved her hand toward my shoulder and I pulled away.

"Just need to lean on you to take my boots off, please. My feet are killing me." I let her. "Scare easily?" she added.

She stuffed her socks inside, slung the boots over her shoulder, and continued walking barefoot alongside me in the grass. "Thanks," she said.

"So, you're going to do something to me that will give me the sight, correct?" I asked as we walked beneath a rising crescent moon.

"That's incorrect, Robbie," she said, and then had a short chuckle. "I won't be the one that does it to you, someone else will."

We walked in silence for another mile or so, then turned down a dirt road by a stream in a dark wooded area. I dislike wooded areas; they disturb me. I'm a city dweller. I avoid jobs that send me off to either deserts or forests. They're always trouble, especially if my quarry finds himself more at home in such surroundings. It can make things complicated. How the hell did one acquire Depriver sight? I was not letting anyone touch me.

We came to a large clearing wherein stood a two-story house with a landscaped garden and smoke coming out of the chimney. "Someone's home," I commented.

"Let's hope it's someone who can help," she replied.

She had a little spring in her step as we reached the porch. She produced a key from its hiding spot. "Shhhh," she instructed. "People may be sleeping."

We went in quietly. She led me into the den, where a dark-haired woman, forty-something, sat cross-legged in an armchair with a book in her lap.

"Terry," Cassandra squealed, and crossed the distance in seconds to carefully embrace her. She gestured toward me. "Terry, this is Robert, Robert, Terry."

I crossed to them, nodded and smiled.

"News on Nicholas?" Terry asked pensively, removing her glasses.

"No, but Deveraux is all over me." Cassandra sighed.

I looked around the place, avoiding their intimacies. There was a nice fire in the grate, lots of books piled about, photographs on the walls. I noticed a telephone and considered using the scrambler to check my answering machines, then decided it would not be prudent. I was less than available at the moment, anyway.

Terry's question, "And what sort of Depriver have we here?" brought me back.

"He's a paralyzer," Cassandra answered without hesitating. Then to me: "No secrets here, Robbie."

"Fine," I said after a pause, then redirected: "What sort of Depriver are you?"

Terry smiled. "No sort at all, sir. I see that you're blind."

"That's why we're here," Cassandra added. "Who's around? Geraldo, maybe?"

"Nope," Terry answered, wrinkling her nose. "Sparrow's here."

"Oh, Sparrow will do just fine, we're not in a hurry. Is he sleeping?"

"He just went upstairs. We were playing cards."

I noticed, on the mantle, a silver-framed picture of Cassandra holding hands with a young man who resembled her. They were standing by the shoreline and she was pointing toward the distance, at a lighthouse. I got the impression that this "safe house" belonged to her family.

"We'll talk tomorrow, Terry. Is my room empty?" We said our good nights and Cassandra led me upstairs. She knocked on a bedroom door and a young, male voice responded, "Come on in."

It was an empty room, save for a hammock inhabited by an Indian kid. American Indian. Looked about sixteen or so, long black hair and high cheekbones. The boy rose, eyes wide, and jumped into Cassandra's arms. "Cassie," he cooed. "I'm so sorry about Nicholas."

He was good-looking, spoke softly, solidly built. I liked him right off.

"I've missed you," Cassie replied, squeezing. "We'll get

him back. This is Robert, he's a paralyzer, twenty minutes, no bad news. Can you sight him?"

"Yeah, sure," the kid replied.

"Sorry," she said then. "Robert, this is Silver Sparrow. He's an Iroquois. Do whatever he says. Sorry I can't stay up to watch. I'm beat. Crash wherever you find an open bed. Okay, Rob? Good night."

She swished out of the room and left me standing, awkward, with the Indian kid.

"So," I said, crossing my arms and trying to sound calm, "how does one acquire this enhanced vision?"

He pulled his hair off of his face. "Well, all you have to do to see is get yourself deprived. Then, as my people would say, it's a gift from the spirit world."

Spirit world. Dandy! I had no intentions of letting him touch me right then and there, and I'd have slit him wide open if he'd taken a step closer. He sensed my tension and went instead to the room's single window and raised it. A brisk, cool breeze entered. He dropped two pillows off the hammock onto the floor and motioned for me to sit. Cautiously, I did. He sat across from me, within arms-length. I was fingering the knife in its sheath against my forearm.

"Do you get high, Rob?" he inquired, producing a joint and then lighting it. "Maybe some dope would loosen you up for this."

"No, thanks," I answered. "Listen, Sparrow, I'm not feeling comfortable about you touching me."

He took a drag and then reoffered it to me, shrugging his shoulders as I declined. "Hey, man, we don't have to do this if you don't want to, but I'm really one of your safest bets if you want to see. Cassie seems to think you need it. I'd trust her if I were you."

Kid, if you were me, you wouldn't trust anybody, ever. "What would I be deprived of?"

"Hearing. Audio. You'd be clinically deaf. I'm good for first-timers. Most people can handle not hearing for a while no problem."

"Duration?"

A fly landed on his leg and he swished it away. "Six to eight hours. It varies with me. Never had a permanent impairment or nothing like that."

Deafness, eh? That leaves me still able to defend myself. "It's kind of hard for me to imagine real deafness," I said.

"Is it?" he chuckled. "Ever been in a sensory deprivation tank? We've got one downstairs. It's great for relaxing, getting in touch with yourself. Cass calls it my casket. She's a claustro, won't go near it. Are you claustrophobic, Rob?"

Note: Cassandra is claustrophobic.

"No," I replied. "Not that I know of." And I recalled the three hours I'd spent curled up inside a dumbwaiter in a hotel in Chicago waiting for a mark I'd ended up bludgeoning to death with his own five iron.

"Let me have a drag off that," I asked Sparrow. He passed it, smiling. I could tell he was already under. The smoke was sweet and stung the back of my throat. I coughed a few times, then took another drag.

"How about this?" he began. "I'll touch you and you can touch me. Will that make you feel more comfortable? I've never been paralyzed and I like to try them all. What's your duration?"

Waitaminute, wasn't that supposed to happen anyway? "I'm confused, Sparrow, wouldn't you automatically be deprived by touching me?"

"Maybe, maybe not, certainly not a full dose. When I'm sending, I'm really closed off to receiving. Everyone's different. Twenty minutes, huh? Is that all? Okay. Cool. What say you, Rob?"

This is what you came for, right? "All right," I said with

a long exhale. "Let's do it. I'll need a few moments to get myself ready."

He nodded and I started heating myself up, concentrating on my hands, a warm ball of energy in my hands, my heartbeat accelerating the energy into my hands, hot hands.

Sparrow moved closer to me and looked into my eyes. His were an odd grayish color with yellowish flecks. He would have to touch me first, of course. Suddenly I felt a burning flash run up my spine, quickly followed by a second. I realized that he'd touched me on the forehead. Another flash, this one much cooler, then several more, each progressively colder, until they were actually chills. A loud explosion; my ears began to pound. I felt as if a vacuum cleaner had been switched on inside my head. I felt my face numbed; my fingers, toes and back prickled. Blue sparkles danced before my eyes. I felt nauseous. The vacuum kept sucking at my ears. I could not reach my hands up to touch them. Then *whoooosh*, like a drain plug being pulled from a full sink, and it was over. Was this how my targets felt when I touched them?

Sparrow's lips were moving slowly, but he wasn't speaking; or rather, I could no longer hear him. The room was dead silent. The only sound I was conscious of was my own rapid heartbeat.

I tried to read his lips: "Feel okay?" I nodded. Then he said, "Touch," indicating my hand and his forehead.

I reached my hand slowly toward him, fascinated that it was back under my control, and touched his brow. "Three minutes," I told him, not hearing my own voice. Weird. I got up and walked to the window, feeling the breeze hit my face. I looked at the woods, the sky, an airplane flying soundless high above.

I turned back to Sparrow and saw him frozen, cross-legged, mid-smile, high as a kite. He didn't seem aware of me at all—off exploring, I guess. I didn't know what to do with myself now that I was deprived. I snapped my fingers near my ears and heard nothing. I left the room and went downstairs. No *creaks* beneath my feet. I passed a clock. No *ticks*, no *tocks*. I went into the empty den and looked at the dwindling fire. No *snap*, no *crackle*, no *pop*. I picked up the telephone. No dial tone. I laughed. Not hearing myself laugh kinda freaked me out. I accidentally knocked a picture off the wall, the glass shattering without sound into tiny shards.

I unlocked the front door and went outside. The wind was so strong it unbalanced me from time to time. There are tiny audible gusts that act as warning signals to the ear that I was missing, Sparrow would later inform me. I was feeling more than a little paranoid, and blamed some of this on the marijuana. I moved around the perimeter of the house, stepping on pine cones that did not *scrunch* below leaves that refused to *rustle*. I half enjoyed all this, but thought, This had better all be temporary, I cannot function with an impairment like this. Calm down, relax, chill out!

I kicked an empty soda can, which sailed off noiselessly into the dark. It began to drizzle and I could really smell the pine trees. Then it began to pour. I was drenched before I made it to the porch. I looked out. Clouds completely obscured the moon. Lightning flashed repeatedly to the north without accompanying thunder, very strange indeed. I watched for a time and became somewhat aware (difficult to explain if you've never felt it) of the way the thunder is anticipated, sounds, and reverberates. It was my favorite part of the experience.

I locked the door behind me and walked the memory-strewn corridors where ghosts of a family still roamed. Sparrow was no longer in his room. Not surprising—I was reasonably sure he'd be up and about by now. At the end of the hall I found Cassandra curled up in a bed beneath an oversized pink comforter, clothes strewn about the room, sleeping fitfully. What's going on in that pretty little head? Hauntings, I'd guessed. Like my own. What kind of childhood would it be in a family with two Depriver children? What kind of guilt descends upon a child who has deprived his own mother of her sight? Rough case.

I remembered that Sparrow's things were set up in the basement and I went down the stairs in the semi-dark to find him. His casket, as Cassandra called it—an apt description—was indeed coffin-sized, and equipped with a polarized glass viewing window. Looking in, I saw him there, nude, dark-goggled, arms outstretched, floating at ease. I wondered what he was feeling. Weightless, sightless, tasteless, smelless, deaf, deprived? He looked so vulnerable. We both had one thing in common, he and I, we both enjoyed using our touch, were excited by it.

The first time I'd enjoyed it was in a little pub in SoHo. I'd just graduated from Columbia and was out on a drinking binge with some classmates. I was drunk. I asked the piano man to play a song, I don't recall what. He refused, adamantly, saying it wasn't appropriate for this crowd. I couldn't let it go. I started asking people in the bar if they would mind hearing the song. They were the usual rabble, people who spent their days slaving in the production of widgets and forget-me-nots, spent their nights trying to forget their days. Unescorted women buzzing around, trying to become otherwise. People spilling their problems over the bar onto me, onto each other, onto the stale-faced bartender. Nobody gave a damn if the piano man played my song. I went back to the piano, put a five in his tip jar, and asked him again. Again he refused, and began to ignore me. He pissed me off. So I touched him on the back of the neck.

He was solid as a rock within minutes, fingers hovering languidly just above the keys, eyes a torrent of fear as I sat beside him and took his wallet and told him a dozen ways I could easily kill him. He pissed himself right there on the bench.

I ruffled his hair and left, thinking, *There's money to be made in this, a great deal of it.*

I watched Sparrow float for a while, then went upstairs and found a bed. Cassandra was standing over me when I awoke, her mouth moving silently. And then, "—et up, Robbie." I could hear her again! Hallelujah!

That wasn't the only thing that had changed. She was glowing. A pale blue. "You okay?"

I nodded, rising, pulling on my shirt.

"Can you see now?"

I nodded again.

"Good, meet us downstairs for breakfast."

She left and I finished getting dressed. My ears were a bit numb, but worked fine. I came downstairs, each creaky step a joy, and found the three of them sitting on the back porch. Sparrow had the same glow, more subdued, a pale bluish outline. I would have counted it as a trick of the sun, save for the fact that Terry wasn't radiating. I looked down at my own hands. Faint, but I was marked as well. This is not good! I thought. They laughed at me, standing there.

"Like a halo," Sparrow called out.

"Or a warning signal," Terry added. "Depriver blue."

More like a homing beacon.

"Morning, all," I said, sitting down next to Cassandra. "Blue's never been one of my better colors."

We ate breakfast, it was pleasant, I really appreciated the taste of the food. They spoke of other Deprivers. I listened quietly, seeming disinterested. All the while, Terry took notes in a leatherbound ledger. Afterwards, Cassandra and Sparrow brought the dishes inside, leaving Terry wide open for interrogation.

"So," I asked cheerfully, "what's your part in all this craziness?"

She pushed her glasses up into the recess of her dark braids and smiled at me. "I'm documenting it. Cataloguing what I can. Helping here and there."

I poured us both another cup of coffee. "How'd you get involved? Have a Depriver boyfriend? Get touched in an elevator?"

"No," she said, sipping and staring out into the woods, "nothing quite so dramatic. I'm a psychiatrist. Cassandra's family brought the children to me when they were young and we all became close. How old were you when you realized you were different?"

Who's interrogating whom? "I was nearly fifteen," I told her, and she reached for her ledger.

"Mind telling me about it?"

"No, I don't mind at all. I'm happy to be part of your research."

"Really," she said, warming instantly. "I'd have thought you'd be more reluctant."

"Nah, I'm the first one to lend a hand to anything scientific. Here, take down my address and phone number."

She really lit up at that, and flipped to the back, jotting down my name in an address section. I dictated a few bits of misinformation while looking over her shoulder at a cornucopia of private listings.

"You don't have a tape recorder, do you?"

"Why, yes, I do," she replied, as if I'd had the idea of the century. "It's upstairs."

"Why not get it and I'll give you the story of my life."

She stood up, beaming. "Great, I'll do it right now."

"Great," I echoed as she walked off. Then I picked up the ledger and scanned the address book for a listing I half suspected would be there. I replaced the book and went into the house.

I told Cassandra I'd be out for a short walk and asked her to please tell Terry that I'd be right back.

Ten minutes later, I found a pay phone by an abandoned gas station that miraculously still worked. I jacked in my scrambler and dialed. A man answered, gruff sounding, all business, the kind of decisive voice I like to hear.

"Mr. Deveraux," I began, with a grin I could not contain. "I've got a proposition for you that's so juicy it's glowing blue. Would you be interested? Great."

THE PEOPLE OF THE STATE OF NEW YORK -VERSUS- DUNCAN CAMERON

PAUL JON EDELSTEIN

Y ou know Amy, if I pull this one off, I will truly be the king." I said, with all the bravado of a good trial attorney.

"Yeah, yeah. I've heard that a thousand times before from people who are now back in the complaint room writing up witness statements," she responded, without bothering to look up from her work. My desk was set flush against hers, but even without anyone sitting at either, it was quite clear whose desk was whose.

"Yeah, but think about it. I'll have the Post and the *Daily News* in here in two seconds. They'll eat this case up. I'll be all over."

"Excuse me, but did you forget about that little evidence problem? And how do you plan on dealing with his defense attorney?"

"I'll figure that out somehow," I said, knowing full well that she was right. The telephone rang. The bureau chief, Lou Grandelli, wanted to see me immediately.

Amy knew who it was simply from my face. She was laughing as I pulled on my jacket and headed out of our dingy office, but I still managed to catch her last dig as I was three steps from the door.

"Good luck, Josh. Better start coming up with a theory. Remember, ancient Chinese man once said: 'Hands only weapon man need to blind attacker.' "

Grandelli was the chief of the homicide division, one of the most powerful people in the Brooklyn District Attorney's office. A renowned trial lawyer, he had started out in the district attorney's office right out of law school, making a name for himself through numerous murder convictions. After a few financially rewarding years as a defense attorney he returned to the DA's office to be second in command to the District Attorney himself, the most glamorous position in the office. Still, he dressed too sharp for an Assistant District Attorney. He wore dark Italian suits, custom-tailored shirts and colorful ties. His jet black hair was always slicked back and his dark eyes and commanding physique were truly imposing, ironically giving him the appearance of the Mafiosi he spent so much time putting away. He'd walk down the streets of Brooklyn at lunchtime followed by an entourage of young lawyers. Everyone would stop and say hello, shake his hand, promise to do lunch, pay their homage.

"Leitner. Sit down. I just got off the phone with the *New York Post*."

As usual, our conversation was brief. Grandelli didn't want me to talk to the press until I had gotten a felony conviction. I needed to help quell the potential race riot which seemed to be brewing regarding this case.

No problem.

I woke up early the next morning, even though it was Saturday. Gone were the days when I could sleep till noon, my body now refusing to break its week-long pattern of seven-thirty risings. I headed out of my apartment and straight for the local greasy diner, grabbing a *Post* on the way. I rarely if ever looked at the front of the paper before I was through with the sports section, reading it literally from back to front. On this morning, however, I noticed the headline blaring from the top paper in the stack outside the Korean grocery:

DEPRIVED OF SIGHT
HOW DID IT HAPPEN?

The words ran above a picture of Jermain Grant with his parents, his eyes bandaged shut. My stomach split open. I flipped immediately to a full-page story on page three, complete with a picture of my defendant, Duncan Cameron, exiting the courthouse with Jacob Weinstein, his lawyer. The article was sprinkled with quotes from just about every person I would need to put on the stand.

"All I know is the old guy swung at Jermain and Jermain went down, man, like someone shot him or something." Derrick Clarke.

"I was right there, but I couldn't do nothin'. It was too late. Dude had already floored the kid with something. I don't know what it was, but it had to be something." Alvin Williams.

"I grabbed him afterwards and he didn't struggle or anything, just asked if he could put back on his glove, which was lying right next to him. Of course, I looked in that glove before I let him get it back, but I didn't see anything in it that could've blinded that kid." Officer Miguel Rodriguez.

"We weren't gonna hurt him, we just asked if he had any change," offered Jermain himself. "No one even had anything out, like a knife or anything. He just swung at me, for no reason. I really don't remember if he had anything in his hand. I don't remember being hit with anything. I didn't feel any metal or anything like that."

Asked by the reporter about mace or something along that line, Jermain squelched that theory conclusively.

"Oh, no. He definitely didn't have no mace. I know what mace feels like. There weren't no mace involved. I'm telling you, he just smacked me, and it was lights out."

Dr. Joseph Felicia, Brooklyn Interfaith Medical Center, stated upon questioning that it was possible that a heavy blow to the head could damage either the optic nerve in the eye or the nerve sheath and blood vessels that surround it, causing blindness. He suggested that, if this were the case, surgery could repair the damage.

They were burying my case before we ever set foot in the courtroom. Each line increased the sound of the blood rushing through my eardrums. Each quote provided terrific cross-examination material for the defense. Each word was further ammunition for Grandelli to assail me with, as there was no way I should've allowed any witnesses under my control speak to the press before they had spoken to me. One day was all it had been, but that one day had apparently been an unusually slow news day, so the *Post* had to come up with something. Why couldn't there have been a nice murder in Washington Heights or something?

Two things caught my eye towards the bottom of the article. First was my name being used, "Josh Leitner declined to comment." That amused me, since it probably would have been my exact response had anyone associated with the press even bothered to ask me about the case. Beside this, slipped into the last paragraph, was a rather arousing quote from a woman who claimed she saw what had happened and was sure she knew how Jermain was blinded. "That old white man has the power. Very strong. You see the eyes. In my country, Haiti, these men they can do all sorts of things just by touching you. Sometimes they don't even need to touch you, just need something personal of yours, like a piece of clothing."

One week later, the case had already been played out dozens of times in the media. The tabloids focused on the "voodoo" angle, but the so-called "legitimate press" stirred up the race issue, with one side focused on the fact that a black kid had been blinded by the white Cameron for no real reason, and should therefore be punished as severely as a black man would be for doing the same thing to a white man. Thank God Amy, who would likely be sitting next to me for the entire trial, is black, I remember thinking.

I read on in disbelief. There were those who advocated the positive results of "vigilante justice," feeling that Jermain had got what he deserved, since he and his friends were obviously looking for trouble in the first place. Jermain's criminal history came to the forefront. He had been arrested three times, before. Two of the cases were sealed, as Jermain was afforded youthful offender status but it didn't mean he would be free from cross-examination on those arrests. The third arrest was, unfortunately, an assault case.

Perfect. Jermain and his friends would be as much on trial as Cameron would be. Self-defense was looking pretty good.

Over the next two weeks, I prepared for trial, speaking to every known witness but still being left without anything concrete to support the assault-one charge which required the use of a deadly weapon. The way I figured it, the jury would be made up mostly of Black and Latino people. If I could prove that Cameron blinded Jermain intentionally, it would likely overcome the self-defense theory. But how did Cameron do it? I simply couldn't believe that the blow itself damaged Jermain's optic nerve. Cameron was too small and fragile to cause such damage. Jermain had fallen back into his friends arms after the contact, screaming that he couldn't see, so there didn't seem to be any way he could've hit his head during the aftermath. How the hell had he been blinded?

I didn't want to think about a plea bargain but the thought flashed in at each frustrating stalemate. There simply were so many ways to lose this trial. The self-defense theory was strong and was gaining favor in the newspapers. The Rev. Malik Brown had led a march through Brooklyn in support of Jermain and against the bias of "the system" which refused to vigorously prosecute white men who assaulted black men. Unfortunately, the good Reverend didn't have to try this case. In response, a protest outside the courtroom called for the dismissal of the charges against Cameron. The chances of finding jurors who hadn't already been influenced seemed pretty slim.

The trial arrived too soon; I wasn't sure what I was going to do that first morning, but that wasn't unusual. My father had been a trial attorney for forty years, and he had taught me that while you could never be too prepared, you still never knew just what was going to happen in a courtroom. You simply had to walk in and feel out the room before you began he used to say. As I walked toward the courthouse with only the Duncan Cameron file in my hands, the press, the protesters, and the curious all mixed together outside, blocking traffic on Schermerhorn Street. There were network vans with antennas three stories high, and extra uniformed police, who were keeping everyone organized. I slipped past the crowd into the courthouse without being recognized, thinking how often I had dreamed about this type of chance. Perhaps this was my fifteen minutes of fame, and here I was, cowering, rather than basking in it. The writers outside the courtroom swarmed, shouting questions I could not answer.

Supreme Court Justice Richard A. Singleton was a large man whose mere presence was intimidating. His dark, resonant voice caused many a talkative attorney to lose his train of thought. I had been before him twice before, with both cases resulting in convictions, so I was hopeful he would at least believe I wasn't here to play games. He read the arraignment judge's notes on the file jacket and glared at me.

"Mr. Leitner, How do you intend to prove the assault one charge." he intoned.

"Well, Your Honor, my theory is that there may not have actually been any weapon at all, but . . ."

"Are you telling me that you don't have *any* evidence of a weapon and yet you're proceeding with this as a felony assault?"

"Yes, but I can . . ."

"I don't want to hear it. I'm not going to argue with you, counselor. What do you intend to show, that this defendant's hands were dangerous weapons in and of themselves?"

The only way to keep the felony charge alive was to go with that theory, crazy as it seemed. A murmur went up from the gallery. A bead of sweat ran down the back of my neck. I turned to look at Cameron, hoping that he might reveal something, but he just sat calmly, looking straight ahead weakly, as if he were sick.

"Counselor, I'm waiting. How do you intend to proceed?"

My father never told me what to say when you want to pass out. "The People request a one-week adjournment for the purpose of bringing in a medical expert." I said.

Defense counsel Weinstein, who had otherwise remained as stoic as his client, instantly jumped up. "Your Honor, we object. The defendant is ready to proceed. This is simply a delay tactic by Mr. Leitner, who obviously can not meet the evidentiary requirements necessary to sustain the charge. If you are inclined to grant an adjournment, then I respectfully request that the charge be reduced from assault one to assault three, as counsel for the People has conceded that this is not an assault one case, based on the facts."

"Counsel," I interjected, trying to break his flow, to do something, anything. "Your client looks ill. I think an adjournment will do him some good."

"I can only take that comment as a poor attempt at humor, which in light of the seriousness of this case, should be considered as nothing other than an insult," Weinstein yammered.

Judge Singleton rose from his chair from behind the bench and stood over us like a great oak tree over two saplings. "Stop. I will not hear any of this. Counsel, your motion to have the charges reduced is denied. The grand jury has spoken and I will not reduce the charge. Whether the People can prove it or not is another story. I am giving the People a one week adjournment for the purpose of bringing in a medical expert, because of the seriousness of the victim's injuries. The People will be charged for the time with regard to any potential speedy trial issues, which do not seem to exist at this point. This case is adjourned until one week from today."

The Judge turned and pushed through a door behind the bench, cleverly built to allow for just such a swift escape.

"So, Leitner," sneered Grandelli, "I heard you asked for some more time on the Cameron case. Why?" He'd summoned me to his office direct from the courtroom. I swear that bastard's telepathic.

"Because I need a doctor."

"Why? Are you sick? You look like shit," he responded without actually looking up at me.

"No, I need a doctor for the case." I said.

"You haven't subpoenaed someone from the hospital? How about Felicia? He already testified in the grand jury. What the hell is wrong with you!"

"Of course I have the doctor that treated Jermain in the hospital, but that's not what I need. I need someone to testify about Cameron."

"What the hell are you talking about?" He stood and took a step towards me as I retreated toward the doorway. "What the hell are you doing to this case? I want to know right now."

"I think he's sick. I think he's got some kind of disease, something that could've been transmitted to Jermain on contact." I don't think I sounded very convincing.

"You must be kidding. Listen, Leitner, I don't care whose kid you are, you better not fuck this case up. You can't put on some fucking ridiculous unexplained phenomena theory, I don't care how good a jury you get, it will get overturned on appeal. You have to stick to the facts. Cameron struck the kid and now he's blind. Who cares exactly how he did it? You got fifty witnesses to that, don't you? That's all you need." His right index finger stuck out from his custom-tailored dark blue shirt and nearly touched my chest.

"Hey! Wait a minute! Wasn't it you who told me, not three weeks ago, that I had to get a felony conviction? Did you forget about the fucking weapon requirement? If I do what you just told me, I can kiss the felony goodbye. Did you think of that, or are you just pissed because the newspapers are all over us?" I could feel the red in my face. The shouting had brought a halt to the offices which surrounded Grandelli's like bunkers on a battlefield. There was a moment of hesitation before Lou responded as he too noticed the six or seven people who were awaiting the next salvo.

"All right. Listen. At this point, I guess you might not get the felony count, but Singleton will never drop the charge anyway so it'll go to the jury. Let them decide. If the facts don't sustain it, so be it. We can't voluntarily drop the felony count, because we'll be torn apart in the papers. So go for it. But just go on the facts. I don't want this turning into a circus. No quacks. No talk show theories. Go with the hands as dangerous weapons. It's all you got."

"But Cameron may not even testify, and you know he has no prior record. We haven't uncovered anything on him regarding boxing or marital arts or any other type of training. I'll never be able to sustain that theory."

"I don't care. It's the only one you've got. Maybe the jury will buy it if he doesn't take the stand to refute it. Either way, it'll be out there, and the jury will hopefully want to hang the guy, anyway."

But I couldn't get the disease theory out of my mind. "Listen, Lou, I think I may have a doctor . . ."

"No!"

"Wait, you don't even know what . . . you can review what he's going to say, then decide."

"Look I just told you what you're going to do with this case."

"But you don't even . . ."

"That's it! No more." His eyes burned into mine. This conversation was finished.

I stormed out of his office and then out of the building, not realizing that some of the reporters had hung around and once again I was hammered with questions I wasn't able to answer. One week later, we had selected a jury and were ready to give opening statements.

I loved my jury. The makeup was perfect for Jermain: eight women, two Latina and six black; five of them were mothers. Four men, three black, one white. The courtroom was overflowing with people and charged with energy. Adrenaline flowed through my body as I paused before entering. I was ready.

Amy was already at the prosecution table. I had asked that she second seat and Grandelli had allowed it, because he liked the appearance we created together. The room grew quiet as the judge entered.

"Trial Part Three is now in session. The Honorable Justice Richard A. Singleton presiding. The People Of The State Of New York versus Duncan Cameron, Docket Number CR-1060. All those who desire to be heard, draw near and give your attention and ye shall be heard."

The Judge took the bench slowly and reviewed a few papers while the tension built in the courtroom.

"Are the People ready?" he asked me politely.

"The People are ready, Your Honor."

"Is the defense ready?"

"The defense is ready, your honor." Weinstein was

dressed in a dark blue Armani suit with a soft red tie and a white shirt. Juries love red ties. Cameron sat at the defense table, colorless.

"Bring in the jury—let's proceed with opening statements," instructed Judge Singleton.

My opening statement was short, growing dramatic only when I pointed out Jermain and his blindness to the jury. Three of the women seemed near tears at that point, and two other jurors glared hatefully at Cameron as I described the malicious blinding. I sat down to a smiling Amy and a message scrawled on my pad: "They hate Cameron and they feel bad for Jermain."

Weinstein slowly rose to do his opening.

"Ladies and gentleman, you have all heard what Mr. Leitner has told you, but what you must remember is that not a single thing Mr. Leitner or myself tells you is evidence. The Judge has already instructed you on that and you all made a promise to me, a promise to my client and a promise to everyone, really, that you would follow the letter of the law, whether you agree with it or not. Now, at this point you may feel sorry for Jermain Grant. It's perfectly understandable. I feel sorry for his injury as well. But what you must remember is that your sympathy must not, can not come into play here. The Judge, when he instructs you on the law at the end of the case, will tell you as much. You are the deciders of the *facts*. The Judge is the giver of the law. If either the law or the facts are not placed into the equation then the system will fail. And that failure will not be limited simply to this courtroom and this case, but will, in fact, fall upon everyone. For we all will have all failed to follow the recipe that has been tried and tested throughout our country's history.

"Now, Mr. Leitner has told you something of what he feels are the facts of this case, but you must remember that he must prove these facts to you. For again, nothing either of us claims is actually a fact until you say it is. You and you alone. Mr. Leitner can not tell what is and what is not a fact. Judge Singleton, most respectfully, can not tell you what is and what is not. *You* must decide what the facts are, based on evidence, and that evidence will come from the witness stand, right here. Now, of course, as you have already heard, Mr. Cameron and myself, we do not have to prove anything to you. We can simply sit here without saying one word during the entire trial and it is possible, likely even, I believe, that the prosecution will not prove their case. Remember that the entire burden of proof rests with the prosecution, and that burden is one that they must meet beyond a reasonable doubt. If you have any doubts at all in your mind when the prosecution rests, than you have no choice but to dismiss their case, no matter how badly you may feel for Jermain Grant. You must say, I am truly sorry about your injury Mr. Grant, but I must dismiss this case. You all took an oath, you swore that this is precisely what you would do.

"I would like you to know some things about this case that Mr. Leitner has *not* revealed to you. First, when Mr. Grant approached Mr. Cameron, he did so with at least two of his friends, who you shall hear from. These three, able-bodied youths menacingly approached my client, whom you can clearly see is an elderly gentleman who requires a cane to walk, and demanded money. These three youths, all with criminal backgrounds, came up to this simple, unimposing, sixty-six-year old man, who was simply minding his own business, they came up to him and said. 'Give us some money!' They will tell you that themselves. What was their motivation? The answer is quite clear, I believe, even without looking into these youths' sordid criminal backgrounds. They were out to rob Mr. Cameron! When he refused to give into their demands, a scuffle ensued, and in the midst of that struggle, Duncan Cameron fought back. He fought back like any good citizen would do. He fought back with all the might his aged body could muster. Jermain Grant was unfortunately hurt in the struggle. Duncan Cameron was hurt in the struggle. Neither person will ever be the same again. For this we can all feel sorry. However, the District Attorney's office now comes to you and asks you to punish Mr. Cameron for doing what any normal, law-abiding, self-respecting person in this city would do. Fighting back! They will tell you that Mr. Cameron's actions were unprovoked and unnecessary? Excessive? Could that possibly be true?

"Ladies and gentleman of the jury, the evidence in this case will show unequivocally that the wrong person is sitting at the defense table. Duncan Cameron should not be on trial here today. He has done nothing different from what any of us would have done under the same circumstances. I simply ask you to listen carefully to the evidence presented, to put aside sympathy and decide this case on the facts alone. If you do, you will have no choice but to return a verdict in favor of Duncan Cameron. Thank you."

"Call your first witness Mr. Leitner," spoke the court.

I looked at Amy and hesitated for a second before calling Jermain Grant to the stand. The mere act of Jermain struggling to take the stand with the aide of a court officer dissipated some of the impact from Weinstein's opening. Whether the jury felt sympathy for Jermain's condition or anger towards his actions would be a key factor in the verdict. My direct examination was short and to the point. Towards the end, I tried to stretch it out, if only to keep Weinstein from beginning what I knew would be a tough cross-examination.

Cross-examination is the skill which divides trial attorneys. With three quick questions, I knew which class Weinstein was in. Jermain, frustrated and angry almost from the time Weinstein stood up, lost control and started kicking and flailing in the witness box.

"Can't you see I'm blind, goddamn it! He blinded me! And all you want to know about is these stupid things that happened years ago?"

Tears streamed down his otherwise dysfunctional eyes. By the time he got off the stand at the close of the day, the self-defense theory had been shackled to the heart of the case. Without Cameron saying a word, twelve pairs of eyes suddenly lost their softness and compassion and instead shifted their powerful displeasure towards the victim rather than the defendant.

Court broke for the day. Although I was relieved to get out of there, from a strategic standpoint I had twelve jurors who were going to sleep for the night with thoughts of dangerous, angry young blacks intimidating, threatening and finally pushing a poor old man into retaliating. The shark like press swarmed outside the courthouse as I attempted to get away. Shouts from supporters of both sides flew by. I had to do something to turn things around. Something dramatic.

"Amy, I have to show them that he blinded Jermain. That Cameron did it, that he knew it could happen and that he wanted it to happen. That's the only way. Without it, I'm finished."

"I know, Josh. I know. But what if it doesn't work? What if the Judge doesn't let you do it? They have no real notice of this so-called doctor you want to call." .

"That's not true. He's on the witness list. They just don't realize what he's going to testify to. There's an optometrist in Manhattan with the same name and I know they think it's him because one of Weinstein's clerks asked me the other day and I didn't really say it wasn't. They have no idea that my Dr. Carl Berenson is . . . um . . . ah . . . ergh . . . well, let's just say he's not exactly in the mainstream of medical theory."

Dr. Carl Berenson had called me constantly after reading about the case in the paper. At first, I dismissed him, along with the comments I'd read about voodoo. After weeks of calls and letters and articles, I still didn't exactly believe Berenson, but his theory intrigued me and remained in the back of my mind as a last-ditch way to prove the case.

"Josh, if it doesn't work, not only are you going to lose this case, you're probably finished in this office. You know that, don't you?" Her voice was full of caring and fear.

"I know. Fuck it. It's the only way. One way or another, I'll make the front page of the *Post*. Amy, you gotta help me with the case law. You know they'll oppose any kind of physical test like this on Constitutional grounds. I already did some of the research and we definitely should win. Just do me a favor and go the extra mile with it, like only you know how. Weinstein won't be prepared for it, anyway. I guarantee it."

The next morning arrived so quickly I didn't have time to change my strategy. I trudged to the courthouse through thick humidity and once again arrived soaked in sweat, only this time I knew that half the moisture came from nerves. The Judge took the bench promptly, Cameron was seated stoically beside Weinstein and, as usual, Amy was spread out at the prosecution table looking ready for a technical lawbook argument. The packed gallery seemed especially hostile, probably because Jermain had been the one put on trial the previous day. I glanced around at the faces of his family and friends, faces filled with frustration and anger. Jermain's lifeless eyes burned into me.

"Good morning, counsel," said Judge Singleton as he

slipped on his black robe. "Is there anything we need to deal with before I bring in the jury?"

"Nothing from the defendant, Your Honor, we are ready to proceed," Weinstein said eagerly, hoping to move as quickly as possible to deliberations while he had a jury looking to punish the victim in this case.

"Well, Your Honor," I said, "I intend to call a physician this morning, a certain Dr. Carl Berenson from New York City."

"There is no objection to this witness from defendant, is there?"

"No, Your Honor," Weinstein said, "but if it will save time, the defendant will stipulate that the complaining witness is in fact blind at the moment. Our own doctors have confirmed this fact, as have the hospital records."

"Your Honor, the People will be happy to accept defendants' stipulation that Jermain is in fact blind. However, we feel the issue is precisely how he was blinded and that this fact is at the heart of the case. If defendant wants to stipulate that he intentionally blinded Jermain, then maybe Dr. Berenson's testimony isn't necessary."

"Well, Mr. Leitner, I hate to disappoint you, but we can't stipulate to that."

"All right, counselor, you may put Dr. Berenson on the stand and, provided he meets the qualifications of an expert witness, we may hear his opinion as to the precise cause of Mr. Grant's ailment."

"Uh ... well, Your Honor, at this point, Dr. Berenson is actually not able to render an expert opinion on causation."

"And, when, pray tell, do you think he will be able to give that opinion, Mr. Leitner? Next week, Mr. Cameron may very well not be here, you know." said the Judge, giving me a clear indication as to how the case was going.

"Your Honor, if you will indulge me for just one minute,

perhaps I can explain. Dr. Berenson is a specialist in the fields of dermatology, infectious diseases and forensic toxicology. His work focuses on reactions between various elements, specifically those found in and on animal skins as well as plants and minerals."

"Counsel, I have a full courtroom here and twelve people in a steamy jury room who don't have time for this. What in the world is this man going to testify to?"

"Well, Your Honor, I'll get to the point. The People intend to show through this witness that the mere touch of Duncan Cameron's skin will cause blindness in a human or animal. That there are certain unique features in the composition of the oils and substances contained in his skin which rendered Jermain Grant blind on the night of May 22nd, 1999, and which could render anyone or anything blind any time it comes into contact with him. The evidence will thus show that the defendant had a unique type of condition dangerous to any and all who came into contact with him, that he was *well* aware of this condition and thus whether or not the complaining witness initiated some type of altercation, this defendant can not claim self-defense, because, as a matter of law, his conduct did not entail self-defense but a premeditated, intentional assault with a deadly weapon. And that deadly weapon is the Defendant himself!"

I found myself conveniently planted directly between a flailing Weinstein and Judge Singleton, my index finger outstretched to the point of near contact with Cameron's nose as the courtroom filled with screams. Bright white shirted court officers moved in quickly to quell the anarchy as the judge slammed his gavel down on the bench. I turned to witness the shouts and arguments, which were primarily divided along racial lines. Members of the press laughed out loud, heads shaking as they scribbled furiously. Amy smiled as I moved back towards our table.

"Now you've done it," she said.

"This it outrageous!" screamed Weinstein. "Your Honor, this is outrageous! Simply preposterous! I . . . this is crazy."

Finally, I thought. Finally a curve ball Weinstein wasn't ready for. I sat down and waited for the Judge to regain control.

"I want to see both counsels in my chambers, right now!" he bellowed. I could only hope that he was angrier at the bedlam in the courtroom than its cause.

Amy and I followed a flustered Weinstein into the judge's chambers.

"All right, Leitner, what do you think you're doing? You can't just throw out insane theories like that without any basis in fact. If the jury was in, I would declare a mistrial." The Judge was not happy, but it seemed like he was at least ready to hear me out.

"Judge, please. Dr. Berenson has the necessary credentials. What we really want to do is use demonstrative evidence to prove his theory—"

"And, just what type of demonstrative evidence would you like to introduce, counselor?" Weinstein interrupted before I could continue. "Your Honor, before we go any further, the defendant objects to anything this witness may have to say, on the grounds that he has not been properly disclosed as an expert witness pursuant to the CPLR. We had no notice of this type of testimony! It's outrageous and poisonous to this jury!"

"The only thing poisonous is the touch of your client!" said Amy, to my great surprise.

"What? Your Honor, I take offense at that type of statement, and so does my client. These two young attorneys are attempting to turn the trial into a circus, and it should not be tolerated."

Defense counsel finally on the defensive. I could only laugh.

"Mr. Leitner, was this witness properly exchanged?" asked the judge impatiently.

"Of course he was, Your Honor," I replied, as Amy handed me proof of service of a copy of the People's intention to call Dr. Berenson.

"Your Honor," said Weinstein, clearly surprised. "Dr. Carl Berenson is a Manhattan optometrist. The Dr. Berenson they intend to call is some kind of specialist, if you'll call it, in something completely different something I doubt is even recognized by the medical profession."

"Your Honor, it's not my fault that Mr. Weinstein has the wrong Dr. Berenson. We never intended to call the optometrist Berenson, simply our own Dr. Berenson. We were never aware of any confusion on the part of defense counsel. If we were, surely I would have cleared it up right away." The sarcasm dripped from my lips.

"Your Honor, this is trial by ambush. You can not permit this."

"Counselor, I can and I will. Although I do sympathize with the strange coincidence which seemingly benefits the People at this time, they did exchange proper notice of this witness. You had every opportunity to determine what exactly he would testify to. I will not permit you to exclude this witness simply because you thought it was someone else. I will have the people exchange this witness's C.V. and other documents relating to his credentials, and I'll give you a short adjournment until this afternoon to review same."

"Your Honor, there is one other thing," I said. "Our demonstrative evidence involves Dr. Berenson bringing to court one of his laboratory monkeys."

"You surely must be joking, Mr. Leitner. Now I do think

you're turning this trial into a circus. What the hell do you need a monkey for?"

"Well Your Honor, it really is quite simple. Dr. Berenson proposes a simple experiment, if you will. We would like to, well, as demonstrative evidence . . . well, we want to have the defendant touch the monkey with his uncovered hand."

"*What!*" Weinstein jumped out of his seat. "Absolutely not. This is preposterous. This is totally improper procedure. There's no basis in law for this type of test."

"We'd also like to have this done in front of the jury," I added.

"*Your Honor.* This is the most outrageous suggestion I have ever heard in my thirty years practicing law. Surely you can't—" Judge Singleton's raised hand silenced the panicked Weinstein.

"Mr. Leitner, I suppose you have some type of support in the form of case law for this type of inquiry. It would seem at first to violate the defendant's right to be secure from an unreasonable search."

I could feel Amy move to the edge of her seat as she chimed in. "Sir, we view this as no different than taking blood from a father to determine paternity. No different from taking hair or semen samples from a defendant for forensic analysis in rape cases. I have fully briefed the matter for your review." She handed over copies of a brief to both the judge and defense counsel. "I would ask that you pay particular attention to *Andre versus Warren,* 1st Department 1995, which held that DNA and human leucocyte antigen blood tests conducted in a paternity proceeding did not infringe upon a father's Fourteenth Amendment right against unreasonable searches and seizures and his Fifth Amendment privilege against self-incrimination."

"Counselor, this is not a paternity case. A man's liberty

is at stake," interjected Judge Singleton responded, but Amy was way ahead of him.

"I realize that, Your Honor. However, in *People versus Nelson*, 2nd Department 1990, the Appellate Division of this district held that the taking of blood and hair samples from a second-degree murder defendant was properly directed. In that case the People properly demonstrated the existence of probable cause to believe that the defendant committed the crime and there was a clear indication that relevant material evidence would be found through such a search. In addition that court as well as the court in *People versus King*, 1994, found that such minimal intrusions occasioned by DNA blood samples did not constitute unreasonable seizures. Although, obviously, neither case involved a situation quite like the one we have here, they seem to indicate that this type of test should be permissible. Here we have at least two eyewitnesses to the defendant's contact with the complaining witness and a simple test involving merely a touch would not be considered as intrusive in any way."

The Judge perused the brief with one hand while his other covered his mouth, thinking, no doubt, about the ramifications of allowing such a demonstration, particularly in front of the jury. But I knew that we were right on the law.

"Your Honor, this clearly violates the defendant's constitutional rights," said Weinstein.

"What does your client have to hide, counselor?" I asked.

Weinstein shot out of his seat, shouting, "What does he have to hide? That's not the issue! This is simply improper, especially when you spring it on us in the middle of the trial. I will ask for a mistrial if this jury is allowed to see such a demonstration, regardless of the outcome."

"What are you talking about?" I replied. "If he touches the chimp and nothing happens, you want a mistrial? I'm basically putting all my eggs into one basket. If somehow Cameron's touch blinds this animal, then you have a problem, but even then he could still beat this charge. If he just touches the damn thing and nothing happens, than *I'm* looking for a new job tomorrow!"

The Judge was pressing his right thumb and forefinger onto the sockets of his closed eyes. "All right," he said, "That's enough, counselors. I'm familiar with this area of the law. I actually wrote the *Conte* decision, which I see you were smart enough to include in your brief," he acknowledged with a smile towards Amy. "I'm going to permit it. Simply having your client touch this animal is not intrusive at all, and thus does not violate his Constitutional rights. We're not talking about removing blood or hair or semen, or anything intrusive to his body. This involves no more of an examination than an identification lineup, as far as I'm concerned."

"*Your Honor!* In front of the jury?" exclaimed Weinstein. "How could you possibly—"

"Counsel, you'll have your exception. We'll put it on the record. You can go to the Appellate Division, as I suspect you will, but I'm going to allow it."

"Your Honor, a monkey? This case will turn on what happens when my client touches a monkey? It's preposterous. A monkey is not a human being. This type of test can not prove a thing."

"Well, counselor," I replied, "if you're so opposed to using the monkey then perhaps you would like to substitute yourself into the demonstration?"

The color drained from Weinstein's face as he retreated to his chair. For the first time, he was without a response.

Judge Singleton quickly severed an uneasy silence with encouraging words for Weinstein. "As far as I'm concerned, you should allow it. I can't imagine it bearing out anything, anyway. Mr. Leitner is absolutely right about one thing, at least. The whole case rides on this. If nothing happens, and I seriously doubt anything will, then the case is, for all intents and purposes, over. I may even set aside any verdict contrary to your favor, in that event. We'll allow this circus to go on, but since this is my tent, we'll do it my way. There will be one touch, in essentially the same manner, duration and force as the testimony indicates to this point. The animal will substitute for the complaining witness for that brief moment, and that's it. Now, since the complaining witness has testified to being blinded instantly upon contact, the same thing has to happen with the chimp, or you're done for, Mr. Leitner."

"I realize that, sir."

"I hope you realize that you're putting your office's reputation on the line along with your own. Does your supervisor know you intend to do this?"

"Sort of."

"All right then. We'll adjourn until two-thirty for Dr. Berenson and his traveling monkeys. I don't want anyone talking to the press about this until afterwards, is that clear?"

"Yes, sir," I responded.

"Your Honor, I must at least ask that you grant us an adjournment for the purpose of briefing the Constitutional issue," Weinstein added weakly.

"No. I have made my decision and it will not change. You have your remedy. You can go to the Appellate Division. I'm allowing it, counselor. Give them enough rope and maybe they'll hang themselves."

"Judge, it's my client that faces the noose. This is not proper."

"Appeal. I don't care. Really, I don't. Mr. Leitner, one other thing."

"Yes, sir."

"What are you going to do when the animal rights activists breathe down my neck for allowing this."

"I hadn't really thought of that. I guess since everyone seems to think that nothing's going to happen, we won't have to worry about it, right?"

I laughed nervously. We were sailing into uncharted waters.

At two-thirty, Dr. Carl Berenson, medical degree from the University of Southern California, six years studying skin cancer at the Hospital for Joint Diseases in Manhattan, ten years studying unique skin disorders in Latin America, three published books and a lot of nonbelievers took the stand. Before we could even get to the test, Weinstein's *voire dire* examination on Berenson's qualifications had exposed him as a bright mind who had clearly fallen from the graces of the scientific community. His theories had never been given serious attention, but had been ridiculed as completely unsupported. Berenson even admitted, on the stand, that he could not medically document how someone could be blinded simply by exposure to the touch of another person, or toxic chemical, as he proffered. A rejuvenated Jacob Weinstein moved again to exclude him, on the grounds that his theories were not grounded in acceptable medical fields.

"Your Honor, I haven't asked him to render an opinion yet," I retaliated quickly. "I could see excluding Dr. Berenson's opinion based on defense counsels' argument, but we've put the doctor on the stand to basically confirm today, here, that his theories are, in fact, grounded in true science. All we ask is for the defendant to remove one of the gloves that he never seems to take off and touch one of Dr. Berenson's subjects."

The room once again came abuzz. I looked at Cameron and for the first time his eyes met mine. I could tell that he was angry.

"Your Honor, once again we renew our objection to this type of unscientific experiment. Further, I believe the comments from Mr. Leitner warrant a mistrial." Weinstein was grasping, trying to preserve every possible ground for appeal. I began to believe that the monkey test was actually going to work.

Judge Singleton had already resolved this issue and he wasn't about to change his decision now. He ordered Dr. Berenson to proceed. With a signal from the good doctor, two assistants appeared at the back of the courtroom, each holding the hands of a four-foot-tall chimpanzee, who smiled at the gallery as a rush of sound built with each simian step. The monkey was called Eve, and had been born and bred in captivity. She was used primarily for cognitive and physical tests, and had been treated well, for the most part, by her handlers. Cameron shrunk at the sight of her and whispered intently to his lawyer. Dr. Berenson first showed the jury how the monkey was in good health and, using photographs of bananas, proved that she could indeed see clearly.

"Mr. Cameron, would you please be so kind as to remove the glove from your right hand and place it on the defense table?" asked Dr. Berenson with obvious excitement.

It was now or never.

"Mr. Cameron, step up to the witness box and place your hand against the left cheek of the animal with medium-type force," Judge Singleton ordered.

"Your Honor, we strenuously object!" Interjected Weinstein.

"You *strenuously* object? I have heard enough objections on this issue. One more objection, strenuous or feeble and I'll hold you in contempt, counselor. Now, instruct your client to step up to this witness box and take off that glove *right now!*"

"And what if I refuse?" asked Cameron. It was the first time I had actually heard his voice and it seemed fragile.

"Than *you* will be held in contempt, sir, and I will instruct the jury that they may make every reasonable inference against you by your failure to abide by my order."

Cameron stood at the defense table. "Your Honor, please. Can I at least speak privately with you?" he pleaded.

"Absolutely not. Sir, I am ordering you not to say one other word but to simply move to the witness box and follow Dr. Berenson's instructions. I will not ask you again."

Cameron refused to move.

"Your Honor, I realize this is not proper procedure, but if you will just allow me to speak with you privately I think it will spare everyone a great deal of trouble."

"Sir, I will ask you once more. You may consult with your counsel if you wish. However, if you do not comply, you will be held in contempt and I will have you removed from this courtroom and incarcerated immediately, until such time as we can have a separate contempt hearing."

Three court officers moved into position behind the defendant. Cameron turned to see the officers, then glanced at Weinstein before facing the judge.

"Your Honor, you just don't understand..." said Cameron with outstretched arms.

"Oh, I beg to differ, sir. I understand that you are pushing my patience to the limit." replied Judge Singleton.

"I am truly sorry, Your Honor, but I must respectfully refuse."

"Sir, you are showing me anything but respect. Officers, remove Mr. Cameron from this courtroom immediately!"

The officers moved to obey.

"This is unfair!" cried Cameron. "Am I not to be permitted to stand witness at my own trial?" His body stiffened in response to the three officer's presence. "I must be permitted to speak! This is an outrage!"

The officers moved to pull him away, one on each side, grasping Cameron's gray suit. Cameron squirmed in their grip and he turned violently to face the jury, breaking free from the two officers.

"I am innocent! I did not intend for this to happen! You don't understand. It wasn't intentional, you must believe me!"

The third officer, the youngest of the three, placed his bare right hand directly upon Cameron's mouth in an attempt to silence him. Upon contact, he shrieked in terror.

"Oh, my God—I can't see! I can't see!" He crumpled to the ground in front of the jury box, hands pushed hard into his eyes as he cried. Gloved court officers swarmed around Cameron, whisking him from the room as the crowd in the gallery exploded past the wood divider.

Judge Singleton unsuccessfully tried to restore order in the court. The room flooded with officers. Sirens wailed outside and an alarm began clanging in the hallway. The officers surrounded Amy and me, attempting to get us out of the courtroom unscathed, but the crowd closed in tighter and tighter until I could no longer see past the nearest white shirt. The blizzard of officers closed in on us and soon I, too, was blinded.

WAITING FOR THE GIRL FROM CALIFORNIA

DEAN WHITLOCK

I cannot tell the story of our meeting. Stories flow, scenes stand out to make an order. I am not sure these are those scenes. I can only sift the images, looking for a common theme, more like poetry, more like writing metaphor. I think this is the story of our meeting . . .

I am waiting for inspiration, sitting and waiting in the study, the little room we use for computers. Outside the window, folded snow drifts in the light of a rising moon. The deep quiet there draws my eyes away from the blank white screen, past frosted panes, to watch blue shadows that glide across the field to the edge of the woods. The cursor lies still. My thoughts are buried in snow, half-deep in winter. The thermometer reads thirty-eight degrees below zero, Fahrenheit. Tiny drafts leak around the ancient, many-paned window. The outside wall seeps cold. My feet are chill and distant.

I am rising, push back the chair, sudden harsh sound. Outside, nothing is sudden, except perhaps the flash of light on crystals of snow as I move closer to the window and peer out through the growing leaves of frost. I crane my neck and squint upward, as though to curve my sight around the eaves, but the moon is too far east. The sky has depth, like still water. Moonlight sheens the surface. I can pick out only the brightest stars, tiny specks drowned deep by the winter moon.

I touch the glass, leaving gray prints in the frost. It burns my fingers. A chill runs down my arm and through my body, but I hesitate to draw back to the warm center of the room. The still silver night hides something. I can feel it waiting, in the blue shadows, under the black archways of the woods, above the long eaves of the roof. There is something just out of sight that likes the cold. My heart quickens, and I consider going out. Considering, not going. My imagination is too great, or too limited. The chill from the window glass stills it.

I turn back to the PC, to stare briefly at the black-lettered keys. The unmarked screen waits for other signs of life in my imagination. The subject of this paper is called time—how odd that sounds. The night outside claims all meaning. I switch off the hooded lamp, leaving screen and window to glow blue in the cold and empty study.

The living room seems hot. The parlor stove radiates heat and smoke, orange flames flickering behind its un-caulked seams. Lou and David crouch on sagging chairs, eyes fixed on the Go board between them, house mates sharing no more than a roof and a game. Lou is rubbing the sides of his forehead, shuttering his face with his hands. A shawl drapes his shoulders. David's fingers tap out computer language on his knees. His feet are tapping, too, muffled by shearling slippers. Stones dot the board in patterns I don't begin to comprehend. That, and Lou's shuttered hands, keep me away. David glances more or less in my direction, smiles blankly, looks back down. They know nothing of the night outside.

Julie lies curled under an old quilt at one end of the couch, surrounded by her ward of rescued cats. Only her face and hands extend beyond the faded cloth and kittens. She reads on, unaware of my entrance. She is fleeing Vermont without me, reading Tolkien. I sit in the battered Morris chair beside her, but her attention is fixed. She is reading Tolkien. I fidget, staring at the cracks in the stove. A cold draft flows down the stairway and into the room. A clock chimes slowly in the landlord's half of the house. Julie turns a page. Lou plays a stone. The fire snaps.

I rise, wandering into the kitchen, where the floor is colder than the study wall. I open the cupboard by the bathroom door to contemplate our dwindling stash of marijuana, hidden in a tea tin. Lapsang Souchong. The smoky tea odor lingers, blending with the sweet-basil smell of dope. Cloying. I glance left, out the window. The night is waiting.

Back in the living room, I study an untidy heap of CDs, consider and reject the radio. I put my back to the ornate little stove and stare at the wall. Julie turns a page. David plays a stone.

Outside, the moon tops the peak of the roof and starts back down.

Outside, shadows shift on the snow. I see this in my mind's eye, wondering what moves in the shadows.

The landlord's clock is chiming. I listen to the bells, counting, but they chime too slowly, as though cold makes the air too thick and hard for bells to sound. I shake myself and step away from the stove. My back is stiff, my calves dry from the iron glow of wood heat.

"I'm going to bed."

My own volume startles me. The rest are unaffected. Lou stops rubbing and waves with his left hand and continues rubbing. David smiles up in my direction and says,

"Ah," as though to a revelation, and looks back down at the stones. Julie finishes her paragraph and marks the place with a long finger.

"Did you get much written?" she asks. Her tone is kind, her round face warmed by faint interest, but the words are a foreign language. No real meaning. Certainly no passion. She is not inclined to join me, and it seems unimportant, almost ordained.

I shrug.

"Sweet dreams," she says, and turns her gaze back to Middle Earth. A cat blinks one eye at me. Another turns its back.

I move a brick from the side shelf to the top of the stove and go to the cold bathroom. I am picking up the brick on my way to the stairs. Julie is turning a page. Lou is playing a stone. The brick is warm, though its glow does not extend beyond my hands. I slip it into one of the flannel sacks Julie makes just for this purpose and hold it to my chest, walking up the narrow stairs.

At the top is a latched door that leads over to the land-lord's side. There are noises behind it, a sound like crying. I hesitate, wondering, knowing it is the girl, but the sound stops and it is very cold in the hallway. I hurry into the bed-room I share with Julie, hurry into my nightshirt, hurry under the many blankets with the brick. The sheets are cold, the blankets heavy. I push the brick down to the foot of the bed, where it warms my feet, slide it up to my thighs. And to my chest. And down to my feet. The mattress is slowly warming and I wonder about the sound of crying.

The landlord and his lady are prone to shouting or singing, not tears. There is a roomer, though, a young woman who inhabits a half-finished space in their attic. I notice her eyes as we pass, and she seems the type to cry, a deep-eyed girl in a thin jacket. There is something about her, about those eyes, I find compelling, but she is more than shy. She avoids us all, her presence known mostly by a rusty Dodge Spirit, half buried outside in the snow. It has California plates. In this cold, the moon seems closer than California.

Moonlight reflected on snow is leaking between the cracks in the curtains on our small dormer window. A line of gray light stripes the ceiling, descending the wall beside me. I stare at it and my eyes dim and something like sleep falls on me. Vaguely, I hear the sound of tears.

Another noise wakens me. The line of light is off the ceiling, is running across the bed. A cat jumps up, circles my feet, seeking warmth. Half alert, I hear downstairs the tap of keys, David working.

But that is not the sound that wakes me. Someone is moving in the room. I turn my head and see Julie, her tall outline faint against the slit of light. And she is not alone. She hugs a smaller figure to her breast. This is what I hear: muffled crying.

"Come," Julie says. "Come to bed. You're freezing."

"I'm sorry."

The voice is high but musical, even through her crying. I recognize in its tone the sad girl from California. Her head is tucked down on Julie's chest, cradled like a rescued kitten. Her face turns toward me. Moonlight shines deep in her eyes, reflecting the path of tears. Julie walks her to the bed, moves a cat, lifts the covers. Cold drafts in around me. I shift over, yielding my warm hollow to the crying girl. Her hand brushes my chest through the nightshirt and she draws back from the touch.

"It's okay," Julie tells her softly. "You're okay with us."

The girl slides in slowly. She keeps a space between us. Then Julie slides in and lets the blankets fall. She lays her arm across the shivering girl and touches my shoulder.

"Okay?" she asks me.

I nod. The girl is a slender line of cold between us, but the shivering slowly stops as she lets herself relax into the warmth. She is crying softly. I don't know why. For a lost lover, perhaps. For her family beyond the mountains. Perhaps for her half-buried Dodge, marked with the plates of a state so far away. I touch my hand to her shoulder, a chaste gesture, gentle, trying to show sympathy. Her weeping smile wakes the knight inside me; I share Julie's need to protect her. She takes my hand in both of hers and holds it on her chest. She is wearing fine gloves, like silk.

Julie's arm lies lightly across her stomach. Our six legs lie close together, warming the foot of the bed. The crying lessens and her breathing is slower and the crying stops and she and Julie are breathing together, asleep. I can feel beneath my palm the heartbeat of the girl from California. My rhythm matches hers. It seems to fill my soul. I am asleep.

I am awake and we three are cupped like spoons. My left arm enfolds the girl from California. I breathe into the nape of her neck, and the scent of her dark hair fills me with sudden wonder at her presence. As if feeling me wake, she nestles back against me. Our night shirts have shifted up in our sleep. Her buttocks press into my lap, skin on skin, as silken as her fine gloves. At the touch a shock flows through my groin, cold and hot, spreading up my body to my heart. I breathe in more deeply the warm scent of her hair. She presses harder and my loins respond. Without thought, I cup my hand over one small breast. She stiffens and I think she is crying again but, no, she is sighing, willing, her nipple firm in my touch, and she is taking me in with an easy arch of her back.

My heart quickens, my mind slows. We lie still, joined as closely as she can bring us, and Julie is sleeping and our breathing joins in rhythm and the warmth between us grows to heat. The girl from California shifts gently, squeezing me with the slightest of motions, a tiny pulse that matches our breathing. I slide my hand down the smooth hollows of her skin, pressing gently with the same pulse in the curling hair that joins her thighs. The cold night backs away from us. All my feeling centers in her lap.

I whisper to her, without sound, moving my lips to tell her how easy it is to love her. I think she nods her head. Her dark hair swirls in my face and I touch her neck with my lips and the breath of ecstasy shudders into me. And her, I feel it in the rhythm of her breath, our breathing. My life continues in the rhythm of her breath.

We are still, lying still, breathing still in slow rhythm, and she draws my hand to her face to kiss the tips of my fingers. Her lips move. I read the words as human braille. *Thank you. I'm sorry. It has been so long. I'm sorry.* And I don't really understand.

Unwanted sleep is claiming the edge of my thoughts, but there awakes in the center a strange, wondering love that does not fade with the shrinking flesh in my groin. I am amazed, both at our loving and at how I feel. I feel like this for no other lover, not even Julie. That love is not less, but I feel it differently—a friendship, not a passion—not like the wonder that lingers in my heart. I do not understand it. I feel the smallest touch of guilt, a distant speck that drowns in shifting light. The room looks different, the cold air on my cheek feels different, transmuted by the woman in my arms. I wish I was watching her face. I wish I was looking into her wide deep eyes, to see the lights that flash in darkness there.

Sleep piles in against my will. I want to tell her I love her. I want to kiss and kiss and kiss away her sadness. I fall asleep instead.

I am waking, slow and sluggish, lying on my side, my right arm numb and heavy beneath me. Across an empty hollow, Julie lies on her back, deeply asleep. The sheets between us are growing cold. The girl from California is gone.

Fighting a weight of blankets and persistent sleep, I rise up on my elbow. Pins and needles torture my waking arm. Cats shift, sullen weights on the covers. The streak of moonlight is gone, but the room is lit with a faint blue glow. The curtains hang wide open.

And I am listening for the sound of crying, but all I can hear is Lou, snoring in the next room, and David's printer, rhythmically churning behind a closed door downstairs. The sounds seem slow as the chiming of a frozen bell. Even the blue light from the window seems slow. I imagine time as something blue and thick, and the thought twists in my mind, confusing me, confounding my need to move, to find the girl from California.

I push from the warm bed into blankets of cold. Cats claim the warm space behind me. The chipped floor boards feel like stone. I pull on wool socks, and pants over my nightshirt. I glance out the window. Stars needle the dark sky outside. Below, dark footprints pattern the bottom of a deep trough that breaks the drifted hollows of snow. It leads past the mounded Dodge Spirit. There, at the far edge of the field, it stops at a pale thin figure poised before the dark cloisters of the wood. She is looking back at my window with shadowed eyes. She seems to glow faintly, blue as moonlight on snow. She is turning, passing under branches into darkness. Snow dust glitters in the air behind her.

I am rushing down the stairs. Behind me, Julie sleeps. Lou snores. David, too, is sound asleep. His printer slogs out unnumbered pages without him. The stove has died to cold iron. The entire house is slow-witted, unknowing.

The kitchen is cold enough to remind me of clothing, to jam my feet into boots and throw on my coat and grope in the box for gloves. I am groping in the dark for my hat and gloves, groping, digging, taking whatever lies on top of the pile. The hat is Lou's, too small. I have one mitten, one glove, both left-handed.

I slam through the doorway and the cold greets me with grim surprise. My bare face stiffens at its touch. I trot through the hard cold down the narrow shoveled path to the driveway, half shuffling in my heavy untied boots. A gap breaks the piled snow beside the buried Dodge, and I push through it into the trough of her passage. My feet sink into her small footprints. The snow is thigh deep, but so dry and light it flows back into the path behind me, as it refills her path before me. Snow floods the top of my boots. My ankles are chill through boots, pants, and woolen socks.

Clouds of snow curl up in my wake as I try to hurry. They hang in the still air, flashing starlight. I can't run—the snow is too deep, the air too thin, the cold too thick. Each breath burns the lining of my nose and throat. I stumble down the hill, and down through deep drifts, and down to the edge of the wood. Her footprints lead into darkness.

I stand at the edge of the wood, the edge of the darkness, breathing hard and trying not to, holding a gloved hand to my face to filter the freezing air. The snow is just as deep under the trees, and the dark is deeper. It is pressing against me, it hinders my wanting to go. I shiver with more than cold. Yes, I am chill beneath my coat and hat, but she wears only a nightshirt. I clench my fists and press on.

I can see nothing. The half filled trough of her passage is my guide. It winds among the trees, tending downhill toward the river. The trunks of oaks and pines loom against the faintly glowing snow, flat black on gloss. Hidden roots tangle my feet. Branches reach at my face. A pine bough springs up at my passing, shedding snow that finds the gap at the back of my neck, a bitter surprise even colder than the dark air. I curse both trees and cold.

Her footprints are at the river. I half fear to see them end at a dark hole in the ice, and I am ready to mourn. But they do not end. Starlight leaking down the river's gap reveals the drifted mounds of rock and shore. The water is capped by an unbroken plain of snow. I feel a breath of relief, but her path winds downstream from mound to shadowed mound as though in search of a doorway. I lean against a barren trunk. I am sweating beneath my coat. The cold seems thicker the farther I come from bed. But I cannot turn back with her path leading on like that.

I step onto the river, slipping on ice beneath the snow. I can hear water rippling somewhere, the only sound beside my straining breath. I am forcing my way over mounded stones, stumbling in snow deeper than it looks, stumbling on rocks that appear to be snow, tripping on snags and tears in the ice. The river runs on beneath me, persistent and slow, its bed stretching out beneath the stars as long as the Milky Way. She can't be much farther—I tell myself that, because I'm not sure how much farther I can go. I cannot even try to run. I am plodding on through dark and snow under the twisting cold river of stars. I am wandering from her path and find myself waist deep in unmarked drifts beneath the trees. It takes an effort to fight back to the river, even more effort to turn away from home and follow it. But I do. I wander. I fight back. I do.

And the path does come to an end at the thin shape of the girl from California, hunched on the river, softly glowing like a dozen other star lit mounds. I am beside her and see her and realize it is her and not a ghost shaped by moonlight and snow. She is wearing her thin coat after all, and a pair of thin shoes, kneeling with her back to me, not moving. She does not see me. She is staring down at her hands, bone white, the gray of weathered bones, her bare skin, gloves gone, bare skin glowing gray blue in running water in a small hole in the ice.

I am yelling, crying, "No! Why? No!" and not really thinking, yelling and grabbing her arms, pulling her up, she is so much heavier in the snow, dead weight, fighting my pull by hanging limp, reaching for the hard silver hole of water with hands gray blue and dying.

I turn her toward me, stumbling, almost falling, and she is looking in my face, eyes wide. I can see them clearly, and they are wide and deep, a rich dark color with lights that seem to flash inside, like dreams. I am filled with a longing that makes me breathless, staring into her eyes, wide, staring back, staring into the river of stars in her eyes.

"Stop," she is saying. "Stop staring. Do something else."

"What?" I reply, staring.

"Look away," she says. "Look down, count your breath, let go of me." She is saying those things and there is an order to them, though I cannot make out the order.

"Why?" I ask, holding her wrists and staring at her bone-chilled hands. "Why are you doing this?"

"You cannot touch me," she is saying. "Do not touch me. I cannot touch you or anyone. I cannot touch."

And I am holding her wrists and asking, "Why?"

"I am a Depriver," she says, softly but with an edge like screaming, like the pain that must be spreading from her half-frozen hands.

I hear that but it makes no sense. "A Depriver?" I say, but words are marching through my brain, words from TV and radio and Web and magazines and federal mailings, e-mailings, voices speaking at work and home. "A Depriver?"

"Yes," she whispers, head down, eyes where I can't see them, the lights turned away. "I'm a Depriver. I am not allowed to touch you. I cannot touch you. I cannot let myself touch you." Even softer: "No matter how much I want to."

And I am testing my senses. Holding her wrists so tightly, not believing her words, I am checking all my senses. Seeing her turned-down head turning back up to watch me, hearing the water splash at the edges of the hole and ripple back beneath the hard ice, smelling the scent of pine and, yes, the musky scent in her hair and tasting in the back of my mouth the sweet, nutty flavor of her neck, her flesh. And feeling warmth, feeling her arch to take me in, feeling . . .

Feeling numbness growing in my body, numbness spreading from my hands and feet toward my center, where panic is flashing in my heart.

But, no, I can feel my heart, pounding hard, feel the cold air passing in and out of my mouth, feel the cold bars of her wrists even through the mismatched left-handed leather that covers my palms. I am feeling the cold and the girl—this woman before me—this person who is changing the very way I feel.

"No," I am saying. "I can see and hear and smell and taste and feel. I am not deprived. You are not depriving me of any sense."

"What time is it?" she asks me.

"What?" I am saying, "what did you say?"

"What time is it?" she asks. "What day is it? What month? When were you born?"

"Born?" I am saying. "I am born. I am here. I exist. I do not need to be born any more."

"You have no sense of time," she says, tells, insists to me, her fists hitting my chest, tears running from her eyes. "I am taking it away from you, depriving you of time, all time, all thought of time."

And I am telling her I don't understand and I don't care and it doesn't matter because I love her.

And she is not talking, not crying, she is staring at me, not moving, only the lights in her eyes are moving, drifting in her glance as she searches for something in my eyes.

And I am telling her I love her, trying to tell her how she changes me, how I am feeling, how she brings wonder to my heart, and I am putting her hands inside my coat against my skin, trying to warm them, telling her how much I love her hands.

And we are kissing, she is kissing me. Her lips are cold and her hands are stone cold on my chest, her lips are warming on mine. I feel her touching me as close as any people can touch, skin on skin, tongue on tongue, cold and warm spreading through me to my heart and mind with the water rippling beneath us and the stars turning slowing in the winding path of the river.

We are kissing and she is pulling back, pulling back, standing at arms length and also huddling within the circle of my arms. Her hair swirls into my face, her cold hands press like knots against my chest, and I can feel her shivering. I am shivering, too, with wonder and cold.

"We have to go back," she is saying. "We can't stay here all night. We'll freeze to death."

It makes no sense, really, but I understand that I am cold and she is cold and there is a warm house nearby.

"Come with me," she says. She is turning me by the hand, leading me back up the river. And I am stopping to give her the mitten from my left hand, putting it on her left hand, taking her other hand, flesh on flesh. I am following, and she is stumbling, so I am picking her up, trying to pick her up. I am stumbling myself and we both sprawl into the snow and slide a long way on the ice.

I tell her I'm sorry, but she is laughing and stumbling

up, me with her, and taking hands. We are half walking, half skating up the river, laughing together, sliding together in long, almost graceful steps, hand in hand. We follow our path up the river, from mound to glowing mound, and she is glowing beside me, all but her blue hand in mine.

We are in the woods and we are through the woods and in the field, pushing up though the light, glittering snow. The moon is halfway down the western sky, and I am checking my sense of direction and congratulating myself. I am not deprived of that or any other sense that I can reckon.

And we are stumbling through the snow bank, past the mound of her buried Spirit. We are stumbling through the door into the cold kitchen that feels hot against our outdoor skin, closing the door on the night and the moonlight. The house is quiet, except for some kind of bell, chiming faintly behind a closed door. But I am thinking about warm drinks, about warming the girl from California. We are too clumsy to deal with stove or kettle, she tries but cannot make her fingers move. I turn on the hot water, watching it run and steam in the warm-seeming kitchen. She shakes me and points to the steam. We are drinking the warm water, I hold the cup for her, helping her drink because her hands will not work and we are both shivering so hard the cup rattles on our teeth, mine and hers.

And we are in the living room, where the stove is cold, but I build up the fire, trying not to clank the doors or drop the wood in the quiet house. And I am pulling an afghan from the closet and an old blanket and we are taking off our clothes and curling up together on the couch, wrapped in the afghan and the blanket, curling up together, face to face, our legs twined, her hands in the warmest space between us. We are curled up together, naked, and my heart and mind are pulsing with her touch, responding, but my groin is cold and my flesh too tired and we are falling asleep together in the warming room. Her hands, too, are warming between us, unknotting, spreading out to lie flat and loose between us.

She whispers in my ear, something about tomorrow. But her voice is fading into sleep and it doesn't make any sense anyway and her voice is fading and my mind is fading, our breath smoothing out into one joined breath.

Julie is coming down the stairs. There is sunlight in the room and I am waking up, and Julie comes downstairs, followed by cats, stands by the couch, looking from me to the face of the sleeping girl in my arms. The girl wakes up and she and Julie are talking. Julie sees the girl's hands and gasps in surprise at the blackening fingers. She reaches out, but the girl draws back, refusing to touch. She says she is a Depriver. Julie draws back.

I am denying it, telling Julie it isn't true, that I am not deprived. I am describing how I feel, how the girl makes me feel, and Julie is watching with wide eyes, with narrowed eyes, with open mouth and mouth tight. She goes into the kitchen, returning with rubber gloves to take the girl's hands, study her fingers, carefully cover them with ointment and bandages. Lou is awake and bringing warm drinks and food. He mutters under his breath and carefully hands things to me to give to the girl from California, who I am feeding because her fingers are bandaged and hurt her, and I am dressing her and hugging her and undressing her and we are kissing. We are in the bedroom with moonlight on the walls, but we are warm in bed, kissing, touching as close as people can touch, lips everywhere, hands everywhere, she is letting me in, breathing ecstasy, her body glowing blue as snow on moonlight.

And I am telling Julie, trying to explain, how it is with the girl and I. We *cannot* not touch. I know the girl is a Depriver, I know that I cannot teach or write or follow a recipe. I know I am missing something, something I can't even understand that I miss, any more than I can understand the chemistry of attraction that makes us laugh together on the river and in the kitchen and the bedroom. But I am trying to explain the wonder and amazement and desire—all the feelings she brings to me, those and mystery, yes, and love. The pure emotions that make up all the rest, that give us passion, that make us human and form our spirit.

But David is gone and Julie is leaving with Lou and her cats, and the girl and I are living here alone. She has only five fingers, three on one hand, two on another. Both thumbs, at least, and it gives her an excuse to be wearing gloves around other people, working, shopping. But she is not wearing gloves to touch me, with flesh as fine and smooth as gloves. We talk and take walks and she tells me stories and I write her poems. Yes, I can write poems. But touching is what we do, she and I and all people, to show how much we love.

This is the story of our meeting, and of our life together. She can tell it better. I tell things out of order. But she is not here, yet. Now. Soon. Always? It makes no sense. She is not here and she is also here.

And I am waiting, sitting and waiting in the small room with the computer. The screen glows with these words. Outside, starlight shines on folded snow, though I also see green grass and bright red leaves and rain and sunshine—all of them are outside my window. And starlight on snow. Blue shadows that glide behind slow drifts. Deep cold. A rising moon.

And I am sitting and waiting for another warm touch from the girl from California.

MARGINAL EXISTENCE

JAN CLARK

"Night, Punkin," Mike said without looking up from the paper.

"G'night, Dad."

A second later, when she hadn't trotted off down the hall to her bedroom, he let the sports section slide onto his lap. Her huge brown eyes looked down at him from beneath a mop of golden ringlets. "You want to tell me something, Tracy?" She nodded, her bottom lip jutting forward uncertainly. "What?"

"Love you, Daddy," she said, then leapt at him, arms extended. She caught him around the neck with a sturdy hug and gave him a noisy wet kiss on his jaw.

When she released him, Mike looked up at her. "What do you want and how much?"

"Dad!"

"Isn't that what all this sudden affection is about?" he asked.

"Well, not exactly. But Lauren just got a new VR set and it really clips."

"I see," Mike said, even though he didn't. "And now you're fishing for one, too."

"Not the one *she* got," Tracy explained, her excitement plainly building now that she had his attention and he hadn't immediately said no. "But it's been ages since I got a VR anything. And there's this one—"

"Isn't your birthday next month?"

"It's sixteen days away, actually. But I already told Mom what I wanted."

"So this is something extra," he said, making sure his tone sounded discouraging.

Her hopeful smile wavered slightly. "Right."

"What about your own money?"

"I've saved up half." She gestured with her hands and her eyes seemed to get bigger, if possible. Mike found himself both amused and mesmerized by them. "Actually, Daddy, I was hoping I wouldn't have to spend all of my money. But I have saved up $75 and . . . I could pay you back after my birthday money comes in."

Mike sighed and wondered whether she'd end up as a stockbroker, real estate agent or a lawyer. He chuckled and shook his head. "I'll talk to your mom about it. But no promises."

"Okay." She smiled. "I love you, Dad."

He nodded, and grabbed up the paper. "Now go on and say good night to your mom."

" 'Kay." She ran off down the hall and Mike wiped his cheek with the back of his sleeve. Though he had nothing to fear from Tracy, he knew the risks of skin-to-skin contact. Hell, he dealt with them every day as an EMT. Anyone was susceptible. Even kids, though they rarely displayed any symptoms.

A few minutes later, Jenna came down the hall, flopped herself in a chair and switched on the stereo screen. She scrolled through the programming menu and settled on a music channel.

He listened to a few lines of the song being played, the Eagles' "Hotel California." Dark and brooding, it was as relevant a comment on today's society as it had been twenty-five years ago. Mike returned his attention to the article on sports injuries. He considered humming along with the tune, but not with Jenna sitting there.

"Anything newsworthy?" she asked.

"Other than Tracy's latest request?"

"You're not going to let her have that VR game, are you?"

"I told her you and I would work out the details," he said.

Jenna sighed. "She's got you exactly where she wants you."

"Maybe. But she's my little Punkin."

"Not so little any more," Jenna reminded him. "She's started borrowing my clothes."

Mike shrugged. He handed her the front section and kept reading. They stayed that way until she put down the paper and switched off the screen. "G'night, Mike," she said.

He glanced up and watched her go, then heaved a sigh and went to check the locks on their front door. As he turned and saw the light in their room go out, Mike wondered when had they fallen into this godawful routine. He knew exactly what would happen in the next few minutes, few hours, probably the next fifty years.

In all likelihood, Jenna had gotten into bed wearing nothing and expected him to do the same. They'd make love, or not. He'd fall asleep. She'd get up six hours later and go to work. He'd get Tracy up and take her to school before he drove his forty-minute commute and checked in at the station. In the following hours he'd triage about twenty people on the way to County Hospital. Then he'd clean up, go for a drink with his squad, come home, eat a late dinner by himself and scan the paper.

Such was his life.

A week later, as Mike sat in gridlock on northbound Interstate 35, he glanced to his left and saw the driver bang his steering wheel in frustration. Sure, it was late, and they hadn't moved in six minutes, but this guy needed to get a grip. Eventually, Mike drove past the overturned truck that had created the bottleneck. He pulled into the parking lot fifteen minutes late and ignored his supervisor's brief comment on tardiness.

After lunch they got a call to a house fire. Two engines were already on scene when his MedUnit arrived. Mike slid on his gloves and mask; while he followed with the equipment box, his partner and their driver rolled the stretcher out the back

The firefighters had pulled three people from the house. Two were kids, the oldest one no bigger than Tracy. The mom had been badly burned on her arm. She had to be in shock and severe pain, but she wouldn't hold still for treatment and kept fighting them, yelling to the firefighter she needed to go back inside.

The man lifted his mask and asked why.

"Gilbert's in there," she cried.

"Where?"

"The kitchen, I think. Oh, God, I can hear him."

Mike strained his ears and heard the sharp whine of an animal. Dog? He thought so. That woman must be crazy to ask a man to go back into a burning house to rescue a dog. Then, to his amazement, Mike saw the firefighter slip his mask back on and head for the house.

Mike checked the younger kid and bandaged his burned

hand. "You a doctor?" the boy asked, looking up at him with pale, trusting eyes.

"No."

"Oh." The boy's expression deflated, but it had no effect on Mike. "That's a good bandage," he offered hopefully, nodding at the gauze wrapped around his hand. "I don't hardly feel it hurtin' now."

"Good," Mike said. He looked up and saw the firefighter carrying a small dog. The woman ran to him and took the puppy, tears streaming down her face. When she seemed satisfied it wasn't hurt, she handed it to the boy.

"He's okay, Pauly. We're all okay. That's all that matters."

Mike looked past them at the house, still engulfed with flames and wondered if they had insurance.

"What the hell? Oh, this pisses me off so much I could scream."

Mike looked up from the paper to see Jenna glaring at him from the kitchen table. "What?" he asked.

"Damn it, Mike. I told you these letters needed to be mailed today. I left them right here this morning."

"So?"

"So, I just found them under yesterday's sports section, Mike," she complained. "Some of these bills need to be paid by tomorrow."

"They'll get over it," he said.

"What is with you lately?" Jenna groused, her wide, demanding eyes snapping at him.

Mike looked up and saw her jaw set in anger. He shook his head. "What do you mean, Jen?"

"Everything." She sighed, frowning. "These bills," She shoved them under his nose. "That newspaper you're suddenly married to. I practically burned the pork chops yesterday—and you ate them anyway without a word. Hell, Mike, we haven't made love in over a week."

He looked up at her. "So?"

Jenna shook her head. "You're not even going to argue with me?"

Mike shrugged. "Why should I?"

"Nothing seems to matter to you. You're like a different person. It's driving me crazy." Jenna huffed and stomped off to their bedroom.

When Mike slid under the covers a couple of hours later, he found she'd not only gone to sleep, she'd worn pajamas. A sure sign he was in the doghouse. Mike rolled onto his side and heaved a sigh. Before he drifted off, he realized her attitude and silent treatment should have bugged him. But it didn't. Not at all.

"I'm afraid I've got some bad news, Mike," his supervisor said after Mike had seated himself in the small, sparsely furnished office.

When Jamar closed the door and came back around his desk, Mike asked, "Was it the Perkins run last Friday? I thought my report said we didn't arrive on scene until after the civies pulled her out of the car."

"You did," Jamar said. "This isn't about that." He sat down and began drumming his fingers on the blotter. The brown skin on his knuckles looked dry, with a whitish cast. Mike wondered what he'd been doing to abuse his hands. Yard work? Jenna had gotten on him about that last weekend. Everything seemed to piss her off lately.

Jamar went on. "It's about the physical you took on Monday."

Mike sat a little straighter. "What about it?"

"You know we do an in-depth neuro study."

"Yeah. So?"

"Your neuro chems are way out the margins, Mike. It looks like you're Deprived."

Mike shrugged. "I don't think so," he said. "It's never happened to me, but I was here when Fletcher and Montez both went blind for a month." He shook his head. "I feel fine. I can see, hear, remember . . . walk, talk . . . everything. No way I'm Deprived, Jamar."

His boss leaned back and frowned skeptically. "You sure?"

"I've suited up for every call. Can't see how I could have even been exposed."

Jamar made a note on a pad. "And what about off duty? Or at home?"

"I know the drill. I risk exposure every day," he recited. "And I can't recall any recent contact with untested individuals."

Jamar shrugged then let out a tired sigh. "And how old is Tracy now?"

"Tracy? Well—" the image of his little girl's innocent hug and kiss flashed through Mike's mind "—she'll turn twelve in a couple of days."

"Okay." Jamar made a note of that and leaned back in his chair. "You say you've got no symptoms. But your chems are low and even I can see you're acting strange." He scrubbed at his chin, then looked Mike in the eye. "I hate to do this, but I'm pulling you off your unit. I'm gonna switch you to dispatch, Mike."

"Okay," he nodded agreeably. "For how long?"

"We'll do a chem run every other day. When you slip back in the margins, I'll put you back on the street."

"Sounds fair." Mike stood and offered his hand, then let it drop back to his side. "Jamar."

"Mike."

After he closed the door behind him, Mike went to his

unit and pulled his personal gear. He inventoried it and stowed everything in his locker, then went up the stairs to the dispatch room.

As he sat at the console, he considered how he'd been acting for the last week or so. Normal, he thought. Maybe a little more relaxed. Nothing much had bothered him, true, but then again he wasn't the type to overreact about stupid stuff. Tracy's birthday was the day after tomorrow. He remembered how he'd felt about her turning eleven, a year ago. He didn't feel anything like that this year. He didn't feel much at all, now that he really thought about it. City traffic didn't irritate him. Neither did Jenna's complaints or Jamar's pronouncement. Even the hard-sell telemarketer he'd talked to last night hadn't annoyed him. Normally, a comment like the one from the kid with the burned hand would have bugged the hell out of him.

"Unbelievable," he murmured. "I guess I am Deprived."

But if he had been Deprived, then by whom? Like he'd told Jamar, his training had taught him to be careful. Even with his own family.

He took half a dozen calls and dispatched them before there was a lull long enough to concentrate on the problem. Everything kept coming back to the kiss Tracy had given him. But she was just a kid. To be a Depriver, you had to be an adult.

More words echoed in his head. Jenna telling him Tracy'd been borrowing her clothes. Tracy asking for the VR game, then bargaining for it like a pro. Tracy complaining that her face was breaking out. Puberty wasn't around the corner any more. It was here.

Mike sat back in his chair. Tracy had become a Depriver. But even that didn't bother him. Still, he needed to protect his daughter from the cruelties of the world. He'd have to get her tested first, though, to rule out the possibility that he'd been Deprived by someone else. He couldn't remember being touched by anyone other than Jenna, but testing her seemed reasonable, too.

More calls came in and he dispatched them. He waited patiently until his break, then took a pad and pen to the lunchroom table and started making a list. How ironic, he thought, ripping the sheet from the pad, being Deprived made it possible for him to deal with this in a calm, logical manner. Normally, he hated being incapacitated in any way. Even allergies bothered him. But this bizarre deprivation was like floating on a calm sea. Both what had happened and what he needed to do were clear, and the sense of righteous indignation that usually clouded his judgment at such brutal injustice just wasn't there.

He would have to get both of them tested. Thankfully, because of his job, he could do it directly, without having to go to a doctor. He'd tell Jenna he'd been exposed to something, then have the lab run hormone and neuro chem checks on their samples. That way, he'd know first and not have to worry them while they waited for the results.

"Quit acting so goofy, Dad," Tracy whined. Having all but worn out her new VR set, they were playing checkers on an old set. Every time she reached his end of the board, Mike played an elaborate fanfare before he "queened" her.

"There's no rule that says I can't have music."

"You are so weird."

She huffed, but he could tell she wasn't mad. He grinned at her across the VR's imaginary board, knowing the computerized expression looked like it belonged on the Cheshire Cat.

"Definitely weird, Dad."

"That's my job, isn't it?" he jibed. Three weeks ago, he

might have hugged her after a comment like that, but now he didn't dare. Instead, he sent his princely VR image forward and ruffled her biker woman character's hair.

"Dad!"

Mike laughed, but felt bereft without that hug. This morning, when he'd gotten up, it felt like a fog had lifted. Colors looked brighter, things registered as good or bad, annoying or pleasant. He'd burnt his toast at breakfast and ate it *because* it tasted awful. The commute to work made him fume, even though he was only five minutes late. He'd argued when Jamar suggested he stay on dispatch one more day. And then he'd snapped at a driver for turning the wrong way, annoyed at not being out there doing his real job.

And he'd loved every minute of it.

Tracy won, mostly because Mike's renewed emotions distracted him. He slipped off the VR headgear and set it down. "It's already seven," he observed. "Mom'll be home in a couple of minutes. You set the table and I'll nuke dinner."

They worked separately but together, Mike's heart aching that his daughter might actually be a Depriver. He wondered how he could ease her into that isolated, encapsulated life. Never to touch or be touched without severe and debilitating consequences.

He leaned against the counter and watched her put the forks on the napkins. The pain in his chest threatened to explode and Mike warred with himself to both hate and cherish this moment. Tears welled up in his eyes and his throat burned. Even as he despised the things he felt, Mike knew he needed them.

Before Tracy could notice him wiping his eyes, Jenna came through the door. "Mail's here," she chirped. "Something sure smells good." She set the short stack of envelopes on the counter and went down the hall to change.

"Goulash," Tracy said.

While she put the salt and pepper shakers on the table, Mike rifled through the mail, snatching up an envelope from Dallas Labs. Fingers shaking, he ripped open one end and shook the letter out.

"What's that, Dad?"

"Nothing," he said, too fast.

Jenna and Tracy's results were printed numerically in four neat rows. He ran his finger down the right column and across, making sure he didn't read the wrong number.

Tracy's neuro chem score was 3.62. Not high, not low. Definitely in the margins. Her hormones were elevated, but he expected that. Puberty was coming on strong. She wasn't a Depriver.

All but floating with relief, Mike scanned Jenna's readout. Her neuro score was 3.470. In the margins, too. But the estrogen score nearly topped the chart. Frowning, he folded the paper and went to find her.

"Jenna?"

"Yeah?" She pulled a T-shirt over her head and bent to slip into a pair of jeans.

"Remember that blood scan you guys did for me last week?" he asked, hoping the anxiety didn't seem too obvious in his voice.

"Uh-huh."

"Got the results." He held out the sheet.

Jenna nodded. "Everything okay?" She squeezed herself into the jeans and, with much wiggling, managed to zip them up.

"I think so." He watched as she bent to grab a pair of sneakers. When she stood, the shirt pulled tight across her breasts.

Mike felt his heart pounding in his chest. "Jen?"

She turned and looked at him, eyes wary. Her teeth worried at her bottom lip. "Is everything okay?" she whispered.

Mike wanted to hold her, to kiss that worried frown from her face. "We're okay," he assured her. "We're fine." He paused, telling himself to breathe. Jenna was making him pay for behaving like such an ass for the past two weeks. "You have something to tell me?"

She nodded. When he smiled, she smiled back, tentatively at first. "I didn't want to say anything while—while you were so—I don't know. Not yourself," she admitted.

"You're pregnant."

"Yes."

One step brought her into his open arms. Emotions dormant for far longer than two weeks surged inside him and he cried against her cheek. However he'd gotten Deprived, Mike didn't care. The experience had taught him to cherish life in ways the past thirty-four years had not. He squeezed Jenna against his chest until she complained.

"You're really happy, aren't you?" she asked, wiping his cheeks.

"Happier than I ever imagined I could be, Jen." Her voice, even her smile, made his pulse rate jump. How could he have lived without being able to love Jenna?

"Hey," Tracy called from the kitchen. "Dinner's ready. I'm starved."

"She doesn't know, does she?" Mike whispered.

Jenna shook her head. "When should we tell her?"

"In a minute—or three." He brought his fingers up and touched her face. Soft. The freckles she hated winked at him like old friends. When had he blinded himself to all these significant details? Her blue eyes smiled up at him, the corners crinkling into crow's feet.

"You are so beautiful." Mike dipped his head to kiss his wife and it felt like coming home.

DON'T TOUCH ME

SEAN STEWART

I climbed up the last few steps of the fire escape to the top of my apartment building, clang clang clang, only to find a hippie girl watching me from the roof. I had never seen her before. She wasn't blonde, like Amy; her hair was short and straight and dark. She was sitting cross-legged, wearing a long green shapeless dress that covered her ankles. She had a piece of printed cloth wrapped around her shoulders like a shawl and she was wearing gloves, long black lacy gloves. She looked totally eccentric to me, especially after going with a girl who really knew how to dress. Amy could have been a model for the Gap.

The good view from the roof is looking north, down the slope of the hill to English Bay and over the ocean to the North Shore mountains. The hippie girl was sitting in my favorite spot, a few feet back from the north edge, in a place where the gravel has mostly come unstuck from the rubbery stuff underneath and you can lie back without getting poked. It's not a big spot, and she was taking up all of it.

She looked at me. She looked tired; her face was pale

and her eyes were dark. Probably needed makeup or something. She held up her gloved hands.

"Don't touch me," she said.

Talk about attitude. "As if."

She continued to display her hands, staring, until I got it. "Oh," I said.

"Duh."

"Sorry." It was late afternoon and the autumn light was turning like a leaf, gold and brittle, glinting off the water in the Bay and the glass buildings downtown. I had Amy's letter crumpled in the front pocket of my jeans. It embarrassed me to know it was there, with this hippie girl watching me.

"Did you come here to be alone?" she said. "I can always leave."

"It's a free country."

"It's very important to find places that are real," she said. "I don't want to spoil this one for you."

"What does that even mean?" I squeezed my eyes shut. "Can we start over? I come up the stairs, I walk across the roof, only I'm not an asshole, and this time I say, 'Hi, my name is Jeff. Did you just move into the building?' " Then like a moron I put out my hand to shake. "Oh, shit," I said, pulling it back.

"You're hopeless," she said. But she was smiling.

Her name was Renata, but she said most people called her Reno. She had come to live with the Olsens in #32. Mrs. Olsen was her aunt. After we had been talking for a while on the roof, the breeze came up and made it too cold to stay outside. That's when she asked if she could see our apartment. I never brought my friends home if I could help it, but it seemed rude to say no.

"I like seeing other people's houses," Reno said. "It's like exploring a new world."

Mom was sitting in the living room watching M*A*S*H through a faint haze of cigarette smoke when we came in. She's had health problems for a long time and she doesn't work, just watches Channel 51. They run the shows she grew up with. She's a miracle of evolution, a creature evolved for her tiny micro-habitat, living on nothing but smoke and TV rays. They say the children of smokers are more likely to smoke, but not me. I sleep with my door closed and my window open. Beer is my vice.

Mom gave Reno a longer look than she ever gave Amy, then returned to watching the 4077th while we went into the kitchen. I wasn't sure if this was discretion or disinterest. Mom can be pretty inscrutable.

"We've got Budweiser, milk, orange juice, Diet Sprite . . ." I rummaged in the shelf over the stove. "Ovaltine—regular, not chocolate—and ginseng tea."

"Definitely ginseng tea." Reno dropped into a chair at the kitchen table and started fingering the day's stack of Lotto cards, the kind with little tabs you pull out and look behind. Dad says the government stole the idea from advent calendars and is using old people's memory of Christmas to rip them off. Mom picks up the instant-win games every time she gets smokes from the Chinese grocery.

There was something odd about the way Reno handled the Lotto tickets, touching each small curled flap, bending it down, then watching it spring up again. She picked up one of the cards in her gloved hand and touched it to her face, letting the little cardboard fringes slip across her cheek. It was kind of embarrassing.

Noisily I filled up the kettle and put it on the stove. "Mom says ginseng is cleansing." I turned on a burner. Gas hissed out and broke into blue flame with a whoosh.

"I've never had radiators before," Reno said. Now she

had her gloved hand on the old metal radiator pipe beside the table. "It's always been baseboard heat."

"Where did you come from?"

"Minnesota."

"Why?"

"My mom remarried and they had a baby. It was okay at first, but now Jackson's two and he won't stop climbing on me. I almost killed him."

"Pain in the ass?" I pulled down the box of tea and a couple of cups.

"No. I mean I really almost killed him." Her voice was flat. "Jackson's a million times better than Don, who's a prick. But he wants to play with me. Even if I wear gloves, sooner or later he tries to kiss my nose or tickle my feet, and then . . ." She looked up. "I take away touch. No feeling. It lasts about two days, for Jackson. He's in hospital now. They're trying to fix his hand. He put it on a burner."

Blue flame hissed and wavered under the kettle.

"He's a really sweet kid," she said. There were a couple of tears on her face. She wiped them off with her lace-gloved hand. "Sorry," she said.

I put the ginseng teabag in her cup. "It's okay to cry," I said. "I hear that's cleansing, too."

I forgot to take Amy's letter out of my pocket and it went through the wash. I stared at it in shock, then tried to open it, heart pounding. I'd left paper to go through the wash before, lots of times, but after meeting Reno I really noticed how it *felt*, parched and . . . brittle-but-felty. Still warm from the dryer. It cracked as I tried to tease it open, tearing along the folds, the tears fuzzy instead of crisp. Amy had written it with the special fountain pen she uses to write in her diary. The ink had run like crazy, smudging the round loops of her considerate but firm kiss-off into unreadability.

Just as well, I guess.

It was four days before I went back onto the roof. Reno was there, squinting in the late afternoon sun. "Don't come up on the weekends?"

"I was at the movies," I said.

"All weekend?" She looked at me incredulously. "What were you seeing?"

"*Patchouli.*" I sat down at looked over at the distant North Shore mountains, feeling sorry for myself. "My girlfriend dumped me. It was kind of our film."

Reno snorted. "Jesus, Jeff, it was everybody's film. How disappointing."

"Sorry I don't live up to your standards."

She looked at me, unimpressed. This time she was wearing a baggy black skirt and a homemade sweater over a lumberjack shirt. Very Minnesota. "Stop looking at me like that," she said. "So I'm not the best sewer in the world." She picked a pebble off the roof and flicked it into the street. "We're not broke or anything. I just think people don't *feel* things enough. They don't appreciate them. But it's important. I don't want my life to be off the rack. When I make my own clothes, it makes them personal. Particular." Reno buttoned up her sweater. I could see flecks of her pale hands through her lace gloves. "*Patchouli.* Christ. Where did you meet this heartbreaker?"

"Amy. We both work on the school paper."

"Jeff Clack, Ace Reporter." She stood up and started for the fire escape. "Come with me. I want to show you something."

"I was nice to you when you were sad," I said, following her.

"Yeah, well, I had a better reason."

It was late October and the weather had turned decidedly chilly. We came out of the alley behind the apartment building and turned down Granville Street, heading for the Bridge. Reno walked fast. She was completely shapeless under her homemade clothes. "Don't you get tired of people staring at you?" I asked.

"If you're a Depriver, Jeff, you're going to get stared at no matter how you dress. So fuck it." Her lips were thin in her pale face. I found myself wondering if she had ever been kissed. Not twice, I guess. "Anyway, once you get in the habit of making everything special, it's hard to go back to the usual crap."

I stuck my hands in the pockets of my jeans to keep them warm and hurried after her. "Like bread," I said. "Have you found the Dutch bakery yet, just across Broadway? Mom sends me there for the day-old. Now I can't eat, like, Wonder Bread."

"Yeah!" Reno glanced over at me and grinned. "Yeah, that's it."

Pigeons swung and fluttered in a gray sky. Scraps of Mr. Sub wrappers slid along the cold sidewalk. Reno strode past the Vancouver Sun building. People saw her gloved hands and stepped well away, staring. I hunched my shoulders, hoping nobody I knew would see me tagging after this Dep bag-lady chick, which in turn made me feel even more like a jerk.

A block past the Sun building she took the stairs down to the pedestrian underpass that ran beneath Granville Street. I hadn't gone that way in years because I hated passing the buskers that used to work the tunnel. Either I had to give them money for the privilege of listening to two minutes of screechy Bob Dylan covers, which made me feel ripped off, or else I didn't give them anything, which made me feel like an asshole. It was easier to cross at the lights on Fourth Avenue.

Reno was already at the bottom of the stairs. "Come on!"

No guitar strumming or bazouki plinking, thank God. I hurried down the steps after her. The tunnel underneath had changed. Obviously the City thought they had graffiti problems. Instead of whitewashing the walls, though, they had stamped them with Christmas trees, about a thousand one-foot-tall Christmas trees, starting at ground level and running the length of the tunnel, both walls, nearly up to the ceiling.

"Isn't this great?" Reno said, grinning. "A mall, see, a mall isn't a real place. It's a fake place. So is Foot Locker. So is MacDonald's." She looked around the underpass, eyes gleaming. "This place is real." She glanced at me again. "Careful." She took off her gloves and touched the wall with her bare hands. Small hands. Amy's fingernails had been long and flat and shiny with subtle polish. Reno's were short and curved and bitten down. I imagined her taking her gloves off in her bedroom, chewing on her fingernails.

She ran her hands along the wall as she walked to the far end of the tunnel. "This is my favorite part," she said, pointing. In the clear gap between the top of the treeline and the ceiling, so high you wondered how anyone could have written it without a chair to stand on, someone had scrawled out three words: GUILT WITHOUT SEX.

I read it three times. "What the hell?"

"I don't know." Reno laughed. She looked over the scrawl again. "You're dying over Wonder Bread, Jeff." She held one small hand dramatically to her forehead. "*Patchouli.* Christ."

"It still hurts," I said.

Her face got serious. "Feel it."

"I don't want to."

"It's yours," she said. "Your life. Feel it. Live it."

Nobody at school saw Reno laugh much. Most people found her stand-offish, and of course nobody gets close to a Depriver, anyway. Apparently in Minnesota they try to keep the Deps pretty integrated, but at our school she wasn't even allowed to attend gym class, for "Insurance reasons."

Amy was unfailingly pleasant to me. Bo, the guy she was dating now, didn't rub it in. I would have liked it better if they had been jerks.

I knew I wasn't in love. First, because I was fifteen and stupid, as my dad said. Second, because when I tried to imagine myself and Amy together in, say, ten years' time, I drew a complete blank. Nothing. So obviously it was just a crush.

Only, what nobody ever mentions about a "teenage crush" is that it hurts as if it were real. I kept waiting for the spasms of desire to go away when I watched Amy with her head over her notebook in class. They didn't. The exact and particular fall of her hair across her cheek filled me with aching loss. The swell of her breast brushing against the desk seemed inexpressibly erotic.

Feel it, Reno had said. I dunno. I got drunk a lot instead.

Back home, nothing changed. Dad stayed out late and Mom sat on the front couch, cheeks hollowing out with every pull on her Virginia Slim. Colored light from the TV winking and gleaming on her face. Watching the shows from when she still had a life in front of her. I wondered what she was feeling.

I have this theory that every kind of pain is real, and everything that happens to you personally, no matter how stupid, feels exactly life-size.

• • •

I ran out of beer and movie money, and *Patchouli* finally closed.

Sunday mornings, Reno went out looking for more real places, and I fell into tagging along. On the second Sunday in November she decided we would go up to Main Street and work our way back through Little India to Chinatown, eating only food we'd never had before.

If you thought Americans like sweet foods, you haven't experienced a Sikh bakery. The food is god awful: hard candies that taste like Worcestershire sauce, slabs of almond jelly, candy-coated popcorn puffs that look like jeweled June bugs, mealy shortbread with Smucker's jam inside, and radioactive balls of dirty orange sugar that are the candy equivalent of hardcore porn, without a scrap of nut or fruit or nougat to make them decent.

We staggered out of Little India on the point of throwing up and got lunch in the New Town Restaurant in Chinatown where we ordered by pointing at things on the part of the menu where no English translation was provided. The best of these turned out to be a bowl of soup that tasted like licorice and had jellied meat-flavored blobs floating in it. We tried to get the waiter to tell us the ingredients, but the only word we could understand was "tendon."

Afterwards we wandered at random, until we found ourselves walking along Hastings Street, past the Victory monument and the blind windows of a closed Army & Navy store. It was sleepy, the way a slummy part of town is before noon on a Sunday morning. Narrow brick buildings with apartments above and pawnshops below, along with a Communist Party Headquarters and a contemporary dance studio. Everything locked up, metal grilles in front of darkened windows, entrance tiles discolored with last night's piss and beer.

I leaned over and peered at something in the gutter. A syringe. I nudged it with my toe and kept walking. "This is depressing."

"It's always the right time to make a wrong turn," Reno said, quoting herself. "This isn't pretty, but it's real. Places like this, you never see them on TV. It isn't a tough enough neighborhood to be in a cop show. Nobody here has any money, so no advertisers need shows about them. Or they don't speak English," she added, as we passed an old Chinese woman on her way out of the Golden Pagoda butcher shop. "They aren't on TV, they don't make the news. The world you live in never touches theirs."

We came to the tiny triangular park in front of the Co-op Radio building. Two old guys played chess at an iron table. Pigeons wandered around their feet. Two other benches were occupied by homeless men, sleeping or trying to sleep. One had a long black wool coat, a toque and a pair of gloves. The other wore an ancient down-filled parka, dirty and spattered with grease and pigeon shit. His head was bare and he kept his hands in his coat pockets. The skin on his face and wrists was gray.

We kept walking. "They feel things," I said. "That's real life, boy. Real cold, for instance. And wet. And hungry."

"I know."

"If you asked them, they'd live in TV in a second," I said. "They'd shop at the mall and live in a big house like the kind in paint commercials. They'd live off the rack in a second. I don't see what's wrong with wanting the same things everyone else does."

"Christ." Reno was wearing her sweater over the long green dress she'd had on the first time I met her. She could have passed for a homeless person herself, or one of the teenagers who hang around the Granville Skytrain station bumming handouts.

I kicked at another syringe in the gutter. "Sometimes I worry that you'll get so caught up in *feeling* things, in going these strange places and living this weird life that you'll get trapped. Once you fall out of everyone else's world—" thinking of Mom here, maybe, as well as the homeless guys "—it's hard to get back. And it gets pretty lonely," I said.

We walked on. Reno said, "Lonely is how you feel when you have to pick up the phone and call somebody, anybody." She looked down at her gloved hands. "Alone is when you know there isn't any point."

Then it rained for ten straight days, morning noon and night. I didn't see Reno around the building much. Mom won thirty bucks on the Lotto. Dad got his hours cut back again. He says it's the Free Trade Agreement.

Finally one day at the end of November the weather turned clear and cold. I went for groceries and made dinner for Mom. By the time I could slip out of the apartment and up the fire escape, it was almost eight o'clock. Full dark. I was only wearing my jean jacket over a shirt and I probably would have turned around and gone back inside if I hadn't been dying for a breath of clean air.

Reno was up on the roof again, standing near the north edge of the building. Wet gravel clicked under my feet as I walked over to her. "Maybe frost by morning," I said.

"Maybe."

We stood a moment in silence, breath smoking. Strips of light lit up the city like a circuit board, shop fronts and neon signs and streetlights. In the skyscrapers downtown you could tell the overtime workers by their lit windows, exposed in identical glass cubicles. A couple of super tankers floated like bath toys on the darkness of English Bay. The stars overhead seemed very small and very cold, white grains of ice in the night sky.

I jammed my hands into my jeans pockets. "Guess what?"

Reno looked sideways at me. "You gave up journalism for a career as a concert lute player."

"Close. Amy asked me about getting back together today."

"Oh."

"I guess it wasn't really working out with Bo."

"Jesus. Hey, this is great news," Reno said. "Just in time for Christmas. They'll be bringing *Patchouli* out on video. I can get you both a copy," she said. She walked a few steps along the roof.

"You sound mad."

"Don't flatter yourself."

I decided to keep still and not follow her. I was starting to shiver in the cold. "The thing is, I'm not sure I want to."

Reno kept her back turned. "Oh?"

"Yeah. I mean, Amy's great. Really nice. Smart. Nice person."

"Great tits," Reno said. "Don't forget that."

"Never," I said. "But when I try to ask myself, where is this going? I dunno . . . And yet, I feel sorry for her, with Bo and all."

"Amy can always find someone to f-fuck her," Reno said bitterly. The cold was making her stutter.

"Hey—"

"It's so easy for someone like her. You think guys hate condoms? How about a whole raincoat. Or a s-scuba suit. Amy, Amy can have anyone she likes. She can have kids. She can h-hold hands in the goddamn p-park," Reno said.

I walked up behind Reno but she wouldn't turn and look at me. "You can—"

"D-don't tell me about my life," she said fiercely. "Go back to TV land, where it's safe."

"Hey!" I put my hands on the bulky shoulder of her sweater. It was the first time I had ever touched her. She was trembling with the cold. "I'm being nice here. Shut up and listen, okay?" Gently I turned her around. She stared at me through narrow eyes. "The thing is, I can imagine being with you in ten years. Because we talk. Because you make me smarter than I am."

"Can you imagine it? I don't think so, Jeff. I don't think you can," she said. "Can you imagine trying to, to m-make love with someone like me? No kids, none, ever. People staring at you all the time, just because you're with me. Even if I moved to the mall, even if I bought all my clothes at Banana Republic, there would always b-be these," she said, holding up her gloved hands. "Forever and ever. I'm not here just to broaden your horizons, Jeff. This is my whole life. Do you really think you could risk any of that?"

We stood staring at each other. I think we were both cold and angry and scared. I still had my hands on her shoulders. Somewhere down below us, Mrs. Olsen was feeding her cat. Mom was sitting on the couch in our apartment, face colored by the flicker of the TV. Dad was out, God knew where. It was warm inside and stuffy and known.

Up on the roof, under the bitter stars, Reno and I were standing close together, closer than we had ever been. Her thin lips looked cold in her white face. As we breathed, coils of steam rose from us, meeting and twining in the air. She was shaking under my hands.

"Don't touch me," she whispered.

THE JANITOR

MAGGIE ESTEP

It was late afternoon and I was mopping the chemo waiting area when a girl blew into the room, threw herself on the couch, and started sobbing. She didn't have any hair, so right away I knew she was a patient. I just stood there stupidly, mop in hand, wondering what to do. I'd been assigned that floor for several months, but it wasn't like I usually interacted with patients. I felt for this girl though. She was young and haunted-looking and her whole body was quivering.

"Hey, hey there, miss, hey, are you okay?" I said, leaning my mop against the wall and taking a step towards her.

The girl looked up.

"Is there anything I can do?" I asked her.

Just then, a doctor walked into the room. "Carla. There you are," she said to the girl.

The girl kept her face buried in her hands.

"Please come back to my office now," the doctor said.

The girl wouldn't look up though and, for some reason, I decided to put in my two cents.

"Miss, the doctor's talking to you," I said.

"I'm not deaf," the girl said, looking up at me.

"Carla, you spoke!" the doctor exclaimed, "You got her to speak," she said, turning to me.

Now both the doctor and the girl were staring at me.

The doctor had intense blue eyes. "Who are you?" she asked me.

"Billy."

"Thanks for your help, Billy," she said, then ushered the now compliant Carla out of the waiting room.

I turned back to my mopping and was lost in the sort of rhythmic thoughts I get when I'm doing my work. After a while, I heard the door open. I looked up. It was the doctor again.

"I'm Doctor Ray. Jody Ray," she said.

"Nice to make your acquaintance, Doctor," I said.

"What did you do to Carla?" she asked me.

"What do you mean?" I said, alarmed. You always hear about lowly hospital employees getting in trouble for inter-acting with patients—which is why I never did. Until today. But you couldn't even call what I'd done interaction.

"She's talking now," the doctor said. "She hasn't spoken in weeks. She said you showed her kindness."

"I just asked if she was okay. That's it. Then you walked in the room."

"Oh. Well. Thank you."

"Sure," I said, shrugging, "how's she doing?"

"She's got about a month to live. I'm trying to help her cope."

"Depriver-related?" I asked.

We'd all been told Deprivation wasn't fatal, but there was no way to be sure this was true.

"No. Just plain cancer," Dr. Ray said.

"Oh," I said then.

"Be well," Jody Ray said, and turned and walked out of the room.

I stared after her for a moment, then went back to mopping.

Over the next few days, I ran into Dr. Ray half a dozen times—which was odd, considering I'd never seen her before in my life. She wasn't the sort of woman you forgot. For one thing, there were the bright blue eyes. Then the hair. Dark red, thick, cut to her jaw. And her legs weren't bad either. At least from what you could see where the lab coat ended.

I hadn't been with a woman or really even looked at one since leaving the circus a year earlier. I'd been the escape artist in the sideshow. I loved my work, but right after I hit thirty, I started getting migraines every time I dangled upside down from my ankles. I couldn't stand the idea of working in administration and, although I loved the animals, I wasn't high up enough in the political pecking order to work as a trainer. So I left.

I'd never really wanted to do anything else and I was just mortally depressed. Until I got this job. I liked the hospital. It was a peaceful, well-lit environment.

One day, after I'd run into Dr. Ray once more, I asked did she want to grab a drink. A few hours later, we were in a diner across First Avenue where they served wine. She laughed at things I said. Her eyes got big when I told her about the escape act I used to do. About dangling from my ankles over a boiling cauldron of water. She liked that. A lot of women do.

After a few glasses of wine, we caught a cab back to her place, an enormous loft in the Gowanis section of Brooklyn. The ceilings were five stories high and there were catwalks and remnants of machinery. Pulleys and such. I guess the place had been some kind of factory and she hadn't done a whole lot to it. There was a bed and a couch and a kitchen, but the rest was just empty space, lots of it.

We'd been there about fifteen minutes. She'd fixed us drinks and taken off her cardigan and her shoes. She had stockings on and I looked at the way her painted toes were bunched up in there, constrained by the nylon.

"You can't be that thrilled with being a janitor," she said, after she'd settled down next to me on the couch.

"It's fine. I like the lighting." I said after a pause.

At first she laughed, but when I failed to join in, she stopped.

"I didn't mean to offend you. It's just that you're not the usual janitor fare."

"Whatever," I said. "I'm an escape artist. I don't know how to do anything else. When my dad left the circus he pulled armed robberies and ended up in jail. He died in jail. I don't want that. I'd rather mop the cancer ward."

"I'm sorry," Jody said, slowly leaning towards me, lips parted, eyes wide.

She reached for me, then stopped herself in mid-motion, her hand freezing in the air.

"You're a Depriver," I said, knowing it irrefutably the moment I saw her hand hesitate over touching mine.

"Yes."

"It'll pass soon," I said, letting her know I'd be interested in reconvening when the contagion had run its course.

"Class C. Sub section two two three point six," she said then, looking at me with her mouth pulled into a sad line.

"What does that mean?"

"You know what Class C is."

"Chronic?"

"And 'two two point six' is incurable. As far as they know anyway."

"And which senses are you deprived of?" Deprivation is

usually fairly easy to spot. In a lot of cases people lose their eyesight or their hearing and it's obvious. With Jody you couldn't tell.

"It's a bit subtler than the standard cases. I suffered transient reconfiguration of neural tissues following non-invasive compaction," she said, looking at me and then staring off into space.

I had no idea what she was talking about but it sounded sexy. I've always loved women who talk in lingo.

She reached for a pack of cigarettes on the coffee table. She lit one and inhaled, blowing the smoke out through pursed lips.

"I was deprived by my ex-lover," she said, eyes narrowing. "Drew was a research neurologist. He stumbled onto a viral strain that affects the brain's frontal lobes. Drew wasn't the type to take precautions. He contracted the Deprivation, then passed it on to me."

"On purpose?"

"I don't know. I suspect so, although he denied it," she said.

A bittersweet smile played over her lips. "It's a mess in there," she said, tapping her forehead, "areas of trauma spontaneously sealed against one another resulting in a high-order failure of inhibition in an attentional set-shifting paradigm."

"Oh?" I said, like I had any idea what she was talking about.

She smiled. "It means I don't have control of myself. I can fly off the handle and have near-Tourretic episodes. Senselessly repeating a motion or a phrase."

She stubbed out her cigarette. She was so beautiful.

"That doesn't sound so bad," I said, thinking of some of the Deprivation cases we'd all seen, stumbling around town, blind, deaf, crazy.

"It might be interesting if it weren't permanent and incurable," Jody said. "As it is, it's ruined my life," she said, tossing her hair back and lighting yet another cigarette.

"How?"

"I've had three episodes with patients," she said carefully, like she was talking to a child. "Flying off the handle. Some little thing they do or say sets me off and I lose any capacity for self-censorship. Last week, I called a patient a psychotic bitch."

"Oh," I said.

"And the hospital doesn't know I'm a Depriver. I try not to touch anyone. I wear gloves if I have to. My chief of staff seems to think I'm stressed out. That my episodes are due to this. I've been put on warning. One more incident and I lose my job."

"Can't you do anything?" I said, feeling my stomach knot up. I wanted her. Bad.

"Not as far as I know. There's no telling how the virus would behave in someone I infected," she said, catching my drift, "it would afflict them differently. But I don't know how. It's Russian Roulette, Billy."

"It usually is," I said, trying to let her know I didn't care. Everything is Russian Roulette; Deprivation just added a twist.

But Jody wasn't going for it. Her whole body was stiff and she had a far-off look in her eyes. I started wondering why she'd brought me here if she was feeling scrupulous about infecting me.

Thank god for the Tourette's-like symptoms. I was trying to convince her it was okay, that I was willing to risk it. Finally, she got angry and started to tic: a lunging motion, her hand darting out and her whole body following it, like she was fencing. As luck would have it, her hand landed on my arm.

"Oh no, Billy, look what you've made me do," she said, pulling her hand away.

It was too late though. We both knew it.

I cupped my hand under her chin and slowly pulled her face to mine. Her lips were stiff at first. I bit them. After a second, I felt her whole mouth relax. I pressed my chest against hers and ran my hands down her sides, squeezing at her narrow waist and then hiking her skirt up over her hips. That set her off. Her whole body came to life and she started ripping at my clothes. In a few seconds, she had my pants off and my cock in her mouth. The sight of her lovely head of red hair bopping at my crotch, combined with the knowledge that she had made me a Class C Depriver, was the most erotic thing that had ever happened to me.

Dawn showed through the immense windows of Jody's loft. Jody was sleeping, turned on her side with her lovely naked ass to me. I got up and walked the length of the loft. I didn't seem to be deprived yet, but I was restless and needed to get home and feed my cat. I scribbled Jody a note with my phone number, then headed for the subway stop.

The first thing I noticed was that my cat started acting goofy around me. Where she'd always been an aloof and independent type cat, now, she followed me around and seemed to listen attentively to everything I said. As a lark, I told her to sit and then gently patted her hind end with a ruler—I couldn't touch her as I didn't want to give her the virus—and she sat. After about a half an hour, I had her fetching toy mice. It was an odd display of feline obedience but not something you'd attribute to Deprivation.

The next day, I had a date with Jody. I'd run into her at the hospital. I was mopping, she was on rounds. She broke off from the pack of doctors, took my elbow, and led me into a utility room where she looked me over and grilled me, asking what symptoms I was having. When I'd convinced her I was fine, I cupped one hand over her mouth and ran my other hand up her thigh and inside her panties. I saw her eyes get big and round. She tried to say something, but lost her train of thought when I unzipped my pants, hiked up the lab coat and the skirt and entered her.

That night, I went over to her place. No sooner had I walked in the door than she was ripping my pants off and blowing me. After a while, I let her lead me over to the bed. She went foraging for something in a closet and next thing I knew she was blindfolding me. I let myself relax into it. Like I was one of her patients. I let her tie me up and I indulged her for a minute, lying there with her straddling me. I guess she'd forgotten I was an escape artist. She laughed when I zipped out of the restraints in five seconds, put them on her, and fucked her until her body was like an earthquake.

The next day, on lunch break at the hospital, I was sitting in the little park out front eating my sandwich when all these squirrels started to descend on me. In a few minutes, close to twenty squirrels were sitting in a semi-circle before me. Looking at me like I was some sort of squirrel messiah.

Heddy, a bedraggled woman who always haunts the outpatient mental clinic, happened to walk by right then. She saw me and stopped, setting her big plastic bag of cans down and folding her arms over her chest.

"The little ones like you, eh?" She said.

"So it would seem," I shrugged.

"You ever try gettin' em' to do tricks?"

"Excuse me?"

"You ever try seeing if you can make the squirrels do tricks?" She motioned at my audience again.

"It's not like I have power over the animal kingdom or anything. I must just smell like an acorn." I told the woman.

"Oh no. You've got yourself a power there, son, nothing to shrug off," she said, gravely nodding her head.

She continued on towards the clinic. When I got up to walk back inside the hospital, the damned squirrels followed me all the way to the sliding doors.

A week went by and I started wondering if that loon woman wasn't on to something. One night, I was in Central Park with Jody, taking her to my favorite secluded havens in the park. I wanted to show her everything. In just a short time she'd come to mean a lot to me. It wasn't just the way she fucked—although that didn't hurt; it was something more. There was a deep wound in Jody and I felt like I could heal it.

We were sitting under a tree, looking at the reservoir, when a handful of squirrels started to gather. Jody made a comment about how tame the park squirrels were. I was a little unnerved. Particularly when the squirrels started coming closer and made Jody nervous. You hear stories about rabid squirrels. I took her hand and led her out of the park.

A few days later, I was sitting eating my lunch outside the hospital and sure enough, the squirrels gathered to fawn over me again. Jody came to meet me and found me surrounded by my court.

"What's with the squirrels?" she asked, sitting next to me on the bench.

"I don't know," I told her, "I can' figure it out. It keeps happening."

I put my hand on her thigh and squeezed lightly. I got a hard-on right away but sex was the last thing on her mind.

"Wait a minute," she said, frowning, "the other night, in

the park, remember? Same thing, all the squirrels came around you."

"Yeah."

"Billy," she said excitedly, "I think this is it, this is your Deprivation."

"What?"

"Shifts within the pre-frontal cortex can literally open the mind up and create new pathways of communication."

"Oh, and what, animals suddenly think I'm Saint Francis?"

"Something like that," she said.

She told me about historical occurrences of this sort of thing, most notably Phineas Gage, a railroad worker in the mid 1800's. An explosion drove an iron rod through his brain but he suffered no immediate adverse effects. After a few months though, his personality started to shift. He went from being a level-headed competent guy to a foul-mouthed degenerate. The only jobs he could hold were working on horse farms. Animals suddenly loved him. Even wild animals. Squirrels in particular. Not that it did him much good. After a succession of horse-related jobs, he ended up doing a stint at P. T. Barnum's museum. He'd stand there telling about his wound and showing off the tamping iron that had traversed his frontal cortex. This didn't make him happy though and eventually, he ended up in San Francisco where he died alone and broke.

"Billy, I can't believe I've done this to you," Jody said, looking more serious and forlorn than I'd ever seen her look.

Hospital employees and walk-in clinic patients were milling around us. A bunch of homeless people parked themselves on benches. And, of course, there were still half a dozen squirrels hanging about, looking at me. I just wished I could do something to make Jody feel better.

"Come on," I tell her, "there are worse things than having animals love you. I can live with this. It's really okay. If I could go back and do it all over again, I would," I tell her.

This only made her sadder though. Her face twisted up and she started crying. I got down on my knees, right there in the little public park, with half the world and a bunch of squirrels looking on. I stared up at her puffy eyes and traced my finger through one of the sooty streaks the mascara had left on her cheek. I've loved three women in my life, but none of them made me feel what Jody made me feel.

That night, at her place, we got into bed and stayed there. Only we're not ravaging each other the way we usually did. We'd made love slowly and now Jody was lying flat on her stomach. She had her eyes closed and I was going over every inch of her, committing each hair to memory, etching every tiny blemish into my mind's eye. After a long silence punctuated only by the sound of my hands on her skin, Jody started to talk. She told me about growing up the only child of two psychiatrists who never spoke to her. She'd left home to go to Vassar, but quickly flunked out. Moved to New York, where she'd held a succession of odd jobs while taking up with various men and women, never sticking to any one of them until she met Drew, a neurologist who talked her into going to med school. She'd fallen in love with medicine and with the anatomy of the human mind, and she started to have hope. For herself. For others. Until the Depriver epidemic struck. Until, everywhere you turned, there was someone walking around in a virally imposed sensory deprivation tank. Jody started to feel rattled then. And Drew had grown aloof. Spent days on end holed up in his lab, doing government-sponsored research. Then infecting Jody with the particularly unpredictable strain of Deprivation. And now, the disease had all but ended Jody's career and she'd passed the Deprivation on to me, the first guy she'd really felt something for in several years.

"You know I wouldn't change anything," I told her again.

She looked at me for a long while but said nothing. We fell asleep holding each other tightly.

The next afternoon, Jody and I had just grabbed a sandwich together when we heard her being paged over the hospital P.A. system. Jody grabbed for a house phone, picked it up, listened, and went pale.

"Carla," she said, then blindly ran towards the elevators, jostling people as she went. I ran after her, just slipping in as the elevator doors closed. I looked over at Jody, but she was just staring ahead.

Ever since the day I'd tried talking to Carla in the chemo waiting room, she'd been getting better, at least psychologically. Jody'd brought her around to where she was cheerful and engaged and, although there wasn't much left of her other than bones and burning bright eyes, at least there were spots of color on her cheeks, little red circles, like targets of hope.

There was a whole team of doctors and nurses in there, trying to bring Carla back from cardiac arrest. But she was gone.

Jody started to tic then, doing that odd lunging motion and blurting out random syllables. My stomach knotted up and I grabbed her arm, trying to make it stop, trying to hide it from Jody's supervisor, Doctor Wool, who was standing right there.

"Doctor Ray? Are you all right?" Dr. Wool said, staring at Jody.

By now, I was acting like a straitjacket, draping my

whole body over Jody's. It didn't help though. The ticking had turned into a seizure, the force of which sent us both tumbling to the floor.

I lay my body on top of Jody's and felt the awful spasms of her arms and legs. Guttural sounds were coming out of her throat and I could feel tears in my own eyes. I looked up at the half-dozen doctors who were just standing there, gaping at us.

"Do something," I said to Doctor Wool.

But he knew. He knew what was wrong with Jody and he wouldn't touch her.

"Somebody help her," I screamed.

An autopsy showed that the Deprivation had literally made holes in her brain, turning it to sponge the way Creutzfeldt-Jakob disease would. I went to look at the CAT scan pictures at the Medical Examiner's office. I needed to see what my girl's brain had looked like. Like somehow that would put closure on the whole thing. It didn't though. I just stared at that strange image, thinking of the face that had been attached to that savagely pock-marked brain, and every part of me ached.

I stayed holed up in my room for ten days. I just couldn't move. I had the deli deliver sandwiches, but I couldn't eat. I'd just lie there, watching my cat. I couldn't cry. I couldn't do anything.

On the eleventh night, I finally went outside. Up to Central Park. I sat down under a tree and in a few minutes, two squirrels appeared. Then some more. Then still more. I could almost feel the odd chemistry in my brain, the strange new way my neurotransmitters were firing, opening up new pathways. And the squirrels definitely felt it.

I started going into the park every night. It was peaceful in there. Sure, there were lunatics lurking, but I had nothing to lose. If someone wanted to slit my throat, it was all the same to me. So of course, no one bothered me. Except the squirrels.

I couldn't touch them, for risk of infecting them, but I started trying voice commands and that worked well.

Now and then, someone would spot me there, sitting under a tree, talking to the squirrels. I guess I just looked like any other crazy person. And that didn't bother me. I'd never been a part of society.

Eventually, I brought some of the squirrels home. At first, I worried that the cat would stalk them, but I told her not to and she didn't. I taught two of the squirrels to ride a skateboard and another to fetch. The rest of them learned to jump through hoops.

One day, Herb, the old drunk from next door, stopped over to borrow five bucks. He saw the squirrels, all loose in the apartment, and all the contraptions I'd set up for training them. He just thought he was having DT's though. No one would have believed it.

The circus people did though. I found out that Hubner Brothers Circus, the one where I'd worked as escape artist, was doing a week stint up in Mystic, Connecticut. I put four of the squirrels in the cat carrier and took the bus up. I showed Gideon, the main administrator, what I could do. I got hired right away.

I came back to the city and packed up my clothes, the cat, and the squirrels. I moved into a trailer with Betty and Theo, two of the clowns. No one had ever done a squirrel act before and the novelty of it attracted a lot of press. Pretty soon, attendance at our little circus started to soar.

Recently, I hired Missy, the lion tamer's daughter, to be my assistant. She wears a glittery cat suit and holds the hoops the squirrels jump through. I also bought my own trailer. It's a nice one. I had cages built in for the squirrels and I have a picture of Jody hanging in the bedroom. This bothers Missy sometimes, but I guess she knows she'll never take Jody's place.

As for the Deprivation, chances are it won't pass. I hope not, anyway. I don't know what I'd do for work if it did.

IDIOTS LOSERS
FOOLS

D. H. RESNICOFF

For over five years, Victoria Myerson had managed to remain untouched by human flesh. She could gauge in an instant how close another person intended to get, who was going to stumble on a stair or try to squeeze in next to her in a crowded elevator. Her gift, her uncanny ability to perceive the slightest nuance, intention and meaning in the set of any human face, was why she had remained undeprived.

Victoria veered off the parched afternoon sidewalk and leaned her way through the heavy glass door of SoHo Naturale. Perfect, she thought, quickly taking in the nearly empty store. Minimal risk. Maneuvering her way easily through the aisles toward the Freeze Bar at the back of the long, airy, pine-floored store, she imagined herself a billiard ball. A well-preserved, forty-five-year-old billiard ball, with naturally blonde hair. The other customers were bumpers with invisible force fields, around which she glided smoothly in her suede booties, avoiding any possibility of an accidental bump or shove, making it look easy. I'm slick, she thought, slick and mean and clean. And, after tonight, away and free.

But now she had one thing on her mind: a Five Senses Herbal Choco Freeze. Only Humongo would do. In minutes, maybe moments, the frothy, mineral-filled concoction would be hers and she could be at the gallery at least half an hour before the opening, lock herself in her office and enjoy her treat in peace and safety.

Behind the counter, a sullen boy in his early twenties turned to face her. He was wearing one of those T-shirts with a large red "D" on it. Above his head, an official government sign read FOR YOUR SAFETY PLEASE ALLOW YOUR SERVER TO PLACE PRODUCT ON COUNTER AND RETREAT BEHIND YELLOW LINE. Victoria flicked her 20–20 natural blue eyes over his insolent face, taking in his oddly prepubescent features, noting automatically the deep grooves beneath his prominent cheekbones, framing the full mouth. A slight increase in the proximity of these lines to the corners of his lips told her all she needed to know. Idiot! He thinks he's superior to me.

When it came to reading people's faces and knowing their thoughts, Victoria was always right. She had made an art of perceiving the potential buyer's slightest nostril twitch signaling a desire to be flattered into a purchase. She knew the downturned mouth of the miser who hated to part with money but desired the status of ownership. She responded with confidential reassurance to the conscientiously wrinkled forehead of the insecure *nouveau riche* and reinforced the proud misconceptions of the hopelessly tasteless. She could tell at a glance what anyone wanted to hear or believe. And that was why she ran one of the most successful art galleries in New York.

"Five Senses Herbal Choco Freeze. Humongo," Victoria ordered.

"Humongo it is. Bran or no bran?"

"No bran. And make sure you mix the ingredients thoroughly. But leave some texture."

The boy turned, slow as molasses, to a gleaming array of mixers and vials of minerals and, with deliberate emphasis, pulled on a thick pair of gloves. Victoria considered doing without her Five Senses Herbal Choco Freeze. No. No. They had not gotten the best of her yet. She would have her treat. She deserved it.

She deserved it because she had put up with so much. Like this little shit with the big "D" on his underdeveloped chest. Losers, all of them. As though aligning yourself with the afflicted would change anything. Bring the world back to order. She wanted to kill them all. And that was why she was going to escape tonight, leaving all the other idiots, fools and losers who lacked her sensitivity behind.

"Hard freeze or soft?"

"Hard. Very hard."

A definite deflation of the boy's cheeks. He would prefer that she say "Please." Too bad. Take that shirt off and shove it up your supercilious little ass! Fuck the Rights of Man and all that constitutional crap. Deprivers should be quarantined and everybody knew it. The Founding Fathers would have whistled a different tune if twenty percent of the colonial population had roamed the streets freely depriving honest citizens of *their* right to see or hear or smell or feel or God only knows what else. Where was the goddamned government when you needed them?

The government had failed to take care of her and now she was going to take care of herself. The U.S. Government would never again see another red cent out of Victoria Myerson. In fact, the U.S. Government would never again see Victoria Myerson at all. Government taxes had ruined her parents' greengrocer business in Astoria and sent them to an early grave. "Get something for yourself," her father had told her. And she had.

"Don't forget the root of elm sapling," she told the boy's back.

Root of elm sapling was good for the eyes, said to make reds redder and greens greener. These sensory boosters had become big business lately, a delicious panacea for the afflicted and nonafflicted alike. Those who could afford it had gone running pell-mell to return to the supposedly care-and-chemical-free days of hunting-gathering, when gnawing on a branch of a certain tree was both nutritious and medicinal. Well, it tasted good, and taste was the only sensual pleasure she knew.

He turned his face in the barest acknowledgment. She watched with satisfaction as the boy's eyes narrowed ever so slightly and his mouth grew broad and flat. Smirk at me all you want, you little piece of shit, I'm getting out.

God, how she despised his generation. They had never known life before the Depriver Syndrome—disease, DNA glitch or whatever the hell it was—hit the planet, and so they wore their tragedy like a personal badge of honor. As though they had the right to be snide, sullen and lazy just because they had never known the freedom to dance on a crowded floor, play contact sports, pet heavily in the back seat of a cab or—the specialty of her generation—meet a stranger and boff his or her brains out and then never see that person again. They had their own code, these kids, and it drew them close together. It made her sick.

The noise of the blender invaded her ears. She felt herself growing warm under her thick, padded jumpsuit. He was ruining it, ruining it on purpose. Her treat!

"That's enough!" she barked, the volume of her voice surprising her for a moment, jogging a memory that once she had wanted to be an opera singer. She had the voice of an angel, her father said. But there was no money and the admissions committees at the right schools had not seen that this angel needed a scholarship. A B.A. in art history from City College provided her with some measure of beauty in her life.

The boy capped off the frothing cup with a sprinkle of bran.

"I said no bran!" she shrieked.

"Sorry." The word flipped like a tiddlywink over his shoulder as he went to pour the cup in the sink.

"No! Give it to me. You've made me late as it is."

But he was already tilting the cup over the sink, spilling the first few brown bubble drops onto the stainless steel.

She was back in her father's store. Instinctively, she leaned across the counter and snatched the Five Senses Herbal Choco Freeze from the startled boy—like her mother would have collared one of the neighborhood jerkoff kids with a pack of Hostess Cupcakes up his shirt—sharply bumping the thin ribbon of exposed skin where her sleeve pulled back from her glove against his own bare flesh. It felt like the brush of a dog's dry tongue.

"Ow!" she blurted reflexively, although it didn't hurt. For a split second their eyes locked. Like lovers, she thought incongruously.

Her tensed body filled with relief. The fear in his deep black irises meant that he was not, to his knowledge, a Depriver. His snickering veneer broke away like cellophane from a candy valentine, revealing two rows of perfect teeth. She was taken back to the days when a smile exchanged with a stranger over some common recognition, some irony, swept away the rigors of city life like an offshore front clears the fog, revealing the striped bathhouse. Coney Island. Mama! Daddy! Look what I found! She wanted to reassure him, hold him, comfort him, give birth to him all over again and raise him in a world without fear. Then the boy's face split. He laughed.

How dare he laugh at her? How dare he. Now she would spend the whole night, the most important night of her life, wondering if she had been deprived. A night when she needed all her wits about her, too. Her father's voice rose in her throat, a soothing antacid.

"Rot in hell, you little fuck," she hissed, quickly looking around to see if anyone she knew had witnessed the incident.

"No charge," he said with a grin.

Oh, the insult! As if money made any difference. The damage was done.

She did the one thing she could do to show this toad, this idiot, this fool, this loser that she was above him and his kind. She pulled out a twenty-dollar bill and tossed it on the counter. "Keep the change," she said lightly, turning on her heel and gliding through the store toward the light of the street. She didn't look back. She knew he would be performing the self-test for deprivation. Modeled on the highway patrol's test for drunken driving, it was a quick way to test sight, balance and general cognition.

He needn't worry. Today was his lucky day. Although medical science could find no proof, Victoria believed that those who became Deprivers had brought it on themselves. Somehow, deep down, they wanted to become Deprivers. And Victoria Myerson definitely did not want to become a Depriver. Victoria Myerson might be known for her ruthlessness in the high stakes world of art, but when it came down to it, Victoria Myerson would never hurt a flea. Commit grand larceny, yes, but inflict bodily harm? No, it wasn't in her.

On the street, she went no more than a few steps before

tossing the bran-clogged Choco Freeze into a trash can. She wanted no reminders of what had just occurred. She turned off the broad avenue and walked quickly down the empty cobbled street. Once bandits and whores, rubes and gentlemen had clotted these streets, mixing blood and semen and smells in the pursuit of pleasure and thrills. Doing unto others in a frenzied dash to be done oneself. She shuddered. How could people have so little respect for themselves?

Victoria unlocked the empty gallery, secured it behind her and walked briskly to the back of the long, tall, white space. She tried, but she couldn't quite block out the monstrosities that hung from the walls of her gallery. Canvasses serrated by bold strokes in blackest tones of blood red and nauseous green, representing human figures, longing, lonely, isolated. Crap. Very expensive crap. She slammed the door to her small office behind her.

Throwing herself onto a plush red love seat, the one luxury in the otherwise efficient room, she closed her eyes, and with a sigh gave into a longing for her wasted frozen treat, letting the craving course through her body, like . . . like something. What was that feeling? Her heart sank and jumped, skipping a beat. Like when she was a child speeding down a long slide. No, she must not have a heart attack tonight! Not tonight, when she would begin the rest of her life. She forced the feeling away, slipping into a brief, relaxing trance by breathing through her nose while humming a Vivaldi concerto. She must remain focused. Aloof. Alert.

Her eyes flew open. Those damn paintings. The damn artist. The damn buyers who chased the pop-culture bandwagon, forcing her to drive the goddamn thing just to make a living.

With great effort, she made herself relax her tense muscles by composing invective in her head:

Kaspar, age twenty-two, the artist whose work will
be auctioned tonight, with twenty percent of the
proceeds going to Depriver Research, has outdone
himself, in a display of primitive morbidity. The
show is expected to reap record windfalls. These so-
called "paintings" crudely illustrate despair and rep-
resent the work of a clever but naive child. Art
should not reflect the misery of life. Art should lift
the human spirit above the grinding horror of daily
life, particularly during an epidemic. Kaspar, a
member of the Depriver School, as it is known, is
immensely popular, supposedly groundbreaking,
and very, very pricy. The self-elected members of
the Depriver School give the wealthy, heart weary
dilettante exactly what he expects, and relieve his
guilt by cleaning his wallet. Cash purchase only.

She sat up, feeling herself again. Opening the small safe
behind her desk, a thin whispering giggle escaped her lips as
she removed an Air France envelope, savoring her immi-
nent triumph. The joke was on them. By the time they got
the punch line, she would be well on her way to a remote,
luxurious chalet in the Swiss Alps, stocked with books,
videos, CD's and enough tinned caviar to last a lifetime. It
was all arranged. A nearby village would supply her with
food and drink and other necessities. And if no cure was
found, well, then, she would live alone, drinking goat's milk
and reading the classics for the rest of her goddamn life.
She figured she had a good thirty-five to forty years left.
Victoria Myerson did not intend to suffer as her parents had
suffered.

She pulled out six one-way airline tickets, an entire row
to herself. She would take no risks, now that she was so
close. Six one-way tickets to . . . What was this, a misprint?

mlohkcotS? This could foil her whole plan. Or was it? No. Impossible.

She blinked, breathing through her nose, humming a few soothing bars of Vivaldi, then re-examined the ticket. Stockholm. It said Stockholm. A deep breath. It's just nervousness, she chided herself, I'm not deprived. To be on the safe side, she leaned back, closed her eyes, stretched out her arms and touched alternate lacquered fingers to the tip of her nose. Perfect. All systems were go.

Outside she could hear the caterers setting up a buffet and the investors chirping at each other with excitement. She put the tickets back in the envelope and returned them to the safe, plunging the key down the front of her jumpsuit, pausing to lower the zipper to mid-cleavage. Sex sells, she thought. Sex and Deprivers. Give them what they want. Removing a small gavel from a desk drawer, she rapped it three times for emphasis. Going, going, gone!

Emerging from her office, Victoria surveyed the milling, pampered, jumpsuited crowd. Fashion follows fashion, she thought. Philistines. Trend-hounds. Moneyed clodhoppers. Losers, all of them. There at the far end of the room were the investors. Cherlyn, Carol and March, wearing X-tra large "D" T-shirts over their evening gowns, acting as though they had painted the canvasses they used to keep their social-climbing legs limber. All told, these well-tucked and plucked matrons had a total of two classes in Intro to Art Theory and five old-money husbands to their credit. Until tonight, they had owned her.

Victoria recalled her first opening, in her old gallery—her own gallery—nearly fifteen years ago. A glorious display of beautiful colors splashed onto enormous canvasses, beautiful to the eye and to the soul. Buyers and artists alike had fought to shake her hand warmly, even touched her back lightly in admiration. Some flirted. She had taken home to her triumphant bed one very young, very eager, very wide-eyed artist, his admiration for her taste vibrating along her naked limbs. And then the Depriver thing had started and the beauty and her gallery came to an abrupt end.

Dull, hollow sounds ricocheted off the walls of the rapidly filling space. At the buffet, a long-haired boy in tight, paint-spattered jeans stood at the center of an adoring circle drinking champagne from a spouting bottle. People laughed and smiled. Kaspar. The hack. Playing the eccentric creator to an audience of fools. Odd, these hangers-on and socialites seemed less opportunistic than usual. Their tight smiles and creased eyes signaled goodwill, not the avarice she had come to expect and exploit. Happy people didn't invest in the Depriver School. Unhappy, angry people invested in despair. This might not be as easy as she had thought. Good thing she had her wits about her.

Kaspar turned to toast the room, holding his glass aloft. His eyes alighted on hers. Yes, he was wearing the damned "D" T-shirt and the all-knowing sneer of his kind. That was a sneer, wasn't it? Was he smiling at her? Smiling at her cleavage? The nerve. He wouldn't dare. Perhaps there was something wrong with his mouth. He needs braces, she thought, and some light plastic surgery, if he wants to turn that ridiculous friendly smile into a proper artist's leer, or hangdog frown, or neutral, holier-than-thou expression.

She examined his face more closely. The glittering, now swarming room seemed to grow brighter, then dim. She was consumed by a wave of nostalgia. And something else. His face, which at first had reminded her of an overly bright iguana, now appeared handsome. Strong nose, sensual lips, the crown of rising hair a bold stroke of masculinity. Her skin tingled beneath her jumpsuit. She felt not unlike she had earlier, longing for her Choco Freeze. What was that feeling? Loneliness? That was out of the question.

She considered running into her office and locking herself in. But it was too late. He was coming toward her. She had to save face.

Then Victoria did something she had not done since she was a blushing schoolgirl at her first dance, in the dress her mother had sewn for her from discount cloth. She panicked. The blood in her head raced to her feet and the room glowed even brighter.

No! She mustered her wits and re-entered her role of Victoria Myerson, the successful, admired director of the gallery. And she stepped forward to greet this young man.

"Fucking hell!" Her father's dying words escaped her lips as Victoria missed the step down onto the gallery floor and went slipping on a soft bootie several yards before coming to rest in a heap at Kaspar's feet.

Victoria stared at the blackness behind her eyelids. The red edges of humiliation threatened to burst into white hot tears. She opened her eyes. Around her the crowd retreated, like water molecules from a drop of grease, the instinct to aid a member of the pack reversed by fear of contact. Then the full-on throttle of Kaspar's largest canvas seared through the wetness blurring Victoria's vision.

In that instant, Victoria Myerson knew that the painting was beautiful. Not just beautiful. Breathtaking. Expressing the emptiness that pressed dully beneath her ribcage. The work of a genius. A genius speaking through his art directly to her and her alone. This knowledge made her reckless, free, like she had felt as a child singing in her parents' store, before anyone had told her she was not good enough.

She heard the soft shuffle of worn boots. A bare hand reached out to her. She removed one glove and stretched forth her own slender, pale hand, and allowed the genius to pull her gracefully to her feet. All around her she heard gasps of surprise and horror.

Gripping Kaspar's hand, Victoria stared deep into the eyes of the man who had created her heart. She felt the warmth of sweaty flesh pervade her body, the firmness of her bones beneath the skin, the matching, secret pressure between her legs. She lifted the hand joined to hers high into the air.

"Ladies and gentlemen, I present to you the greatest living artist: Kaspar!"

The crowd burst into applause, and then a roar so profound she imagined that it echoed down the canyons of the city, proclaiming, *Yes, in spite of everything, we will go on. We will go on!*

The evening flew by, so much like the old days. How quickly the auction went. How like a dream. The slam of her gavel. The money joyfully poured out of unsnapped briefcases, the revelry, even the dancing, cautious at first, then more raucous, reckless, the buyers gathered in a swaying mass, repelled and attracted electrons, around her and Kaspar, the brave couple who bumped pelvises in a brazen declaration of freedom.

How quickly, how easily she bid a grateful and unsuspecting Cherlyn, Carol and March adieu for the last time. How natural it seemed to tell Kaspar of her plan and convince him that he should join her in the welcoming mountains of Switzerland, where he could paint, his genius safe and flourishing. How simple and right it seemed to leave twenty percent of the proceeds in the safe and write a company check to Deprivers Research.

Then, oh, then! The rushing urgency of taking the artist between her legs. How like her first memory of running into her father's strong, capable hands and him lifting her up and away from earth. For the first time since she could remember, she sang: Kaspar! Kaspar! Kaspar!

Yes, thought Victoria Myerson, at peace with the world, glancing back from the glowing clock on her bed stand to the fringed eyelashes of her genius lover, I will have his child.

It was barely morning, but it was time. The sack of millions secured, the one thin suitcase parked by the door, the cab called, she drew gentle circles on the bare shoulder of her companion.

"It's time," she breathed in his ear. "Put on your shoes, we're going to the airport."

Kaspar opened his eyes. In the predawn dimness of her bedroom Victoria could just make out their roundness, the tension in his fluttering lids, his lips stretched open and across his teeth, so much like the despairing figures in his work. Loving the man more, if that was possible, she leaned closer, to bestow a kiss on his upturned face.

He turned his head, looking into the distance over her shoulder. Sometime in the night, Kaspar had gone blind.

RENT MEMORIES

KEITH AARON

The barren road reminded Raitchel of her empty life. The trees flew by her like the days in the years, short stubby vapid looking trees.

She had sent Jonathan spinning through fugue. And Stephanie. And Mandy. It was enough.

Jonathan, her first tender moment; he had leaned into her at the shore, on the tall lifeguard chair, the air salted, the storm coming, and kissed her softly, so, so softly. She remembered the dizziness, the floating, the perfection of it. She'd raised her hand and touched his cheek and . . . No! No! don't pull away, it is perfect, it is perfect!

But he did pull away. He'd pulled away and said,

Who are you?

Who am I?

Yes, who are you? She remembered the confusion in his eyes, the utter detachment. And the loss in her—that kiss gone! She'd told him his name and where he lived, walking with him. Then he'd remembered. But he never remembered that one decent perfect thing in her life. And what remained indelibly within her was the eerie horror of him being wiped clean like a crashed hard-drive.

That was Raitchel's seventeenth birthday. Her first date.

And then she'd gone home to her bastard father.

She looked at him now. Disgusting, hairy animal, with that cheap fucking cigar. And that smell, that rotten smell of booze, an old drunk's stench.

Yeah, home to Daddy.

She'd cried all the way and he was gin drunk when she came through the door; drunk and staring into space. He'd looked up, red with toxic sweat.

How was your date you little whore—just like your mother, that fucking bitch. Happy fucking birthday . . .

She'd flown up to her room to make God hear, with tears and more tears. *What happened? What happened to Jonathan? Why? Why? Why?* God, she wanted that kiss back.

The brand new black Chevy Blazer ate the open road. Her father's latest birthday bribe, his bullshit contrition for twenty-four years of hell. She felt the rage like evil in the pit of her.

Upstairs amidst helpless tears she'd found the keys to his first bribe, a shiny Mustang key on a Mustang key ring, with a card that said, Happy Birthday, Dad.

Bleary and spent, she'd fallen asleep. A soft knock awoke her. *Hey, sweetheart, let daddy in, baby. Come on, baby, let daddy in.*

No no no no no, please no, please God no, not tonight, not tonight, please not tonight!

And then pounding like thunder. *Open the door you fuckin' slut! Open the door before I break it down. Open this fucking door!*

There was a boom and a crash, the wood split and the door smashed against the dresser.

It's time to thank daddy for his birthday gift. Happy birthday to you happy birthday to you happy birthday dear Raitchel . . .

Raitchel remembered how clear it had been that night. She could feel the horns of that crescent moon as if they were pushing through the top of her skull.

Her father was through and sleeping. She'd grabbed the keys to the Mustang and eight hundred dollars in cash intending never to return and driven to Stephanie's. She'd thrown the pebbles at the window pane until the light went on.

Wanna go for a ride in my new Mustang?

A new Mustang? Oh yeah, happy birthday you lucky bitch.

Yeah, lucky me, Raitchel thought.

Ok, give me a minute.

Steph—Steph! Bring something to drink. Something. Anything.

Oh, I don't know Raitch, my father checks that kind of thing.

Just do it, Steph! I mean, come on, it's my birthday.

Raitchel smirked inside as she remembered that bottle. Bacardi 151, dark, horrible, and completely effective.

Raitchel had parked the Mustang near a playground at the edge of town, clutched the bottle, full past the label, and killed the ignition.

Let's go walk by the bay for a little while. And she'd unscrewed the cap and thrown it in the back seat.

Raitchel pulled hard on the bottle—too hard—she'd felt it rising like an acid lump in her throat. She'd choked it down, choked it down with all her might, felt the warmth of it hit her stomach and spread. She passed the bottle.

Happy birthday to me, happy birthday to me . . .

It's a real nice car, Raitch.

Yeah, the bastard outdid himself.

Stephanie had turned up the rum and taken a long sip too, coughed a little. *God, this stuff is awful.*

Is it? I can barely taste it. It just burns on the way down, like it's eating you.

They'd sat on the bulkheads. The tide was high and the water lapped. The lines holding the boats in their slips and on their docks had creaked in tension, creaked to ripping, unravelling.

Raitch? Raitchel had started, jumped, as if the sound of her name were a snapping boat-line, and she were half adrift in the dark water, the strong current pulling heavily by her, putting immense fathomless pull on her last line. She felt the wind pick up, the nerves stretch in her head and spine.

Huh? Raitchel drank more. More burn, more pain, another piece lost to the torrent.

Raitch? What are you doing in September? Stephanie took the bottle, turned it against her lips, sucked it down, gagged a little, hating it, but drinking to drink with Raitchel. She'd seen the look in Raitchel's eyes, an empty sliver in the moonlight, and she'd chilled. Something was going to happen. She knew it.

College up north. Computer science. Boston University. I got the letter the day before yesterday. Raitchel had said the words, but remembered how far away they seemed, as if Stephanie were across the world and the words were creeping like heat through cold metal. She'd held out her hand for the bottle and drank, and she pushed back the seeping cold in her heart, and the one-fifty-one seemed to add more than it stole. They'd sat in silence for a while, drinking.

How about you? Stephanie was her friend. Raitchel knew she should care. But she didn't. She'd thought she should feel guilt for not caring. But she hadn't. Raitchel was scared. She'd needed Stephanie, needed her to help blunt the sharp edge inside her. She'd felt like she could cause pain.

I want to go to college close by so I can be around my brother and sister, when my brother left for school I missed him terribly. My dad wants me . . .

Raitchel had left, though. She'd taken another pull from the bottle, handed it to Stephanie, and stood.

Hey, where you going?

To the swings, come on.

Stephanie had turned the bottle up to her lips again and stood, and felt the ground reel beneath her. And she vomited, having drunk far too much and far too fast.

Raitch! She'd moaned as she tasted the horror. *Stupid stupid stupid. Raitch*—and heaved again. And again. *Raitch?*

When Raitchel had found Stephanie she was passed out in the dirt, with vomit and spit dripping from her mouth and hair.

Stop it! Stop it! Stop it, Raitchel cringed from the past, from the grotesque disease of her memory. The sun was all but gone to her right, the last arc of it going behind the dunes, hiding behind the Earth. Her father reached over and pushed the lighter in. Raitchel's face screwed.

"You got a fuckin' problem with that?" he snapped.

Stephanie's head rocked in her lap and she was wiping her face with napkins, and when clean stroking her face and hair and telling her it was alright, caressing her, trying to help. Stephanie breathed deeply, regularly, passed out, and Raitch held her till morning twilight, absorbed in the stroking of Stephanie's face, in the quiet rhythm of the setting moon.

When Stephanie began to stir Raitchel whispered to her.

Steph, I think I'm going crazy. I feel myself slipping away. There is no one. No one. I have no one. I know you're

my friend, I know it, but . . . you can't help . . . and Jon-
athan? What happened? He was the best thing . . . it was
perfect . . . and my father . . . oh, what am I going to do,
Steph? What am I going to do? I can't figure out . . . And she
tilted back the last inch of the rum and felt it tingle down
into her—*I just can't find me. My mother must have taken*
me with her. I just can't figure out—

And Stephanie groaned, she looked up into Raitchel, but
with nothing, not a ripple of recognition, of reason, of anything. Like Jonathan, but so much worse. *Stephanie?*
Stephanie? Stephanie opened her mouth as if to speak.
What came out was cooing and crooning. Not a word.

The nightmare of the past pulled Raitchel from the road,
almost to her death.

"What are you fucking crazy, bitch?! What are you
doing? Stupid." Her father grabbed the wheel and swerved
the car back into the lane. She had control again of the
Blazer, her heart beating like a piston. She slowed the car.
She reached into her purse for a cigarette, a long slender
More and pressed in the lighter.

"That's it, smoke like a whore."

"Fuck you," said Raitchel. She said it before she knew
what she was doing. And before she knew what was happening she felt the slap on her mouth, hard. The car
swerved, the cigarette smashed. She looked in loathing at
the beast beside her. The blood rushed to her lips and face
and she felt the sting.

So she said it again. "Fuck you." Next it was a clenched
fist, and it hit her in the right temple. She slammed hard on
the brakes and the truck skidded. Too late she realized, he
was wearing his seat-belt.

"You bitch, you bitch, you ugly whore bitch," he raged.
As the car came to a stop, he grabbed her hair and pulled

her up from the driver's seat, against the seat belt, pulled her until her hair ripped. "Bitch," and he yanked. "Bitch," as he unclasped her seat belt. "Bitch," as he twisted her out of the seat. Raitchel could do nothing. She stared to the front, a torn ragdoll caught in the jaws of a terrier. He heaved her up and threw her into the back of the Blazer.

"I'll show you how to fuckin' drive," and he hit the gas hard. The wheels chirped against the pavement as he spun the steering wheel to the right. The truck bumped hard off the empty parkway and onto the sandy grass of the shoulder, into a gap in the stubby trees. "I'll show you, bitch whore slut-cunt. We're gonna have a little picnic. You can thank Daddy for the Blazer, for four years of Boston University, you fucking bitch. Didn't phone even once. Didn't you miss me?"

He held her head by her hair between the two front seats. "Is this what I get for thanks—fuck you? Fuck you? Is that all you can say, fuck you? I'll show you fuck you!" And he stopped the truck behind the trees and dragged her, helplessly, through the driver's side door—and Raitchel withdrew, exchanging pain present for pain past.

In the guilt ridden gift of a Mustang, Raitchel and Mandy drove to Boston to check out the university. But they left late, a spontaneous thing brought on by a fifth of Seagrams. Drunk, they pulled and swerved off the highway up near Albany, to eat some eggs, to buy more booze.

A mile off the highway, on a road with broken streetlights, was a Seven Eleven and a dirty looking all night diner called Time Gone By, or TGB's. It was a greasy little place, patronized by a few greasy little people. Mandy and Raitchel walked in.

Bells went off in Mandy. *This place doesn't look so good, Raitch.*

Why? Eggs are eggs, what are you worried about? Raitchel smiled.

What are you two pretty little ladies doing? The guy dripped and oozed off the counter-stool, meeting them before they sat.

Nothing, stranger, Raitchel said, and she turned from him to face the booths, pointing one out to Mandy. But the other hand she ran up his slimy thigh, over his wrangler bulge. *Nothing until I finish my eggs.* Raitch left him and sat with Mandy, walking her most languid seductive walk across the filthy floor, looking up at Marilyn Monroe.

What are you doing, Raitch? That's the most degenerate looking reptile that ever slinked through the dark. Look at his hair, for Christ sake! Mandy laughed, but it was nervous and halting. Looking at Raitch, she saw a darkness behind the drunkenness. She knew Raitch had been missing a few of the essentials lately, knew it from the way she made love to the Seagrams. But this . . .

What are you going to do with him?

I'm going to fuck him, and then I am going to steal his fucking mind!

What are you crazy? You're going to screw him? Don't you know . . . What? Her eyes bolted open.

Raitchel couldn't wait for eggs.

I'm hungry, she said, and got up. She moved to the man, whose eyes had never left her, and ran a finger under his chin.

Skip the eggs.

He slithered and bucked, coming inside her, as she felt him pulse within her, as she felt herself on the edge, she put both her hands on his face and held it between them, held him and jammed her hips and thrust herself around him. When the Mustang stopped moving, the man's brain had been completely fucked out. He drooled like a child. He could not talk, work the door handle; he couldn't remember his pants, or his shirt, or his name: nothing. Raitchel slipped on her panties under her little lycra skirt, grinning.

How 'bout a ride to some dark road up north? Raitch had dropped Mandy at the nearest bus station, then dropped the slimy dumb fuck off somewhere south of Boston.

Why don't I just do it? I know I can do it. I can strip this motherfucker to an infant in an instant, a touch, a pretended moment of tender mocked capitulation. I can place my hands upon his head like I've done to all the others and destroy him: destroy him utterly. Why don't I just do it? Raitchel raged indecision. She could think of nothing but his destruction and could do nothing for fear, for love (*love?*), for some inexplicable barrier of morality.

Because he is my father? Is that reason enough to spare him what I've done to others for the sheer thrill?

He spit his spite, though the angry words bounced unaffecting in the Blazer, like an insane man in a padded cell, "My father told me not to go near that whore-bitch-of-the-earth mother of yours, said my useless wasted life would continue being useless and wasted if I married her. But he was wrong. Oh, he was so wrong. Your mother gave me the finest piece a' young ass I ever had!"

He laughed. He laughed through that fat fucking cigar, laughed through Raitchel, bruised from the neck down, bruised so bad she could hardly work the gas pedal.

She could say nothing. She could do nothing. She felt the sand down her back, felt the slimy grit of him between her legs. She felt the anger of the raging helpless well within her.

All he had taken from her ripped through her blackened heart: the joy of her childhood, her successes, the few memories she had of her mother, whose face was fading to be replaced by the bastard face and the bastard words of the bastard beside her; he had taken all those and what was left was a hungry maw of a soul; bastard. Even Stephanie, who had lost everything, who's in the fourth grade again, has more. And what've I got?

The sun was gone, the trees dark shadows, amorphous black, the outlines rising and falling between the highway lamps and the stars.

"Raitchel, why don't you try to go to grad-school local. I mean, why go so far away. There are plenty of good schools in New York. We should really . . . I mean, I've been seeing someone, a specialist, a man who says that with time . . ."

MAN DEPRIVED OF HIS WHOLE LIFE

The paper told the story of a man who had been wiped clean, never to recover; permanent brain damage from a chance brush with a Depriver in the subway: one of those human-like creatures with the power to destroy neurological structures.

So fucking what? What about the bastard who deprived me? And she threw the paper down on the sofa and stood. She went to the full length mirror hanging on the bathroom door and looked at herself. She teased her long thick curls, ran her hands over her thighs, trim and tight in black jeans, and for the thousandth time she clutched her own face, squeezed it, tried with all her concentration to make herself forget it all.

Damn! Damn! Damn! She looked back to the mirror and straightened herself. She heard crying across the hall, weeping and bawling. She grabbed a bottle of peppermint schnapps.

The woman had lost her grandchildren, lost them to drugs and stupidity. Weak and pathetic, Raitchel thought.

She went across the hall and knocked on the door. The elderly woman answered, drying her eyes.

Hello, I heard you crying. I thought maybe I'd offer you some schnapps, maybe it would warm you up, help you to forget . . . Raitchel was invited inside.

*Oh, you are so kind, thank you—*but her eyes welled up again, *you know, they . . . they . . . they were about your age.* An eye filled up, tears Raitchel envied slid down the woman's face.

It's ok. It's ok. Raitchel went and helped herself to the kitchen, brought in two glasses, poured. *Try some of this, it helps me to forget.* And she handed the old woman a nice double.

You're Mrs. Holt. My name is Raitchel. I'm sure everything will be okay. Raitchel walked toward the mantle. Pictures and sentimentalia lined the walls, were displayed on and along the brick of the fireplace: husband, brothers, sisters, smiling, grandchildren, black and white antique photos in antique frames of antique parents, grandparents.

Yes, it'll be ok Mrs. Holt.

How, child? How? I've no one now. I've no one. What am I to do? All that I am and all that I could ever still hope for was in the souls of those dear children. It is as if I had died.

You're a sentimental woman, Mrs. Holt. I guess, in some ways, that is good. But let's have a toast:

To memory, the stuff of guilt and pain and remorse, mourning and nostalgia, of grudge and vengeance, of heartbreak and loss; and to the longing for the release of oblivion. Cheers.

Raitchel swallowed her double and put the glass on a small round table of pewter frames and baby pictures. Mrs. Holt looked at Raitchel, desperate eyes registering desperation.

Raitchel softened and moved closer. She held Mrs. Holt's gaze and placed her hands on the old woman's face, cradling it, like a mother. The old eyes ebbed. Eighty-seven years slipped from them and into the oblivion of the forgotten.

Good-bye, Mrs. Whoeveryouare. And Raitchel picked up the two glasses and the bottle and left the room. She then packed a bag, put on long black gloves, and in a once beautiful Mustang, left Boston forever.

"Why in the name of anything decent in the world would I want to live anywhere near you?" Twenty minutes left, thought Raitchel. Twenty minutes left, and this ride through hell is finished.

"Look you little bitch—I'm sorry. I mean, Raitchel, I just think it would be right if you helped me. I've lost a lot of time. We've lost a lot of time. I thought that this weekend we could just try—"

"Just try!" Raitchel choked on the words; for a second she thought, she hoped, she had felt tears, but no—"Just try? What the fuck was that that just happened? Just try. Fuck you. I'm going as far away from you as I can get. I despise you. I despise you so vividly that it has spilled over onto the rest of the fucking world. Just try. Specialist. You don't need a specialist, you need to be fucking executed."

Raitchel looked at her father. She hit the lighter and pulled another cigarette from her bag. She saw the man stiffen, saw the red come to his face, saw the clenching and unclenching of his fists. The lighter popped and she lit her cigarette. She rested her smoking hand on her bare thigh, caressed her bruised leg. She saw his torment.

He mumbled something.

"What did you say? I'm sorry, I didn't hear."

"Nothing, I didn't say anything." But she saw the muscles tighten in his jaw, the sheen of perspiration on his fore-

head. It was quiet in the truck, a numbing silence punctuated by the rhythmic slapping of the tires on the concrete
grooves. The turn-off was just up ahead. Raitchel smoked.
She felt the dangerous tension, the pressure building in her
father. He was going to pop, to break, as sure as her past had
broken her. It was just a matter of time.

He always carried a few gin miniatures for just such
occasions, which he popped and chugged. After the second,
Raitchel felt his glare. She pressed on the gas, hoping to
reach her aunt's before zero hour. He drank the third and
was cracking the fourth when he said:

"You're not going anywhere." He lit his cigar. "You're
not gonna slut around Boston or California or anywhere
else, except right here. You're my little slut. Daddy's little
girl."

Raitchel turned off the parkway, then turned again and
started up a long gravel road. Then again into a long rock
driveway. Before her was a beautiful cedar beach home, her
father's sister's, and the commencement of her soul's
wrenching; the first tender cabana horror with her father;
her mother drinking butler-brought exotic cocktails in the
chaise lounge with the bitch aunt.

They got out of the truck, and her father, with that stupid fucking smirk opened up the trunk and heaved up the
cooler of blue-claws. And Raitchel felt something break
inside of her. She felt her past course through her like high
voltage, stunning her, the montage of memories that are
supposed to flood those who are about to die, a rush of
anger and horror she could not contain. She looked at her
father with both hands on the cooler.

"You want to try again? Start over? Okay. Let's then
start from scratch." Twenty-four years of hatred and abuse
lashed out and she slapped him with all the force she could
collect, slapped him right across the face and watched him

reel. She knew the power and effect of a touch from her upon the head. She had watched it grow. She saw his eyes vacate. He clutched the cooler because he didn't know enough to drop it.

"Maybe this time you'll do it right."

THE LIEUTENANT

HARRY TURTLEDOVE

Jerry Daniels drove his beat-up little Toyota east along Victory past the library, past the police station next door. Smoggy summer sun blazed down on the San Fernando Valley. People on the street mostly wore as little as the law allowed, though nobody except a few obvious couples walked very close to anyone else. Jerry eyed a pretty blond girl whose halter top and tight denim shorts left next to nothing to the imagination.

He sighed wistfully. He was twenty-one, blond himself— well, sandy-haired—and no less horny than any other twenty-one-year-old guy you've run across lately. She might have thought he was cute. But even if she were wearing nothing at all, even if they got together in privacy, what could he do? "Ruin her for life," he muttered, and flicked on the left-turn signal.

Hip-hop blared out of the car stereo's speakers. The in-crowd, of course, listened to bang these days, not hip-hop any more. He imagined himself part of the in-crowd. In a way, that was even sadder than imagining himself alone with the blond girl.

"Not gonna happen, Jerry," he said as he turned onto a side street. For excellent good reasons, he spent most of his time alone—he'd never make a mall rat—and talked to himself a lot. "Get used to it. It won't. And believe you me, it could be worse."

He parked outside an apartment building, one of the many that marched north up the street. They dated mostly from the 1970s, pre-dawn, and had seen better days. The white muscle pickup parked in front of his car wore two bumper stickers: TO HELL WITH THE AMERICANS WITH DISABILITIES ACT and DEPRIVERS CURED BY SMITH & WESSON.

"Fuck you, pal," Jerry said as he put the Club on the steering wheel—it was indeed that kind of neighborhood, even with the police station only a couple of blocks away. When he got out of the air-conditioned Toyota, August heat smote with full force. His jeans and chambray shirt only made things worse. So did the microthin, almost invisible gloves on his hands. The latexoid made him itch, too, but he'd do worse than itch if he didn't wear the gloves. He might hang or burn or end up in one of those fancy new relocation camps from which nobody ever seemed to emerge.

A dog trotted past. It ignored Jerry. Up in an olive tree, a hummingbird zeebled. *This is my place*, the rusty song said. *Everybody else go away*. When he was a kid, Jerry had never imagined he could be jealous of a hummingbird. But where was *his* place?

The telephone pole in front of the apartment building had a Depriver warning stapled to it. This being L.A., the warning came in English and Spanish. Anybody could be a Depriver. Anybody at all.

Up the stairs Jerry went. He had a card key to let him

into the building. An Asian woman came down the stairs toward the entry. He held the door open for her; he'd been raised polite. "Thanks," she said, and went on by. A middle-aged Hispanic guy built like a brick churned up and down the pool on endless laps. A couple of lazier men and a dumpy, middle-aged gal courted skin cancer in the lounges on the nearby decking. One of the men waved to Jerry. He raised a hand in return, then went up the steps two at a time.

Apartment 268 was on the left-hand side, at the back. He knocked on the door. A gray-haired, square-jawed fellow in a short-sleeved shirt and polyester pants let him in. The guy was exactly what he looked like: a plainclothes cop. "Hello, Jerry," he said around a cigarette. "You're right on time."

"Hi, Sergeant Turner," Jerry answered. "Those things aren't good for you, you know." Talking to anybody who knew him and was willing to look him in the eye—though Turner hadn't offered to shake hands, even though he had to know Jerry was wearing gloves—was rain in the desert for him.

"Everything okay by you?" Turner asked. "Boys on surveillance haven't seen anything to sneeze at."

"Everything's fine," Jerry answered. "And I do appreciate that you guys keep an eye on things for me." He meant that. Nobody hassled him, the LAPD least of all. Compared to the furtive lives most Deprivers had to live, he had it made. *Of course, I'm useful to them*, he thought. *I'm damn lucky they decided I was useful to them instead of giving me a fatal accident or something.*

"Willie and Contreras and the Lieutenant are in the bedroom with the asshole," Turner said, and jerked a thumb toward the back of the apartment.

"Okay," Jerry said. Turner said the same thing every time. "What did this one do?" Jerry asked; he had a morbid curiosity about such things.

Turner didn't satisfy it, answering, "What you'd expect. We don't give you a buzz when we catch 'em playing horseshoes."

"Horseshoes," Jerry said tightly. "Right." He started back toward the bedroom. "Let's get it over with." Turner followed, carefully, keeping a couple of feet away from him.

Jerry grimaced. Everybody who knew what he was acted like that around him, even though he wore gloves and long sleeves. He hadn't asked to be a Depriver. He didn't want to be one. He would have given anything not to, in fact. But God, or Whoever, didn't cut deals like that.

"Hi, Jerry," Carlos Contreras said when he came into sight. Contreras looked like a Mexican-American version of Sergeant Turner. Willie Peebles was black and a few years younger, but also stamped from the same mold. He waved to Jerry, pink palm out.

The Lieutenant stood by the bed, effortlessly in charge of everything. Jerry had been in his office, in the station around the corner. He knew his name was Jason McNabb. But nobody every called him by his name. He was just . . . the Lieutenant. Tall—six-four, easy. A black pompadour that added another two, three inches. Lean. Handsome, in a stern, long-faced way. A slash of a mouth. A blade of a nose. Eyes like gray ice, but a little colder. And a voice . . .

"Hello, Jerry," he said. Had he said, *Take out that machine-gun nest, soldier,* Jerry would have charged first and asked questions later, if he lived. It was that kind of voice.

"H-Hello, sir," Jerry stammered.

The Lieutenant held out his hand for a pre-dawn handshake. He had no fear. He was perfectly confident Jerry would never dare touch him ungloved. His grip said how strong he could be without showing how strong he was. He pointed to the other man in the room, the bastard on the bed. "There he is. Do what you do."

"Hello, hello, hello," the fellow said, a whacked-out grin on his face. They'd have fed him roofies or something like 'em before they brought him here, something to keep him from remembering what went on. This was all highly unofficial business. *As unofficial as cops taking good care of a Depriver instead of giving him one in the balls*, Jerry thought. Yes, he knew when he was well off.

"What did he do?" Jerry asked.

"What you'd expect," the Lieutenant answered, as Sergeant Turner had before him. His mouth narrowed further. Jerry hadn't thought it could. The vice officer's eyes grew colder, too: another surprise in the range of possibilities. "Statutory rape."

Jerry nodded. This was the mildest thing they'd brought him here for. The serial rapist. The pedophiles. The fellow who'd gone and . . . He scrunched up his face. He didn't even want to think about what that fellow had done. Well, he wouldn't do it again, even if he did get out of jail one of these years.

"Come on," the Lieutenant said crisply. "Do it."

"Yeah, come on, babe, do it," the guy on the bed said, his grin getting even wider. "Sweet little tits, ride my pony." He bucked as if a girl were riding him.

Slowly, almost as if doing a striptease, Jerry peeled off one of his gloves. Turner and Contreras and Peebles all took an involuntary step backwards. The Lieutenant never stirred. Only his eyes were alive. He might have been watching a beautiful redhead shed the last of the lace and the ruffles. Jerry took off the other glove. The Lieutenant nodded. He licked his thin, thin lips.

"Hold him, boys," he said.

The three cops grabbed the guy on the bed. It could have been done better-none of them wanted to get anywhere close to Jerry's naked hands—but the guy was too zoned to fight back much. In fact, he kind of dug it. "Ooh, baby!" he said. "You into b&d? I tie you down next, okay?"

"You see," the Lieutenant said to Jerry, his voice even colder than his eyes, nothing but disgust on his bony face. "He deserves every bit of it."

"Yeah." Jerry nodded. He knew what he was going to do to the guy on the bed. He wanted to despise him. Wanted, hell—he *had* to despise him. To do that . . . He asked the Lieutenant, "How old was the girl? Eleven? Ten? Younger?"

Before the Lieutenant could answer, the guy on the bed let out a mournful bellow: "Seventeen? You outa your fuckin' mind, man?" He might have been talking to the cop who'd busted him, not to the ones who had him now. "She hadda be twenty-two, twenty-three, maybe twenty-five even. Way she was pourin' down the tequila at that party, she . . ." He lapsed into babbling that didn't make a whole lot of sense.

He couldn't have been faking that, not with all the shit he had in him. Jerry turned to the Lieutenant. "Isn't this kind of tough?" he asked. "Seventeen—especially if he didn't know she was seventeen . . . and this?"

"It's just as much against the law as if she were eight." The Lieutenant's voice had not an ounce, not an inch, of give in it.

Jerry wasn't surprised. Imagining the Lieutenant yielding . . . He shook his head. He couldn't do it. Imagining the end of the world came easier. Even so, he tried again: "But . . ."

"Jerry, you've helped us before," the Lieutenant said. "You take care of . . . problems we have in a way that courts can't—and can't authorize, either. You've made the streets of

Los Angeles a safer place. And we've played ball with you, too. Right?" When Jerry didn't answer right away, the Lieutenant's voice came like a whipcrack: "Right?"

"Yeah—uh, yes, sir," Jerry said miserably. "But Jesus . . ."

"You don't cooperate with us, Jerry, we don't cooperate with you," the Lieutenant said. "Hard row to hoe for Deprivers these days. You don't know what a hard row it is. If you want to find out, though, you can. That'd be real easy."

Jerry shivered, although the apartment's air conditioner had seen better days. When they caught Deprivers—the ones people didn't lynch first—they put them places where they couldn't do any Depriving, except among themselves (and who cared about that?). Or maybe they said they put them in those camps, but something else really happened. Who could know for sure? Jerry couldn't, but he had a good imagination.

"Do it, Jerry," the Lieutenant said. "Do it right now."

The guy on the bed giggled. "Yeah, sweety-pie, do it right now."

"Jesus," Jerry said again. "If she was seventeen, if he didn't know . . ." He looked toward the Lieutenant. That was a mistake. The Lieutenant's face promised him a world of trouble if he didn't do exactly what the older man told him to do. And he knew the Lieutenant meant it, too. The Lieutenant didn't promise what he couldn't deliver. That was one of the things that made him so scary.

You know all the things that can happen to Deprivers. The Lieutenant didn't even have to say it again. Just looking at him made Jerry say it to himself. *Or maybe you don't know all the things that can happen. Maybe they'd come up with something special, just for you.*

He wanted to cry. But he wanted the cops to leave him alone. He wanted everybody to leave him alone. And when he did what the cops wanted, they did more than leave him alone. They took care of him. They did things for him. How many Deprivers, anywhere in the world, could say that?

"Sorry, fella," he told the guy on the bed, and leaned forward and yanked his T-shirt out of his jeans. The guy giggled some more. Slowly and deliberately, Jerry set the bare palms of his hands on the other young man's hairy stomach.

His touch was gentle. Even so, the guy on the bed howled like a wolf. "Hold him!" the Lieutenant said sharply. The cops did hold him. He was still way too high to fight back.

But he tried. They always did. Jerry wondered how the guy knew. He wondered how any of them knew. When you were deprived of sight or touch or hearing or smell or taste, of course you knew you'd lost it. But none of those was what Jerry took. Jerry Deprived a man—or a woman, as he'd found out the worst way you could find out—of something even deeper than any of those. Jerry stole the ability to desire, to want, to get hot . . . and, as far as anyone could tell, it never came back again.

No wonder the cops don't want me to touch them, he thought. *If I were in their shoes, I wouldn't want to get touched, either.*

The guy on the bed kept howling. He knew what he was losing. Jerry didn't know how he knew. Drugged up as he was, he couldn't be horny. But he knew. Every one of them had known. It was going, going, gone.

"What does it feel like, Jerry?" the Lieutenant asked. "What does it feel like to take *that* away?"

"It doesn't feel like anything to me," Jerry said. The Lieutenant always asked that. "Just . . . touch. I don't get off on it or anything."

"I can't believe that," the Lieutenant told him. "I just

can't believe it." He always said that, too. "You're taking it away. It can't just go nowhere. You've got to feel *something* when you do it."

But Jerry just shook his head. "I keep telling you and telling you, it's nothing to me. I wouldn't even know I was doing it if it wasn't for what other people do."

Would the Lieutenant keep after him? He sometimes did. Not always, though. And not today. He just said, "Well, you've done the city another good turn. Here's one more scumbag who won't be molesting innocent people any more."

She was seventeen. He didn't even know she wasn't legal. For that, you had me make sure he can't even think about getting his ashes hauled for the rest of his goddamn life? For that? Jerry'd already spoken up once, though— twice, even. The Lieutenant didn't want to hear it. Why should he? The Lieutenant didn't have to pay attention to a lousy Depriver. A Depriver had to pay attention to him.

Jerry did pay attention to the Lieutenant—to the sheen of sweat on his forehead, to the sheen of saliva on his thin lips, to the gleam that made his eyes look a little less cold but no less dangerous . . . and to the bulge in his pants.

Realization smote. *He didn't have me come here for this guy because the fellow was a dangerous pervert. He started me with guys like that, yeah, but not this one. The one reason I'm here with this poor, miserable bastard is that he gets off watching me deprive guys.* Jerry wanted to be sick. *Christ! Talk about perverts!*

The guy on the bed wouldn't remember how this had happened to him. All the drugs the cops had given him would make sure of that.

Jerry, now, Jerry would never forget. Not if he lived to be ninety, which wasn't likely, not for a Depriver.

"You did a good job," the Lieutenant said, his voice

breathier, warmer, moister than his usual hard-guy rasp. "You did a hell of a good job. Congratulations."

Inside the crowded little bedroom, time seemed to slow down for Jerry. Sometimes the wink of an eye in which choices get made can look like days, even years, from the inside. But only two questions really mattered-or rather, one question and one answer.

What will they do to me?

Who the fuck gives a damn? What can they do to me that's worse than what they just made me do to myself?

With a broad smile, Jerry said, "Thanks," and stuck out his hand.

And, automatically, the Lieutenant took it.

FOR GOOD PEOPLE LIKE YOU

JONATHAN SHIPLEY

Where's Hennesey, anyway?" Craig muttered as he and Cheryl sat sipping Cokes in the Dairy Queen parking lot. It wasn't like Hennesey to stand up friends. "He said eight o'clock."

"Let's just go," Cheryl shrugged. "Joan says he's been getting really preachy anyway. She's thinking about breaking up with—"

Shouts echoed across the parking lot. Craig hopped out of the car for a better look. "Some commotion over by the drive-through window," he reported. "Sheriff's people or Texas Rangers fighting with someone."

"Oh, right," Cheryl nodded. "That's where they had the sniffer stationed." She glanced at her watch. "I need to get home. I've seen Public Safety roundups before. Doesn't look like Joan and Hennesey are going to show, anyway."

"They're bringing sniffers here?" Craig grumbled, sliding back into the driver's seat. The DQ had been the high school hangout as long as anybody could remember—something sacred. "Since when?"

"Since last month, idiot. As in the Public Safety Emergency Procedure. You need to get out more, Craig."

Maybe he needed to get out less. The thought of a sniffer being close by gave his stomach the flutters. Sure, they were just people, but then again, so were Deprivers. He wanted them all out of his life, wanted things to be normal again, like it was before the epidemic. He could count at least a dozen people he knew from the Grange and church and shops around town that had been fingered by sniffers. People he'd known all his life.

Still, what was the alternative? If Public Safety was rough on Deprivers who tried to pass, it was for a reason. Unlike some bleeding heart liberals at school, Craig did not believe it was a narco-sicko plot to take over the country. Deprivers were a real threat to the health of the community. He just wished Texas in general and Parker County in particular didn't have so many residents turning freak.

"Craig?" Cheryl was waiting.

"Oh, sorry. Just wishing things weren't so bad." He gave her a sidelong glance. "So what else was in the emergency decree? It must have come out when I was visiting my dad in Decatur."

She mulled a moment. "Let's see—sniffers in public places, automatic detention, crackdown on teen Deprivers who've just turned."

"Yeah, right." He'd never even heard of teen Deprivers.

"No, seriously. Public Safety has cleansed eight kids over at Consolidated just since the program started. Why else do you think the game was called last Friday night?"

Craig just shrugged. He hadn't heard why their Consolidated High archrivals had postponed. It had been a first.

"Their varsity lost six key players to Public Safety. Why do you think everyone was talking about—oh, never mind. You are so unplugged, Craig, I'm surprised I go out with you."

"Yeah, me too." But his mind was elsewhere. Six of Consolidated's key players turned freak over the last month? That was too weird to comprehend.

"Watch it!" Craig snapped as someone shoved against him in the hall the next morning.

"Watch it yourself, dep!" the guy shot back and kept on going.

Craig froze a second, then bristled fiercely. "Hey, you're the dep!" But he'd lost the timing. It was a stupid thing to call people anyway.

"Varsity dep!" the same guy called unexpectedly from up the hall. "Turns out all you jock types are just waiting to waste out. Just like Hennesey."

Hennesey? Craig felt a chill. He turned and hurried back up the hall, until he spotted someone on the varsity. "Hey, Miller," he called. "Heard anything about Henn–"

One look at Miller's face told everything. Hennesey really *had* wasted out.

"When?" Craig muttered uneasily.

"Discovered last night at the DQ," Miller shrugged. "Spot check by Public Safety."

The Dairy Queen. That was *Hennesey* last night?

Miller fidgeted. "Bagged him right there in front of his date and everyone and dragged him off to detention. Big scene."

Craig shuddered at the image of the varsity co-captain dragged out of his own car on a date. First Consolidated, now their school. Normal, OK guys turning freak overnight— already it was giving the varsity a funny rep. People must be thinking Deprivation was contagious, which was impossible.

At least, it better be impossible. These were guys he'd been rubbing shoulders with for years. It made Craig a little nervous about the headaches he'd been having lately.

Maybe that was how it started. He shuddered and shook his head. The headaches could just be midterm exams. If he could loosen up, it might be OK.

Trudging outside, he climbed into his pickup and roared off the lot, as if speed and noise could make up for the general confusion he was feeling. Hennesey—who would have guessed? Smart, athletic, champion of the underdog. None of that would do him any good now. Craig was really going to miss Hennesey.

A group of guys huddled by the school steps the next morning as Craig walked up.

"Hennesey had been having freak attacks for weeks," one of them said. "Talked to some elementary kids who know his little brother, who said he'd wake up gasping in the middle of the night . . . headaches all the time."

Craig shifted uneasily.

"Think the kid knew his brother was a dep?" someone asked. "Joan sure didn't. Imagine her shock when her boyfriend turned out to be a freak."

"Yeah, real shocker," someone else added. "Just one more reason for rounding up all the deps and shipping 'em south."

Craig drifted down the hall. He could guess there'd be a lot of dep bashing over the next few days—almost like a ritual of relief among edgy ex-friends. It left a sour taste, both for Hennesey's sake and for reasons closer to home. Six first-string players at Consolidated in one month. What if his own headaches were more than headaches? What if *he* was wasting out?

He wasn't sure what drew him to the other end of the hall after everyone had split after school. But Hennesey's locker was right there, staring him in the face. Craig stared back for a few minutes, looked around to make sure he was alone, then gave the lock a tentative jerk. That was too much to ask.

Plan B was just as good, anyway—the ole varsity locker roster. Strictly unofficial but very useful for circulating homework assignments around the team. Craig found Hennesey's name on the photocopied list and dialed in the combination.

He swung the door open and frowned at the chaos of books, papers, and Gobstoppers. It looked just like his own locker. He poked at a few piles, wondering what he was looking for. But he couldn't let it go. Ten minutes later, he was still there, rifling through Hennesey's things.

Finally, there it was, tucked inside a Calculus book. A federal pamphlet from the Justice Department, *Deprivers' Rights and Responsibilities Under the Law.* That was so like Hennesey, with all his politically correct views—a real flaming liberal for this part of the country. The very title was inflammatory. In Parker County, deps didn't have any rights, except maybe the right to get dumped in the Detention Center. Hennesey had scrawled notes all over the cover, something about Texas-style detention centers being reviewed by the Supreme Court. Funny how that bit never made the local six o'clock news. There was more about due process and *habeas corpus*, which eluded him, but then again Craig had slept through most of Government last semester. But he got the general idea. Stuffing the pamphlet into his letter jacket, he shut the locker and headed for the parking lot.

What really bothered him about the pamphlet was that Hennesey must have known what was happening to him weeks ago if he'd had enough time to write off for information. But that didn't fit if Public Safety was catching kids just as they turned. Despite popular gossip, Hennesey hadn't been acting weird before that bolt out of the blue at the Dairy Queen. The pamphlet didn't make sense.

At some point—Craig didn't remember making a conscious decision—his drive home turned into something else. He was in the highest risk group in the community. He had to find out what was happening to the team, maybe happening to him. And he figured the only person who'd know about turning freak was someone who'd just been through it.

A new billboard had been erected on the other side of town, right by the junction with the interstate. DEPT. OF PUBLIC SAFETY it read. CLEANSING PARKER COUNTY FOR GOOD PEOPLE LIKE YOU! Part of the new public awareness campaign. Craig himself had one of the orange BETTER SAFE THAN SORRY bumper stickers. Now he was wondering if he might be sorry.

He passed the billboard going south and headed for the open country. The exit wasn't marked, but everyone knew where the new construction had been going on. The Detention Center slid into view along the gravel road, all tilt walls, concrete, and barbed wire. It was supposed to be like a nursing home with twenty-four-hour medical care. Looked more like a prison.

He'd had a long enough drive to think about what to tell the guard at the front desk.

"I need to see a recent admit—Hennesey. He walked off with his girlfriend's ring—they traded rings, you see—and she wants it back. Her mom went ballistic when she heard a family heirloom had ended up here. I volunteered to get it back, despite the danger—" Craig did a little jock swagger to underscore the point "—now that Joan's available, I got reason to help her out. How about it?"

The guard bought the story. Why not? It had pretty much happened that way with Cheryl's old boyfriend, who'd moved to Seattle. Or maybe the guard was just bored. Inside, Craig was offered an orange safety suit with helmet and gloves. Considering what was at stake, he couldn't imagine any visitor refusing. A single touch from any of those Deprivers inside the compound could maim in ways he didn't want to imagine.

"What about . . . them?" Craig had asked the attendant. He noticed the inmates didn't have any protection. "What happens if they touch each other?"

The man shrugged. "Doesn't happen much. But if it did, I guess it would teach those freaks the kind of hell they give normal people."

Craig shut up immediately, though he had a couple of other questions. This place didn't have answers, just attitude. And he really hated the thought of Hennesey being at risk from other Deprivers. Just knowing that an accidental touch from the person next to you could render you blind or deaf or crippled . . . Craig shook his head. Even a Depriver shouldn't have to go through that day after day. He finished sealing his safety suit and was let into the "patient" rec room.

He noticed the chairs were arranged as far away from each other as the walls permitted, and wondered if that was the staff's doing or the inmates'. He took a good look at the shabby green walls and barred windows, and tried to visualize what it would be like to be stuck here day after day. With a shudder, he quit trying. He was having way too much luck.

After a few minutes, Hennesey showed up, looking years older, though it had only been a week.

Craig moved closer. "Hi . . . uh, Hennesey. It's me."

A bit of interest sparked in Hennesey's tired face, but he seemed to have trouble focusing. "What are you doing here, Coraghan?" he mumbled.

"I . . ." No excuse was going to cut it. Not in this place.

"I found the stuff in your locker," he finally said. "I've got questions."

The conversation rambled. Hennesey was obviously doped up, but the more he talked, the more his words started coming together. After fifteen minutes, he almost sounded like himself.

"Okay, here it is," Craig blurted out during a lull in the small talk. "You wasted out, and this thing seems to be spreading. How do I know if I'm next? What do I look for?"

Hennesey massaged his temples with a forefinger. "I'd tell you if I knew. I never saw it coming. They just came and got me."

But the pamphlet? Maybe Hennesey was so drugged up, he didn't remember. Craig cleared his throat. "Uh, I found this pamphlet in your locker."

Hennesey gave him a funny look. "The pamphlet wasn't about me. It was about all the people getting rounded up by Public Safety. Public Safety has been violating civil rights all over the place." He gave a bitter laugh. "Ironic that now I'm the one who needs the help—and that there's no one to help me."

That sounded too much like a hook. The last thing Craig needed was getting dragged into some ACLU lost cause when his own future was so shaky. He glanced awkwardly around the room, saying nothing. It didn't help knowing that Hennesey would have been fighting like gangbusters for him if the situation had been reversed.

"What about the team?" he asked after a moment. "What's the connection? Fungus in the locker room?" The joke sounded flat, even to his own ears.

"It has to be coincidence. Even Public Safety admits that Deprivation is not contagious. But hell, if I had it to do over again, I'd quit the team in a heartbeat, just on the off chance. Think about it, Coraghan. You've still got a choice."

Except that Friday night football really was Craig's life, unlike Hennesey, who had student council and honor society and all that other stuff going for him. He was just playing football because in a small town everyone played football, unless . . .

Craig sucked air. "How many of the deps—sorry, Deprivers—over at Consolidated were brains?"

"They all kept solid grade points, if that's what you mean. I knew most of them through National Honor Society."

"Political activists?"

Hennesey snorted. "In this part of the country? The most you can get away with around here is a mild-mannered petition."

"But were these guys active like you were—you know, editorials in the school newspaper, arguments in the halls?"

"Maybe."

"Don't you see?" Craig insisted. "The connection isn't the team—everybody plays football. The connection is a bunch of smart guys asking too many questions. Maybe Public Safety got pissed."

"But that would mean—" Hennesey's face rolled through a series of expressions, ending up in total confusion. "That means it's all a setup. I'm not a Depriver—maybe half the people here aren't really Deprivers!"

Craig had only thought this through Step One. Step Two terrified him. "Sounds like a narco-sicko plot to me," he muttered under his breath.

Hennesey started laughing, a strange sound in that grim, barred room.

"Hey, shut up," Craig hissed. "The guard thinks I'm here to dump on you."

"But that's it, isn't it? Everyone was panicked, wanted to be safe again, so Public Safety pulled on the jackboots and really cleaned things up. And I believed that crap. I thought I was infected."

"We don't know for sure," Craig cautioned. "We're just guessing."

Hennesey paused and nodded. "You're right. But we can find out." He held out his hand, ready to shake. "And that's our *de facto* proof that Public Safety is victimizing innocent citizens."

Craig looked at the outstretched hand. *Aw shit,* he thought. Hennesey was probably dead right, but it didn't make the moment any easier. But the thought kept surfacing that if the situation were reversed . . .

With a sigh, he loosed the arm seal on the safety suit and pulled off a glove. "I never did like you, Hennesey," he muttered.

THE COMPANION

LISA D. WILLIAMSON

The grass leading down to the pond has that too-wet, Crayola green color that it gets in the early spring. The willow by the edge leans gracefully over the water, shading two swans that desultorily look for food.

The tree reminds me of an old adage, the one about how oaks are strong, but they break, where willows survive because they bend. I think that willows probably break, too. It just takes longer.

Jack reaches up as if he has been reading my mind, as if to pat my hand. But our habits are too ingrained and he merely rests his hand on his own shoulder.

This little, insignificant movement jolts me. Even so small a gesture will be impossible soon. My brief stab of self-pity turns to guilt. And I resent the guilt. Not an easy time for Jack and me.

Jack has Multiple Sclerosis, a hideous disease. It takes everything from you, but slowly. This is what God would have done to Job if he'd thought about it. Of the many diseases you could name from in the latter half of the twentieth century, this one is particularly cruel, because you can only sit and watch as everything leaves you. Your abilities, your self-control, your freedom, your friends. Only your mind remains, a silent, screaming witness.

There is, however, one disease that is worse. Depriver Syndrome.

And Jack has that, too.

It's almost like a bad joke. Jack and I, in our better gallows-humor moods, wonder what will happen next. "Bad luck comes in threes" has a particular resonance for us.

In unspoken agreement, Jack and I prepare to go back to the car. After a long, dull winter, we have tried to escape our cabin fever by running away to the park. But by the time I load up everything, Jack readies himself, and we get his motorized wheelchair situated into the van, we're both exhausted and testy. Neither of us trusts his go-cart in the wet earth, especially after his last spill, and my shoes always seem to fill up with cold, muddy water no matter how careful I am, but still we go, day after day. It's marginally better than staying home, where we have long since run out of things to say to each other.

It's not so much that we have stopped loving each other, but I think the hurt is so overwhelming, we've each had to insulate ourselves from it, which means isolating ourselves. And what good would talking do, anyway?

As we pull back into our parking space at the apartment complex, we see Mr. Bradley. I know he doesn't lie in wait for us, but sometimes it's hard to believe that the frequency with which we run into him is mere coincidence. But even Mr. Bradley couldn't be that relentless.

He's an ordinary looking man, with a round face. It's a shame that he and Jack are adversaries. They are the only two at this end of the complex who are at home during the day. Mr. Bradley, although only in his fifties, has a severe heart problem that renders him as disabled in his way as Jack. But the two will never be friends. Mr. Bradley has made Jack his obsession, rather than a companion.

In a way, it's my fault. At the beginning, when we first moved in here about three years ago, I tried to make Jack and Mr. Bradley friends. It seemed so perfect. They are both so alone in their illnesses. I tried to orchestrate a friendship, not realizing how jealous Mr. Bradley was of Jack. Jack has me. Mr. Bradley has no one. He is too bitter, too angry to be able to accept Jack. So, instead of finding the perfect solution to Jack's isolation, I have really screwed things up.

Mr. Bradley is convinced Jack is a Depriver.

"Jack," Mr. Bradley nods as he watches the van's lift settle Jack onto the ground. "Rebecca." He nods to me as well, but does not once take his eyes off Jack. "Getting any better, Jack?"

"MS is not something that gets better, Mr. Bradley," I say bitterly as Jack and I go up the ramp to our door. Mr. Bradley knows that, of course, but our conversations are always about what we don't say, rather than what we do. And we have to handle Mr. Bradley carefully—no pun intended. Right now, he's looked upon as the community eccentric, and we want it to remain that way. The moment someone starts paying any attention to Mr. Bradley, we're in serious trouble. We've seen what's happened to other Deprivers.

It's hard to say which came first for Jack, the Depriver symptoms or the MS. I think it was the Deprivers, and that that was what brought on his MS, but Jack thinks perhaps he'd already begun feeling the MS symptoms, and it just hadn't registered yet. Since they both center on the nervous system, I think they're intertwined, but we may never find out.

The first documented case of Deprivers was discovered about fifteen years ago, in the late nineties, although now there are apocryphal reports of possible cases as early as the fifties, generating new speculation about Deprivers being a nuclear-caused mutation.

The early days were crazy. People were in such a panic, they never stopped to have a rational thought. Deprivers were shunned, persecuted, locked up, or murdered, depending on what neighborhood, state or country they were in. All sorts of wild rumors sprang up, as well as instant "experts." And, of course, there were the religious zealots. You'd have thought that God would get tired of sending diseases down to punish people, but the righteous seemed to know better.

Although Jack and I weren't particularly caught up in the mass panic, Deprivers was something you thought about—you couldn't help it: Every second ad on the bus, every other public service announcement on the radio, and every headline, day after day, screamed and warned and howled about Deprivers.

The theories went from the thoughtful to the ludicrous. Agent Orange, nuclear mutation, Iraqi bacterial weapons were all examined and discarded as causes, and then taken up again in a new wave of hysteria. Genetic mutation, a new super-race, God's punishment, all these and more were introduced as the theory of the week, fanning the madness further.

We used to sit with our friends and discuss these theories, how ridiculous they were. Of course, we never see our old friends anymore.

Crazy notions and superstitions cropped up weekly. People were afraid to use public bathrooms. It was said that if a Depriver touched you, there was a permanent scar on that spot. My personal favorite was the blue flash. That is, until Jack and I were almost caught.

Jack had just confessed to me the previous week that he

was fairly sure he was a Depriver. That sounds silly. With all the hysteria, you'd figure you'd know instantly. Not true. Contact has to be skin-on-skin, and not every contact will bring about an episode.

We were still newly apprehensive, looking for signs, wary of contact with strangers. Jack was fairly certain he had the kind of Deprivers that paralyzed people, the kind that deprives the sense of touch, which causes all sorts of chaos in the nervous system. Jack didn't know about the MS yet. He was still walking at that point.

A little boy ran up to us on the street downtown. I remember him now as a round, piggish-looking child, but that may be hindsight. He stopped dead in front of Jack, pointed at him, and screamed, "Mommy, that man has a blue cloud around him!"

Everybody had heard the rumor that once you've been Deprived, you can spot Deprivers because of a blue aura that surrounds them. Like the Caribbean's Green Flash, or UFOs, there's never been any proof, but in those days no one needed proof of anything.

My heart stopped. I looked out of the corner of my eye at Jack, who was equally stricken. We stood there, feeling everyone's gaze on us, unable to move. Not knowing what to do.

The moment stopped when the boy's mother slapped the child on the back of the head and snapped "I told you not to do that, Brendan Michael. Cut it out." She grabbed him by the hand and dragged him off. Jack and I remained motionless, while the people around us visibly relaxed and moved on. But it was these near-miss episodes that drove us further into isolation.

Winter was always the best. You put on gloves, scarves, hats; you bundled up so no one could touch you. The summers were a bit dicier. We stopped using public transportation and Jack refused to go to the pool. I told him it was ridiculous—Deprivers couldn't be caught in a pool, but it was one of those idiosyncratic fancies I couldn't argue him out of.

The MS has made our life hell. Visits to the doctor are usually okay. Not that the doctor knows—we have learned from all the stories we've heard not to confide in anyone. But doctors, already cautious from the AIDS epidemic, have swathed themselves to the eyeballs and are fully protected. So too the dentists and any other healthcare providers. It's the other people.

They see Jack in a wheelchair, and they stretch their hands out to help him. It's as if everyone feels nobody could be inflicted with two horrible diseases. If only that were true. Jack has assumed a haughty don't-treat-me-like-an-invalid kind of attitude, which is antithetical to his nature, and obviously hurtful to the people who are trying to help him. But in today's atmosphere, one can't afford sentimentality.

Once inside, I make dinner, our usual macrobiotic one of brown rice and vegetables. Neither of us thinks it's doing anything, and the meal fails to satisfy, but somehow we are unable to stop. It's like wearing your lucky socks. You just do it.

The long evening stretches ahead. I'll go to sleep in a couple of hours, before heading out to my job. I'm a computer programmer, and can fortunately work in the dead of night when Jack's safe. I stopped sleeping well years ago, so I barely notice my moments of snatched sleep.

A warm, damp breeze wafts in from the windows. Jack looks at me questioningly. I think sometimes he's amazed I've stood by him, and he's afraid to ask for anything directly. But I nod, and we prepare for one last foray outside today.

There's a lot we don't discuss. I'm sometimes amazed

myself that I've stayed. Not that I feel there's any other choice, but I do on occasion wonder how other people handle a Depriver relationship. Why do I stay? If not me, then who? Do I ever feel trapped? In all honesty, yes. But not by Jack. And Jack is just as trapped as I am.

I open the door and let Jack go down the ramp first. When I turn back from locking the door, there is Mr. Bradley on the sidewalk in front of us. How does he do that? Why is he always around? Is he, perhaps, the third part of our bad luck?

We start on our walk, Jack and I, shadowed by Mr. Bradley. Although I refuse to look at him, I know he has his eyes locked on Jack. He always does. But when he speaks, it's to me. It's as if Jack and I are one being in two bodies. In a way, we are.

"Association meeting's tonight," Mr. Bradley says. There is a monthly meeting for the people who live in this complex, a homeowners' meeting for grievances, information, and general gossip. We avoid it, as we've learned to avoid every social gathering. Mr. Bradley attends each one. Jack is his favorite grievance.

"I know," I answer, looking down at Jack. He smiles slightly. Thank God the neighbors all think of Mr. Bradley as a bit nutty. Jack and I used to have an act. I would dramatically touch Jack, skin-to-skin, then hope and pray nothing happened. It was our little game of Deprivers Roulette that had convinced the neighbors that Mr. Bradley was eccentric.

"I know about Anita Sanky, down by the 7-Eleven." Mr. Bradley lays this bombshell out for us with calm satisfaction. "She still can't use her right arm."

Neither Jack nor I knew the woman's name, but we certainly remember the incident. It was last month, on our way home from an outing. We stopped at an unfamiliar convenience store a few miles out of town for some groceries. As usual, there was someone who wanted to help Jack. I normally can run interference, and Jack's aloof attitude staves off whoever I miss. But there was an older woman who slipped in between our defenses.

Before we knew it, she took down the box of rice Jack had been reaching for, laid it in his lap, and stroked his cheek.

"Is it MS?" she asked. "My son in Augusta has it. What a terrible thing, poor dear."

We were rooted to the spot in horror, but only for a second. Jack murmured something and I walked in a wooden, cautious-but-hurried way to get the door. He put the rice on the counter on his way out, and we were in the van and away from the store faster than we would have thought possible. Fortunately, the van was parked at the side, so we were fairly certain that no one would be able to identify us. We might have used the store once in the ten years we'd lived in the area, so they didn't know us there. Plus, since Deprivers is such an iffy thing, the woman might never know she'd touched a Depriver. We scanned the newspapers for the next few days, but saw nothing.

Obviously Mr. Bradley knows more than we do.

Jack and I had stopped, and now I turn to look at Mr. Bradley. He has been hounding us from the day we moved into this complex three years ago. We have been so careful, but nothing protects against an obsession.

I think of begging. But looking at Mr. Bradley's obdurate face, I don't even bother.

"I knew it all along," Mr. Bradley whispers at me, while he looks at Jack. "I knew you'd slip sometime. I heard about Anita from a friend of mine the other day. No one knows but me. I'm the one who figured it out. Everyone else will know tonight."

I step forward. I am afraid. Who wouldn't be, who's seen

what has happened to Deprivers and their protectors over the last years? But the fear is subsumed by anger.

"Damn you," I say. I grab him by his shirt. I only realize how forceful I'm being when a button pops off. Sparse, surprisingly dark hair shows through the gap. But I'm beyond proprieties.

"Damn you," I repeat, more loudly this time. "Is this what it's all about? You'd ruin our lives so you can tell everyone you knew it all along?"

"Why should he have everything? I have nothing." Mr. Bradley says this defiantly, but there's an underlying whine to his voice that enrages me further. Especially when you consider all that Mr. Bradley has that Jack does not.

I only know I'm shaking Mr. Bradley when Jack's voice penetrates my consciousness. I look at Mr. Bradley, whose face has become white and sweaty. He grabs my hand, where I am still holding on to his shirt, and slowly sinks to the ground.

"My pills," Mr. Bradley whispers shakily. "I don't have them. They're in my house. You have to help me." His head drops against the sidewalk with a small thump. His labored breathing seems very loud in the evening air. I look, but no one is around. No one has seen.

I look up from where I'm squatting next to Mr. Bradley's supine body. It's the first time Jack has been taller than me for a while.

"My God, Jack, I've killed him."

Kneeling by Mr. Bradley, holding his hand, I keep an eye out for passersby. Has it really come to this? How will Jack and I cope with this latest disaster? Mr. Bradley truly is the third part of our bad luck.

I can't seem to let go of Mr. Bradley's hand—not so old-looking, the skin a bit papery, a few age spots, but not so old.

Jack moves his chair closer to Mr. Bradley and looks

down. Mr. Bradley's chest is moving up and down in a strained, unnatural rhythm.

Jack, moving slowly, leans heavily against the handlebars with one arm so he won't fall, and reaches down to Mr. Bradley. He holds my gaze while he slips his hand through the gap in Mr. Bradley's shirt and places it gently but firmly over Mr. Bradley's heart.

"Not you, Rebecca," Jack said. "Not you."

We watch as the paralysis takes hold. And I look back up at Jack, my eyes filling with the tears I haven't shed, not once in all these years.

THE ONLY ONE

LEAH RYAN

I hear vague strains of country music over the PA. It's the radio. The reception is bad. I finger the two-dollar cassette tapes near the register, while the worker kid behind the counter eyes me suspiciously. *25 Favorite Harmonica Tunes. Convoy and Other Trucker Hits.* But then there's George Thorogood. What's he doing here? *Bad To The Bone*, I think. But that tune isn't on the tape. It's a collection of early stuff. Probably lame. But for two bucks . . .

I can feel this trucker's eyes on my head. It's like a laser beam that I can see. I decide to pass on the tape. "Pack of Marlboro, box," I tell the worker kid. He reaches. I glance to my left and I see that the trucker is dawdling by the window decals, waiting to make a move. I get my cigarettes, thank the kid as cordially as I can, and head into the coffee shop.

It's full of truckers. A few families. Locals, they come here because they know all the waitresses. Both the waitresses are probably thirtyish but look older, with washed-out blond hair that they color at home in the kitchen sink while their kids sleep and their husbands channel surf in the next room. I find a seat in a booth and pick up the huge laminated menu. I'm more interested in having a smoke, so I light one. The waitresses sprint around like deer.

"Coffee?" My waitress asks, eyeing my gloves.

"Please," I reply, smiling, hoping to ease her discomfort. I could have ended up like that, if The Institute's experiment had worked. Normal. Right. I look at the menu again. Not hungry. Since I took up smoking again I'm skinny as a rail. I look younger than I am. I open my wallet to see how much cash I have. Ten bucks. I'll have to hit the ATM. I'm not sure how much money I have in the bank, and I don't know if the truck stop ATM will tell me. I figure I'll just have coffee and leave a good tip.

Putting the wallet away, I glimpse John's picture. I can't resist taking a long look, even though I don't want to. I hate this picture, but it's the only one I have of him so I keep it. The picture was taken at The Institute, just after they cut his hair. John had beautiful hair, thick and straight and chest-nut brown. When he was committed, it hung down to the middle of his back. I told him once it was the color of one of those shimmering brown carriage horses in Central Park. We were kids then. He'd never been to Central Park. I told him we'd go when we got out of there. I said "when," not "if," even though I didn't know if we ever would. In the picture, he's sitting in the cafeteria, wearing a Pearl Jam T-Shirt under his pajamas. Even though it's a long shot, you can see the black circles around his eyes. You can see his Adam's apple protruding more than it should. In fact, you can even see its shadow. But John is smiling. It's a real smile, not a picture smile.

"Want some company?" the trucker asks. He's the one that was eyeing me before. He doesn't fit the typical middle-aged jowely trucker profile. He's maybe thirty-five, blond and not bad looking.

"No thanks," I say without guile. He sits down anyway. I put out my smoke and immediately light another.

"That's bad for you, you know," he tells me. I glance at the square bulge in his breast pocket.

"So I've heard," I say.

"You look like you're just wandering around here all alone," he says. This is a lousy line to use on me if you want to be my friend. I'm alone, yeah. But I know what I'm doing.

"I'm fine," I tell him.

"Coffee?" The waitress asks him.

"Yeah," he says. "Two eggs over easy, bacon, home-fries . . ."

"Wait a minute," I interrupt. "You're not sitting here."

"I'll come back," the waitress says, and she glides away.

"I was hoping you wouldn't mind," he says. "There aren't any other booths left."

"I don't want to be nasty," I begin. "But I'd really rather not have you sitting here."

"I'm not going to bite you," he tells me.

"I'm sure you're not," I say.

"You meeting your boyfriend here?"

"No."

"On your way somewhere?"

I don't say anything. I pick up my menu.

"Just trying to make conversation," he says innocently.

"I don't want to make conversation," I reply. "If you need to sit here, okay. But whatever else you have in mind, conversation or whatever, just assume I'm not interested. Okay?"

"Deal," he says, and hails the waitress. I know this isn't going to work, but I'm sick of arguing. I look at his hands. They're thick and blunt, with short, manicured nails. Clean for a trucker. He lights a cigarette.

John's fingers were long and thin, like the rest of him. At sixteen, John was six-foot-three. His hands were rough and shiny from working in the dishroom of his mother's restaurant. When he arrived at The Institute, I'd been there for six months and I hadn't said a single word. They had my case history on their computers; they knew everything there was to know. Still, they wanted me to talk. I wouldn't. First they tried to reason with me. Then they tried drugging me. They tried locking me up in solitary for days on end. One morning they let me out and sent me to the caf for breakfast. They didn't explain—I wondered what they were going to try next. I walked into the caf and there was John, sitting with a bunch of other kids. An instant celebrity. He was drumming on the table with his hands, recounting a concert he'd recently been to. I walked right over to him, my heart pounding.

"Hey, you," John said.

"She can't talk," one of the other kids told him.

"She's a dummy," rejoined another.

"Can't talk, or don't talk?" he asked, looking at me.

"Who cares?" one of the kids said.

"I think don't," John said. I let him meet my gaze. I felt myself starting to smile. He made room for me on the bench next to him and I sat down.

"She killed some guys," one of the kids said.

"Cool," John replied. I could feel the heat from his arm on mine.

John said later that when he first saw me, something went "click" in his head.

There's nothing clicking in this trucker's head. More likely in his boxer shorts. He mops up egg with his toast, not talking only because his mouth is full. After he's done he lights another cigarette.

"Married?" he asks.

"Separated," I say. Well, gone, anyway. I'm gone. So I guess we're separated.

"Legally?"

"Why, you shopping for a wife?"

"Not me," he says. "Free agent all the way."

"Smart."

"You ever cheat on your husband?"

"That's none of your business," I say. The waitress takes away his plates.

"I'll take that as a yes," he says. I tell him he can take it any way he wants to. The waitress comes back with the coffee pot and the trucker tells me he's headed west, to Chicago, making a stop in Kalamazoo. My heart starts to pound. Shit. That figures.

"You're more than welcome to join me," he says, reaching for his wallet. I gnaw my thumbnail and think. Dr. Salzberg lives in Wheaton, a suburb of Chicago. If I can get to Chicago, I can probably get on a bus from there. It shouldn't cost too much. I remember that I have to check my bank balance. I pull out my crumpled ten and the trucker waves it away. "I'll get this," he says.

I look at him. He's probably all right, I think. Lots of truckers are just desperately lonely. Many of them will just settle for having some company, someone to talk to. The real psychos are cruising the highways in cars looking for someone to mess with. If I can set some ground rules with this guy, I figure, I can get to Chicago fast and cheap, which is what I came here for.

"Listen," I say, "I'd love a lift to Chicago. We can talk or whatever. But I can't fool around."

"No problem," he says.

"I really mean it," I tell him. "It isn't even just that I don't want to. I can't. It's a long story. You have to know up front that it's out of the question."

"Sure thing," he says. I know he's going to try anyway. But I also know that I could report him for picking up a passenger and he could lose his job. It's a trump card I can pull out later if I need to.

"I just need to hit the bank machine," I tell him as we rise from the table.

"You bet," he says. "But don't worry, I'll take care of you."

Truckers do that. The single ones spend all their time on the road, making loads of money. Then they forget how to spend it. Whenever I traveled by truck, I was kept fed and stocked with cigarettes. This used to make me nervous, until I realized that most of them didn't expect anything in return, other than the comfort of having someone there to ride beside them and help them stay awake. I'd rather let a trucker feed me for a week than let a guy buy me a beer in a bar.

Seventy-three dollars and fifty-seven cents. I withdraw ten bucks, wincing. It's all I have in the world. I've been closer to the edge before, when I was younger. But that was different. I was used to it, and I felt like I had nothing to lose. It didn't matter, somehow.

The trucker buys us each a carton of cigarettes and a six-pack of RC Cola. He fuels up and I hoist myself into the passenger's seat. I'd forgotten how huge eighteen-wheeler cabs are. It makes me feel tiny. I'd forgotten also, about the vibration. If it's just right, it makes my cheeks and neck itch.

The great thing about riding with truckers is that it makes you hard to find. It had taken a week for the cops to find me after the last incident, fifteeen years ago; the one that had landed me in The Institute. I was one of the first hundred kids to be sent there, and one of the last to leave before they shut it down.

After breakfast the day that John arrived, there was a recreation period. We were released into a yard that was surrounded by a high fence topped with razor wire. John and I sat on a bench.

"What do you do?" he asked.

"I blind. Just for a couple hours." Talking felt strange. I hadn't spoken in a long time. My voice was hoarse.

"Me, too," he said.

"No shit?"

"No shit."

"How'd you get here?" I asked.

"I was using it as, like...a party game. We'd get wasted...and then I could get them blind. Kids told their parents. They came into my math class and carried me off one day."

"Ugh."

"How about you?"

"Oh, it's a long story."

"So does this place, like, suck, or is it just my imagination?"

"It, like, sucks," I said, and smiled. "What have they done to you so far?"

"They put these electrode things on my head. And they give me pills."

"What kind of pills?"

"Blue caps. And triangular white pills."

They were trying out a new treatment on him. A special thing just for boys.

"You have therapy yet?"

"Yeah," he said, "But that's easy. I just tell them what

they want to hear. You know. I deprived because I was insecure. I really want to be normal. I don't need to be special.
Blah blah blah."

"Right."

"I'm going to jam out of here so fast," he said. Then he
paused. "You don't talk, huh?"

"I hate them," I said simply.

"You gotta start talking, babydoll. Just play their game
for a while. Then you can get out."

"They won't really let us out until they know we can't
deprive anymore. The psychology is just part of it. They
want to fix us. Physically."

"Whatever. We'll be out in no time. Promise me you'll
start talking. I'm not leaving you in here."

"Maybe. I hate them though. They're evil."

"So what? It doesn't matter. Just tell them what they
want to hear."

"It won't be enough," I said. His gloved fingers reached
for my hair, then stopped and fell into his lap.

"Were you born with it?" he asked.

"No, I got it when I was twelve. You?"

"Born freak," he said.

"Can you meet me after lights out?" I asked.

"Thought you'd never ask," he said. "Where?"

"The lock on the laundry room was broken last time I
checked. I've been in solitary, so I don't know if they fixed it
or not."

"We'll try it," he said. The buzzer sounded.

Telling them what they want to hear is a trick I learned from
John. The trucker asks me about my husband and I tell the
parts of the truth that I know he'll like.

"He was my foster brother," I say. This is true.

"Wow," says the trucker.

THE ONLY ONE

"I was raised in an orphanage." Lie. I was raised by my natural parents, until they disowned me. "I was sick for a long time, in the hospital." Sort of true. "I was taken in as a foster kid when I was a teenager." True. "There were three boys and me. I was the only foster kid. The middle boy was about my age and we kind of fell for each other." Lie. He fell for me. Rather, he fell for the idea of me. He fell for pity. He pitied me and he pitied himself. He learned this from his parents, who had taken me in after seeing my picture in the newspaper. "I got married at eighteen." True.

"Any kids?" he asks.

"No." Not much sex, either. He was scared by the blindness. More often, he'd quietly masturbate beside me. I don't know if he thought I didn't notice, or if he didn't care. As for me, I'd just lie there and think about John. I used to wish that I could blind myself, so that maybe I could make love to my husband and pretend.

"I lied before," the trucker tells me now. We're tailgating a Subaru, scaring them to death. "I am married."

"Oh, really?"

"She goes with other guys all the time. Thinks I don't know. I know."

"Are you sure?"

"Oh yeah. I'm sure." The Subaru changes lanes and the trucker accelerates.

"That's too bad," I say.

"How 'bout if we just kiss with our clothes on? I promise I won't . . ."

"No," I say. "Sorry. It's nothing personal, really."

"Okay. Hungry?"

"Kind of," I lie. I'm too anxious to be hungry. I'm thinking about the note I left on the kitchen table, weighted with a crystal salt shaker we'd gotten as a wedding present:

203

I'm Very Sorry. I Had To Go.
Thank You For Understanding. I Love You.

Lie.

He downshifts, and we pull off the highway into a truck stop. It's dusk. Cars fly by. I get the loneliest feeling all of the sudden. I climb out of the truck and I realize that there are tears rolling down my face. I can't control it. I reach for my cigarettes. The trucker comes around to my side, thinking he needs to help me down. He doesn't know I'm an old hand. He sees my tears and he reaches for me, a reflex. It's a good reflex. I don't cry often. The few times I cried in front of my husband he couldn't deal with it, said he didn't know what he was supposed to do. It's safe to let the trucker hold me, so I do. He's put on a jacket. I realize I'm cold. It only takes a few minutes for me to stop crying. I get my coat from the truck. Miraculously, the trucker asks no questions. I go right to the bathroom and clean myself up. When I sit down at the table, I'm starving.

"Get whatever you want," he says.

"Thanks," I say.

"Are you okay?"

"Yeah, I am. Thanks. Sorry I lost it like that. It just came out of nowhere."

"No problem," he says.

"Hey what's your name?" I ask him, deciding to have a chicken sandwich and fries. I don't usually eat meat but tonight I feel depleted.

"Dan," he says, and smiles. "What's yours?"

"Linda," I say quickly.

Lie.

"You're one of those Deprivers, aren't you?" he asks. I nod.

"Must be rough," he says.

"It's interesting," I tell him.

The waitress arrives before he can ask any more questions. On the spot, I decide to have a milkshake.

"Go for it," Dan says.

By the time we get back on the road, it's dark. I ask Dan if he minds if I sleep for a while. He seems surprised that I ask. He doesn't mind.

After bed check, I tiptoed to the laundry room and pushed the door. It was open. John was already there, sitting on top on a washing machine, his long legs dangling almost to the floor.

"Hey, babydoll," he said. We both wore The Institute's regulation nightwear: long-sleeved pajamas not much different from what we wore during the day, white cotton socks and soft white cotton gloves. He hopped off the machine and came toward me.

"I want to kiss you," he said.

"Wait," I told him, and started unbuttoning my shirt.

"Yeah, yeah, we should see each other before our lights go out." Impatient, I pulled my shirt over my head. I wasn't embarrassed or afraid. When I kissed him, the room started to darken.

"Can you see me?" he asked.

"A little," I said. "Can you see me?"

"No. It sucks."

"I'm stronger than you," I teased.

"Oh yeah?" he teased back, pushing me gently against a dryer. I could still see the faint outline of his facial features. I was losing it, though.

"You're fading," I said.

"No, I'm not," he replied. I lost all my sight and I didn't

care. The concrete floor was cool and smooth. I kept one hand buried in his hair, thinking about the color I knew it was; the color of the horses.

"I wish I had a cigarette," I said later.

"That's so corny," he said.

"No it's not."

"I guess you should know. I've never done this before."

"You liar," I said.

"Yeah, you're right."

"How many girls have you done it with?" I asked.

"Just two."

"Including me?"

"Three. You're the best."

"Oh, cut it out."

"No way, it's true." I felt his hand on the back of my neck.

"Did it scare them?"

"Yeah. I tried to, like, warn them. But they were scared."

"How about you?"

"What?"

"How many?" I sensed him leaning up on an elbow. We were lying on the concrete floor.

"I dunno," I said.

"Don't know or don't want to talk about it?" he asked. I didn't say anything. "It doesn't matter," he said.

"I don't think I want to talk about it."

"What if this is the last time we get to be together like this?" he asked. I knew that it very well could be. If we got caught, they'd watch us like hawks. Restrict us, put us in solitary. Anything could happen. I wanted to tell him, suddenly. People knew, but I'd never told anybody. I'd never said the words. I tried to form the words in my head. It took a while.

"Babydoll?"

"Hmm?"

"Sleeping?"

"No," I said. "Thinking."

In Kalamazoo, I check the ATM again. One thousand, sixty-three dollars and fifty-seven cents. My husband. He's deposited a grand into my account. Stunned, I don't withdraw anything. It occurs to me as I remove my card that he could be trying to trace me. Would he do that? I'm not sure. I don't touch the money. I let Dan buy me dinner again. He doesn't seem to mind. He tells me more about his wife, how he'd gotten shitfaced when he found out about her and this other guy. Then he found out there had been others, and he got really shitfaced. I tell him that my husband and I didn't really understand each other, we'd gotten married too young. This seems to make sense to him.

I have to hide in the truck while it's weighed. We're not far from Chicago. I'm getting nervous. I have to get the address. Then I have to get there. Once I'm there, I'll know what to do.

"Is Chicago your final stop?" I ask Dan once we're back on the road. The landscape is dull and flat.

"After I unload, I go back to Buffalo. I have two days off. Then I do it again. Why?"

"Just wondering."

"You visiting family . . . or friends in Chicago?" he asks.

"My only surviving relative," I say, "lives in Wheaton." The lie comes easily.

"Wheaton. That's a suburb, right?"

"Yeah, it's not too far."

"How you getting there?"

"Not sure yet."

"Are they expecting you?"

"Not exactly," I say. "It's a great uncle. He's widowed, retired. A Doctor."

"You surprising him?"

"Yeah."

"Well, don't kill him," Dan says.

"What?" I say, alarmed.

"You know, with the shock. Don't give him a heart attack."

"Oh. I won't." The sun is coming up. I feel tired again.

"Why are you so quiet?" John asked me after about ten minutes.

"I feel sick," I said. I really thought I was going to throw up.

"Take some deep breaths," he said.

I tried. The sick feeling came and went as I told him. I told him everything. How my father would take me for drives in the country when I was a kid and how he did things to me. How I found out I'd become a Depriver at a junior high school dance when I touched a boy I liked and blinded him. How I ran away from home and started hitch-hiking all over. How I figured out that if I got into a car with a guy and he made a move on me, I could touch him, blind him, jump out of the car and watch him crash. How I had a system. I'd get out of my seat belt if I was wearing one, and unlock the door. I'd get him to slow down, one hand on the door handle. I'd tell him about all the things I was going to do to him. Then I'd touch him, grab his hand. And jump. I'd roll into the ditch and then I'd watch. I could have died, but I didn't care. Some of the accidents were bad. Sometimes people died. I told him how I'll never drive a car, ever. How I felt safe in trucks because they were so big and truckers were always nice to me. Truckers would hide me. Of course I got caught eventually, and sent to The Institute.

I told him how I liked watching the accidents. I'd see my victim careen into the wrong lane, or slam on the brakes and skid. I'd watch the chain reaction. It was the panic that got them, more than the blindness.

I didn't cry when I told him. My sight started to come back when I was through. Still blind, he reached for me and buried his face in my hair. The concrete floor felt hard and I leaned into him.

We got caught. They found us just like that, naked on the floor.

"You could rent a car in Chicago," Dan suggests. We're on the expressway on our way into the city.

"I don't drive," I tell him.

"Right," he says. "That's why you're here."

"Right."

"Well, it was nice having you," he says. I can tell he means it.

"Thanks," I say. "I really appreciate it."

"Well, how are you going to get there?" he asks.

"Maybe take a bus," I say. I'm really not sure.

"I can take you if you want," he offers.

"It's the suburbs, though," I say. "You can't take this thing there."

"I can get you close, probably."

"It's out of your way."

"It's no big deal," he says. "I'm in no hurry to get home."

They put me in solitary for a week. Meanwhile, they used John as a human guinea pig. When they let me out at breakfast time, I found him sitting in the caf by himself. His hair was cut short. He was so tired he could barely sit up. That was the day they were taking pictures. In the picture, it looks like he's smiling for the camera. But really, he was smiling at me.

Dr. Salzman was the director of The Institute. I found him hanging out in the day room, trying to be cool with all the kids. I asked him what they were doing to John.

"We're trying to cure him," he said. "Just like we're trying to cure you."

"He looks horrible."

"The treatment for boys is different, you know that." He rose from his chair.

"Not that different," I said. He led me out into the hall.

"Your problems are more psychological. Look at you. You're talking. You're getting better. John's problems are more physical."

"That's bullshit," I said.

"Did you ever know anybody who had cancer? Doctors give them drugs that sometimes make them sicker before it heals them."

"Yeah, I know about that. You're telling me you're giving John chemotherapy? He's not sick."

"It's not chemotherapy. It's like chemotherapy. We know what we're doing. I'm sorry, I have an appointment, I have to go. Feel free to approach me with any other questions you have." He broke away from my angry gaze and strode down the hall. The next day, John was in the infirmary. He was there for four days. I visited for the one hour per day that was allowed. I told him about the carriage horses. He told me about the click in his head. They put all the pictures they had taken up on a bulletin board in the day room, and I stole the one of John and the one of me. I was on probation, and this got me another week in solitary.

I knew he'd be dead when I got out. It was an unfortunate accident, they said, something about a heart condition that they didn't know he had. Really, they just killed him with drugs. Experimenting. Trying to find a way to normalize us all, at any cost.

"I'm not even really sure where my uncle lives," I confess to Dan.

"Can't you just call him?"

"I really want to surprise him," I say. We devise a plan. Dan leaves me at a diner, goes to make his delivery. I use the phone book. I get the address, and then find a store nearby. I call the store and ask for directions. I hit the ATM and take out three hundred bucks, which is my daily limit.

John wouldn't want me to kill Dr. Salzman. Even if he knew that five more kids had died after him. Revenge wasn't John's style. It's mine.

When Dan comes back, I buy him a meal. I tell him I have the directions, that there's a truck stop near enough to the house that I can call a cab and get there easily. I can't believe he wants to do this for me with no promise of sexual reward. Then the questions come.

"So what do you do?" he asks.

"For a living?"

"No. You know . . ."

"Oh, that. I don't really like to talk about it, actually."

"Would it kill me?"

"Only if you were driving," I say.

"How long . . ."

"No more questions," I tell him. "I'm sorry."

"Okay," he says. But I know it isn't over.

It takes us about half an hour to get to Wheaton. At the truck stop, I call a cab. I hug Dan when the cab comes, thank him for everything.

"How long do you think you'll be?" he asks.

"Just a short visit," I say. "he's old. Maybe an hour."

"I can wait for you," he says.

"No, don't do that," I say. It strikes me that neither of us really have any place to go.

"Maybe I will."

"You can if you want," I say. I'm not sure what I mean by this. I wave good-bye from the cab.

Dr. Salzman is sitting alone in front of the television on a quiet suburban street, just like a retired murderer should. The door's open. I push the screen door in and yank the gloves off.

"Hello?" I call sweetly.

"Hello, who's there?" he replies.

"It's me," I say, stepping in to the living room. He's shocked. We didn't part on especially good terms all those years ago. They kept me pretty sedated after John died but Dr. Salzman knew I hated his guts.

"Oh. Well. How are you?" he starts to rise from his chair.

"Oh, don't get up," I place my bare palm on his bald head and push him back down. He's blinded immediately. I grab an urn from the mantle that I'd spotted on my way in. I assume it contains his wife's ashes.

"You killed the only one," I say as I bring the urn down. I want him to know why I'm killing him, even if he doesn't care.

When I get back to the truck stop, I see that Dan is still there. He's leaning on his truck. He waves when he sees me. He wears sunglasses. I wave back from across the lot, use my gloved hand to shade my eyes.

What now? I'm not sure. I have a thousand dollars and no plans. I find myself walking toward him.

I've never been to Buffalo.

ANGEL

JANET HARVEY

ARE *YOU* AT RISK?

LEARN TO RECOGNIZE THE WARNING SIGNS OF UNDIAGNOSED DEPRI-
VATION:

- * LOSS OF PERIPHERAL VISION
- * IMPAIRED HEARING OR RINGING IN THE EARS
- * NUMBNESS IN THE EXTREMITIES

IF YOU BELIEVE THAT YOU, OR SOMEONE YOU LOVE, MAY HAVE COME
INTO CONTACT WITH A DEPRIVER, CALL THE DEPRIVER INFORMATION
NETWORK AT 1–800–DEP–INFO. WE'RE HERE TO HELP.

Fitz was, frankly, sick of it. The warning signs. The
public service announcements. The cheap lawyers, the
foot treatments, the skin doctors. The rush hour ride
had become one long gauntlet of inexorable human contact,
deodorant smell, screaming brakes and bad design—all of
which grated intolerably on Fitz's nerves.

More than usual, he thought *More than it used to.* He
shut his eyes against the fluorescent glare, focusing on the
work he still had to do on the account that was due today.

Five initial concept designs for the toothpaste company. So far he'd come up with four, and three of them, he knew, were too daring.

"Fitz, these are good, but they're too sophisticated for the target audience," Gordon would say. "Orville & Johnson are known for delivering consistency—clear, commercial, solid designs. You need to make it more accessible, bring it back to the audience."

His eyes flew open as the subway ground to a stop at his destination. He left the train and moved swiftly, in the crowd, up the stairs to work. *What is wrong with me?* he thought. *It's her it's her.* He stepped into the dirty morning air, thinking *she started it—no, she's the cure. The cure that makes it worse.* He pushed through the revolving glass door and into the office building.

It's ridiculous to blame her, he thought, switching on the computer. *I mean, come on. It's not like the subway doesn't get on a lot of people's nerves.* He went about his morning routine, getting his coffee, tuning in the alternative radio station and shutting his office door. Insulated from the rest of the office, he settled down to finish design Number 5, willing himself to finish *something* before the design meeting at three o'clock. He stared numbly at the open Adobe files on his screen, wrestling with the persistent desire to go back, to curl up in her bed again and let her take it all away with a touch of her hand.

Good God, he thought, *it's only nine in the morning. . . .*

Fitz rubbed his eyes, covered his face in his hands. He could barely remember the last time he'd allowed himself to get excited about a design, to let himself believe that his excitement about a project would communicate itself to a mass audience. His job sucked, his wife was a stranger and he hadn't had a vacation in years.

* * *

And that's what drove you down there in the first place, wasn't it?

The night he met her, he'd had a shitty day at work—screaming phone calls from the account rep because Fitz was working up to the deadline, the whole concept shot down in the end, three weeks' work wasted. Gordon, smug: *Well, we're not all here to serve your artistic agenda, Fitz.* He'd left the office at five, for once—burnt out, exhausted, in need of a drink. He called Ben, the only one in the old college crowd who was really living the kind of life that they had all joked about in art school. Working in a gallery, hanging shows for minimum wage, eating rice and beans, and painting. Ben could give Fitz what he wanted: a few shots in a smoky basement room talking art among people who didn't have to wear ties. Fitz's wife had been sour when he told her he was going to meet Ben (*"You never talk to me about art any more"*), but Fitz didn't care. He was going to do something for himself for once, goddamn it.

Ben took him to some alternative jazz joint downtown. Plenty of raveling sweaters, bare flesh, matted hair and tattoos, smoke and spilled microbrews. After a few drinks, Fitz was feeling expansive, freer than he'd felt in months. He and Ben talked excitedly until well toward midnight, not even noticing when the trio for the late night gig came in to set up on the small stage. And then the warm deep cello tone of her voice ran through him like a sword and he looked up, and he saw her: tall, defiant, her shorn head framed in the amber background gel.

She was breathtaking. Large dark eyes and full lips, a slim, willowy figure, long-fingered hands that handled the mike gently. And a deep strength that pulled him in—her expression, her flashing eyes, her hands. And her voice. Her contralto voice like a river of honey pouring over him, wry, defiant, vulnerable, passionate, reeling around the tight arrangements, rising to a scream, blending with the deep thrumming bass or the throaty saxophone. Fitz had never even liked jazz, but this was something else. Strong as a narcotic, lethal as speed metal, the trio wailed on their instruments like no jazz band he'd ever heard. The muscular, confident music reached into his gut, breaking open something that had been locked there. The same feeling of pure pleasure he'd once felt only when he lost himself in the colors of a composition, resonating inside him. He felt like he was gasping for breath.

"Fitz?" Ben was looking at him funny. "Don't you have a wife in Westchester, or something?"

"Knock it off, Ben." Fitz reached for the shot of single malt on the bar. "It's a purely aesthetic affinity."

"Well, that's good, 'cause there's something you ought to know about Lydia."

"Lydia?" Her name was Lydia. "You know her?"

"Down, boy." Ben took a swig of his beer. "She's untouchable."

"What, she's gay or something?"

Ben gave him a serious look. After a second, it penetrated Fitz's euphoria. He turned back to the stage in shock.

"Tragic, ain't it? I had a crush on her, too. But believe me, you don't want to go there. She's a mess because of it. Comes off like some kind of *femme fatale*. She's got all these little alternative boys all over her all the time. There's something kinky going on there, but I really *don't* want to know what it is." Ben took another swig of his beer and studied his friend's face. "But I suppose you just want to, like, *congratulate* her on the music, or something."

Fitz spun around, an agonizingly hopeful look on his face.

Ben sighed. "Oh, Jesus."

She was talking to the other band members at the end of the set when they approached her. The saxophone player turned and saw them first. "Hey, man." He and Ben embraced. Lydia stood apart, regarding them evenly.

"Hey, Brigand. Lydia. This is my friend, Fitz."

Fitz put out his hand. "Hey. I really enjoyed the music."

Lydia looked at his hand, then back to his face. Her dark eyes flashed as she smirked. "Thanks." She moved off to the bar. The crowd parted around her.

Fitz moved after her as she ordered a drink. "I'm sorry. I didn't mean to—"

She glanced at him over her shoulder. "It's all right, really. Thanks. Nice to meet you." She turned back to the bar and he felt himself dismissed.

"I mean—I just really wanted to say—" *I'm babbling. She thinks I'm a total idiot.* "It was great. Really great. You've got a gift."

She turned and stared at him, then threw back her head and laughed derisively. "Yeah, I guess you could call it that!"

"I'm not talking about the Depriver thing," Fitz said, suddenly angry. "I'm talking about your music. It's good."

Lydia stirred the lime into her gin and tonic and regarded him dispassionately. "Nice suit," she said. "You industry?"

Her eyes were mocking him. His suit. His embarrassment. Fitz pulled himself up. "No," he said. "I'm not industry. Just a square who tried to pay you a compliment. Have a nice evening."

He turned and started to walk away. "Hey," came her voice, behind him. It was as if the warm contralto had laid a hand on his shoulder, and it gave him the chills. He turned around. She indicated the stool next to her with a tilt of her head.

"There's no need to get your knickers in a twist. Have a seat."

He returned and sat down.

"You'll have to excuse me," she continued. In the raucous bar her voice seemed to reach its own level, like water; concentrating on it, Fitz felt everything else blur into soft focus. "I misinterpreted your interest. And I don't like to get personal with just anybody."

"Yeah, well, just 'cause I have a tie on, don't lump me in with the schmooze hounds, okay?"

Lydia's eyebrow arched. "Touchy bastard, aren't you?"

"Takes one to know one."

She looked at him suspiciously. "And are you one?"

"One what?" Fitz was confused for a moment. "A Depriver? Oh, no. No I'm not." Seeing the relief in her face, he asked, "Does it make a difference?"

Lydia shrugged. "They come to the gigs, looking for some kind of answer."

"What do you mean?"

"I have this sort of following, because of the music. I have this website. I'm out about it, you know, the Depriver thing. So other people . . . other Deprivers . . . they hear this and they seek me out. They think I've found some secret they don't have."

"The secret to what?

The mocking smile was back. "To being able to live with yourself."

"And have you?"

She shrugged again, smiling. "Maybe I have, maybe I haven't. I don't know. I'm not doing anything they couldn't do. And I'm not trying to make a statement, or anything." She sipped her drink. "I just got tired of trying to pass."

Fitz studied her. Every time she shifted her position at the bar, she was careful not to touch anyone else. And there was anger beneath the lazy mocking smile, passion lurking behind her eyes.

"You don't like talking to them," Fitz observed.

"Who?"

"Other Deprivers."

"Oh, well, you know." Lydia made a waving motion, as if pushing away some invisible thing. "I just don't need to get into the whole touchy-feely-support-group thing. I've been to those meetings. Everybody sitting around moaning 'Why me?' and feeling sorry for themselves. What a waste of time. I make my music. I live in my reality."

"And that reality is?"

"I am who I am. I do what I do. The same thing that makes me dangerous makes me extraordinary. It's just a fact of life."

"But isn't your reality lonely?"

Something flickered across her even smile, but it stayed in place. "What do you mean?"

"Well . . . you don't like other Deprivers and you don't like squares. Is there anybody you do like?"

Lydia threw back her head and laughed again. "Oh, that—hey, I have plenty of friends." She tilted her head toward the room. "I choose my own company. And my company chooses me."

She smiled at Fitz. He felt flattered, warmed, to be included in the circle of her attention. Suddenly, Ben slapped him on the back.

"Okay, cowboy, time to hit the trail," said Ben. "I'm taking my boy home, Lydia, before you seduce him."

"We were just having a nice conversation," Lydia said, smiling.

Fitz wanted to stay in that dark room with the honey-dripping voice going on and on, but his life and obligations beckoned from Westchester and Ben was never going to let him stay. He put his name on the mailing list and promised to come to the next gig.

"Thanks," Lydia said, as he was leaving. The genuine warmth in her voice when she said it gave Fitz a moment's pause.

"For what?" Fitz asked.

"For wanting to get to know me as a person."

In retrospect—after the tears, the recriminations, the blackouts—those words gave him nothing but pain. *Yeah, but you couldn't just leave it at that, could you?* For days afterward, he couldn't get her out of his mind. Waiting and waiting for the flyer—rushing to the mailbox every day, wondering if his wife had intercepted it, and, thinking it was a mistake (*"Fitz doesn't like jazz"*), throwing it out. Kicking himself for not getting a phone number, then kicking himself for even *thinking* about getting a phone number. Finally, he remembered. Of course! *The website.*

He typed her name into the search engine and up it popped: the Lydia Frank home page. Seeing her picture download onto his screen at work gave him a jolt. *"Lydia Frank and the Screaming Sirens, @ Tonic, November 12th."* Well, there was the gig. He clicked on the hotlink for Lydia's name.

Music is all about feeling, he read. *In that respect it is the purest of all art forms, because when you take away everything else—the words, the arrangements, the performance itself, you're left with nothing but pure emotion. That's what I try to get to in my work. And that's why I like jazz— the purity of expression allows me to explore various tones and colors, and take the emotion as far as it will go.*

When I tell people I'm a Depriver, they see that as ironic—that my music inspires feeling, but my touch takes it away. I see the two things as complementary. My particular thing is to take away bodily sensation—to make people go numb. You're still conscious, but you can't feel anything. It's been described to me as a sensation of lightness or weight-lessness. I like to explore that edge with people. Because when the other senses are taken away, the pure experience of the music is heightened.

She hadn't been surprised to see him, right at the front table, drink in hand. When the show ended she walked up and smiled at him, with the same regal regard.

"Hey," she said.

"Hey."

"You left your friend at home tonight?" Her eyes were probing his, but the smile remained frozen on her face.

"He had some things to do," Fitz lied. "He sends his regards."

"Mmm." Lydia watched the drummer dismantling his set. "I have to help the guys break down, but what are you doing later?"

"Nothing. Why?"

"You want to go to a party?"

They walked over to the East Village with the rest of the band without exchanging a word. Fitz tried to join in the banter of the other band members, but he couldn't seem to engage in small talk with Lydia. She didn't seem to mind. She just strode alongside him in the cold November air with a little smile on her face, her hands thrust deep into the pockets of her wool jumper, her head muffled in a big black scarf. It wasn't until they got to the apartment on 13th Street and they were alone again, in a corner of the dark-ened living room, that Lydia spoke.

"You saw the website, didn't you?" she said.

Fitz nodded.

"And you're curious, aren't you?"

Fitz said nothing. Lydia sighed.

"Okay," she said. "Well, I should warn you. It's kind of addictive. I-"

"You know, I don't get it," Fitz interrupted her.

Lydia blinked. "Don't get what?"

"Why all the warnings? Why all the testing? I mean, you put yourself out there this way, you go through all this trouble to make sure people know you're a Depriver. And then when people try to talk to you about it, you get all ticked off because they see you 'that way.' I mean, for somebody who's supposedly found the secret of being okay with yourself, or whatever, you've got the biggest goddamn chip on your shoulder that I've ever seen in my life."

Lydia said nothing, but in the darkened room Fitz could feel her hostility brewing on the other side of the couch.

"Does it occur to you that maybe some people *would* like to get to know you as a person, if you just stopped being so defensive all the time?"

"It's not a chip," she said finally. "It's part of who I am."

"It's a *fluke!* An accident of *birth!* And you've made it the center of your life. You've even got a webpage devoted to it, for Christ's sake."

"The webpage weeds a lot of people out," Lydia said. "And I don't have to repeat myself over and over again. It saves me a lot of trouble."

"A lot of pain, you mean."

"Yes. That, too." Lydia leaned forward. "Look . . . what's your name again?"

"Fitz."

"Fitz. You've asked me for an explanation. I'd like to give it to you."

"Okay," said Fitz.

Lydia pulled her hands out of her pockets—the long-fingered hands Fitz had admired onstage—and clasped them in front of her. Her knuckles were white.

"The last time I saw you, you asked me if my reality wasn't lonely. It is. When I was fourteen years old, I discovered that I couldn't touch another human being without making them fall over senseless like a sack of grain. I had to find other ways to touch people—with my music, with my voice, with my presence. So I learned. All of that took discipline and control."

She gazed down at her clasped hands and opened them.

"Eventually I learned to control this, too."

" 'This'? The Depriver thing?"

"To a point. Not stop it, exactly. Just kind of manipulate it a bit. I was in music school, with this guy, and we . . . we used to experiment with it a bit. With the Deprivation. I found out that I could hold off on it, at least for a while. Slow it down. Kind of like . . . like when your leg falls asleep. It sounds stupid, but when we would do it with the music . . . it got pretty intense."

"The pure experience of the music."

"Yes." She smiled, twisted her head away in embarrassment. Fitz squinted at her in the darkness.

"My God," he said, "you're blushing!"

"Yeah, well, you know. College. We were really young."

"What happened to him?"

The shrug. "He took off a long time ago." She looked up at him, tight smile, eyes flashing. "He couldn't handle it."

"Didn't like it any more?"

Lydia shook her head. "He liked it too much."

There was loud laughter across the room, and both Fitz and Lydia looked up to see a couple in the kitchen, dancing. The girl was drunk and laughing. The boy spun her in a circle, then hugged her close.

"After that, I—well, I guess I got kind of bitter. I started drinking a lot. I would take guys home from bars. They were curious, you know. One-night stands, pretty easy to deal with. And there was a kick to it. I have to admit I got off on the power. I started writing my own music, and got better and better at the control. The manipulation. But—"

"But it wasn't real."

"No." She looked up at him. "Fitz, you have to understand. There's a whole underground out there, of people who get off on this shit. I mean, they seek out people like me."

"But it's not making you happy."

In the darkness her large eyes were black and deep, pleading with him. "What can I do? I can't change who I am."

The drunk couple in the kitchen were screaming with laughter, tickling each other. Lydia glanced up at them and winced.

"Do you want to get out of here?" Fitz asked.

"Yes. Please."

They walked together through the bare trees in Tompkins Square Park. The cold wind was refreshing after the warm, smoky party, and Fitz breathed deep.

"So." Lydia cocked her head at him, smiling. "Did that satisfy your curiosity?"

"Yes," said Fitz. "No. I mean—" He stopped, put one hand on Lydia's covered arm to stop her. Her eyes softened.

"Look," he said. "I have to admit, I *am* curious, and I know you'll just think I'm another perv for saying that. But what's made me curious doesn't have anything to do with your—"

"My 'gift'?"

"The Deprivation thing. It's your music, it's your voice, it's—I don't know what it is, but—Lydia, you shouldn't sell yourself short. You're an amazing person, with incredible talents, and from what you've told me you're a very strong, courageous, loving person. You want to touch people. And there's no reason in the world why someone shouldn't love you for who you are."

Lydia laughed bitterly, turning her face into the hood of her shawl. "Sure," she said. "You say that now. Afterward..."

"Afterward is—look, let's get something straight: I'm married. I have a life that doesn't include you. What can I say, it's there. But I'd like to be your friend."

Lydia looked him over evenly. "And you'd like me to touch you."

The wind blew through Fitz's coat and he shivered. "Yes."

Lydia just looked at him for a moment, calculating. Finally, she turned and walked toward the northeast corner of the park. When Fitz didn't follow her, she turned back.

"Come on," she said.

They walked side by side without speaking, until they came to a storefront on the corner of 13th and Avenue D. Lydia pulled out a ring of keys on a chain and unlocked the padlocked gate over the front door. She reached up and turned on an overhead light.

It was a bare, whitewashed storefront, clean, sparely furnished. The front window was boarded over and painted white as well. Aside from some shelves of books and CDs on the walls, there was nothing in the room but a chair, an elaborate sound system, and a big waterbed in the middle of the floor.

"Welcome to my studio," she said, smiling wryly.

Fitz smiled. "Kind of '70s, isn't it?" he said, indicating the waterbed.

"Ever been on one? It's a trip. Lay down. Take your shoes off, though. I don't want you waking up in a puddle."

Fitz positioned himself awkwardly as the water rolled beneath him. Lydia strode briskly around him, in her element; she flipped a few switches and the amps and speakers hummed into life.

"I've had a few drinks," she said, reaching over her head and rummaging among the CDs. "Sometimes that affects how it goes, but I'll try to stay focused." She pulled out a CD and turned back to him. "Any requests?"

"Just as long as it's yours," said Fitz.

Lydia smiled. She turned off the overhead light. Fitz could still see her dimly in the glow from the amplifier. There was a click, and a deep thrumming bass came out of the darkness. A ripple in the water mattress and Lydia was straddling him in the bed.

"Comfortable?" The voice rolled over him, thick and sweet, as the water rolled beneath him. Before he could answer, he felt a tug on his shirt buttons and then her fingers brushing down his chest.

It wasn't like anything he had expected. It was as though her fingertips were draining away all the tension from his body . . . the awkwardness, the aches and pains, the screaming account reps, the dirty subway tunnels, his wife's stinging comment over coffee that morning, the bills—everything was flowing and pulsing out of him in a ribbon of light. And then, nothingness swelled up within him like an immense wave.

My God, he thought, *this isn't like having your foot fall asleep at all . . .*

Then the wave broke and dragged him under and he was submerged, suspended in a deep blue void where nothing existed but her voice, singing within him until he dispersed and was carried away.

* * *

"Hey."

He was aware of his body again, tingling back into being along the edges of his nerves. He felt incredibly light, weightless; his lungs effortlessly took in deep gulps of air. Someone was poking him gently through the blanket. A voice tugged at his consciousness from far away. He felt the water rolling beneath him and remembered where he was.

"Hey."

He opened his eyes and, blinking, saw nothing but darkness.

"What time is it?" he asked thickly.

"About five."

He began to make out the silhouette of a head bending over him, surrounded by a faint penumbra of blue light, like a halo. Lydia's concerned face came into focus.

"You okay?"

Fitz smiled and reached out for her, like an infant. "Angel," he murmured. He stroked the side of her face, which—he realized, for a moment—looked very, very sad. And then he slipped outside of himself again.

When Fitz woke up the next morning, Lydia was already out of bed and two cafe leches to go were steaming on top of the amp. She was fully dressed and smoking a cigarette, watching him.

She got up and handed him the coffee. "How are you feeling?"

"Pretty great," said Fitz. He sipped, handling the cup gingerly in the rocking waterbed. He half expected Lydia to come back to bed, to curl up next to him and ruffle his hair, but she sat down in the chair again. He felt a bit awkward.

Lydia was appraising him emotionlessly, like a doctor

examining a patient. "I was a little worried about you last night. You were out for a long time."

"Afraid I wasn't coming back?"

Lydia didn't smile. "It's usually an hour, tops," she said. "You went away for three."

"Well, what do they say when you oversleep? My body probably needed it." Fitz smiled mischievously over the cup.

Lydia abruptly stood up and walked toward the bathroom. "You should drink your coffee and go," she said softly. "Your wife is probably wondering where you are."

Fitz was taken aback. He decided not to argue. He got out of bed, found his clothes in the corners of the room. Lydia said nothing as he was getting dressed. When he left, she didn't ask him when he was coming back. But she stopped him at the door.

"There's one more thing you should know. They tell me there are side effects."

"What, permanent loss?"

She shrugged indifferently. "No one's had any permanent damage yet—at least none that I know of. Other stuff. Kind of like withdrawal."

"Withdrawal?"

"You'll see."

During the next few weeks, Fitz's world changed. Nothing could puncture his sense of well-being. For the first time in months, he felt as though he could see clearly, that everything was manageable somehow. When he got back into the office he plunged into his work, whipping out some of the best designs in his career. Nothing Gordon said could derail him; he'd simply nod, smile, and get back to work. Even his relationship with his wife was better. He was kinder to her, able to listen to her worries about the business she was starting without feeling pressured to remain in his job.

Somehow this allowed him to justify lying to himself. So what if he took time off to go see Lydia, if it made him a better husband and a better designer in the long run? Didn't he need something for himself?

He would go to Lydia's gigs, occasionally going home with her and having long talks over coffee and beer about music, art, life. He really did want to get to know her as a person. But more and more, the little sessions in the Avenue D studio began to take over their relationship, and it was becoming harder and harder not to see them for what they were. During their encounters on the waterbed, Lydia became cold and remote, dispassionate—almost a different person. It made Fitz feel weird about it. Dirty. The lack of endearments afterward he could write off to her condition, but he could feel her keeping him at an emotional distance as well. The more he needed her, the more he could feel her indifference coming up between them like a wall. When he confronted her about it, he was met with the same shrug, the familiar sarcasm.

"You said it yourself," she told him, "You have a life that doesn't include me. What can you give me? Why should I open myself up to you?"

"Because that's what people *do*, Lydia," he said. "They open themselves up to each other. That's part of being human. That's part of being a friend to someone."

"It's not what I do."

"Jesus Christ." Fitz sighed in exasperation. "What do I have to do to make you trust me?"

Lydia looked at him. "You really want to know?" she said.

Fitz looked at her. He nodded.

"Don't see me for six weeks."

Fitz laughed. "More testing? Boy, you don't give up, do you?"

Lydia's eyes were steely. "Six weeks. Six weeks clean. Can you do that?"

"What do you mean, can I do that? Of course I can do that."

He'd started out smug. Of course he could do it. His intentions were pure; he only wanted to get to know her as a person. But after two weeks it started to creep in. The petty annoyances. The little insults. Small noises began to grate on his nerves, make him jump. He found himself enervated and exhausted by four o'clock in the afternoon. He would play her CD at work constantly, but that didn't do it. He started to send her emails, to call. She didn't answer.

Finally, after four weeks he was at her door, banging. When she opened it, stone-faced, he was nearly frantic. She pulled him inside and bolted the lock behind him. His heart was pounding and his mouth was dry.

"Please," he said, clutching at her like a baby the moment they were in the door, pleading, mewling. "Please." And then the oblivion he craved hit him, and he slumped to the floor.

He woke up in the darkening room, straight again. There was a lump on his head where he'd hit it on the radiator. It was dark. The clock radio said it was seven o'clock. In the fading light, he could make out Lydia's smoking form against the wall. She had taken his shoes off and moved him to the waterbed. It occurred to him that in his grasping desperation she could not have gotten any pleasure from their encounter, and he wondered how much she ever got. He sat up.

She didn't say anything. He saw the glow of her cigarette, and then a puff of smoke tumbled into the slant of light.

"Lydia," he said, "I'm sorry."

"Not as sorry as I am," she said.

Fitz sat at the end of the waterbed, fumbling with his shoes. He wasn't sure what to say. Pangs of guilt shot through his calm, but once again he was thinking clearly. When he got his shoes on, he went to her. She wouldn't look him in the eye.

"Lydia, one of us has to end this."

He could feel, through her shirt, how tense she was. So tense she was shaking. Painfully, Fitz wished that he could take it away with a touch, as she had for him.

"I'm sorry. I thought I could take away your pain, that I could help you. But I only seem to cause you more."

"No," said Lydia, shaking her head but still not looking at him. "That's not true."

"It is true, you know it."

"Oh, Jesus Christ," Lydia spat out. "For god's sake, please don't feel *guilty*."

"But I do!"

"You're not causing me any pain. Really, it's all right. I can handle it. I can—"

"No, let me finish. This isn't right. You know it's not right. I know it now. You proved it. I mean, look at me, Lydia. You're right, I'm no better than a junkie. I thought I was. But I can't keep doing this to you. It's not fair to you. And it's not fair to my wife. I've been using you to deal with my own problems."

On this, Lydia turned and stared at him, her eyes glassy and horrified.

"I've become addicted—and you deserve better than that. You deserve love. Real love. And I'm not the person who can give it to you. I thought I was, I set myself up to be, but I'm not."

"What are you saying?" Her voice cracked.

"I'm saying—Jesus, Lydia, I'm saying I care about you too much to keep fucking you, that's what I'm saying."

Tears welled up in her eyes, and in a moment of dawning horror Fitz realized why.

"Oh, my God," he said. "That's what *he* said to you, isn't it?"

The tears were flowing down her face and she didn't stop them. Fitz began backing toward the door.

"Oh, Jesus," he said, "I'm sorry. I'm *really* sorry. This wasn't what I—"

"No, please, don't go, don't—"

She lunged toward him in the half light and before he knew what happened he felt her grab him. A sonic boom like a thunderclap went off in his head, then blackness.

He came to on the floor three days later, every muscle in his body aching, Lydia squatting against the wall beside him.

"It's Sunday," was all she said. Then she opened the door and walked out.

Fitz took the hint and left. When he emerged onto Avenue D, groggy and thirsty, dawn was breaking. He got himself a coffee and made his way to a train, trying to think of a good excuse for being gone all weekend.

What if it had been Tuesday? he thought. *What if I had missed work . . . ?*

That was when he noticed that two fingers of his right hand had gone numb.

He got back to Westchester and let himself in, took a long hot shower to wash off the smell of the studio and Lydia's cigarettes. He crept into the bedroom where his wife was still sleeping. Even in sleep, her face looked tense and worried. Fitz stroked her hair and she murmured sleepily and snuggled close to him. Her face relaxed. For a moment, he savored the fact that he could hold her, just hold her, and that his presence made her feel secure. He curled up next to her in the bed, warmed by a sense of relief that the affair with Lydia was finally over.

Four weeks later, at three o'clock in the conference room: the account rep stopped in front of design Number 5, a closeup of two mouths at the point of touching, a man and a woman. The caption, in block letters: CONTACT.

"It's visual," said the business manager.

"It's sexy," said the account rep.

"Not in bad taste?" said the business manager. "I mean—well, you know."

"Screw that pc shit," said the account rep. "This is advertising. Everybody wants contact. The Deps can buy toothpaste as well as the rest of us."

Fitz sat at the end of the conference table, saying nothing, rubbing the outside fingers of his right hand and staring off into space.

At five, drained, exhausted, Fitz came out of the conference room, shut off his computer and called his wife. "Are you coming home tonight?" He could hear the brittle sound in her voice. It was an old dance. "Yes," he said. And he always meant it when he said it.

He wanted to come home to her and the normal life. He meant to. But something in him went down to 14th Street and bought a newspaper. He sat in Union Square Park while the numbing city noise went on all around him. Sat on a bench in the darkening, chilling air, rubbing his numb hand and pretending to read, when in fact he was simply staring at another *advertisement* which seemed to scream up at him from the page in black and white newsprint while he struggled to tame the beast inside him and shut out the noise.

Fitz rubbed his eyes, looking up from his paper, and his

attention was suddenly arrested by a girl with pink hair and a motorcycle jacket, slightly chubby in her black leggings and combat boots. She was crossing the street, and he could see, around her head, a faint penumbra of light. At first, he thought it was the light reflecting off her hair, punked out and dyed pink like ratty fiberglass. He blinked for a moment and rubbed his eyes. As she cut across the intersection toward Third Avenue, his heart sank. It was still there. And it was definitely, distinctly, blue. The same halo. Lydia's halo. A squatter chick. Fitz put down the paper and followed her.

He stayed about a block behind her as she moved down Third and then cut over, east, toward Loisaida. She ducked into the crowd on St. Mark's Place and blended into the sea of black leather. He would have lost her except for the aura. It was as though he could feel it, not just see it, as if he was homing in on something. Like a target. Like radar. That aura bobbed through the sea of MC jackets and Fitz staggered after it like a man in a desert chasing a mirage.

She turned left on Avenue A and slowed her pace a bit. Fitz caught up with her, keeping a distance of about five feet between them on the less crowded street. Suddenly the girl stopped to read some flyers pasted outside of a coffee shop. Fitz hesitated. He hadn't expected this. He suddenly realized that he had no idea what he wanted from her, why he had felt compelled to follow her. Should he talk to her? Go into the coffee shop? What would he say? *"Why do you have a halo around your head like my ex-girlfriend?"* Before he could figure it out, she turned and looked him boldly in the face.

"Yeah, what?" she snapped. Her summary gaze told Fitz that she was used to this sort of thing.

Fitz's awkward reply showed that he was not. "I . . . I'm sorry, I just . . ."

The girl smirked, crinkling the edges of her liquid eye-liner. She looked him up and down. "Oh." She tossed the pink hair out of her eyes contemptuously. "You're one of *those*." And then her face twisted into an unexpected snarl. "Listen, creep, let me tell you something. You can see us. Well, we can see you, too. A mile away. So go get your kicks somewhere else. *Hag*."

The angry girl flounced into the coffee shop.

That did it. Fitz headed toward Avenue D.

In a way, when he saw the storefront, he was surprised that it was still there—that it wasn't all just something he'd dreamed up, months ago, out of the depth of his desire for nothingness, for oblivion, for release from his everyday life. Like a man in a dream, he knocked on the door and she opened it. Lydia seemed as unsurprised to see him as he was to see her.

He went in without a word, and she shut the door behind him.

SUFFER THE LITTLE CHILDREN

TANANARIVE DUE

Laurel pushed open the vestibule door with one hand, clutching a bag of yellow onions and hot peppers from the market with the other. In the foyer, her twelve-year-old granddaughter lay sprawled across the floor, her suntanned arms and legs splayed awkwardly, her mouth half agape. Her eyelids fluttered rhythmically, as if from electric pulses, the only sign that she was alive. It was just enough to keep Laurel from fainting.

"Get away from the door," said an authoritative voice. "Close it behind you, quick."

Laurel looked up to see a child, a black boy her grand-daughter's age or even younger, in front of her. A loud crash from the kitchen—something aluminum clattering across the floor—startled her further.

"Do as he says, lady," came another too-old voice, this one from the stairway. "Close the goddamned door. If not, we torch this house. You and that kid and everything inside here will be ashes in two minutes flat."

The voice belonged to a girl, her blonde hair in a blunt cut, tall enough to be fourteen, but with the round face of a baby.

Laurel dropped her grocery bag to the floor with a cry of dismay and shock. It was all too much. She'd heard about gangs on the television news, down in Miami, but she'd never imagined there might be a gang in Live Oak. And what had they done to Gwen?

"What's wrong with her?" Laurel asked, her arms curled outward, away from her chest, as if she were still clutching the bag.

"You deaf, lady? You wanna be? Read my lips—*close the door.*" The black boy again.

"You tell me what's wrong with her," Laurel hissed.

"Oh, Jesus Christ. Why is it nobody in this house knows how to follow simple directions?"

Yet another voice—slightly older, husky—and it came from directly behind Laurel. A smooth palm, tattooed with a wildly gazing eyeball, angled toward her face.

It didn't take Laurel long to learn their voices. Not much later, she learned their names, as well.

The one who had blinded her was Jose. He'd touched Gwen, too. "It was him, Gram, the one with the eyeball on his hand," her granddaughter had whispered into Laurel's ear while they huddled together beneath the blanket at night, trying to sleep but unable to, because of their racing, frightened brains.

The blonde was named Jen, and she was thirteen, not fourteen, Laurel had been told nastily when she asked. The black boy was Mercury; he spent most of the time in the room with them, breathing quietly just inside the closed door. There were two others, who'd been in the kitchen orig-

TANANARIVE DUE

inally: Sean and Shane, twin brothers. According to Mercury, they were the only documented twins like them in the continental United States.

When all the other voices had been accounted for—Jen, Mercury and Shane arguing over what television program to watch in the living room; Sean and Jose running water and flinging dishes carelessly in the sink in the kitchen— Laurel heard scurrying at night. There must be more of them, in the attic. Still, she wasn't sure. She wasn't sure about the first thing any more.

"Gram," Gwen whispered on the third night, her voice trembling with excitement, "I can see the moonlight through the window. And the red curtains. It's blurry, but I can see it. Can you?"

Laurel had to feel her own face to know whether or not her eyes were open. They were, and all she could see was murky darkness.

"No, sweetie. Not yet."

Gwen began to cry, the muted, private little sobs she'd perfected the first day, when Jose threatened to slap her silly if she didn't shut up. Laurel stroked her granddaughter's hair, picturing the silky brown strands, and told her not to worry, Jose had said it might take a while.

Actually, what Jose had said was that it might take forever.

By the fourth day, there were definitely more of them. Twice a day, Mercury came to feed Laurel and Gwen, the sort of food children ate—salty chips, overly sweet Chek sodas, hot dogs wrapped with plain white bread, spaghetti from cans that were at least two years old—odds and ends she'd stocked in the house for the days Gwen came to visit, or kept in case of a hurricane or, she told herself ironically, some other emergency. Then he sat with them, and Laurel asked Mercury how many others were in the house. But, despite his overall politeness, Mercury never answered her.

Still, she knew more than she let on. She'd explained it to Gwen as best she could when they were alone, from what she'd read in the *New York Times* and *Newsweek* online over the past few years. There was a scientific name for these people, as well as several slang terms, some of them vulgar, but Laurel couldn't remember any of those. They'd been born with this odd condition that made their skin dangerous; you weren't supposed to touch them, except with gloves. Many of them had been sent to facilities—properly compensated and cared for, of course—so scientists could try to find vaccines, treatments and maybe, hopefully, a cure.

But Laurel had never met one before now. And it had never occurred to her that some of them might be children.

"Be careful, Mercury," Laurel said, feeling the weight of the boy as he sat at the edge of the bed. "You're too close to Gwen." He'd gotten bolder in the last day or so, making himself more a part of their company. Apparently, he'd also been exploring the medicine cabinet in the downstairs bathroom. He smelled just like Phillip's old fragrance she hadn't thrown out after he died.

"Stop worrying so much, lady. You sound like Grandmama used to. I got clothes on."

"And he's wearing gloves. Green ones. Right?" Gwen said. Picturing them in her mind, Laurel knew they must be the gardening gloves she kept on her kitchen window sill.

"Yeah, right. Not bad for a little blind girl, huh?" Mercury said, angering Laurel.

"How many fingers I got up?" he went on, sounding genuinely encouraging now.

"Four?" Gwen sounded hopeful.

"Nope. Look harder."

"Three?"

"Yeah! You doin' all right. You just gon' need some glasses, that's all."

Laurel heard feet pounding up and down the hallway outside the closed bedroom door. The whole floor seemed to shake. Picture frames clattered above her headboard. Something crashed outside the doorway. Sounds of laughter and grunting, and bumping against the wall. Laurel tried to blot out the images of broken china and glass littering the hallway and living room.

"Would I go blind again if you touched me, Mercury?" Gwen asked.

"I ain't gon' touch you, so what's the difference? And nobody else will, neither, as long as you stay in here with your grandmama and don't be a pain."

"But would I?"

"Nah. With me, your ears would ring, probably, that's all. My baby brother went deaf, but that's just cause he was so young. Babies and old people . . ."

"Babies and old people what, Mercury?" Laurel asked, for the first time in a long time sounding like every one of her seventy-four years. She wondered if her irises were still blue, or if they'd been washed of color. Already, blue was hard to imagine as anything other than the brightly exaggerated hue from a cartoon.

"Babies and old people get stung worse. Pow. *You* know. Right?"

"Yes, I do," Laurel said, biting her lip, feeling much angrier than she sounded. "Tell me who you are. Tell me why you're here."

"Just a little party, right? That's all," Mercury said. The bed shuddered as he stood. "Just a place to be."

"Where were you before you came here? You all know each other. Where do you belong?"

"Lady, what did I tell you about all those questions? You need to back off. Ain't nobody gon' hurt you or her. Just let it alone."

"Babies and old people . . ." Laurel repeated, feigning a smile, but all the while glaring at the void, terrified. She felt her old self clawing at her heart, screaming for escape from the darkness. She had to shut that self away. They're just children, a calmer voice inside her said.

"Mercury, will you read it to me today?" Laurel pleaded.

Mercury sucked his teeth loudly. "I already told you, those words are too hard for me."

"I need to hear it, Mercury. Gwen and I both need to, and so do you. I'll help you with the hard words. Spell them out, and I'll tell you what the words are."

He sucked his teeth again, trying to make up his mind. Then she heard the gently fanning pages of the book she kept on her nightstand. Mercury began reading, his voice low and detached, choosing a line at random.

"My soul waiteth . . . for the Lord . . . more than they that watch for the morning . . . Let I-S-R-A . . ."

"Israel," Laurel said.

". . . Let Israel hope in the Lord . . . for with the Lord there is mercy . . ."

It was the Book of Psalms, just as she'd hoped.

Laurel knew it was only a matter of time before they would want the password for her ATM card. It was probably just as well, she decided. It would be a relief to have some real food. It was a shame she'd never had a chance to make the spicy spaghetti sauce she'd been planning when she came home from the market. The onions and peppers must still be lying on the floor in the foyer where she'd dropped them. The thought made her woozy.

"Son, could you do me a favor and bring us a cooked chicken from the deli right inside the market? We need more substantive food. We're always hungry."

"Barbecue," Gwen whispered in her ear.

"Bitch, the only thing I'm about to bring you is a concussion," Jen's voice shot back. Laurel heard the contents of her purse fall to the floor. Jose snickered in the doorway. Whatever this group was, Jose was in charge of it, she'd figured out. She wished Mercury were here. Mercury would sneak in a barbecued chicken and share it with them.

"Toilet paper, then. Please? Our bathroom is out," Laurel said.

"Yeah, whatever. We got that covered. Just shut up," Jen said. It was so hard to imagine those harsh words coming from that angelic face, that looked as young as Gwen's. Jen's name even rhymed with Gwen's. She felt a dull pang in her chest that, for once, wasn't heartburn.

"What happened to you, sweetheart?" Laurel said, before she could think better of it. "Tell me what's happened to you. Were you sent somewhere? Because of your condition? Did you run away?"

Silence. Laurel braced herself for a blow. Were Jen and Jose looking at each other? At her? Would one of them touch her again? Laurel heard herself pressing on, even though she'd decided not to speak again.

"I'd like to know. Where are your parents? Where are the people who love you?"

"You know what?" Jose said, sounding closer than before. "We got about twelve different kinds of hell waiting for you outside that door, you old cunt, and all we gotta do is touch you. Why don't you just shut up and be glad all you lost is your eyes? Wouldn't have lost that much if you'd listened to plain English in the first place."

Laurel felt Gwen's tiny bones, trembling beside her.

Jose's voice always had that effect on her. Gwen's vision improved a little each day, but Laurel knew her grand-daughter would never be the same after this. The bad things that happened in childhood were like no others. She wrapped her arm around Gwen, drawing her close against her breastbone, until she could feel Gwen's driving heart-beat. You poor, scared child, she thought. But she wasn't thinking of Gwen.

"I'm sorry you had to touch me," Laurel said. "I was in shock. I didn't react quickly enough. How could I know? So I made you do what you did, and I know you didn't want to, but that's neither here nor there. I think you should have someone. All of you. You're children."

"Oh, yeah, poor us," Jen said. "Man, Jose, let's go. Before the store closes."

"And my granddaughter needs some real food. One of you should bring us a whole chicken from the supermarket deli," Laurel said. "Barbecued. Please."

"Bitch, what did I just say?" Jose said.

But something in his voice told Laurel he would bring it.

After a week had passed, Mercury told Laurel they would be moving on soon. He was very talkative, and Laurel under-stood why when he was close enough for her to smell the beer on his breath. "We don't like to stay more than a week," he explained. "It's no fun after that."

"What's the fun of it?" Laurel asked him.

"You know, just hanging out. Doing what we want. Being free. That's all."

"And your families don't miss you?"

"Lady, my family wouldn't even know me if they saw me. Didn't you hear me say I made my baby brother deaf?"

"But you didn't mean to."

"Yeah. And?"

"Mercury," Laurel said, "how old are you?"

"Why are you always asking that?"

"Please tell me."

Mercury suppressed a burp. "Ten," he said.

"And how long has it been since anyone hugged you?'

"Nobody hugs stingers, fool," Mercury said, laughing. "You crazy?"

"Well, if I were younger and I weren't so frail, I would hug you, Mercury. Because that's what I'm supposed to do. But I'm afraid to. And I'm sorry for that. I'm really very sorry."

Mercury's laugh was more uneasy now. "Why you sorry? No one told you to hug me."

"But do you understand what I'm saying? You *should* have someone to hug you."

Mercury didn't answer. He sat at the edge of the bed, smelling strongly of cologne older than he was. After a moment, she heard him sigh. "Yeah, I guess so."

Gwen was sleeping; Laurel could feel her granddaughter's breath rising and falling against her bare forearm, warming her skin. It was hard to keep track of time without light. Dinner had been hours ago, so it was probably after midnight. Laurel sat with Mercury in silence, listening to the television blaring downstairs, and the raucous laughter echoing through her hallways. It sounded like rage. And pure joy.

ELLIS ISLAND

JOANNE DAHME

From the outside, Mark Hanson's house looked like all the others in this Brooklyn neighborhood—tidy twin bricks with front porches boasting views of front lawns with neat gardens of rose bushes or hedges or Japanese Maples which just about took up the entire yard. Hanson's had a tree—and a yard full of wind chimes.

The chimes didn't surprise Detective Grundy. He had seen them at other Deprivers residences. Deprivers liked things that touched. Hanson's chimes were all sizes and materials—metals, ceramics, shells. A few hung on the Japanese Maple. A number of them hung from plant hooks lodged into the ceiling of the porch roof. One even hung from the top of the rainspout at the point where it met the roof. That took some effort, Detective Grundy thought as he stood on the sidewalk, squinting at Mark Hanson's front door as if he were trying to see through the brick walls.

Grundy was forty–three years old. He'd been assigned to Depriver Enforcement after promoting out of Rape Investigation. He'd gone through extensive training–spending time in deprivation tanks and interviewing Deprivers and their victims. He'd even practiced going without touching anybody for days, which wasn't that hard for him. Grundy was a loner; he'd thought he could probably be a law-abiding Depriver, although he realized it must be more difficult if you really couldn't touch anyone.

Then he'd started tracking down Deprivers who'd broken the law. The cases soon made him emotionally weary and ambivalent. His last case had involved a young mother who had only found out she was a Depriver when she bathed her three-year old child and blinded him. The woman had tried to hang herself with the belt from her bathrobe.

Mark Hanson was twenty-five, a Depriver for about ten years who had never touched a soul. Now, suddenly, he was touching at least one person a day. Yesterday, a young woman in the subway had collapsed after Hanson, who was sitting beside her, had bent down, as if to tie his shoe, and touched her on the ankle. She'd been wearing a pair of jeans and sneakers, but no socks. The woman described Hanson's touch as a "caress," which had given her the creeps even before she stood and discovered she had lost all feeling in her legs.

Two days ago it was an old man with whom Hanson had shared a table in a fast-food joint. Noting that the old man had some hamburger bun crumbs on his chin, Hanson had wiped them away. The old man had only recovered his sense of taste early this morning.

Before he actually touched them, Hanson would sketch a portrait of his victim the size of an index card somewhere at the scene of the crime—on a wall, a table, whatever was convenient and usable. In each portrait, the victim was surrounded by a golden aura and had a look of contentment. The old man noticed Hanson scribbling something on the corner of the table, but didn't want to seem as if he were staring.

Grundy looked up. The sky was filled with dark, storm-like, slowly skimming clouds. Grundy sighed and approached Hanson's house. A sudden gust set the chimes clattering, as Grundy ascended the porch steps and knocked at the door. An elderly woman who lived in the twin on the other side of the porch railing opened her door.

"He hasn't been home for days," she told Grundy, without waiting for the question.

Grundy nodded, then asked, "How has he seemed lately? Anything out of the ordinary?" He didn't bother to explain why he was here and why he cared. The neighbors always knew.

"A little agitated lately, that's all," she said, squinting her eyes as if to conjure up Mark Hanson as she'd last seen him. "But please be kind to him. He's a nice boy. Gets my groceries for me sometimes."

Grundy nodded in acknowledgment, and the old woman slipped back inside her house.

It only took Grundy a minute to pick the lock and push open the door. His senses were assaulted by the pungent smell of acrylics and oils. Hanson's living room was a gallery, filled with large and small canvases jostling for attention. A TV sat atop a night table with an easy chair in front of it. An old desk with a PC occupied a corner. That was about it for the living room. The dining room at least claimed a table. Grundy couldn't see into the kitchen.

Hanson obviously liked vibrant, hot colors—reds, yellows, oranges—and images touching. Hands beckoned from a rectangular canvas that hung on the wall of the stairway to the second floor. Easels in the middle of the living room held two canvases, one of a Fifth Avenue sidewalk filled with jostling, weary-faced crowds, the other of a concert, youths passing squirming bodies over their heads. From where he stood, Grundy could see portraits of friends embracing, mothers with children, wrestlers in the ring, doctors with patients. He didn't need to step into the room to absorb this celebration of touching humanity.

The pager on his belt vibrated. He checked the number. Headquarters. Before he even dialed the number on his cellular phone, he knew what the call would be about.

Hanson had struck again. He was at Ellis Island, probably checking his roots, the lieutenant snorted into the phone. He was sending a copter to the nearest ballfield to pick Grundy up.

The graceless copter created a mini-hurricane as it landed on third base. Grundy held onto his hat, the one vanity he allowed himself. The pilot eyed him skeptically as he climbed into the cockpit.

Grundy extended his hand. "Detective Grundy, Depriver Enforcement," he said rather grimly.

"Hi. Joe Fisher." The pilot shook Grundy's hand vigorously, then motioned him to strap on his seat belt. The copter lurched into the air above the Brooklyn ballfield. Grundy felt his stomach sink.

"Apparently this Depriver guy touched a few people just before getting off the ferry. Created a lot of confusion, which made it easier for him to slip off the boat once they reached Ellis Island," Fisher explained.

This didn't sound good. Why would Hanson act so carelessly, with so many people around and nowhere to go? Grundy stared ahead, as if trying to read the sky. He didn't like these angry clouds, but Fisher didn't seem impressed.

The Statue of Liberty came into view and for a moment Grundy was overwhelmed by its massiveness. At the rate they were flying, Grundy was sure they would crash right into her. He closed his eyes to block her out. When he looked again, a swarm of media copters hovered over the island, some of them only yards away from the statue's spiked crown. He almost felt sorry for the print guys, who didn't stand a chance of getting out here as fast. Fisher swore at them as he looked for a good spot to land.

The Island Director stood anxiously at the base of the pedestal, in front of the Statue's entrance. He was obviously waiting for Grundy. A ring of at least fifty of New York's finest surrounded the base of the statue. Grundy was surprised by the magnitude of the crowd pushing against the police to catch a glimpse of the depraved Depriver. There must be at least two hundred people. Didn't they have better things to do? They were all animated, their mouths forming angry words, which Grundy couldn't hear. The noise of the hovering copters drowned out all other sounds.

The statue had been evacuated. A number of people claimed that they'd seen the Depriver touch the security guard at the entrance. A few witnesses said that Hanson had a canvas knapsack over his shoulder and was carrying a gym bag. The guard was no help, as he couldn't hear any of the questions the cops were asking.

The director had no patience for this sort of thing. He grabbed the detective's sleeve as soon as he reached him. "Are you Grundy?" he shouted over the roar. Grundy nodded, looking up at the statue's torch. Those nasty storm clouds seemed to emanate from it like smoke. A lot of stairs to climb, Grundy thought, hoping that the elevator would work, although he knew it wouldn't. Hanson would have made sure of that.

"What are you going to do?" the director shouted impatiently. "We know he's in there."

Grundy looked at him evenly. "I'm going in after him, since the Depriver Task Force hasn't arrived yet."

The director was sweating, despite the April chill. Grundy gave him a job to keep his mind occupied.

"Look, make sure these cops keep everyone else out. When the Task Force gets here, let them in. You got it?"

The director solemnly nodded his head.

Grundy turned and walked deliberately toward the entrance at the base of the Statue, trying to ignore the crowd straining to press in, shouting tips on how to catch the Depriver. He felt his spastic colon kick in when he reached the ticket booth. Christ, rape had only given him heartburn. Grundy grimly touched the handle of the magnum strapped to his chest under his left breast pocket. He breathed deeply, and proceeded past the ticket window into the Statue's entrance.

The reception area was mostly dark, save for the light that filtered through the glass door. Hanson had killed the power. Here, within the massive maw of the statue, the chopping of the copters sounded like a million marching feet. He wouldn't hear Hanson if he were sneezing beside him. Grundy was almost tempted to yell Hanson's name up the length of the long, winding stairs, but he didn't think the Depriver was simply waiting somewhere to reach out and grab him. Hanson was obviously busy.

Grundy took another deep breath and proceeded up the stairs, guided solely by the eerie red emergency lighting. The stairway was wide enough to accommodate two medium-sized people, and the steps were evenly spaced, so Grundy fell into a natural pace. He paused for breath only when he reached the first landing and spied the first Polaroid, taped crookedly to the wall. The photo showed one of Hanson's ferry victims, a man, crumpled on the floor, his face turned towards his aggressor, eyes wide and pained and accusing. No sweet sentiments here; Hanson had changed his M. O. Grundy pulled the photo off the wall and slipped it into his jacket pocket.

By the time he reached the Statue's head, Grundy had found five more photos, which he meticulously collected. He stood on the deck within the Lady's great head, his heart pounding from exertion. At least in here there was light; it oozed grayly through the many wire-mesh openings in the crown. One panel on the side of the Statue's raised right arm had been kicked out.

The deafening media copters buzzed around the Statue's head like supersonic bees around a hive, cameras trained. Hanson must be out there somewhere, visible to them. Grundy crossed the floor to the open panel in the crown, carefully leaning out to inspect the view, his face and hair buffeted by the powerful, capricious winds blowing in all directions. The air smelled like gasoline. Dark clouds menaced the copters. One of the pilots was gesturing toward the torch. Grundy looked up and felt his heart skip.

Hanson was standing on top of the iron fencing that circled the torch's platform. He was wearing a safety belt, tethered to what Grundy couldn't tell, and struggling against the wind to throw a black shroud over the flames of the torch.

Grundy stared at Hanson's back, a mixture of awe and sadness momentarily dulling his police instincts. He watched the strong, lean body for a few seconds, Hanson's shoulder-length black hair whipping in the wind as he symbolically extinguished the flame. Inspecting the black cloths fastened across the Statue's eyes and mouth below, Grundy realized with a start that Hanson must have rappelled down the face. His task was almost completed. But what would he do for a finale?

Grundy crossed to the stairway that would take him to

the torch. The metal gate making the torch inaccessible had been kicked in. By now he knew the width of the Statue's risers and took them two by two without a thought. By the time Grundy had exited the arm's stairwell to stand on the outside platform of the torch, Hanson had finished his veiling.

Grundy stopped in his tracks. Hanson's boyish face was smiling down at him from the top of the fence railing. Portions of the fence on both sides of Hanson were missing. He seemed to be standing on a single panel. His belt was tied to the torch, directly below the flame. Remarkably, he seemed able to maintain his balance despite the wind.

He grinned proudly at Grundy. "I'm just going to give them a few more minutes," Hanson shouted. "Just enough time to get some good footage. I have enough explosive to blow away at least the torch—maybe the arm and a few copters, if I'm lucky. So you'd better get back down." He kept turning his head as he spoke, to keep the hair from his eyes.

"Hanson . . . Mark. You must stop!" Grundy shouted. "You don't need to do it this way." He had no idea what other way Hanson might express himself. He just wanted him to believe there were better ways. But Hanson wasn't in the mood.

"I can't stop, you stupid bastard! You may as well tell me to stop breathing. Goddamn you!"

Thunder rumbled in the distance. The hovering copters seemed to be furiously berating both of them. Without thinking too hard about it, Grundy stepped onto a part of the platform that was missing a section of fence, almost directly beside Hanson, and offered up his hand.

Hanson looked down at Grundy, genuine surprise on his face. "Why now?" he shouted.

"Because I need to know to be better," Grundy answered as honestly as he could.

A sudden burst of wind pushed him from behind and

Grundy was shocked to realize that he was slipping off the platform. He grasped desperately at the section of railing below Hanson's feet and found himself dangling four hundred feet over the harbor, his right leg splayed on the torch's platform, his left leg kicking at the air. He struggled against the wind to heave himself back onto the platform, his fingers clutching at the openings in the iron fencing. The iron lattice work was thin and sharp at the edges, slicing his hands. His fingers felt slippery and cold from blood.

Hanson unhooked the line from his safety belt and jumped to the platform. The copters roared about them in delirium. Hanson reached out his hand to Grundy, careful not to touch him—yet. Grundy knew he couldn't pull himself back unaided. His grasp was slipping. But he was also afraid of what would happen once he held out his bloody hand to Hanson.

"Goddamn you!" Hanson screamed. "It's your choice, man."

Grundy let go of the fence and extended his hand as he felt his weight tip to the nothingness below.

Grundy lay in a hospital bed, his back propped up by too many pillows, his hands wrapped in gauze, like a mummy's. It was weird, he thought, not feeling anything—not his sliced hands, or sprained ankle, or bruised back. He had lost all physical sensation. His doctor was pretty sure that, like most of these cases, his loss of feeling would only be temporary, but insisted that Grundy stay in the hospital for the next couple of days, just to be safe.

Grundy had his own room in the hospital. Everything seemed so white and sterile—the bed sheets and cover, the walls, the curtains over the closed windows. Only the TV blaring from a corner shelf high above his bed had any real color. Grundy was watching CNN. It kept showing the same footage, over and over again: Hanson duct taping the Statue's eyes and mouth. Hanson throwing the black tarp over the torch. Hanson leaping to his death after he'd pulled Grundy back onto the platform.

Grundy closed his eyes. He wondered if the lack of physical pain could make the emotional pain sharper. He felt guilty. Why did Hanson save him? Was it that he couldn't pass up the opportunity to save a life, instead of taking something from it? But Hanson was a Depriver.

Maybe Hanson had deprived him of something besides his senses—his ability to ignore his emotions, to keep his conscience at bay. Maybe now, because of Grundy, the Depriver laws might change.

Grundy clicked off the TV and rolled over onto his side. He'd have to wait until tomorrow to find out.

DEATH GODDESS OF THE LOWER EAST SIDE

LINK YACO

Maria Tereza Lopez sneered and the teenagers flinched.

These New Jersey weekenders, in their shopping mall leathers and designer surgical gloves, liked to take the F train to the Village and play tough, hip, and dangerous. When Maria saw this kind of would-be sense-Dep punk, it really rankled her. For Maria was the real thing, the genuine item. While these pampered kids played at being sense-Deps, Maria had to live it, and it wasn't a fun happy thing, you know.

So Maria played with her protective surgical glove, rolled back her lips in a sleepy, death's-head grin, and leaned a little closer to the straight kids from New Jersey. They recoiled and muttered among themselves. Maria had her bad ear turned toward them, but she could imagine what they were saying.

"Deppie hag!"

"I think she wants to touch you! A love touch!"

The kids got off the subway at the next stop. As it happened, it was Maria's stop, too, so she got off after them and watched them glance worriedly over their shoulders. She considered following them, just to freak them. But she was already late for work, so she booked—and stumbled over something. Her degraded tactile sense had let her down again and she acquired yet another bruise, just because she wanted to get to work a few minutes faster.

She needn't have bothered. No one noticed or cared if she was late. It was only a waitressing gig, and business was always slack at Cafe Nil, here at the ass end of the East Village, in NoHo, north of Houston. Why she'd bothered getting two master's degrees was a mystery. No one would hire her once they read her job application and saw her medical background (legally required, under threat of heavy fine and/or imprisonment). Well, really, she knew why she'd gotten her degrees. It was to put off having to deal with the real world. Not that finally graduating, over a decade ago, had actually brought her down to earth. East Village was Fantasyland, and Cafe Nil was the information booth.

The sun was down by the time Maria walked down into the small, half-submerged cafe, but it was actually darker inside than out. A few naked sixty-watt bulbs hung from the ceiling in the rear and the candles on the tables had not yet been lit, so the peeling black paint on the walls absorbed almost all the available light.

There was a sudden motion in the rear. Maria's night vision was shot; she had to strain to make out that the movement of Jake Nada, coming from behind the bar. He was a good-looking geek. Fortyish, but still youthfully slim. Most Deps were. The sense of taste degraded pretty quickly and food lost its attraction. His hornrims and ponytail enhanced his youthful affect. He looked like a kid, not the owner of the cafe. He tossed her a dirty apron. "We're overstaffed, as usual. If you want to quit early tonight . . . and maybe have dinner with me?"

Maria frowned, then turned her good ear toward him. He repeated himself. Maria tied on the apron slowly. "Haven't we been through this?"

Jake grinned innocently. "It's just dinner. I'm not going to screw you blind."

She turned away. "Maybe. I need the hours, though. We'll see."

Jake said something, but she couldn't hear and didn't care. She knew that he gave all his employees more hours than he needed to, because it was a Dep joint. Jake was a Dep, as was everyone who worked for him. They all had trouble getting by. He paid them as much as he could, but a Dep joint didn't make much money. All the customers were low-rent types—underemployed Deps, liberal young (and consequently undersalaried) activists, and the occasional wacky dep-chaser, neurotic, thrill-seeking, self-destructive weirdos who got off on the romantic danger of a Dep's company. Only the chasers ever had any money, and they tended not to spend it on cappuccino and pasta salads.

Maria halfheartedly hustled to get some tables, but the other waiters and waitresses were pressing harder than she was. After two hours, she had three seatings. One was an earnest, skinny, youngish woman who wore no makeup and had the frames of her glasses taped together with duct tape. She wore no gloves, so was not a Dep. She was with an older man with a gray-streaked beard, a beret, and gloves. Then there was a thirtyish Dep guy, in leather pants, with an eyepatch and a hearing aid, sex-hound, on the make for some fatalisticaly horny Dep woman. Finally, there was a creepy-looking plump guy, with big wet eyes, wearing a T-shirt with a corporate logo, who could have been any age from twenty to fifty.

Not a pleasant crew. The creep disgusted her, the earnest young woman depressed her, and the horny Dep pissed her off. Pushy, manipulative, predatory Dep dicks like him had cost her eighty per cent of the hearing in her right ear, and lately she was experiencing major color loss in her right eye as well. She was only just barely forty and she had the sensory facilities of a pre-Dawn octogenarian.

"Cortical stimulation . . . hypothalamus . . . no effect on the speech center or any of the memory functions underlying the affected areas . . ."

Maria could hear fragments of the young woman's patter. She was probably an NYU grad student, to judge by her academic but naive rap. Maria had a Masters in bioscience and had heard all the theories.

". . . chemical inhibitors but no detectable trace . . . yet if it is a stimulus electrical in nature, why then . . ."

There were no answers. Dep syndrome remained a scientific mystery despite billions in research. Maria had pursued the empirical grail for years until it became obvious that it would lead to neither enlightenment nor a job. Then she'd moved on to history, thinking that the vast panoply of human experience would shed some light on her existential predicament, even if her physiological state was the real question. But she'd ended up learning about the longbow at Agincourt and Neolithic tin-smelting—nothing that relieved her own isolation. No one is so deprived as a Depriver.

She looked around the cafe. A room full of lonely people is just as empty as a broken-down flat on the lower East Side. She might as well be home, back in Alphabet City on Avenue D, watching *Seinfeld* reruns, nursing her bruises, which she could feel, even if she didn't have enough tactile sense left to avoid getting them in the first place.

"Miss? May I have another G-and-T?" The fat creep caught her attention. She got him his gin-and-tonic and deliberately sloshed a little of it when she thumped it down on the table in front of him. The creep was ogling her. She was forty-something and her frizzy dark hair was graying, but she had the same figure she'd had in grad school. And maybe her black jeans were a little too tight. And she wasn't wearing a bra under her light cotton shirt. Face it, she was beautiful. The poor creep couldn't help but stare.

She sat down at an empty table and sipped a Coke with lots of ice. The only way she could taste anything these days was if it was cold. She nibbled at some cheese, but tasted nothing. She gazed up at the TV over the bar.

Jake sat down next to her.

"Remember when we were kids and there were a hundred cable channels?" he said, somewhat rhetorically.

Maria grunted. "How could they afford to generate all that programming in the old days?"

"Economics were different. Advertising actually brought in revenue. Not so much disposable income these days. People don't blow it on pocket fisherman and memorial china sets. Which leaves us with less to do on a Saturday night."

"I can tell where you're going with this," said Maria, standing up. "We've been there before. It's too damn dangerous. My doctor says that if I have one more contact, I might permanently lose my left eye."

"But we can be safe," protested Jake. "I'll wear a condom. We'll keep our gloves on."

Maria laughed. "Safe! One little slip, that's all it takes. The tiniest contact. I love you, Jake, but don't tempt me. Now leave me alone. I gotta work." She walked back to her wait station and pretended to fold napkins.

She noticed a new bruise on her arm. When had she gotten that? One of these days she was going to walk into something serious. Or a fire would start and her fading sense of smell wouldn't alert her until it was too late. Or she would stop eating completely, and not even feel the hunger pangs as she starved.

The creep had finished his G-and-T. Maria went over. "You're a goddeth," he lisped.

"Excuse me?"

"I'm thorry, I mean sorry. I just think you're very attractive."

Shit. Another Dep-chaser. "Want another G and T?"

The creep nodded disconsolately and Maria turned away. She could feel his eyes on her jeans as she moved.

"The nature of the mind's method of information transmission had lately been assumed to be essentially chemical in nature, with attendant electrical phenomenon. Deprivation Syndrome changed all that. We've been forced to reevaluate everything we know about neurology. Don't you see what a boon Deps could be to medicine if everyone wasn't afraid to use them in test situations? Just think of what we could find out about the basic processes of the brain!"

The NYU kid was excited. Her Dep friend, older, wiser, and burned out, nodded tiredly. He knew that nothing was going to change. He sipped his decaf and told the kid, "You know, the AMA is always going to treat Deps like they're a disease to be cured. They look for retroviruses, genetic links, and enzymatic reactions, but they never experiment with Dep exposure under control circumstances. Public outrage would blow their funding, maybe their careers. To deliberately expose a straight to a Dep would be viewed as akin to Nazi camp experiments or the CIA LSD projects."

Jake Nada cornered Maria again. "I was just kidding, you know. I've been having vision problems lately, too. I can't risk any more loss. I really just want to have dinner. Nothing else."

"Nothing?" Maria was skeptical. Jake had lured her into bed before.

"Nothing. That's why they call me 'Nada'!" He looked so guileless.

"That's not your real name, you poseur." Maria hesitated. "What's this about your eyes?" she asked softly.

Jake produced an utterly phony, devil-may-care grin. "Ah, I've lost most of my color vision . . . in both eyes."

"Most?"

"The only color I still sometimes see is blue. 'Auras,' like the fuzzie-wuzzie New Age types say. Only it's not mystical crap. I see them on everybody, straight or Dep. And on electrical appliances. I think maybe I'm picking up heat signatures."

Maria was a sucker for Jake's puppy dog act. When he played helpless, she went all gooey inside. Maybe just dinner. It would be nice to get totally dosed on over-priced table red and pour her heart out.

The NYU kid was waving for a refill. Two more tables walked into her section. Tourists. And two horny sister-Deps joined the Dep-on-the-prowl. Suddenly, the place was packed.

"Gotta go, Jake. Maybe it'll slow down later."

Fortunately, it didn't. She'd managed to slip out of Jake's clutches once again. She had forgotten that it was Memorial Day weekend, and everyone was in town. Sometimes the Village emptied out on the holidays; other times, everyone seemed to decide that the roads and airports would be too crowded, and stayed in town. This weekend was one of the latter cases.

The creepy Dep-chaser ordered another drink. He was really getting plastered. "You're goddeth," he slurred at Maria, "I mean, a goddess."

"Shut up, you drunken asshole," Maria snapped at him.

"I'm thorry." His eyes grew moister. "I didn't mean to bother you. Let me make it up to you!"

"*Perfecto*. Why don't you buy a round for the house?" suggested Maria, who knew how this one went.

The creep pulled out a handful of plastic. Maria snatched a Mastercard and took off.

"The AMA is so closed to alternative medicine. There is a wide spectrum of therapies that could help Deps. You know, acupressure can enhance sensory impression."

The NYU kid was turning out to be a homeopathic freak, too. But Maria was so grateful that she had stopped reciting her Sunday supplement catalogue of Dep medicine, that she brought the girl a bottle of the good Chardonnay, not the house white, paid for by the creep. The grad looked surprised. She said something. Maria turned to her good side. The kid looked serious. "I said, 'Thanks for the bottle.' You got hearing problems? Because I know some pressure sequences that will enhance recuperative powers in the five senses. You want me to try?"

Maria smiled weakly. She'd had this carrot dangled under her nose many times. She'd tried every goddamn remedy in the book. Healing crystals, mantras, vitamin therapy (which consisted, she discovered, of taping a bottle of vitamins over the affected area), solar treatments, gluten-free diets. You name it. Screw it, what did she have to lose?

"*De aqcuerdo*," she said, only slightly wary. "But be careful. I don't have any insurance, you know. If you touch me, it's your problem."

"Sure, sure." The kid pulled on a pair of surgical gloves and gestured for Maria to sit. "I want you to concentrate on your breathing. Bring the good energy in and push the bad energy out." She pressed a spot on the back of Maria's neck and another on the side of her nose. Maria could barely feel the touch. But she didn't tell that to the kid. She just tried to relax and think of her breathing. Good energy in; bad, blue energy out. She imagined her Dep aura being dispelled, blowing away like blue vapor.

The kid pressed gently at her for at least five minutes. It was really getting boring and Maria was neglecting her tables. She was just about to call the whole thing off, when the kid removed her gloved hands. Maria started to stand.

"No, wait." The kid put a thumb in the center of Maria's back and with her other hand, she squeezed her elbow. "Your energy is blocked, you see, so we have to open up the channels."

Maria heard someone snickering. It was Jake. She glared at him, then realized that he was standing on her bad side. "I heard that!" she yelled at him.

"I'm sorry. You just looked like such a simp, sitting there with that New Age straight squeezing your elbow, I couldn't help it."

"No! I mean, I *heard* that! With my bad ear!"

"Ni puta idea." Jake shrugged and went back to tend bar. He wasn't impressed by temporary recoveries, Maria knew. All Deps faded in and out. But he wasn't going to spoil it for her. For just a moment, she let herself believe that this meant she could risk a little intimacy with Jake. Maybe they would have more than just a late dinner. Not that the idea of eating seemed that exciting. She nibbled at some cold cuts to keep her going in the meantime.

As the evening wore on, her hearing got stronger. Weird. Maybe the daffy little woman from NYU was right. Maybe acupressure could counter the danger of sex. It was past three a.m. by the time they finally closed. Jake yawned and gave her a weary half-grin.

"What happened to our late dinner?"

Maria rubbed her eyes. "Maybe tomorrow, if it's slow."

Jake laughed. "A slow Sunday night here? What are the odds, do you think?"

Maria booked. She was lucky and found a cab that was willing to carry a Dep . . . and willing to go to Avenue D past three in the morning.

While she fished for the keys in her purse, she thought she heard footsteps. She turned quickly and saw a bulky figure duck into a doorway across the street. Nuts. She should have had her keys ready before she got out of the cab. The Lower East Side wasn't any more dangerous by night than by day, but it certainly wasn't any less. Some types around here were so desperate, the threat of a Deprivation didn't mean a thing to them.

She quickly got the door open and stumbled up the six flights of stone stairs to her little flat. She took a few deep breaths, then ran a bath in the tub that sat in the middle of her kitchen. She put on a CD of music from her childhood— the Blowfish reunion album—and got into the tub. Her feet and lower back were killing her, but she could hear the music with crystal clarity, her bad ear working just fine now. It brought back happy memories of her early adolescence, in the Dawn days, before her Dep tendencies had surfaced. She shuddered when she remembered the terror of brushing her bare elbow against her mother's arm and seeing her stumble as her vision flickered. Within a half-hour, she was blind. It lasted for days. The shame, the fear, all came back to Maria. That boy she'd been, sort of, dating, what was his name? Carlos Greenburg. The little rat had never come near her again. But the myth of Deppie fecundity had brought lots of others around. Scum, all of them.

So much for nostalgia. She dried herself off and killed the CD. The sky outside was getting light. Time to crash. When she closed her eyes, the world flared blue and then disappeared into murky fuzz.

A particularly intense sex dream about a group encounter woke her late the next afternoon. Funny, there were more people in that orgy than she'd slept with in her entire life. Jake had been in the dream, as well as the dark, bulky figure she'd glimpsed across the street last night.

She spent the next several hours watching videos of old network shows. A lot of cop things, pre-Dawn, many of them shot in the Lower East Side—*NYPD Blue, Law & Order, Plato's Law*—all of them trying to appear dark, seedy, and scary. But anything from the pre-Dawn days seemed innocent by today's standards.

That evening, she hopped the F train back up to NoHo. The streets were largely empty—it was too early for the dinner crowd. As she walked the last few blocks to Cafe Nil, she thought she heard heavy footsteps, just out of sync with her own sneaker-clad tread. Whenever she looked around, however, the sound stopped and no one was in sight.

NoHo was generally safe, as long as you dressed sleazily enough. If you dressed like someone who might have money, you could be in trouble. She was wearing her faded, worn, ripped black jeans, unwashed since yesterday, and a neon pink lycra tube top, to attract tips. Hardly a fitted suit. She picked up her pace a bit and in a few minutes ducked into the safety of the cafe.

"Maria! *Come esta?*" yelled a cheery Jake.

She caught her breath. "I think I'm getting auditory screw-ups. I thought I heard someone following me."

He frowned. "You can't be too paranoid. Better let me see you home tonight."

She laughed. "Jake. I may be in more danger from you."

He laid one of his patented Nada grins on her and she bought it. "*De aqcuerdo* you can walk me to my door tonight. But no farther."

"And dinner?"

"Dinner if you're good."

"And a spanking if I'm bad?"

"Don't be so fucking precious."

Maria sized up the room. She was the only wait staff on the floor. The cafe was empty, except for a white-caned Dep bum nursing a cup of cold coffee.

"You think we might get a repeat of last night's business?"

Jake shrugged. "I doubt it. That was awful fluky. If the overweight Dep-chaser hadn't bought for the room, I doubt we'd have kept them in here."

"*Coño!*" cursed Maria. A large, dark figure had just entered the doorway of the cafe. "It's him! The bastard that's been following me!"

"Excuthe me, mith. Are you open yet?"

It was her chubby admirer from the night before.

Jake chuckled. "We're open. In fact, I think we owe you one. It's on the house." He turned to mix a G-and-T.

Maria leaned over his shoulder and muttered. "This is not funny, Jake. I think he's been following me. There's nothing cute about some wacked-out customer stalking you after work."

Jake looked up, apologetically, but just then a cohort of regulars walked in. Maria slammed her fist on the bar top and headed over.

An hour later, the place was empty again. Even the plump Dep-chaser had taken off, and none of the other wait staff had shown up. They often didn't on Sundays. There was little business and they had big hangovers to deal with.

"That's it," declared Jake, "We're closed. I'm sending the cook home. Let me get you something from the kitchen, and then I'll take you home."

He locked up, and then fixed them an elaborate chicken salad. Maria felt certain he would lay it on thick with the wine and candles, but he skipped on both. And he was uncharacteristically quiet as they ate. She chewed her cold chicken salad slowly. It tasted all right, if a bit metallic. Finally, she could stand Jake's silence no more.

"What's with you? *Qué?* Where's the usual chatter?"

He forced his grin. "Just thinking, is all, *amiga.* I've been getting the flickers in my right eye today. Makes you think, no? As much as I want to, sleeping with you is just too dangerous. You are right. So this is what I have decided."

Maria raised her eyebrows. *"Qué?"*

"We should get married."

She looked into his big, dark, unblinking eyes. He was serious. *"Otay,* I give. What is your reasoning here? I mean, if you've decided that sex is out, how do you get from there to marriage? This is a conceptual leap unprecedented even for you."

"Why, thank you." He grinned, looking more like his old self. "My thinking is this: We like each other, maybe even love each other. We're both lonely, getting to a certain age. Now that we're agreed that sex is out of the question, the last impediment is removed from a marriage of true minds. We may not be able to touch each other, but we can still give each other company, warmth, reassurance."

Maria sighed. "You're just being romantic. You know what Dep marriages are like. Within a year we'd either be basket cases or at each other's throats.'

"Just think about it, that's all I ask."

"Oh, baby, you're so fucking corny. No wonder I love you. Come on, *pronto,* take me home."

It was still early, not even midnight, so they decided to walk. It was a nice night and the walk was only, maybe, a half-hour. Jake looked scummy enough in his sleeveless, threadbare denim jacket that no one would bother them.

"Do you hear that?" Maria's bad ear was ringing with imaginary echoes on their footsteps.

Jake stopped. "Auditory distortions again? Wait a—what's that?" He squinted at a doorway behind them.

A large, dark figure stepped out.

"*Coño!*" yelled Maria and ran. Jake screamed, "Shit!" and ran after her.

This time, the heavy gait of their pursuer was clearly audible. As big as he was, he was not clumsy. Nor was he slow. Within a dozen yards, in the space of seconds, he caught up with them.

Maria's scream was cut off in a choking sound as the big man grabbed her throat from behind. She kicked backward, struck something, and broke free. She fell to the ground, coughing and crying and fighting for air. Out of the corner of her eye, she saw Jake had fallen next to her.

The big man stood over her. He spoke. "Touch me."

She coughed out phlegm and managed to croak, "What?"

Jake started to stand and the big man slugged him in the belly. Jake folded in half and settled down like a slow-motion film of a building demolition.

The big man spoke again. "Touch me! You know you want to! You like to take our eyes, our ears, to steal our thouls. So do it!"

Maria spat at him. "You freak! I know who you are!"

The heavyset Dep chaser sank to his knees and grabbed her by the throat. "You're a goddeth."

Maria couldn't breathe. She grabbed his wrists and tried to pull them away. He didn't even notice her efforts.

"You're so pale . . . so slender." His moist eyes were glazed over.

Maria brought her wrist to her mouth and bit the edge of her surgical.

The big man shook her violently. "You know you want to!"

Maria pulled her hand from her mouth and the glove peeled away. She slapped her open palm against the big man's plump, pale face.

He fell to his knees and clutched his eyes. "My eyes! I can't see!"

Jake, meanwhile, had managed to stand up again. He pulled a glove off and swatted the fat man's jowly features. The big man grabbed the side of his head. "My ears! I can't hear! You've taken my ears as well!"

Jake and Maria stepped away from the deaf and blind giant, who was crawling around on his knees and flailing his hands. "Where are you? Take the rest of me! Come back! I am yours!"

Jake muttered, "He's had a lot of contact in his time. Otherwise he wouldn't have reacted so quickly. I'm betting that he's going to have permanent loss. He's probably got some heavy taste, touch, and smell degradation as well, but he won't notice that until later."

Maria turned away and vomited up her chicken salad. She wiped her lips on her shiny pink top. "Let's go home."

When they got to Avenue D, Jake went up the six flights of stone stairs with Maria. She heard every step clearly, in both her ears.

When they climbed into bed and made desperate love without kissing, without touching, she felt everything was going to be all right—finally, everything all right. She arched wide her legs beneath him and pressed against him. Her shirt rode up and so did his and she felt the naked flesh of his belly press against hers. And her left eye clouded over forever.

But she didn't stop—there was no point in stopping now. She wrapped her legs around him and accepted, even embraced, her blindness. Tomorrow she would try to convince herself that it was all worth it. Jake was a mighty fine fuck. Almost worth losing everything for.

Almost.

SHARED LOSSES

BOB MAHNKEN

Jeremy disappeared for two, three days last week. It may've been two, felt like three: hard to tell, exactly, because he's my clock. Ever since he's been old enough to talk, he's told me when it's light or dark, or what the sky looks like . . . not that I really need him to: I can hear the birds in the morning and the peepers at night, and smell the cool gray metal of rain on the breeze. But while he was gone my sleep got discombobulated, and the dreams were all the bad kind.

I can still see, in my dreams. That's how I know what Jeremy looks like: from touching his face and dreaming about him. Those are the good kind of dreams. The bad ones are all about his father . . . whichever one of those rogue bastards was his father, I mean.

The shrinks and quacks were all very quick to explain what had happened to me, back in those black months before Jeremy was born. They're always that way, though, always in a big hurry to explain to a person what's wrong with her, using those words they use to keep anyone from knowing what they're talking about. Hysteria. Trauma. Projection. Disassociation. I said it was a load of shit then, and time has shown me right. And of course, instead of admitting they never knew what they were talking about in the first place, they've all simply switched specialties: now they're advocates for the kind of scum who made me what I am today. The Deprivers don't deserve censure or exile, they say; it's a disease, they say. No shit, says I. No shit.

Jeremy's fifteen this year, and I've never been more worried. Soon I'll have to explain it to him, why we live the way we do, up here in these hills in this tarpaper hellhole with no one closer than five miles across the woods. A child can't understand these things, but an adolescent must, I suppose, if he's to continue growing. The shrinks and quacks say that his is the age when the condition generally develops, and while they've said a lot of things over the years which have proven to be claptrap, I can't take the chance that they're right about this. They say puberty is the last safe time, so I've been keeping close watch on Jeremy these last few years . . . as much as I can watch anything, that is. I don't know what I'll do if worse comes to worst; but I don't want him out in the world till I know what he is.

He's at that questing age, though. I tell him how important it is that we stay up here, away from cities and highways and people, but I haven't been able to tell him why. I don't have any trust for newspapers or TV; they're useless to me, but I listen to NPR and get enough of what passes for information these days that way. They still can't tell us where these people came from, or how they got the way they are, or how long it's really been going on; they won't even admit they don't know anything, just reel off a bunch of statistics. I was raised to view statistics as just the third kind of lie and nothing has changed my view. They say most deprivations are temporary; only one in ten is permanent, or likely to be permanent. More bullshit. But the shrinks and quacks have been assigning arbitrary numbers to everything longer than I've been around, and folks listen, I guess. Let them take their chances; I know better.

We're not completely isolated up here. These hills are dotted with exiles, folks who came up here when the world started to get out of control, when you couldn't be sure, anymore, about anyone: not the guy on the bus next to you, or the woman making change in the drugstore ... or a mad pack of Blinders on a Saturday night spree. Old Harley Fenton has a place across the ravine where he lives with his wife, Emma, and five or six big dogs. Emma has to be careful, because she was deprived of her sense of touch. This was years ago, before they came up here; the shrinks and quacks must've had a good time trying to figure that one out. Harley keeps a close watch on her, too, because she can't feel anything, anywhere in her body; she could fall down and break her leg and never know it till the gangrene set in. In a way, she's worse off than me, but at least she has Harley. Harley's a crusty old misanthrope, probably made worse by having a wife he can't pleasure, but he takes care of her. She was deprived about the same time as me, back when the government was calling the problem Sensory Deprivation Syndrome (SDS), and they were still trying to blame it on radiation, or acid rain, or cholesterol. They didn't try to pull any of those old saws on me, of course, because my problem was simple: I was just hysterical. But no one ever heard of hysterical numbness, so Emma had SDS.

I was never hysterical, and I never had any doubt what caused my blindness: it was a direct result of being caught on a deserted loading dock behind the Fairview Mall by a half-dozen vicious, giggling punks. When the first one touched me, it was to throw me down where they could get at me easier; things started to get dark as soon as they got to my skin. By the time the sixth one rolled off me, and all I could hear was their laughing and all I could smell was my fear and blood mixed with their mutant spunk, I knew I'd never see again. They tore my sight from me like a cheap trophy, and psychology had nothing to do with it.

The funny thing is, they caught a few of them. They were brought to trial and released, as scum like them usually is, and the lawyers made a big fuss about the idea of testing them for disease: said it was a violation of their rights. Like they have rights and I don't. Like they're worth protecting and I'm just some random nobody who got in the way, even though all I wanted was to get in my car and go home. Those lawyers are the same people who now hold their hands (well, not literally) and commiserate with them about how awful it must be to have to hear the President use words like "quarantine," as though wearing latex gloves and staying the hell away from people is somehow worse than being the guest of honor at a gang-rape, or never seeing another sunset.

I was thirty-six when it happened. Felt the clock ticking; how's that for irony? There I was, worried I'd never have a child, and here I am now, north side of fifty, worrying what he'll be when he grows up. If he grows up.

When he finally did come back, he tried sneaking up the hill quiet. He's learned to sneak through the woods quiet as the breeze, but I smelt him before I heard a sound. I may be old and peculiar and blinder than a bat, but I know the smell of my own whelp when he's upwind. I took down the old Ithaca shotgun I keep over the door and fired a blast in his general direction to let him know how mad I was and to remind him, maybe, how much I hate to be snuck up on, even if I can smell him. After that I heard running and some crashing through the underbrush, and was about to call out,

"What the hell's going on?" when I caught another whiff, a human smell separate from Jeremy's. Whoever it was probably hadn't expected to be fired upon. Jeremy should've known better. I sat down on the porch to wait while every so often his voice drifted up to me, insisting that it was all right, she didn't mean no harm

I decided to help him out a tad. "How many times I told you not to come sneakin' up here like some animal?" I yelled.

Jeremy answered after a moment. "Goddamn it, Ma," he cried. "How you know you ain't gonna hit me?"

" 'Cause I know where you are and I know which way I'm facing," I called back. They were closer now. "Who the hell's with you?"

They were coming straight up the path now, two of them, Jeremy and the other, and I knew what he was going to say before he said it. "Just a girl, Ma."

Just a girl. Just as plain and simple as that, as if there's nothing at all peculiar about disappearing for two, three days and coming back with a stranger. I didn't need him to tell me she was a girl. I could smell her.

"She's scared of you," said Jeremy. And she was: I could tell she was dragging along behind him, afraid to come too close.

"She oughta be," I said. "Where'd you get her?"

"Place about thirty mile east," he said, sitting down at my feet on the squeaking, broken step. "Yesterday afternoon. She was all alone, hiding in this burned out old farmstand by the road."

"Why didn't you leave her there?" I demanded.

Jeremy didn't answer right away, and I wished I could see his face. Then he said, "She was all dirty and scared. I don't think she can talk."

"You touch her?"

"What?"

"You touch her skin? At all?"

Jeremy hesitated again; I didn't think he understood what I was asking, but then he said, "You know, Ma, I ain't completely ignorant. I know about you, and Mrs. Fenton and them others."

"Well, if you ain't ignorant, then you're stupid," I said. "How do you know she's safe?"

"She's just a girl, Ma. Younger'n me."

"Maybe she was yesterday, but I smell the blood on her."

Jeremy fell silent again so I didn't say any more, just listened to his breathing, and the girl's. Hers came in short, sharp gasps: she was frightened and exhausted, and stank of menarche. "Can you talk, girl?"

I heard her move, and then Jeremy began to laugh. "She can't see you," he said, not to me.

Then, laboriously slurred, from the girl: "I can talk. I can't hear."

Jeremy was still giggling. I cuffed him on the head. "What's wrong with you?" I said.

"I've been talking to her all day," he said. "With my back turned. I thought she was mute."

"She probably thought you were an idiot," I said. I turned my face toward the girl, or toward her smell, anyway, and slowly said: "There's a stream on the other side. Would you like a bath?"

"Yes," she said. "Thank you."

Jeremy made to stand, but I grabbed him. "She'll find it," I said.

"But"

I covered my mouth as if to cough and said, "Never mind, boy. We need to talk."

Soon he'll ask me if he can keep her. Like she's some dog he found.

Kyre moves listlessly through the tall grass and weeds behind the strange old woman's ramshackle hut, looking for what she imagines will be a clearing where the water is. She won't hear the running water, has never heard anything subtler than, say, a shotgun blast since birth, though in her dreams she seems to understand the beating of her mother's heart. She hasn't had a clear picture of her mother for years, though she's trying now that her new friend has brought her before the strange old woman. The strange old woman who knows, whose mouth asked him if he'd touched her without knowing or caring if she saw or heard the question.

The sound of the old woman's gun had shocked and frightened Kyre, because she'd heard it. She doesn't know why she heard it, can't imagine that she might hear something else some day. She hadn't heard the mob that came to their house five winters ago and she didn't hear the noise the house must've made when it finally collapsed into a burning wreck of random timbers. She was spared the screams of her parents, though in the aftermath she came to realize that they'd been bludgeoned to death while she hid in the farmstand. She's survived since by living the way they taught her: off the land, and the farmstand has remained sort of a sanctuary to her. She's never wandered this far toward the setting sun, though, and as she creeps to the edge of the sparkling brook she finds that she's almost giddy from the trust she's put in the boy. Why follow him, when she's run from every other human since the fire?

She wades out into the stream, feeling the gravelly mud of its bed squish up between her toes. The water is achingly cold, but she knows she'll get used to it in a minute: water is always like this, in her experience. Slowly she lowers herself into a crouch in the deepest part of the stream, watches amused as her garment billows up around her before it soaks. Shivering deliciously, she runs her hands all over herself, rubbing off the dirt she's picked up and probing experimentally at the warm place between her legs where she's been bleeding. She has no idea what she could've done to herself to start it bleeding but senses, somehow, that it's all right. Almost the way she sensed that the boy was all right.

He'd caught her sleeping and hadn't killed her, of course, was the main reason.

She ducks under the water and scrubs her face and hair and when she surfaces, Kyre realizes that the boy's mother is standing there at the bank of the stream, holding what looks like a large smock of some sort. Peering at it, she realizes it's a faded old dress; nothing much to look at, but better than the filthy rag she's been wearing. The strange old woman's mouth says something but Kyre can't make it out. She leaves the garment in the grass and turns to go.

"Thank you," Kyre calls out.

The strange old woman stops, and maybe she says something but Kyre can't see it, then continues back up toward the house.

The girl, Kyre, wasn't much good in the kitchen at first but proved amazingly resourceful in terms of finding things to eat. The raw materials she brought were strange and wonderful; evidently her years as a wild child stood her in good stead. Once I taught her the fundamentals of boiling water we had a vast array of wild vegetables and weird, steamed roots on our table. She can catch rabbits barehanded, too, and she's teaching Jeremy how, which will save on ammunition. She doesn't talk much to me, except to say please and thank you, but she talks to Jeremy and he talks to me.

Her parents, evidently, were Deprivers. According to her story, they lived quietly in the woods, much like we do, on the fringes of a settlement to the east where there's something more of a sense of community than we have here. She's always been deaf, she says, but her talk of her mother's heartbeat makes me think she wasn't deaf in the womb. Maybe it's just my imagination but I can't help thinking that they deafened her after she was born. I'm torn; I don't know what to think. You can't not touch a baby, not if you want it to live; but it's horrible to contemplate that she might've been normal if she'd been taken away from them at the moment of birth.

I also can't help wondering how they affected each other. If one or both of them were Deprivers, what happened when they touched? I've begun to question everything I've believed all these years. Could it be that they simply accepted the handicap they brought on each other, or were the effects really only temporary, as the NPR says they sometimes are? Could there be deprivations milder than mine, or Emma Fenton's? Why was Kyre able to hear the shotgun, that first day? Could it be that her deafness will abate as time goes on; could it have been the cumulative product of continuous contact with a weaker strain? Did they pass the disease on to her, the way I've always feared would happen with Jeremy? Is it even possible? Or do two wrongs, genetically, make a right?

Too many questions because of this girl. They keep me awake at night, and they've shaken up my dreamlife. Nothing's cut and dried anymore, even when I'm asleep. It used to be either good dreams or bad, either Jeremy or those wild, blinding scum who sired him. Now I have these wild flights of fancy, plotless conjectures about the world and the future, which blur the line between sleep and waking: I lie there in the dark—and it's always dark, of course—and suddenly realize that I'm awake and thinking when I thought I was asleep and dreaming.

Kyre's period came and went and now I have two teenage time-bombs in my house. I don't know what to think anymore. I've dressed Kyre in shawls and every damn thing and I've forbidden Jeremy to touch her skin, and I try to be near one of them all the time but I don't know how long I can prevent them getting at each other. The well of hormonal activity, that pit of horniness we call adolescence has been known to overcome a mother's will before. My own mother feared that sailors would get me, or that I'd give myself to drunken boys in parked cars. And I did, too; but things were different then. I don't know why I haven't sent her away.

Jeremy's learned always to be careful to face her when he speaks to her, and the way they talk is like nothing I've ever heard: like they've known each other their whole lives. Maybe it's just that they were both isolated from what we still call civilization. Maybe they just have more in common with each other than I'll ever have with anyone. Maybe I'm jealous; I'm not so blind as not to see that.

Jeremy woke and heard his mother talking to herself in the dark again. It'd become a nightly event in the weeks since Kyre came, and it gave the boy a creepy sensation. He lay there on his cot and listened to her for a few minutes, like he always did, and when he was sure she was still asleep he rolled over and tried to put it out of his mind. He couldn't, though, not completely: too much had changed, it was too strange to see his mother talking to someone else, or listening for noises other than his own. And that expression she sometimes got on her face when she listened to Kyre and him talking . . .

He couldn't sleep. He listened to the darkness, heard the rise and fall of his mother's breath punctuated here and there by a fresh spate of disturbed mumbling and he knew, as he knew every night now, that he had to get outside for a while. Outside there was moonlight, and the breeze, and the call of the nightbirds, and the sleeping form of Kyre in the lean-to he'd made for her. She wasn't allowed to sleep in the house: Ma said it wasn't safe. Jeremy wouldn't fight her on it. There was no point, and maybe she was right.

He sat up on the cot and swung his legs over the side and listened to Ma going on in her sleep about shrinks and quacks and shysters and the NPR, and a chill ran up his spine. If she was getting funny he didn't know what he'd do. Maybe she'd always been funny and he'd just never had anyone to compare her to before now. He stood and softly padded on bare feet to the door. It creaked slightly as he opened it, but her mumbling continued unabated and he went out.

Outside there was a blue-white glow over the land and the chill breeze of late summer brought him fully to life. He heard the gurgling of the stream out back and the steady pulse of the crickets, and smelt the rich grass and wild lilacs which grew so lush and brilliant by the shithole. He leaped off the porch to avoid the squeaking, broken step and landed in a crouch, like a spider, in the cool, packed dirt of the path. His pliant young muscles contracted and expanded and he was up, springing to a run and dashing madly into the tall, wet grass toward the lean-to. When he was in sight of it he threw himself to the ground and rolled over and over, crushing wildflowers and thriving, fragrant weeds beneath him till his chest and back and arms were streaked with dirt and green and smeared with succulent plantblood, and then he rolled to a stop on his stomach and stared over at the lean-to. His skin was tingling with grass and earth and he faced the open side of the shelter where a glowing white flood of moonlight fell on the sleeping girl, and he lay there watching and breathing with the exhilaration of being young and alive and at one with the night, studying the luminescent form before him defined by that perfect, curving line where her body met the light and that equally perfect, curving shadow where it didn't, and when she woke up, he knew it.

She rolled upright in one motion and looked directly at him, like she'd known where he was, and he watched her breath in the rise and fall of her young breasts in the moonlight and in the interplay of light and shadow beneath them. He found his own breath was matched to hers, and when she then spun on her haunch to face him fully and said, "You smell like flowers," he crept forward on his elbows and knees till he was close enough for her to see him speak.

He said, "I couldn't sleep," but she couldn't hear him because the moon was at his back.

"I can't hear you," she said, reclining on one elbow. Her hip described that perfect curve again.

Jeremy crawled sideways, flanking her, and got his face in the light. "I couldn't sleep," he said again.

"I know," she said, smiling. She stared at him, fascination in her glance. "You have a light around you," she murmured.

He smiled, but had no idea what she meant. "Maybe it's the moon," he said.

"No," she said, leaning toward him. "You have it in the daytime, too."

The first time she touches him, the world goes red. It's brighter than anything, but the red makes it tolerable, and she can't look away in any case because it's there when she closes her eyes, too. It's like a flashing light, a bright, fiery flood rushing through the center of her head and expanding in all directions, and the feel of his hand on her shoulder is like the caress of a thousand friendly pinpricks. They crawl together, and his arms around her make her shudder and twitch, as the beating of blood in her ears joins the flashing in her head in a lunatic marriage of sense gone mad. She drags her fingers down his back and feels the muscles there, and the broken grass and dirt and the sudden sweat as he convulses against her and she feels the sound he's making, deep in his chest, and when their mouths meet all is darkness and the pounding of her heart, and the smell of crushed wildflowers. The rest is touch, and more touch, until she can't stand it anymore and she breaks loose from his embrace and crawls out into the night.

Kyre lies there in the cool grass and feels the gentle throbbing which courses through her body: she is terrified and elated and overcome by a feeling she can't name, and all she can do is lie there and twitch and moan and smile. She doesn't see the strange old woman storming up to the lean-to, can't hear her screaming at Jeremy.

The first time she touched him he felt a savage beating in his ears, louder than a thousand drums and ringing clearer than a shotgun blast, and the crickets and the whipporwill and the breeze in the trees seemed to explode in his head in a fierce cacophony. His hand on her shoulder made her jump, and when they crawled together her body felt so supple and so right in his arms that it didn't shock him when she shuddered against him, mad and twitching, and dragged her fingers down the length of his back. He heard her gasp and then he didn't hear anything, and their mouths met and they moved together in soft, pulsing agony until, with a cry he felt rather than heard, she flung him from her and crawled off into the moonlight.

He watched her go, feeling hurt and annoyed, and

stared at her as she rolled over in the grass and gazed up at the sky with unseeing eyes, and then he understood.

He didn't hear his mother, didn't even look in that direction.

It's looking to be a harsh winter this year; harsher still it'll be for spending it alone. I never really figured on being all by myself out here, though I suppose it isn't much different from the way it was when Jeremy was little. It seemed somehow more natural then, though, like it was easier to take care of myself and him than it will be just to take care of myself. It just made more sense, somehow.

Harley Fenton's been up to chop some wood, for which I'm grateful, and a few other folks hereabouts've come through with some meat and produce. I don't eat much, anyway, so it really doesn't take a lot to keep someone like me alive. They've stopped asking me about Jeremy, since I've never had anything to tell them. Gone is gone, and the more someone doesn't come back, the less anyone expects him to.

It's been quiet up here since they've been gone. I still listen to the radio, and it still beams gibberish into my house from the outside world. Reports from the city of stupid, thrill-seeking kids in sex clubs who become permanent Helens by triple-dripping with Blinders, Beethovens, and Harpos all at once; garbled analyses from state-funded liberal sociologists explaining why, exactly, this period in the history of the disease should be called "sunset" instead of "twilight" or "Thursday"; meaningless statistics read from cuecards by steady-sounding, disinterested radio airheads. No explanation for what happened here in my neck of the woods, so I guess I'm the only one who knows. I suppose I live my story by myself out here. I suppose everyone does, somewhere.

I was sitting on the porch about sun-up of the morning

after that night, cradling the old Ithaca in my arms as I rocked back and forth, wondering about the future and waiting for something to happen, when Kyre came wandering up. I smelt her coming: the smell of dirt and sex and wildflowers. The smell Jeremy'd had on him the night before. We'll be a fine pair, I thought: both of us blind and one of us deaf, to boot. I wondered if she'd still be able to find all those plants and roots. I figured rabbits were out of the question anymore, all things considered.

"Where's Jeremy?" she said, coming to rest in the shade of the house. I couldn't see any point in answering: she'd been blind as a bat when I stood over her in the moonlight: hovered over her smell and screamed at her, and she never made a sound or a movement. "Where *is* he?" she said again, like she could tell I hadn't said anything.

I turned toward her smell. The shotgun across my lap seemed suddenly too heavy to be there. I sighed. Kyre said, "What is *wrong* with you?"

"Jeremy's gone," I said, more to myself than anything.

"Gone where?" she said.

My blood went cold on me, all of a sudden. The world stopped making any sense at all, even to me, out here alone on the edge of it. "You can see," I said.

She snorted girlishly. " 'Course I can see," she said.

"Jeremy deprived you last night."

"Not for long," she said. "I was scared at first, and things are still a little blurry, but it's clearing up." She paused, and I think she shrugged her shoulders. "Daddy used to do it to Mama sometimes. Those days he couldn't hear."

I nodded, thinking how sad and stupid it is that no one understands this thing, and brought up the barrel of the shotgun to fire at her voice. I remember thinking: I'll bury her next to Jeremy, since he'd probably want it that way.

Goddamn them.

PRECAUTIONS

KIT REED

"D on't touch that," Mother said, and I didn't. "Don't go near that. You don't know what's going around."

Well, we all knew, or we sort of did. Meet one of Them and you can lose your senses, all except the sense that you have consorted with one of the corrupted and now you are an outcast, one of Them.

"I love you," Mother said to us. "I'd rather see you dead."

There is a pestilence ravaging the land, one day you're fine; meet one of Them and the next day you wake up staggering around like a blind man or a deaf one because you caught It and blind or deaf is what you are.

"They may look like you or me," Mother told us, "but they don't *do* like we do." That was the day she cut her friends off except for the phone, even though Margaret and Etta were clean as anybody and her best friends in the world, the world being where Father went that I am not allowed to go.

You could catch It!

"Better safe than sorry," Mother said. She loved her friends but she wiped off the mouthpiece every time they talked.

Then Margaret met one of Them and we heard that she went deaf; whether or not she did, Mother got scared of picking up the phone. Once They make contact, you catch it before you even know. And poor Etta, she was nice to One and she lost her voice. When Mother didn't call, Etta and Margaret started writing to her, but you can't be too careful. When you're scared of germs after a while you start getting scared of everything that germs might have come near. You're scared of germs coming off of people and you're scared of germs getting on things like letters, even though the letter carrier has strict instructions to put your snail mail in the De-con box outside of the front door.

We count on De-con to keep us safe.

The De-con box cost us a heap of Father's insurance money, but it is a fantastic service that allows us to go on living the way God meant us to, Uncontaminated, with all our senses intact.

That and the care Mother took, starting the first day the bad wind blew in from somewhere else and changed the world.

"Disease," Father said when he got in from work that day.

"Daddy, Daddy!" Billy and me clamored around his legs.

Mother yelled, "Don't touch him!" and yanked us away.

Father said to her, "So, you heard."

"I heard. Terrible new disease in the universe."

"It isn't bad," Father said. "It's just confusing."

"Don't try and kid me," Mother said. "I saw it on the TV. And you were just out in it."

"I didn't go anywhere, just to the office."

"On the bus. That's one hotbed of infection. All those

people, breathing on you. Who knows what you picked up? And the office. That's two. Out of the hotbed and into the incubator. The work place. The TV says the workplace is the worst." She handed Father his walking papers and shoved him out the door, which she locked and bolted. We heard a screech. He got hit by a truck.

Of course we cried, but when it's a matter of your own health and safety, you shut up fast. Mother pulled herself together. "I'll keep you safe," she vowed. "No matter what it takes."

"Okay," Billy said, "Me and Dolly are going out in the yard."

Mother grabbed him. "Not on your life! Something terrible could happen to you and you wouldn't even know."

"But I want to go out and play." Billy always was rebellious. He looked ready to hit and yell.

"Not now," Mother said. "You either, Doll," she said to me. She shuttered the windows. She mounted a defense missile on the front porch roof, *in case*, and showed us how to use it. She sealed us in. "You'll thank me later. This is for your own good."

"When?" I was scared and excited. Less excited than scared.

"Soon, I promise, just as soon as they get all these people put away."

It was a little song she sang to keep us safe: "As Soon As They Get All Those People Put Away." And every night we had a little party, cookies and ginger ale. We put on costumes and made jokes. Once a month we tested the defenses. Ready. Arm. Everything but fire. If one of Them tries to get in . . .

She made paper hats for us. "Aren't we having fun?" Mother said. She was laughing and laughing. "Aren't we having fun!"

So Billy and me, we stayed in, and I can tell you we were damn glad. We saw the ravages on TV. "Just as soon as they get all these people put away." Truth? I could hardly wait.

But here's the trick of it. You can't get people put away when you don't know which ones they are.

Mother said we wouldn't be in here long, but she worked on our armaments while we slept. It's been a while, but at least I'm safe.

So we have Mother to thank. And De-con. We never touch anything They touched.

We order from Web-TV, no problem, De-con guarantees that no germs get into your food and none come in on the clothes you ordered off the web or from the Shopping Channel and what if it's maybe a little lonely you can count on emailing eBay or Amazon.com and they'll mail you back. Or, and this is great! With the Shopping Channel, you can phone in and sometimes they put your phone call on TV. Imagine. You can tune in and hear yourself talking to the shopping host right there on the air! Plus, you get safe, germ-free delivery of anything you want, from your Albanian Aardvark to a Jivaro shrunken head. Who needs to go out? Our lives were full!

I guess.

It's interesting, sitting there in front of the TV-puter most of the day. You're, like, *connected* to all the billions of others for as long as you stay logged on but you can't touch them, and this is weird. I was sitting in here protecting all my senses from contamination and all I wanted was to be touched.

I guess Billy did too. He said, "I want to go out and meet some people I'm not related to."

Mother smacked him. "No way."

Oh, but we were safe. So safe! See, hear, feel, taste, touch, *have* anything you want. Get excited ordering it and then get excited waiting for it to come. Well, anything that got delivered to the De-con box and made it through the double-sealed de-germified air lock in our front hall. But what's the point of the perfect dress if nobody sees you in it except your brother and your mom? Billy and I would have had friends, I would have had guys to go out with, except she had yanked us out of school.

And I will tell you this about it. Mother did it because she loves us but home education is the pits. The whole world going on outside, we saw it on TV and on the web, and us stuck in Father's den, which she had converted to the schoolroom, us and Mother. Sitting too close and breathing the same stale air.

"What do you think, class?"

"I don't know. What do you think, Mom?"

It got old. Billy was the first to crack. First it was him ogling all these women on TV.

"Stop that. That's just *Baywatch*," Mother said.

"I don't care what it is, I want to go to the beach!" He meant he wanted to go out in the world and consort with jiggly girls.

"That show's so old those girls are probably dead." Mother said, "Girls aren't like that any more."

"Prove it." He was ogling me.

I started to cry.

Mother smacked him. "You leave your sister alone."

The next morning he was gone.

It's amazing how he got out. He made it through the airlock and out of the De-con box. I tried but I was getting hips and boobs and they were getting in the way. Every once in a while he would phone, but Mother wouldn't let me talk.

"That was your brother," she'd say. "He's lost his senses. He wants to come back but I'm warning you: *no matter what he does or says, don't let him in.*"

It's okay, I didn't miss him too much. I went out on the Internet and met a lot of cool guys. Amazing what people will tell you when they can't see you. Amazing what you tell them.

Then Mother got sick. How I knew she was sick was, she started teaching me how to run the world: where the money was, the pin numbers for all our accounts, how to make e-transfers to keep the De-con service and how to pay for the food and the clothes she ordered for us and how to accessorize. The jewelry she'd gotten from the Shopping Channel, she divided into two heaps.

"This is for you." She swept one pile my way. The other, she kept. "I'm going to be buried in this."

"What's buried?" I said.

"Don't worry," she said. "Wherever God takes me, I promise, I'll protect you to the grave."

I did like she wanted. I took the DigiCam and after I did her makeup and laid her out in all her jewelry and the Melissa Rivers kaftan with the solid gold trim, I took lots of pictures and I posted them in the right place on the Web. Then I did like she ordered and put her down the Dispos-All a little bit at a time. The bones I left in the De-con box and the De-con company took them away. He said through the intercom, "Are you OK in there?"

"Never better," I said.

Except it was really quiet in here.

After she died everything was pretty much the same. Stuff kept coming—clean and safe. But safe turned out not to be enough. Except for the necessaries, I left off shopping. It was quiet as hell.

One day at delivery time I left the air lock open, and when the De-con signal went off to tell me the outside box was opening, I stuck my head in the hole so he would hear me direct. "Come on in!"

"Lady, you shouldn't do this. You could catch something."

"You're bonded," I told him. "It's okay."

"You got no idea what's out here."

"Cute guys," I said. "I saw them on TV."

"But some of them are carrying terrible diseases. Women, too!" He sounded muffled; okay, he was talking through his De-con filter mask. In the surveill camera, he looked like he was wearing a gigantic rubber glove. Since Mother died, I haven't talked to anyone direct and I was starved for it. Just me and one other, naked face to naked face.

"No problem," I told him. I was wearing Mother's Pamela Anderson outfit from QVC. "I'll stay away from them."

"Precautions," the delivery man said. "No telling what you might run into out here."

"At least I'd be running into *something*," I said, but I took his word for it and let it go by. Along with the days. Along with a lot of other days.

Until I found the ad on the web. SEX AND GLORY, the header ran. SAFE AND TOTAL LOVE WITH THE PERFECT PARTNER— GENDER APPROPRIATE.

I read the disclaimers. I gasped at the down payment. I sold everything on eBay and took all the money to do it.

I ordered a guy.

The De-con truck pulled up on the morning appointed. The assistant driver ran a forklift around and unloaded the crate. There were air holes in the crate, it was strapped with warning tape: DO NOT BEND. THIS SIDE UP. I saw it on the surveill TV.

The driver said through the intercom, "I got a questionable delivery."

"No questions. I ordered it."

"It won't fit in the De-con box."

"You can set it down out there and leave." Mother taught us to be cautious. "I'll bring it in."

"You shouldn't come out."

"Okay, okay," I said. "You can just open it and leave."

"No way! The crate's been damaged. De-con guarantees protection and no way am I going to be liable. God knows what could have gotten inside."

"I don't care."

"Lady, anything that happens to you comes out of my hide. I can't leave you alone with this thing. You could sue the company."

"I'll take the responsibility."

"Sorry, ma'am." He gestured to the assistant and they started to put the thing back on the truck. I armed the defense missiles and blew both of them away.

It took all the tools in the basement to get the front door open, but I finally managed. I pushed it aside and I came tottering out. Me, Dolly Meriwether, alone out in the world. It was weird! The box was sitting right where the delivery men had left it. I thought I heard thumping. It seemed to bulge. My guy. There were air holes, all right, and there were plastic kibbles dribbling from one corner where the crate had smashed. There was also a warning label: MANU-FACTURER NOT RESPONSIBLE FOR DAMAGED GOODS OR CONTAGION INCURRED IN TRANSIT.

I put my mouth up to the hole. "Can you hear me? Are you in there?"

I thought I heard a voice.

Oh Mother, I was so excited! I could almost hear Mother hissing, "Leave it alone, Dolly. That thing is full of germs!"

"I don't care!" I opened the box with the crowbar. The sides fell away. Plastic kibbles cascaded down. He was standing there smiling in his orange coverall. "Hello."

Mother hissed from beyond the grave. "Don't touch that thing, you don't know where it's been!"

My guy stepped out of the kibbles. He was nice and apologetic. "I'm here on approval. Truth in advertising, I have to tell you this. If the seal on the box is broken, your product may be contaminated. You can return it and get your money back."

I looked at the corner of the crate. "No problem," I said.

"Look," he said. "I was in a warehouse with a bunch of. Um. I'm sorry, I might have it too."

"No problem," I said. I grabbed his arm and yanked him inside with me. "Kiss me," I said.

"Even if I'm . . . ?"

I shut his mouth with my mouth and it was the best thing I ever tasted in this world. Then sirens started blaring, and guns I didn't even know were in the walls around us slipped out of their slots—the automatic firing squad Mother had planted in the middle of some long-dead night. I heard a hundred clicks. The weapons arming.

I heard her voice: *I told you I'd protect you to the grave!*

"I love you!" I yelled at him as a hundred triggers drew back. "Save yourself! Get out!"

But I knew it was too late for both of us.

RED DEVIL
STATEMENT

JANET ASIMOV

This is a camp as in concentration," I said, tugging at the shiny stainless steel LD bracelet on my right wrist. Of course, it would not come off. "We are the victims of a devilish plot to trap us here . . ."

"Please, Becky. Don't use the word devil. It hurts."

Pete was right. Until we became Long-Deprived, we were co-owners of the popular restaurant Red Devil, named after my hair and Pete's specialty. We actually had our own website, and a best-selling cookbook (which did not reveal the recipe of the specialty).

I was manager, hostess, part-time cook and taster. I could tell even better than Pete whether or not his latest creation was a masterpiece or merely superb. Then came deprivation. I could still get sour, sweet, bitter and salt sensations from my taste buds, but it's hard to judge great cooking when you have olfactory loss equivalent to—no, worse than—a bad head cold.

A different deprivation afflicted Pete. After being

deprived, he could see colored objects only in what he claimed were shades of gray, each peculiarly nauseating to him when the object was a colorful food item.

He sought psychological solace in more or less colorless meals composed of items like clear soup with cellophane noodles, coconut and cabbage coleslaw, steamed cauliflower head festooned with creamed slices of chicken breast and surrounded by white rice mixed with white beans. Desserts suddenly became champagne gelatin, vanilla ice cream, rice pudding with white raisins, and angel food cake iced with white chocolate.

I was told—I couldn't tell—that everything was perfectly seasoned and delicious, but patrons objected.

They objected with particular vehemence to the loss of our Red Devil Statement, an incredibly rich chocolate cake full of cherries and rimmed with little devils, their forked tails hooked together. Pete invented the cake after I'd said we ought to have a signature dish, a culinary statement that would make us famous. He wanted devils made of white chocolate with red hair suspiciously like mine, but I made him make them red all over.

To pacify the angry patrons, deprived Pete went back to cooking the Statement and the rest of our menu, with me helping the help and checking to be sure everything looked right. And we dutifully showed up at the local D-monitoring station every week, as was required by law.

Most of the deprived lose their senses of whatever for only a short time, but when your deprivation lasts longer than six months, the D-police (wearing heavy-duty rubber gloves) solder an LD bracelet on your wrist. They then inform you that you'll suffer less prejudice if you move to an LD camp. It is a command, not a suggestion.

Although LD deprivations tend to be quite selective—never total blindness or deafness, for instance—it's now known that the Long-Deprived are more likely to become like the dreaded Deprivers, infecting anyone they touch. The D-police pretend that putting bracelets on us and sending us away will ensure the safety of the general population, but unfortunately nobody has ever been able to track down all of the original Deprivers, those who infect but have no deprivations themselves.

Try keeping a restaurant open when you're wearing an LD bracelet as well as gloves, even if people know that food prepared by a deprived cook is not dangerous.

Our deprivations began one night when I dragged Pete out of the kitchen (he thinks meeting people is my job) because we were asked to go to the table of someone who'd come in without a reservation and had already paid for his expensive meal in cash. As we approached he stood up—a fit, handsome older man with thick silver hair and an air of persuasive benevolence.

"Looks as if he ought to be preaching on TV," I muttered. Pete moaned slightly. He knows me.

"I congratulate you on a mighty fine dinner," the man intoned, his strong, slightly syrupy voice sliding out as if he'd used canola oil on his vocal cords. "And I'm sure this pretty little lady keeps the place running. Those little devils—hair the color of yours, m'dear. It's a cake fit for a god."

"Oh?" I said.

I was about to ask him sarcastically if he thought he was a god, when Pete hurriedly said, "Thank you."

Suddenly the man reached out with both naked hands and grasped our wrists just above our protective rubber gloves. "Congratulations," he said, looking into our eyes.

Nowadays nobody lets a stranger touch him, but Pete likes to believe the best of people, so he said nothing and I was too appalled to do anything but croak "Hey!"

But the man was already on his way out, and within a few hours our deprivations began.

Six months later, after being labeled LD, we found that we'd been assigned to camp LD3, once a Catskill resort. We were to be the new cooks.

It probably won't be too bad," I said, because Pete looked stricken, "It's near our beloved Manhattan, and I suppose it will have a big kitchen as well as trees and mountains and babbling brooks and . . ."

"We'll hate it," Pete said, but we went, and we did.

The Catskill scenery was admittedly scenic, but the hotel was ancient and I dreaded seeing the kitchen. In our room, Pete tried to console me.

"Everyone here is Long-Deprived. At least we won't have to wear gloves, or worry about touching or being touched."

I looked out the window at a view of gardens with a backdrop of wooded hills, while Pete inspected the small lunch laid out for us on the table.

"Becky, I think they're giving us a demonstration of how much they need us here."

He was right. The sandwiches were composed of processed cheese and mashed baked beans on sliced white bread.

After we'd worried down the sandwiches, I sighed. Pete touched me and said in my mind, *I love you Becky, no matter what.*

I love you too.

Ever since we fell in love at the culinary institute, Pete and I have been able to sense each other's emotions—I gather that lovers are usually good at that—but after being deprived, we found that we were telepathic when we held hands, or any other portion of our anatomies, and tried to communicate.

I kissed him, and we went on from there. Later, when we were resting from our athletic endeavor and wondering if there was time for another, a bell in the corridor chimed twice, followed by a vaguely familiar voice saying through the room's loudspeaker, "Everyone will now assemble in the ballroom for the Communal Hour."

"Sounds ominous," I said.

"Let's give it a chance," Pete said, predictably.

We dressed and went down to an enormous round room where hundreds of LDs sat on folding chairs, too busy talking to each other to pay attention to us as we came in hand in hand like two frightened children.

"Everyone seems happy," I said. *But they're probably brainwashed, or on drugs.*

Becky!

Okay, okay, but we're in a crazy prison, Pete.

At least we're together.

A little tearily, I squeezed his hand in gratitude as we made our way to a couple of empty seats.

I looked around and couldn't help shuddering. I also didn't care who heard me. "Pete, right now I'll trade deprivations with you. This room is pink and orange with spangles hither and yon. And—*ye gods! There he is!*"

The man who deprived us had emerged from a door at the back of the platform. When he held up his hand, the ballroom went into hush mode.

"Greetings. The Communal Hour is adjourned. For those of you here for the first time, I am Director Marvel."

No bracelet, Pete. He's one of the Deprivers, and he did it to us deliberately, to get good cooks.

Director Marvel pointed at us. "Let me introduce two new members—master chef Pete and his red-haired assistant Becky. We expect great things from them."

Everyone looked at us and applauded.

"Now we will form our Community. Meditate on Joining."

All bent their heads, except for me, because I hate being told what to do when I don't understand what's going on, and Pete, who is a non-joiner.

"Meditate on joining what?" I asked.

Director Marvel said, "It has been discovered that latent telepathic ability is augmented by deprivation, particularly in the Long-Deprived. Scientific studies of telepathy are proceeding in many of the LD camps, but here in LD3 we are attempting something more."

"Hear, hear!" shouted a few people, and everyone clapped again.

"We work towards becoming a superorganism that will soon encompass all the LD camps..." Director Marvel said sonorously. I almost expected organ music to begin.

"Today the LDs, tomorrow the world?" I shouted. "And with you as Dictator? Marvel, that sucks!"

The Director bestowed on me a smile full of pity, as if I'd just crawled in from a planet of the mentally deficient. "Try to understand that the telepathic Long-Deprived are the future of humanity as a superorganism..."

"But you're not one of us!" I shouted. "You're not Deprived. You are a Depriver...!"

"As are all of you now," Marvel said. Everyone nodded.

"...and you're creating a blasted cult with you as a god, you devil."

"Speaking of devils," the Director said with another icky smile, "Becky and Pete have a secret recipe for the most marvelous devils food cake I have ever tasted. Wouldn't we all like it if they made the cake for tea time?"

Everyone dutifully shouted "Yes!"

Pete and I shouted, "We won't!"

"In the camps, the Long-Deprived must work. You will

make us cake for tea time as well as soup and a nourishing main dish for tonight's dinner."

At which point two burly men in blue overalls took us to the kitchen, a large room with nobody else in it. It had a great deal of reasonably modern kitchen equipment that was fairly clean—perhaps the LDs had never used most of it—and seemed to be well-stocked in spite of the lack of imagination of the previous cooks. The burly men proceeded to lock us in.

"You see, this is a prison," I said.

Pete's jaw jutted out, a sign that he was seriously annoyed. "We're going to do something about that."

"What? The windows have bars and we can't go back to Manhattan. I suppose there are other LD camps . . ."

"Becky, you make chicken stew and sweet potato soup while I bake the Statement. Several Statements." As he kissed me, I heard, *And we're going to take over this joint.* He likes old-time gangster films.

"Yes, we might as well help out, love." *Because if we don't take over I'll be tempted to poison Marvel's food.*

At tea time, the door was unlocked and the Director strode in, sniffing the air. "How delicious! You've made your famous cake after all."

"Yes, sir" said Pete, improving the act. "Have we done it in time for tea?"

"Indeed you have," Marvel said. "So glad you've decided to cooperate. You won't be sorry that you are helping sustain the embryo superorganism of LD3." He stroked my hair. "I have always appreciated electric red hair, and sister, you have it."

Pete gently led me away from Marvel. Attached to his hand, I heard him clearly in my mind.

You didn't put anything psychoactive in the cake, did you?

No, Pete, your masterpiece stands on its own. Marvel really is the pits.

I'd bet that as an original Depriver, he's not telepathic.

With the confidence of someone who possesses a private means of communication in the face of the enemy, I smiled winsomely at Marvel and said, "Pete and I are going to enjoy cooking (*the power of cooking, Pete*) for a superorganism, dear Director. Will you help us carry the cakes?"

In the full ballroom, where tea had already been made with electric hot water containers, the still warm Statements were received joyfully.

After people had finally stopped munching, I went up on the platform. "Listen, everybody, if you want to be a superorganism, you've got to Join in the way the red devils on the cake are joined . . ."

Marvel got in front of me. "Becky is new to camp LD3. She doesn't understand that I am in charge . . ."

"You shouldn't be," I said, stepping around him. "You're not one of us. You're a non-telepathic Depriver. You can't Join. You just want to control those of us who can."

"Now see here, little lady . . ."

I'd already noticed that the two guards had eaten more cake than anyone. I waved to them. "Boys, take him to his car and send him on his way, or Pete and I will never cook another thing for camp LD3."

A rather pudgy female shouted, "Get rid of Marvel! I never liked him since he deprived me when I was trying to check his credit card at the supermarket. We've been persuaded that he's helping us, but we are his victims!"

"That's right!" yelled a man. "And since great food helps turn humans into a civilized society, the cuisine of Pete and Becky will nourish our superorganism."

Everyone clapped. Charismatic preacher-types are all very well, but they can't beat good cooking.

Marvel said plaintively, "But can't I leave with the recipe for Red Devil Statement?"

"No," said Pete.

Marvel was escorted out while the audience laughed.

Someone said, "Show us how to Join, Becky!"

"Pete and I have found that we have better telepathic communication when we touch. So, everybody hold hands, all around the room."

The reluctant ones insisted on a vote, but when the majority ruled yes, the nay-sayers gave in. It was like that scene when the Declaration of Independence is made unanimous, only this time it was a declaration of dependence.

Unfortunately, holding hands and meditating did not produce the anticipated results.

What's wrong? Pete asked me. *Why aren't we a superorganism? Becky, you and I so easily become part of each other, but I don't feel oneness with anyone else ...*

Before I could answer, I heard dozens of people saying, out loud, "We heard that, in our minds!"

Everyone began to cheer and talk about how we'd do it again, next tea time—providing Pete made more Red Devil Statements.

We had to promise, but that night Pete and I clutched each other closely and talked about how scared we were.

I'm not sure I want to lose my identity in a superorganism, Pete.

In a way, Earth is an organism and we're part of it. Besides, when we talk like this, we're still who we are— aren't we, love?

I went to sleep in his arms, and the next day we both cooked superbly for all the meals, and at tea time there were more Red Devil Statements.

When the last crumbs were devoured, everyone eagerly joined hands again.

Then it happened. Each of us, in our minds, in whatever language we used, heard the following:

Welcome to your free sample of the Galactic Wide Web. To be admitted on a permanent basis you must join the Galactic Federation. Please state your telepathic address now.

Everyone in the ballroom gasped. We all knew that everyone else knew.

Pete said, out loud—but we all heard it telepathically, too—"What does the GWW offer?"

Trillions of data bases, comics, games and other websites that can be yours, plus low cost accommodations at any of our far-flung resorts . . .

"We don't have faster than light drive!" shouted a teenager.

Easily remedied. Warp drive specifics are provided as part of the package of joining the Galactic Federation and getting on the GWW.

I broke the link and stood up, not touching anyone. "We have not made a superorganism. Our linked telepathic minds have merely acquired enough hard drive to log onto a blasted galactic commercial website! And joining a Galactic Federation will probably mean a new set of taxes . . ."

But there were mutterings from the ballroom. "I want alien comics!" and "Why can't we go to a new resort?" and "Games!" It's true that some of the brainier LD's did opt for acquiring new scientific information, but the rest were giving in to crass commercialism.

Even Pete said, "It might be interesting-and helpful to our careers-to experience Galactic cuisine."

I gave in and joined hands again. *Our local address is LD3, planet Earth. What's the price of joining the Galactic Federation and getting on the GWW?*

One of your planet's treasures, the worth of which to be decided by the multi-species committee of the GFED.

So Pete gave them his secret recipe for Red Devil Statement.

At the next tea time link, we were told that our planet had been accepted into the GFED. Hurriedly, we of LD3 informed the UN, which had a global fit, but gave in.

Since anyone with enhanced telepathy could enjoy the GWW, the formerly dreaded Deprivers were soon in great demand. The one we knew visited LD3, marching into our kitchen with a broad smile. He was still handsome and fit, but his silver hair had been dyed bright red.

"Greetings, folks. Now aren't you glad I came to your restaurant that night?"

"No," Pete said. "My Red Devil Statement isn't mine any more, and Becky and I are much too busy trying to teach alien cooks who warp over to learn how to cook or modify human cuisine, which seems to be going over big in the Galaxy."

"Now, now, I have a proposition. You see, the millions I've been making lately are coming to an end . . ."

"You've been charging for depriving people!" I said.

"Certainly. But Earth's population is pretty well deprived, so to improve my financial future I've located a planet that has a cure for sensory deprivation."

"No one wants to be cured," Pete said.

"But this cure leaves the enhanced telepathy intact. Here, try it." He handed us small vials with funny tops. "Just press the small end and the medicine is delivered into your system through the skin."

"They did that on *Star Trek*."

"It works."

We tried it. Pete could see the full beauty of the chocolate Statement he was making, and I could taste it again.

"You'll make more millions from this, Marvel, so what do you want from us?" I asked, because if there's one thing I've learned, nothing is free.

"Ah. Merely the means to do good to Earth."

"Oh, sure."

"Listen—you two are now the most famous humans, and cooks, in the Galaxy as well as here on Earth. I want you to alter your cake. I'll sell it here on Earth as a new version of your famous Red Devil Statement, improved for humans."

Pete hates being told to alter any of his recipes. "I don't want to."

Marvel showed us another vial. "I've come across an alien gene that when ingested by a telepathic human will cause said human to be permanently linked to all other gene-enhanced humans. Instant oneness . . ."

"Your old superorganism," I said. "We won't . . ."

Marvel ground his teeth. "You idiots—I could run around polluting all the water supplies of Earth, but that would take years, and with an efficient delivery of adulterated cakes ordered from your website, our planet will soon become a superorganism whether it wants to or not. Then Earth will take over the GFED. Yes, today, Earth—tomorrow, the Galaxy. I'll expect only a moderate cut . . ."

Suddenly I felt pity for him. "Marvel, since you and the other Deprivers have no telepathic talent, you won't be part of any superorganism."

"No, m'dear, I won't. I'm just a disease carrier. But it's lucrative."

Let's try it, love. Okay love. Serve the Deprivers right.

Pete made the cake and things progressed—if you want to call it that—as Marvel predicted.

The rich Deprivers now patronize the most expensive

Galactic resorts while Earth plunges into superorganism hood.

Pete and I have not eaten any of the new cake.

Being alone together is our Statement.

GIFTED

DIANE DEKELB-RITTENHOUSE

I knew her by the white gloves, gloves with tiny pearl
buttons, gloves befitting a lady from an earlier time.
They were made of real silk, not the synth-fabs to which
most of the world, even those of us with a semblance of
wealth, had been reduced. Those bits of white cloth were at
once badge of shame and badge of honor. Erica Pierce was
no ordinary Depriver.

A synth-crystal glass of the modest champagne our
publicity director favored for these events held in one silk-
swathed hand, she gestured fluidly with the other, engaging
our maestro in animated conversation. Light cast by hundreds of enameled Gala fixtures seemed to shimmer in the
thick, red-gold hair curving to her shoulders as she nodded
her head and laughed. Illya Rothman joined in her laughter, inclining his head graciously to accommodate her
diminutive height. Even in four-inch heels she came barely
to his chin.

But he would not take her hand.

There was no need for me to approach. Several of the

other musicians scattered throughout the reception room atop the just completed San Francisco Symphony Hall noticed my entrance and signaled. A dozen different groups were ready to welcome me. But something about those elegantly gloved hands, the sweet tone of her laughter—or perhaps, more prosaically, something about the soft drape of lime-green silk against her body—caused me to ignore the beckoning gestures, the glittering lights of the city beyond the windows, and drew me, instead, across the length of the faux-marble floor toward her. Rothman smiled his approval as I approached. I rarely troubled myself with the patrons, and usually kept the required appearances to no more than a quarter hour.

"And here is our prodigy," Rothman said heartily, making an expansive gesture of his own. For a moment my smile became a bit strained, until I realized he intended no irony.

Erica Pierce turned and looked up at me, still smiling, her plain features made almost pretty by the warmth and vitality of her expression. Small as she was, she should have conveyed an impression of fragility, or delicacy, but she was too vibrant for that. It did make her seem younger, though. I knew that she was twenty-seven, but anyone seeing us together, not knowing who we were, might take me for the elder. Like most natural redheads, she was freckled. An endearing flaw of pale brown dots decorated her cheek. From my own, not inconsiderable, height I gazed down at them in something akin to fascination. Not noticing, or perhaps diplomatically ignoring, my unusual interest in this particular patron, Rothman continued. "Ms. Pierce, please let me present Stephen D'Amico."

"A true pleasure, Mr. D'Amico," she said. Her voice had the pure tones you can hear if you tap flawless crystal. She dipped her head in a polite salute, but did not offer her

hand. "I was fortunate enough to have been in Munich in
'75. I will never forget your performance there." Again, the
laughter, rich and full throated, nothing giddy or coy. "You
must hear that from everyone. About Munich."

"Not nearly often enough," I returned politely. Impo-
litely, I extended my hand to her. I ignored the glare Rothman cast at me, and watched as her brown eyes widened,
her smile fading just a little, the freckles more apparent on
her slightly paling skin. But, protected by silk, she hesitantly
responded as I had hoped. "I've heard of you as well, Ms.
Pierce," I said, not shaking her hand but bowing over it in
the approved Old World fashion. "Let me say that the honor
is mine." Her response was polite but subdued. Having gone
far enough, I released her.

"Stephen will be opening our season, of course," Rothman said, a little too jovially. His glare was intended to
remind me not to offend someone from whom we were hoping to elicit a sizable donation. Erica Pierce's family was
very old money indeed, the sort for whom patronizing the
arts was almost a requirement. My family was new money,
and I didn't control any of it. My father did. And he was not
interested in giving more than token patronage to the Symphony. Rothman knew where his best interests lay, and was
still trying to repair any damage my forwardness had done.
"You must bring your children to see Stephen play," he said.

Her children. The two hundred students of the Pierce
Institute. All of them deaf.

"That would be wonderful," Erica Pierce said, vibrancy
restored. Her interest in the Symphony went a little deeper
than the requisite *noblesse obligé*. Erica's father had dabbled—
brilliantly—in the arts. His career as a concert violinist
ended abruptly when, at age six, Erica first exhibited the
Depriver Syndrome by inadvertently deafening him. Her

career began when she made something of a crusade out of enhancing the ability of the deaf to perceive sound. The Pierce Institute, opened three years previously, was one victory of that crusade.

I knew, from the countless holo-journal articles on her, that the Depriver syndrome presented itself in Erica Pierce in very well-defined ways. First, it was localized entirely in her hands. She had no need to wear the "Safe-t-Skin" body envelopes, or "skinnies" which came between most Deprivers and the world, and which had driven more than a few of them to madness. Gloves provided all the protection she, and the law, required. Second, her syndrome was one that was target-specific. Without gloves, Erica could caress your face, touch your arm, clasp your hand, and you would be unscathed. But if, bare-handed, she touched, however lightly, your ears, you would become instantly, permanently and profoundly deaf. She always wore gloves.

According to all the holos, her father never blamed her for his loss. But she blamed herself. Like so many Deprivers who first learn of their—power? ability? curse?—when it has a devastating affect on a loved one, Erica Pierce was initially swamped and overwhelmed by an ocean of guilt. Unlike them, she did not drown in it, but swam upward to safe harbor.

She began studying sign language at age eight, aural sciences a year later. By the time she was twenty-one, she had earned her Masters degree in Audiologic Therapy and begun the work which would lead to the founding of her Institute. Like me, she was called gifted.

Still, one would not expect a twenty-year-old musician, declared four years previously the world's greatest living pianist, to court her company. She must have wondered why I did.

I blame it still on those white gloves, the shimmer of light in her hair, the drape of green silk. The truth is, Erica Pierce charmed me, utterly. I set out to charm her back.

It should have been easy, but wasn't. Women had climbed, clawed and caroused their way into my bed from the time I was fifteen, while hers, by all reports, went unshared. Experience was in my favor. But Erica Pierce was not an ordinary woman at all, and apparently as practiced in rejecting as I was in accepting.

"I'm a bit old to receive red roses from you," she said primly when I linked her to see her reaction to my first floral tribute. At least, I imagine she thought herself prim. Her lovely voice belied it. I heard her undistorted by the technology connecting us, and detected something that was not as prim as she would have liked, something vulnerable and yielding. The holo-image projected by the computer link in my hotel room showed her in her office at the Institute, looking hardworking and reserved. The sleeves of her tailored cotton shirt—again real cotton, not synth—were rolled up, and her hair was drawn back and up in an old-fashioned braided coronet. Her gloves that day were cotton. I decided to trust what I heard, not what I saw.

"A beautiful woman is never too old to receive red roses," I said. "Have dinner with me tomorrow."

"I'm not a beautiful woman."

"You're not looking at you through my eyes. Eight o'clock?" She said no. I sent yellow roses next. She said no again. White roses followed. Still she said no. I brought the next roses, rare Venus Blue, personally.

"Perhaps you prefer lunch?" I offered, with a rueful grin.

"Mr. D'Amico," she started. I cut her off.

"Stephen. Four dozen roses ought to entitle me to a 'Stephen,' if nothing else. If you won't come to lunch, will you at least have coffee?" I could feel my grin spreading into a more genuine smile as I saw her resistance begin to waver. "Please?"

Her laughter, when it came, was as rich and full-throated as I remembered. "Good lord, you are persistent! All right. Stephen. Dinner at eight." At my look of surprise, she added, "I'm not one for half measures, my boy. You might want to remember that."

"Duly noted, ma'am."

This time her smile made her beautiful enough to break my heart. "Scamp," she added.

Dinner was at a restaurant overlooking the ocean. Her dress that night was a simple linen sheath of beige shot with gold threads; her gloves, soft kid.

"How did you know?" she asked me when she saw where we were going.

"About the ocean?" I responded, helping her down from the skimmer resting a few inches above the ground. "The interview in *Perspectives*. It had a good holo of your beach-front home. Nice."

"The holo of your penthouse in Manhattan wasn't bad, either," she rejoined.

"My parents' penthouse," I corrected.

"You don't live there?" She seemed surprised.

"I live there," I said neutrally.

"But you must have a residence here, as well. You're in our orchestra, after all." She gracefully avoided asking the obvious question: why wasn't the *wunderkind* of '75 play-ing with the Metropolitan in '79? Or the London Philhar-monic? Or any other premier orchestra, instead of the merely respectable San Francisco Symphony?

"Nothing permanent," I said about my living arrange-ments. Nothing to be contested when I come of age, I thought. "I prefer to engage a suite at the new Palace during the season."

"Ah. You've a taste for luxury," she said teasingly.

"Could you doubt it?" I returned. Over dinner, I proceeded to show her how luxurious my tastes could be.

Afterward, I persuaded her to walk with me on the beach. I could not persuade her to kiss me, and because I wanted to do so very badly, and knew there would be other opportunities for persuasion, I didn't press the issue.

The next day I was off for the required bimonthly visit "home." It was slightly more appalling than usual. I could hear the music while I was still in the lift-tube to the penthouse. So much for hush-mode. Of course it only grew louder as I approached the door, pressed my thumb into the indentiplate and stood still for the eyescan. The door slid back and the sound assaulted me full force. The system was, of course, top of the line, as was everything else in the penthouse, from the faux-wood wall paneling to the museum-quality reproductions of nineteenth century Persian carpets on the floors. Every note sounded as if the piano itself were in the room. And every note drove a separate knife into a yet-unclosed wound. The Munich concert, of course. A deliberate choice. My father, dressed casually in dark brown synth-wool slacks and ivory synth-silk shirt, was seated in his personal-fit lounge chair, reading one of the news holos, a mug of coffee near to hand. He barely glanced at me when I walked into the room and tossed my accusation at him.

"Why shouldn't I listen to your better work?" he replied in the unexceptional, mild tones that only betrayed their angry reproach to the initiated. I was well initiated. Edward D'Amico and I were, in temperament, nothing alike. As was reputedly true of my distant Italian forbears, my emotions run too near the surface, and I trouble to hide them only when the need to do so is paramount. My father's emotions are always hidden, to be revealed only when it is to his advantage to do so.

Our dissimilarities of personality made me all the more uncomfortable with our similarities of appearance. The same tall, trim build, the same firm jaw and wide brow. Most especially, for my sins, the same thin mouth, cold gray eyes, and pale blond hair. His was going to gray already, at forty-two, despite rejuv treatments that I knew to be state-of-the-art.

"Listen to those damned cubes as much as you please when I'm not here," I said bluntly. "You know I can't stand it."

He didn't even bother to set aside the holos. "As your father, I think you should be reminded that you are capable of more than you are currently achieving. Much more."

That about tore it. "Don't you bloody tell me that I'm capable of more. I know how much more I wanted to do and how easy it was for you to stop me. So if—"

"You should know better than to distress the boy as soon as he walks in the door, Edward," my mother said. She floated into the room on a cloud composed of *Triste* perfume, platinum hair, and opalescent chiffon. Rejuv took rather better on her than it did on my father, and she was often mistaken for my nonexistent older sister.

Adele—it was impossible to think of such a creature as "mother"—was not happy when I argued with my father. She threw him a vaguely reproachful glance and drifted toward me to place a vaguely maternal kiss on my cheek. "As you," she continued, "should know that your father only wants what's best for you."

"Should I really?" I asked. But I kissed the cheek she proffered before she glided away. The rest of the visit went along the same predictable, uncomfortable lines.

When I returned, I went straight to the Institute.

"I just needed to see you," I told Erica when she let me in to her office. "Can I take you to lunch?"

She was quiet for a minute, looking at me, and I could

almost feel the exact moment when she decided to ignore her better judgment, the part of her that felt no female Depriver should encourage the friendship of a younger man who wanted to be more than a friend. "Okay. In about three hours. When it's lunch time."

I laughed at myself on that one. "Damned time differential always gets me."

"The dangers of bicoastal living in the age of instant transport," she said sympathetically.

Our lunch soothed me, restored my balance. My performance that night was up to par, or at least my new par. She was waiting backstage.

"You're very good," she said. It wasn't kindness. I was very good. And that's all that I was. I smiled and kissed her hand again. But it was several weeks of dinners, lunches, performances, trips to museums and the beach and the theater and the park before she let me do more. When she finally allowed me to kiss her, I drank her in as if she alone could sustain my soul. But I hadn't completely overcome her reluctance.

"Even without the Depriver syndrome, there's the age difference," she would argue.

"What age difference?" I would counter. "You have no idea how young you are, and I—I was born old." She didn't believe me.

It didn't matter. I was utterly committed to my campaign and eventually triumphed.

The first time we made love, she was uncertain, touchingly concerned that I would find that her silk gloves detracted from the experience.

"I don't give a damn about your gloves," I told her, kissing her. "Take the bloody things off, if you like."

"I can't! The Depriver laws! If I accidentally—"

"Shh," I hushed her, and closed her mouth with another

kiss. "I don't give a damn about the Depriver laws, just now, either."

But she did, and there was a bad moment when I thought I had lost her, thought she might get out of the bed, pull on her clothes and flee. I pulled her tightly into my arms and told her, "The only thing I do give a damn about, right now, is how you feel against me, how you will feel beneath me, how *you* will feel, being beneath me."

It felt like heaven.

There are those who will say I need not explain, but how can you understand what came after if you know nothing of how it was between us that first time? How it was between us every time.

We had gone to my suite after what had been one of my better recitals, when I was too drained to suffer dinner in a public place, too wound up to go right to sleep. We'd ordered from room service, and ate seated on a couch facing the large windows which showed the lights of the city spread beneath our feet like a carpet of jewels. We had wine with our meal, and perhaps I drank more than usual. In a bit of lover's silliness, I began feeding her from my dish of ripe raspberries in champagne cream, pressing each tiny, succulent fruit into her mouth with fingers which caressed her lips after she had demolished the treat in delicate, ladylike bites. I watched her eyes widen, her mouth soften as I continued the caress, replacing my fingers first with my mouth, and then my tongue. She tasted faintly of cream, but far sweeter than the berries.

My attentions were just a little more determined than usual, and her resistance was just a little less. It wasn't long before I simply gathered her into my arms, still kissing her, and carried her from the couch to the bed. I began undressing her, and she began to help. When she had nothing left but the gloves, and I had nothing left at all, she grew less certain, and almost left. But I soothed her back into passion. And then, of course, neither of us was soothed.

She felt like heaven, her skin softer than any silk or flawlessly synthesized replacement. She burned like raw spice eaten unaware, and yielded like an ocean drawn back from the shore by the inexorable pull of the moon. In ancient rhythms, I followed after, into the wet, warm welcome of her body. I knew better than to move quickly, was prepared for the momentary resistance of the thin barrier. I distracted her with kisses, with caresses of her most secret, sensitive flesh, until she yielded that last bit farther and I pushed through, catching her cry against my mouth. Now I was deeply inside her, part of her, shuddering with the effort it took not to move, to allow her to adjust to my intimate invasion. With a little gasp she shifted beneath me, lifting her hips, inviting me to take up again the momentarily abandoned rhythm. I kissed each freckle on her cheek, rained more kisses on her temple, the side of her jaw, her neck, down to one breast, where I teased the nipple with my tongue. She responded instantly, her legs wrapping about my waist as she drew me further in. Moon and tide, we moved together, slowly at first, building to a shattering tempest, a storm at sea. Erica Pierce felt like the completion of my own flesh, like the other half of my soul, like the one person in all the world with whom I could share myself.

Those months before I turned twenty-one were halcyon, idyllic, never to be forgotten. As we grew closer, I spent more and more time at the Institute, learning sign, watching her work with her students, her hands swift and white as doves. I think what I admired most about her work was that no matter how tragic their stories, no matter how unlikely the possibility of a cure, Erica was never less than enthusiastic about what each student could accomplish. Those at the Institute were the ones for whom, by and large, modern science had no answers. The ones for whom circuitry implants, nerve-path restructuring and genetic enhancements were not possible. Some came to her seeking pity, but she told them there was no dearth of it elsewhere. She had no pity to spare for herself, or for them. She offered them hope instead. Erica renewed and restored her students, and did the same for me. To the extent that I was capable of being renewed and restored. Which wasn't enough at all.

The critics were not kind. They acknowledged how good I was, and lacerated me for having fallen from the heights when I had been not merely good, but brilliant, innovative, and as one of them put it, approaching divine. Now, I was derivative, mechanical, polished.

Soulless.

"You mustn't let this get to you," Erica said to me as we lay in her bed. She was snuggled against my side, her gloved hand drifting soothingly across my chest. "The career of every artist has its peaks and valleys. And you, no less than I, have no idea how young you are."

"You don't understand," I said. "It isn't the critics I care about. Or what they say. It's what I know to be the truth."

"And what is that?" she said, her tone lightly teasing, an indulgent parent allowing a child to express a fear so that it could be soothed away with kisses.

I looked into her eyes, then, into the tenderness of their brown depths, and told her bluntly, "The truth is that I can't hear the music anymore, not in my head, not where I need to hear it so that I can make it come out in my fingers and hands. And that is why I can't play."

She stopped the soothing gesture, sitting up a little.

"Then you must listen until you hear it again," she said before she kissed me.

I am widely supposed to have carefully planned what ultimately happened well in advance. But I didn't. It was only days before my birthday that she found the cubes, quite accidentally, when I asked her to choose something to put on the system while we read the Sunday morning holos. I didn't know until the first seductive chord—the chord I had intended to be seductive—played.

"Would you mind choosing another cube?" I asked tightly.

"But why? What is it? I've never heard—"

"Please," I managed. She complied. But she didn't let it rest.

"Don't tell me that's not your playing, because I know better. I remember every note I heard in Munich. What I don't recognize is the composition."

"Mine." I admitted tersely, getting up from the couch and walking away.

"You compose?" she asked. I could hear the delight in her voice. I turned to face her.

"No. I don't."

She was, as she had been called, gifted. I didn't need to explain. "Because you can't hear the music anymore," she whispered, delight yielding to sorrow in an instant. "Oh, my dear . . ."

I told her the story, of course, the story which has by now become well known. My father's ambition, his disappointment when his own abilities fell short. His—satisfaction?—when he realized I could achieve his dreams for him. The relentless training, the playing and replaying of virtuoso artists going back to Van Cliburn's work a century and more in the past. And my own joy, at first, in what I could do. Until I began to find other music, other artists. Until I realized there was something I wanted to do even more than I wanted to play. The compositions. The music that was not classical, or not classical as he understood it. Music influenced by the Korean Atonalists of the early twenty-first century, the Russian Primitives of the '30s, the South American Swing Revivalists of the '60s. And, of course, the North American Rebel Rock artists who continued to redefine what music is.

Edward D'Amico wasn't fond of that sort of music, and it was no part of his plan that I should develop interests in it. So when he found my compositions and realized I was spending studio time on them, he took the steps any loving, concerned parent would take. He had his lawyers inform the company holding my contract that I would never cut another cube for them if they allowed me to continue to "waste my time" on my own music. I was to play the classics as I had been trained to do. As I had loved to do. But when it became all I was allowed to do, I no longer could.

It wasn't deliberate at all. I still loved the first wave legends, like Liszt, Rachmaninov, Tchaikovsky, and enjoyed playing them. I was angry at my father's actions, but at sixteen, I thought it merely a matter of time until I was old enough to do things my way. But somehow, long before that time, the music deserted me. To this day, I don't know why.

I only know that I became a deaf man in a world of sound, sound which clouded and obscured the strained and distant notes hovering just beyond the limit of my hearing. Until something in Erica's discovery of those cubes, in her instant understanding of my inner deafness, connected all the pieces for me. By my twenty-first birthday, I understood how to get the music back.

The fight with my father went rather better than planned. I placed the envelope beside his plate when I came down to breakfast.

"Aren't you the one supposed to be getting cards?" he asked, eyeing the rather thick envelope suspiciously.

Adele, in a dressing gown of lilac crepe, smiled calmly,

pouring herself a cup of tea. "I rather imagine that's your *congé*, Edward dear."

"My what?"

"Legal papers firing you as Stephen's manager, voiding your concerns in his business enterprises, and setting you up with a nice allowance that will ultimately prove inadequate to your needs no matter how generous it is. Oh. And the deed to the penthouse. Isn't that right, Stephen?"

"Ah, Adele," I grinned. "You constantly amaze me."

"Yes, my heart. Where did you think you got it from if not from me?" The ensuing battle was predictably loud and unpleasant. I'm not sure whose betrayal angered Edward more, mine or Adele's. She was the one, he discovered, who had begun to prepare for this day by hiring her own lawyers on my behalf at almost the same moment he had hired lawyers to manage the not inconsiderable fortune I had begun amassing five years before.

"Are you coming with me to San Francisco?" I asked her after he had stormed off. Adele surprised me yet again.

"Don't be foolish. I do love him. In my fashion."

I asked Erica to wear her green silk, saying that the restaurant we were going to was a surprise. She didn't balk too badly when we got to the transport center. I think she suspected Munich. Tahiti never entered her mind. But it has one of the most beautiful restored beaches in the world.

At every interview since, I have been asked what cube I chose to play as we ate our private meal on the balcony of our room, overlooking the ocean. The truth is that I *cannot* remember, and Erica *will* not. It has no importance to either of us. What is important is that I did not lock the hotel room door. And that she had no idea what I planned.

She stared at the ring—sapphires surrounded by diamonds in an antique style called "deco"—for a long moment before she let me put it on her right hand.

"But if you can't ask me to marry you yet, why—"

"Because I am asking you to marry me. I just don't want you to give me your answer yet. This isn't your engagement ring."

That caused her to raise a brow in disbelief. "Bloody good imitation, then."

"Do you love me?" I asked, with sufficient gravity for her to realize this wasn't the usual lover's rhetoric.

"Passionately," she affirmed. "Despite my better judgment."

"I'm going to need you to remember that. And I'm going to need you to remember this: I love you. You are the other half of my soul, and I would be utterly desolate without you."

She tried to make light of my intense mood, but I would have none of it. "Well, then, lucky for you I have—"

"I would be lost. And damned. Because I need you to help me. Your whole life has been given over to helping the deaf perceive sound. I need you, in so many ways, to help me hear the music once more." She looked at me then, with a sort of sorrowful tenderness, and I think she was remembering what I had told her about the fight with my father, the years without music. She still did not understand.

She gave me the gift of her tears and the gift of her mouth, but the final gift wasn't freely given at all. I wrested it from her by main force. The attendants, brought, as I had known they would be, by her screams, had no trouble opening the unlocked door. They found Erica sobbing despairingly as I held her naked hands hard against my ears, murmuring over and over that I was sorry, and that I loved her.

Tahiti has the most liberal Depriver laws in the world, and of course I made sure that there was never a question of whose action this had been. But that is all widely known, now. As is the fact that she came near to hating me for what I'd done to her, for my betrayal.

There was no question of forgiveness. Whatever lies I had told myself beforehand, one look into the haunted depths of her eyes brought home what my miracle had cost Erica. No matter that what I had forced her to do had almost exactly the effect I intended. No matter that I could hear the music once more, pure and unobscured. No matter that my gift returned, almost completely, and that I used it to bring the San Francisco Symphony back to the forefront of the musical world. I had betrayed her. I have spent every waking moment of the past ten years trying to make up to her for that brief and brutal act.

That wasn't the only price I paid. When I tried to go back to the compositions I had been forced to abandon, I found I could not. Every note I set down seemed banal, false. That part of my gift seemed forever lost to me, and it made the pain of losing Erica that much harder to bear.

So I spent two years as a man without a soul, condemned to the outer darkness, a denizen of hell. The critics adored me. Work having become my only solace, and an eternal punishment, I produced cube after cube playing every classic that had been written for, or could be performed upon, the piano. I reinterpreted them all, because the way they could sound was so much clearer in my mind, now that I could hear nothing with my ears. Every day brought a studio session, or a recital. Every night brought one more unconnected computer link, unopened letter, unaccepted bouquet.

Until the dozen Venus Blue roses were returned by the florist. I remember looking at the white silk ribbon confining the stems and the pain rising up inside me until it swelled into one crashing wave and the music I had not been able to hear broke over me with drowning force.

I wrote the Venus Rose Sonata that night, knowing, *knowing*, that it would be the last composition of my life.

The critics were beside themselves. "Masterpiece," they called it. "Genius." they said of me. And once again, "Divine." It was absolutely no comfort. Only after I had regained my gift, and only after I had paid the price for it, did I understand what the true gift had been all along.

I stopped trying to link computers, write letters, send flowers. I spent more and more of my studio time alone, without sound techs or other musicians to give me feedback on my work. And several months after the release of the Sonata, I looked up from the keyboard and Erica was there. I could just see a drift of champagne-colored organza float through the studio door as Adele made her exit.

Erica's face was drawn, her eyes somber. She didn't move for a few moments, then lifted her white-gloved hands and signed to me.

"Is there one reason in the world why I should forgive you?"

I signed back. "No. There is no reason. But I hope that one day you'll forgive me, anyway. Because if I am in hell for losing the other half of my soul, then you must also be suffering. And I never wanted you to suffer. I never wanted to do anything but love you. And hear the music."

"You wanted to hear the music more than you wanted to love me." she signed fiercely.

"That isn't true," I signed.

"You are the reason I am suffering!" she signed back. How could I deny it? Erica was weeping by then. I tried to put my thoughts into words. And it seemed that what I had to tell her must come not only from the hands that I now used for speech, but from the voice that had already begun to lose its sharp-edged clarity, that I had to communicate in every way open to me.

"Hearing the music is what I am," I said to her, fighting for every syllable. "Loving you is who I am."

For a moment, she seemed to grow angrier, shaking her head, turning away. But halfway to the door she turned back. I opened my arms and Erica walked into them, and we knew, both of us, that we were home, whole, complete.

So, that explains why Tahiti, and why my house was built on the beach here. Adele visits from time to time, when that minor prince she married after my father's death doesn't require her for some state occasion. She likes it better than the Manhattan penthouse, she says. After three years here, I went back to those abandoned compositions, and found notes that were neither banal nor false. The critics have exhausted their superlatives, but that matters less to me than it ever did. I am often asked if I regret that I can't listen to cubes I've made, or to the new compositions by the artists who influenced my own work. There's nothing to regret. I can hear them perfectly when I look at the notations.

That is everything of importance there is to tell. Just as well. They'll be back in a few moments. The beach at sunset is her favorite time.

She's not one for half measures. She told me so from the first. When Erica forgave me, she held nothing back. Oh, there is a shadow. She cannot give me forgetfulness, after all. Sometimes, I see the sorrow in her eyes and wish I had found some other path, even though I know there was none left to me. But the shadows appear so rarely, now.

I can see her coming back along the shore. She smiles and waves to me as I stand in the doorway, and the little red-haired girl walking with her breaks away and runs toward me, laughing. I can see her lips shape the word "Daddy," but I don't need that to know what she is saying. I can hear it quite clearly, in the silence I have imposed upon myself. No one but Erica believes me when I say I knew it before anyone told me it was true. But I have always known.

She has her mother's voice.

FREAK

WILLIAM F. NOLAN

He was brought into the building by an Enforcer who waited in the long sterile corridor while Kal Adams faced the Compdoctor.

He knew he'd end up here. It was inevitable, given his shattered emotional state. His rage had been steadily increasing and he was very near Breakpoint. And why not? It was a near-miracle that he'd endured this long.

He'd been forced to wear a Skinsuit since he was one. Which was unheard of, since the Depriver Syndrome seldom manifests itself before puberty, and *never* during infanthood. Except in his case.

Except for Kal Adams.

During his first birthday party Kal's mother had kissed her baby son in happy celebration, and was instantly struck blind. Not for hours or days, but permanently. For the next three years, until she died with his father in a gyro crash, she had remained utterly sightless.

"I was too young to remember it," Kal said, sitting on a steel chair directly in front of the Compdoctor. "I only know how I was treated. They put me in a Suit and I've never experienced a human touch since that day."

"I can understand," said the doctor. "I know just how difficult it has been for you."

"No, you don't," said Kal flatly. "You're a machine ... lights and circuits and relays. You can't appreciate what it means to be afflicted as I am."

"You are quite wrong, Mr. Adams," said the doctor. "I have been *programmed* to understand."

"It's not the same," said Kal, staring dully at the audiowall. Its banked lights glimmered and flashed in pulsing rhythms.

"You are obviously a very disturbed young man," said the wall.

"I'm twenty now," said Kal. "For the past nineteen years I've been isolated, denied genuine human contact. I've never held a woman's hand ... felt the warmth of her skin ... caressed her face. I feel as if I'm buried in a pit of darkness."

"Unfortunate," said the wall.

"Why *me*?" asked Kal. "Why did this awful thing happen to me?"

"Every Depriver asks, 'why me?' It is a universal question."

Adams shook his head. "I'm not like other Deprivers. They've all had normal childhoods, years of human contact before their affliction set in. But I've been inside this Suit all my life, wrapped in my protective cocoon." Kal lifted his right arm, shiny and layered; lights gleamed from the Suit's armored surface.

"And you are bitter regarding your condition," stated the wall.

"Damn right I am! It's all I think about anymore, the cruel injustice of it ... the *horror* of it."

"It is good that you are here," said the Compdoctor. "You have reached a state of potential violence."

Kal glared at the wall. "Society did this to me."

"Not so," the doctor declared. "Society is not responsible for your genetic structure."

"I don't understand this world," Kal said, a hopeless note in his voice. "We've got a space station on the Moon. We've built hive units on Mars. We're at the technical edge of star travel. Yet . . . still no cure for Deprivers."

"Science does not have all the answers," said the wall. "There are problems that are unsolvable."

"I don't believe that," said Kal Adams. "This society doesn't *want* to find a cure for people like me. The world needs a minority to kick around and Deprivers fit the bill. Most people feel smug and superior to us. We're the underdogs, the scapegoats."

"That is, of course, neurotic nonsense," said the wall, "stemming from your aberrated mental condition."

"I'm not insane," Kal protested. "But I *am* enraged. My God, I was just twelve months old! I was robbed of my childhood."

"And now you feel like striking out," the wall said. "You are at Breakpoint."

"Which is why they brought me here, right?"

"That is correct. When a Depriver reaches Breakpoint he or she is sent to me for help."

Kal laughed harshly. "Help? No one can help me, least of all a talking wall."

"You are mistaken, Mr. Adams," declared the Compdoctor. "I shall administer a tranc dosage that will lower your emotional drive level."

"You intend to numb my mind . . . put me into Sleep-state?"

"That is the only remedy," said the wall.

"And what if I don't want to be drugged? What if I refuse medication?"

"You have no choice," the wall told him. "You should have remained in D-Colony. Most Deprivers are content to be among their own kind."

"That was agony," said Kal. "I couldn't take it."

"You are a misfit," the wall declared. "A man on the verge of committing an anti-social act. Sleep is better than Termination."

"Not for me, it isn't," said Kal.

"I repeat, you have no choice in the matter."

A silver panel opened in the wall directly in front of Kal Adams, and a long metalloid tube snaked out, capped by a glittering needle.

"This injection will solve all of your emotional conflicts," said the wall. "Hold out your right arm. And do not be concerned about the Suit. The needle is designed to penetrate."

Adams stood up. "To hell with you! I won't be drugged!"

"Then I shall summon an Enforcer and he will—"

Kal Adams picked up the steel chair and smashed it into the wall. Lights exploded. Circuits shorted out in sizzling, sparked showers. An alarm bell keened.

The exit door was flung open by an armed Enforcer who brought his laser to firing position as Kal slammed him across the skull with the steel chair.

The Enforcer went down and Kal grabbed his laser. He brought down a second Enforcer with a cutbeam blast from the handweapon.

The Suit was restricting his movement, and Adams used the laser to carefully cut it away from his body. Now he wore only boots and a shortsleeve tunic. For the first time in his life he was able to feel the stir of air on his bare skin. Marvelous!

Enforcers were closing in from both ends of the corridor. They'd terminate him. He knew that. But he had no regrets. He wasn't afraid of Termination. Better than Sleep. At least he'd die with his mind intact.

Then, a female voice from a side door: "Hurry! *This* way!"

A woman in a light blue flogown was gesturing to him from mid-corridor. Adams ran to her and she waved him through the door, slam-bolting it behind them. "In here," she snapped. "Quickly!"

The room had served as a sensory lab. Crowded with open Thinktanks and exotic equipment.

"Who are you?" Kal stared at her. Stunning. Young. Beautifully-figured. Dark-eyed.

"I'm Zandra, and I can get us out of this building."

"All the main exits are blocked by now," said Adams. "There's no way out."

"But there *is*," countered the girl. "Trust me."

They moved through another door into a narrow transport corridor. She sprinted ahead, urging him to follow.

"Why are you doing this?" he asked. "Why risk your life for me? I'm a Depriver."

"I know who you are," she said as they raced along the narrow passage. "You're Kal Adams."

"But how—"

"You're one of a kind. Unique. I heard about you, got curious and comped your statrecords."

"You work here?"

"Not exactly. I'm part of a lab experiment. But there's no time for talk. We have to escape."

"There's no escaping the Enforcers," said Kal. "Even if we manage to get out of the building they're bound to find us. Enforcers are everywhere. They'll terminate us both."

"Just do as I say," she told him. "Here . . ." She was tugging at a panel in the flooring. "Help me with this."

Together, they loosened the panel, pulling it free. A flight of metalloid steps spiraled downward. "There's a maintenance tunnel below that leads to the street."

"How do you know?"

"Because I've been planning a way out." she said. "I comped the blueprints, and they show this tunnel running under the length of the building."

They hurried down the twisting stairs and began to move cautiously along the dim-lit passageway.

"I've been in comp-contact with a group called the Outsiders," Zandra told him. "Do you know about them?"

"I've heard rumors," said Kal. "Anti-system rebels. Operating against the state."

"They'll help us," she said. "They hate the Enforcers . . . hate what the system is doing to block the cure."

"What cure?"

"For Deprivers. They're working on a cure for the affliction. And they're close to a breakthrough."

"My God, that's wonderful!"

"After we made contact I told them I wanted out of the experiment, and they agreed to help. I planned on making my run this weekend—until you popped up. I recognized you from your statshot, and I knew why you were here. For Sleep."

"Yes." Kal nodded. "And I refused."

"I'm just glad I came along when I did."

Kal smiled at her. "I'm beginning to think we have a chance."

"We *do*," she said vehemently.

They'd reached the end of the tunnel. A steel ladder angled up to an exitplate.

"Once we're on the street," said Kal, "what then? Where do we go?"

"I know where," she said. "I'll take you."

Kal didn't argue. Maybe this remarkable young woman *could* lead him to the Outsiders. Why not take the gamble? Most certainly he was doomed without her.

They exited the tunnel at a street level some three hundred feet beyond the rear of the building. No Enforcers were in sight.

"They won't expect us to come out at this point," declared Zandra. "They'll figure we're still trapped inside."

"So we have breathing space," said Kal. "But my stat-shot will be all over the city by now. They'll be watching every possible escape route."

"I have a plan," she said. "If it works we'll be clear of the city."

"Well, I just hope—"

Kal's words were cut off by a sizzling burst of laser fire that chopped the grass inches from his left foot. A second beam caught him in the left shoulder.

"Take cover!" yelled Kal, diving behind a transit vehicle and pulling Zandra in close behind him. Another beam scored the roof of the truck.

Ahead of them, across a grassed verge, three Enforcers were advancing at a run. Kal scrambled into the truck's controlseat with Zandra.

"Can you drive this thing?" Her tone was desperate.

"Just keep your head down." Kal powered the truck forward in a skidding arc that quickly separated them from the trio of Enforcers.

"Tell me!" snapped Kal. "Which way now?"

"Stanton Square. The park . . . behind the old carousel."

"They'll have ground units out," said Kal. "Don't know if we can make it."

"*Try*, dammit! It's not that far." Then her voice softened. "How's your shoulder?"

The laser had cut deeply into Kal's flesh; the wound was raw and bleeding.

"I'm all right," he said.

Ten minutes later Kal pulled the truck to a stop in Stanton Park. To their left, the silent carousel baked in the heat of day, its mirrors shattered, painted wooden horses cracked and fading, with the floorboards of the abandoned ride warped by wind and rain.

A door opened at the inner section of the carousel, and a tall, sour-looking man in black came out to meet them.

To Zandra: "I see you arrived safely. Who's your friend?"

"Kal Adams," she told him. "He's a Depriver."

The hard-faced man looked at Kal. His eyes narrowed. "I've heard about you, Adams. Afflicted from infanthood. Unique case. What are you doing with Zandra?"

"Trying to stay alive," said Kal. "When I wouldn't accept Sleep they were going to Terminate me. Zandra got me into the clear." He hesitated. "Are you an Outsider?"

"That's what I'm called by the system. My name's Hollister."

"I won't shake your hand," said Kal.

Hollister nodded. "Follow me," he said, entering an overgrown section of heavy-growth woods.

In a small clearing, under a protective cover, a twin-thrust gyro was waiting for them, its rotor blades turning lazily in the heated air.

"This will take you to our headquarters near Bend City in New Oregon," said Hollister. "You'll be safe there."

"What about Airscouts?" asked Kal. "They'll be on full patrol."

"We're invisible on their scanners," said the tall man, helping them aboard the gyro. "We'll be well under their air-detect range. Believe me, they won't even know we're in the air."

"Looks as if you've got everything figured out," said Kal.

"Not everything," said Hollister, strapping himself into the controlseat, "but we're making progress. One step at a time."

The canopy rolled back and they lifted away, rotor blades slicing the sky.

In the passenger section Zandra opened a side panel and removed a flesh-repair kit. "Now . . . let's see about that shoulder."

Kal flinched back. "Don't touch me!" he warned her.

"Afraid I'll go blind?"

"God knows I wouldn't want to do that to you," he said.

"Not to worry. I'll be fine." And before he could stop her she'd laid the wound bare, spreading a healing paste over the laser cut.

"I don't understand," he said. "You're touching my skin, and yet—"

"And yet I'm not afflicted," she said. Zandra smiled, continuing to work on his shoulder. "I'm in no danger. Only humans are affected by Deprivers."

He stared at her. "You mean . . . that you're a . . . a *machine?*"

"Not quite," she told him. "I'm a freak . . . a Composite. Parts of me are robotic, but my main components are human tissue. Muscles . . . skin . . . bones. I'll age normally, grow old and die someday. Just as you will. But I'm not human in the exact sense you are. And I'm immune to affliction."

"Incredible," Kal murmured.

"After I was born ... constructed might be a better term ... they were going to experiment on me. That's when I began planning my escape. Fortunately, I was able to take you with me."

She finished with his shoulder, sealing the wound. The skin looked pink and fresh.

"There," she said. "You're good as new."

"I ... I don't know how to thank you," he said. "There's no way I can—"

She put a finger to his mouth. "Hush!" And, slowly, she caressed his cheek.

He took her firmly into his arms. "I've never kissed a woman ... never felt a woman's lips on mine. And—" he hesitated, felt himself trembling "—suddenly, I'm ... I'm afraid."

"Don't be," she said, pressing her body to his.

She kissed him. Deeply. Warmly.

And the world became a very bright place for Kal Adams.

THE CENTER FOR
DEPRIVERS
CONTROL

CASEWORKER
BIOGRAPHIES

Steven-Elliot Altman ("A Blind Virgin Like a Loaded Gun") is the creator of the Deprivers universe and artistic director of the project. He is the author of *Captain America is Dead* and *Zen in the Art of Slaying Vampires*. He is very honored to have worked with each of the writers involved with the project, salutes their charitable souls, and hopes that this compilation will inspire other writers to institute similar projects.

Janet Asimov ("Red Devil Statement") has published twenty books, many short stories and articles, and an (ongoing) seven years' worth of science columns for the *Los Angeles Times* Syndicate. She lives in Manhattan, close to Central Park and Lincoln Center—also within walking distance of the American Museum of Natural History, soon to have an annual Isaac Asimov Memorial Lecture.

Jan Clark ("Marginal Existence") is currently jet-setting the science-fiction conventions and enjoying the success of both her debut science fiction novel, *Prodigy*, and its newly released sequel *Earth Herald*, both published by ROC. Jan lives in Ft. Worth, Texas with her husband and two children, holds a BFA in theatre and is a survivor of breast cancer.

Joanne Dahme ("Ellis Island") is the author of two science fiction novels, and her short stories have appeared in several anthologies, including *Thirteen by Seven*, and the notorious *Night Bites*, an anthology of vampire stories by women. She holds a degree in civil engineering from Villanova University and a Masters in journalism from Temple University. She lives in Philadelphia with her husband and son and, when not frightening us, heads the Public Affairs Division of the Philadelphia Water Department.

Diane DeKelb-Rittenhouse ("Gifted") is the author of numerous science-fiction and fantasy tales, including "To Die For," her contribution to the *Night Bites* anthology. She lives with her husband, underground comic book writer W. E. Rittenhouse, and their daughter in Pennsylvania.

Tananarive Due ("Suffer the Little Children") is a former *Miami Herald* columnist and the author of two ground-breaking novels, *The Between* and *My Soul To Keep*. She's been a finalist for the Bram Stoker Award and was also a contributor to *Naked Came the Manatee*, a collaborative mystery novel featuring several Miami writers.

Katherine Dunn (Introduction) is both a novelist and a journalist. Her novel *Geek Love* was a finalist for the 1989 National Book Award and a finalist for the 1989 Bram Stoker Award.

Paul Jon Edelstein ("The People of the State of New York vs. Duncan Cameron") is a trial attorney in Brooklyn Heights, New York. He's a partner in the Law Firm of Edelstein & Faegenburg and handles civil, criminal and matrimonial trials. This was his first successful science fiction trial.

Maggie Estep ("The Janitor") is a novelist, musician and performance poet. She was a featured performer at Woodstock 2 and Lollapalooza, and has appeared in the PBS series *The United States of Poetry*, as well as on MTV with her band. She reads her work to charmed audiences in clubs, theaters, and universities throughout the United States, Canada, and Europe. Her novels are *Diary of an Emotional Idiot* and *Soft Maniacs*. She has released two

CDs: *No More Mr. Nice Girl* on Imago Records, and the new *Love Is A Dog From Hell*, on Mouth Almighty/Mercury Records.

Keith Aaron Gilbert ("Rent Memories") holds a Masters degree in English from George Mason University and now lives in Seoul, Korea, where he teaches English to refugees.

The late Edward Gorey (ILLUSTRATOR) had written and illustrated over 100 miniature masterpieces treasured by legions of fans and discriminating collectors before his untimely passing in 2000—*The Object Lesson, The Gashlycrumb Tinies,* and *The Unstrung Harp* to name a few. He had illustrated and designed hundreds of additional books for others. Millions enjoyed his work on theatrical productions, most notably the stunning, 1978 Tony Award-winning *Dracula.* He was perhaps best known for his *New York Times* illustrations, and for the macabre cartoons that graced the opening of the PBS television series *Mystery!*

Janet Harvey ("Angel") got her MFA in Fiction Writing at Columbia University. She writes Batman comic books, most recently "I Cover the Waterfront" in *Batman* #569—the first adventure of the new Batgirl—and "Lucky's Seven," a Catwoman story in the *Batman 80-Page Giant.* As multimedia editor at DC Comics, she also co-authored the CD-ROM adventure *The Multipath Adventures of Superman: Menace of Metallo.* Her play, *The Temptation of St. Antony,* last appeared at the NY Fringe Festival in 1997. She lives in New York City.

Bob Mahnken ("Shared Losses") is an Off-Off-Broadway playwright whose works include *Burnout* and *Drunks With Guns*, winner of the 1994 Access Theatre Award for best new play. He recently completed the screenplay for Bill Pullman's first feature as a director, the forthcoming *900 Women*.

Patrick Merla (EDITOR) is the editor of the groundbreaking anthology *Boys Like Us*, the author of *The Tales of Patrick Merla* and the editor of *The James White Review*. His literary essays, interviews, and film, theater and book reviews have appeared in *Saturday Review, New York Newsday, Men's Style Magazine, Out, Christopher Street, New York Native, Interview, Theater Week,* and *House Beautiful.*

William F. Nolan ("Freak") is the author of over sixty books in the genres of science fiction, horror, and mystery. He writes extensively for films and television and is a two-time winner of the Edgar Allan Poe Special Award. His work has appeared in over a hundred publications, ranging from *The Magazine of Fantasy and Science Fiction* to *Playboy*. As an editor, he produced highly influential collections such as *Alien Horizons* and *Man Against Tomorrow*. Perhaps his best known works are the trilogy of novels set in the universe of a former Sandman named Logan: *Logan's Run, Logan's World,* and *Logan's Search.*

Kit Reed ("Precautions") is the author of twelve novels, including *Captain Grownup, Catholic Girls,* and *J. Eden.* She is a Guggenheim fellow and the first American Recipient of a five-year literary grant from the Abraham Woursell Foundation. Her stories have appeared in venues ranging from *The Yale Review* and *The Missouri Review* to *The Magazine of Fantasy and Science Fiction, Omni, Asimov's SF* and *The Norton Anthology of Contemporary Literature*. *Little Sisters of the Apocalypse* was a finalist for the Tiptree Prize and "The Singing Marine" was a finalist for Best Short Story at the World Fantasy Convention. Her newest collection is *Seven for the Apocalypse*.

D. H. Resnicoff ("Idiots Losers Fools"). Winner of the 1995 New York Women in Film and Television Scholarship, Debra Resnicoff is completing her MFA at the Columbia University Film School. Her feature comedy *Jessica Rose* for Darling Point, LLC was filmed in 1998 in Manhattan. Her one-act plays have appeared at the Samuel Beckett Theatre, Manhattan Class Company, Columbia Dramatists and various regional theatres.

Leah Ryan ("The Only One") has had her fiction and poetry appear *in Sojourner, Affilia, Ararat, [sic], The Amherst Review*, and in the anthology *Through the Kitchen Window*. She writes a regular column for *Punk Planet* and edits her own 'zine, *Violation Fez*. She is a Juilliard Playwright, a graduate of the Iowa Playwrights' Workshop, and a recipient of numerous playwrighting awards for her works produced in Chicago, New York, San Francisco, and London.

Karl Schroeder ("After the War") is the second SF writer to come out of the small Mennonite community of southwestern Manitoba, Canada (A. E. van Vogt was the first). He now lives and works in Toronto, where he has taught writing, written and published numerous short stories and one novel so far. In 1993 he won Canada's top SF prize, the Aurora Award, for the short story "The Toy Mill," which he co-wrote with David Nickle. Karl is currently the president of SF Canada, the national SF writing association of Canada.

Jonathan Shipley ("For Good People Like You") has had his fiction published in numerous venues; including *Dragon* and *Marion Zimmer Bradley's Fantasy*. Jon also teaches at a private school in Fort Worth, TX and is an accomplished musician.

Sean Stewart ("Don't Touch Me") is a two-time Aurora Award winner for his first two novels *Passion Play* and *Nobody's Son*. His third book, *Clouds End*, made the Locus recommended reading list. Now in soft cover, *The Night Watch*, is the sequel to his popular, hair-raising 1995 novel, *Resurrection Man* (Ace), a *New York Times* Notable Book of the Year. His newest novel, *Mockingbird*, was a finalist for the 1999 World Fantasy Award. He lives in Monterey, California, with his wife and two daughters.

Harry Turtledove ("The Lieutenant") is the author of novels such as *The Guns Of The South, How Few Remain*, and *Into The Darkness*, as well as the Hugo-winning novella "Down in the Bottomlands." He is an escaped historian who lives not far from the area where his story for this book is set. He and his wife, writer Laura Frankos, have three daughters.

Dean Whitlock ("Waiting for the Girl From California") had his first story, "The Million Dollar Wound," appear in a 1987 issue of the *Magazine of Fantasy & Science Fiction*; it was reprinted in *The Year's Best Science Fiction*, Fifth Annual Collection. His story "Miriam, Messiah" was also published in the *Magazine of Fantasy & Science Fiction*, 1988, and reprinted in the German anthology, *Das Weihnacts-Buch Der Phantasie*. "Iridescence" appeared in the January 1989 issue of *Asimov's Science Fiction Magazine* and was reprinted in *Aliens*. It was a finalist in Asimov's annual readers poll for Best Short Story in 1991.

Lisa D. Williamson ("The Companion") is the author of *The House that Jake Built*, featuring sleuth Valerie Duncan, and has won several awards for her fiction. Her short stories have appeared in several anthologies, including *Night Bites* and *Out for Blood*. She lives in the Philadelphia suburbs with her husband and two sons.

Linda K. Wright ("The Penitent") alternates between horror and mystery with short stories in several anthologies, including *Night Shade*, *Out for Blood*, *Thirteen by Seven*, *Hen's Teeth*, *Death Knell 2*, *Night Bites*, and the German version of *Night Bites: Mittersnachtkuss*. Her literary work has been published in *The Princeton Arts Review*, *The Seattle Review*, *The Maryland Review*, *Cyber Oasis*, *Echoes*, and *Slice of Life* (Canada). Her mystery work has appeared in *Murderous Intent*, *Belles Lettres*, *Sleuthhound*, and *The Case*. Awarded the 1995 Charles Johnson Award for Fiction, she is a former Vice President of the Delaware Valley Chapter of Sisters in Crime.

Link Yaco ("Death Goddess of the Lower East Side") has written comics for Fantagraphics, Gladstone/Hamilton, Dark Horse, and several other companies; his most recent work is *The Science of the X-Men*, a scientific examination of the popular Marvel Comics characters and their mutant powers, co-written with novelist Karen Haber. He has been a copywriter for Barnes & Noble and Columbia House, a newspaper journalist, a magazine entertainment writer, a technical writer, and a copy editor for educational material. He has a Masters' degree in Telecommunications and was a technical manager at MIT for five years. He has written for independent films and videos that have appeared at the Institute of Contemporary Art in Boston, The Eröffsnungs Festival in Frankfurt, Germany, and the Ann Arbor 16mm Film Festival. Link lives in Greenwich Village with his wife, Susannah Juni, a senior officer at an independent film company.

ACKNOWLEDGMENTS